WATERSHED

A NOVEL

WATERSHED

DOREEN VANDERSTOOP

Freehand Books acknowledges the financial support for its publishing program provided by the Canada Council for the Arts and the Alberta Media Fund, and by the Government of Canada through the Canada Book Fund.

Canada Council   Conseil des Arts
for the Arts   du Canada

Alberta Government

Canadä

Freehand Books
515–815 1st Street SW   Calgary, Alberta   T2P 1N3
www.freehand-books.com

Book orders: UTP Distribution
5201 Dufferin Street   Toronto, Ontario   M3H 5T8
Telephone: 1-800-565-9523   Fax: 1-800-221-9985
utpbooks@utpress.utoronto.ca   utpdistribution.com

Library and Archives Canada Cataloguing in Publication
Title: Watershed / Doreen Vanderstoop.
Names: Vanderstoop, Doreen, 1962– author.
Identifiers: Canadiana (print) 20190213981 |
Canadiana (ebook) 20190214007 | ISBN 9781988298597 (softcover) |
ISBN 9781988298603 (EPUB) | ISBN 9781988298610 (PDF)
Classification: LCC PS8643.A585 W38 2020 | DDC C813/.6—dc23

Edited by Barb Howard
Book design by Natalie Olsen, Kisscut Design
Cover photo © Amy Covington / Stocksy.com
Author photo by Courtney Barr
Printed on FSC® recycled paper and bound in Canada by Friesens

For Neil and Betty Vanderstoop,
forever generous with their stories

1

THE FAINT HISS OF AIRBRAKES sounded above the wind. Willa Van Bruggen looked eastward and shielded her eyes against the May morning light. The sun lay low in the sky – a beautiful, terrible, celestial raspberry coloured by dust and by smoke drifting in from forest fires in Northern Washington State and British Columbia.

Crystel Canada's double water-tanker hove into view at the top of the hill, the shine of its silver barrels dulled by the dusty air. Airbrakes again – intermittent now, like sharp intakes of breath – as the rig inched down toward the Van Bruggen farm. Drivers had to keep their speed in check, so water surges didn't send the vehicles careening out of control.

Last night's conversation with her only son had been running through Willa's mind all morning. Daniel had video-called her to share the news about getting an interview with Crystel Canada.

"I'll be working for the federal Crown corporation keeping Southern Alberta from turning into Death Valley," he said. Daniel shook his head as if his point were obvious and he didn't understand why she wasn't getting it. She wasn't. She wanted him back. Needed him to help them keep the farm afloat. Daniel tried again. "It's like a banker getting a job with the Bank of Canada or an art dealer with the National Gallery of Canada. Crystel operates for profit at arms' length from government, but the feds guarantee the cash flow in case of financial trouble. They won't let the water pipeline fail."

As he spoke, her mind drifted back to a time when she and young Daniel crept into the loft of the hay barn to check out a new litter of kittens. She'd marvelled at how gently his little fingers stroked their silky fur. But he was strong-willed, too—always arguing that he was ready to take on the next big farm job. Back then, she couldn't imagine he'd ever leave.

He told her the job with Crystel would be a dream come true.

Smile, Willa commanded herself. Congratulate him. But the muscles around her mouth refused to budge.

The phone screen relayed the hopeful twitch of his eyebrows. "Aren't you happy for me?" he asked. "I can finally start to tackle my debt."

"Of course I'm happy," she said, the words like a mouthful of sand.

Daniel ran a hand across the top of his head and let it nest in his thick hair, as yellow as ripe wheat. His blue eyes shone. "My master's is paying off. And I've made great contacts. No one is hiring, but my friend, Percy Dickenson, got me this interview. Brilliant guy. Double majored in political science and hydrogeology. Now he's a bigshot in the provincial water ministry."

"I'm glad you can get on top of your debt." Her tiny image in the corner of the screen looked glad, didn't it? "I just wish you were coming home."

Daniel's face disappeared as he tilted the phone away. She saw the dingy ceiling tiles in his basement apartment, then his face filled the screen again.

"Listen to me, Mom. I'm a professional now. I don't want to fight dust and wind on a few lousy acres of dried-out farmland. I want to help everyone. I've been looking for a year. A lot of grads from the Class of 2057 are still out of work. They'd kill for this opportunity. I can't make ends meet with half shifts at the Breakfast Barn."

Neither spoke for a full uncomfortable minute.

"I'm staying in Calgary," Daniel said.

Now, Willa's eyes followed the water truck as she pulled her dual-cartridge dust mask over her head. Her fingers fumbled with the webbed strapping that always tugged at her unruly curls. "Damn this thing," she muttered. Still, it prevented Valley Fever. Few Albertans were immune to the fungal disease that had migrated north from Arizona. Her sister, Sophie, had barely survived it.

Daniel's description of home had stung Willa. The place where he'd nurtured those damn cats, torn down old sheds, built new ones, branded calves once upon a time — all of that reduced to 'a few lousy acres.' He'd once sniffed at a pitchfork full of timothy grass and said farms had the best smells in the world. Willa tried to associate "hydrogeologist" with the deeply familiar image of Daniel as a boy, but the two concepts flowed through her mind like water and oil.

As she snugged the floppy silicone mask around her nose and mouth, a desert whitetail landed on her arm. Another import from Arizona, but this one a hard worker that devoured hundreds of flying insects a day. The dragonfly wriggled its wide, black-tipped wings and chalky body. Willa had heard somewhere that they were territorial. She could relate to that. Her head began to ache. She checked the straps to make sure the mask wasn't too tight. It wasn't. When Willa looked up, she froze. Where the water tanker had been, an army tank now ripped through the barbed wire fence around the field. Bounced wildly through fallow ruts and divots. The main gun pointed at her. Caterpillar treads churned up the ground like enormous black teeth.

Willa staggered backward and toppled over. A horn blasted and airbrakes screamed. She turned slowly to find herself an arm's length from the front bumper of the water truck.

Alain Dupré jumped out of the driver's seat and ran to her side. "Willa, you all right?" Alain's dust mask muffled his voice, but his Quebecois accent was thick with fear. "*Tabernac* — I thought you were going right under my goddamn tires." He shot a frenzied look toward the house and the barn.

Willa sat up and pointed at the field. He looked over with a puzzled frown. She said, "I ... I saw a ..." Where the tank had been, a dust devil pirouetted across the field.

"What the hell you talking about, Willa? You fell like a sack of hammers."

She shook her head and scanned the smooth ground by her feet. "I must have tripped over a rock. I'm tired. Not sleeping well."

Alain helped Willa to her feet and held her elbow. He glanced back at the farm buildings again.

Willa took one long gasping breath through her mask and smacked her hands against her dusty jeans. "If you're looking for Calvin, he's in the barn. I'm fine." Her and Alain's masked voices sounded half-dead in her ears. "Just fine." She waved him on. "Go, go. Do your job already."

He backed away slowly, then climbed back into the cab and threaded the tanker truck around the house to the cistern. Willa followed, massaging her temples. The day before, she thought she saw a coyote in the milking shed. A week ago, the sink and mirror awash with blood as she brushed her teeth. The illusions hadn't lasted long but seemed so real. Maybe she'd contracted Valley Fever despite the mask. Could the fungus make a person crazy? She'd never heard of that happening, but perhaps it had mutated during its migration, now able to wend its way into a person's neural pathways. She'd have to search that.

Alain hauled the heavy hose off the truck toward the pipe that led to the underground cistern. He inserted the nozzle into the pipe and turned to Willa. "You're pale as milk."

Willa shrugged. She waved away a fly that buzzed around them. "Like I said — not sleeping. Thanks for coming a couple days early. I should be asking how you are."

He nodded. "*Dieu merci*. Getting my strength back. Valley Fever's a bugger. Felt like I had the flu for four months. Didn't want to wear the mask before, but I sure as hell wear it now." Alain pulled his phone out of his pocket and slipped off the dust cover. "I've got you down for five cubic metres."

Willa nodded.

Alain walked over to the truck to set the gauge and start the flow. His dark hair spilled down his neck in sweaty strands. His work boots left deep, clear impressions in the fine dust that swirled in constant clouds and settled around the house. Willa's grandfather had died when she was ten, but she remembered how he used to trumpet life's endless possibilities by saying, "They put a man on the moon." Willa imagined that's what a boot print on the moon would look like. Alain walked back and squeezed the nozzle, sending a thick stream of water into the cistern.

The splatter rang deep and distant, an echo of the long voyage that had brought the Pacific Ocean from Kitimat, British Columbia to the foothills of Southern Alberta. The water travelled through the Northern Gateway pipeline that nanobots had cleared of natural gas. ("From hydrocarbons to Adam's ale," one headline had read.) After being desalinated at a plant in Bruderheim, Alberta, the water travelled by pipeline to Red Deer, and by truck to their farm near Fort Macleod. All thanks to almighty Crystel Canada.

"Do you have enough monochloramine additive?" Alain asked.

Willa nodded again.

He peered into her eyes. "Maybe you should talk to Dr. Clyde about sleeping pills."

His stare unnerved her. "I will, but, for heaven's sake, quit your fussing," she said, trying to sound casual. "Fatigue can make the mind play tricks."

He pulled his mask down around his neck and grinned. His teeth and the halo of clean flesh around his nose and mouth shone bright in his grimy face. "These are crazy times, so if you're losing it, you fit right in."

Willa listened to the water, an abundant sing-songy splash.

"The pipeline extension is set to hit Calgary by end of October," Alain said.

Willa shook her head. "The Northern Water Army is fighting it. They say Northern Alberta will suffer if they have to fill a pipeline to the south with their water. Imagine that — *their* water. As if we're second-class citizens not entitled to our fair share at a reasonable price." The pitch of her voice rose involuntarily. "They're threatening to blow up the new section south of Red Deer. Yesterday, the headline on their website read: 'Crystel filling water trough for dead horse.'"

Alain's tone turned soothing. "Crystel is looking out for us, Willa. The feds appointed Adam Landrew to head up the Crown corporation because he's tough. They'll get those *maudit* terrorists under control ..."

His words reassured her until they trailed off, sucked into a vacuum of doubt.

"Did you see the billboard ads the NWA put up in Edmonton and Red Deer?" she asked, her voice still more shrill than she intended. "A picture of a desert with the words 'Would you put a water pipeline across the Sahara?'"

Alain rubbed his forehead. "I don't know what to say, Willa."

He held out his phone. Willa's hand trembled as she placed her index finger on the fingerprint scanner. *Cha-ching.* One thousand dollars further in debt. She'd have to tell Daniel they were close to losing everything. That they needed him to come home to help them make ends meet.

Alain read her mind. "Times is bad, eh? Did you hear about the fight at one of the Calgary water stations? Some guy got knifed for jumping the queue."

Willa nodded. "Died in hospital overnight. I wish Daniel was here, safe and sound."

She and Alain combed the sky for rain clouds. A common reflex among the people of Southern Alberta now. Like compulsively checking the same place over and over for a lost object, certain it will be there the next time. Clouds did skitter across the sky sometimes. Occasionally they dropped a little moisture. More often than not, they swept by in long mares' tails, disappearing as if attached to stampeding horses.

"Calgary is a lawless place full of drunks and thugs," Alain said. "Glad I don't deliver to Calgary water stations. Bad enough seeing your neighbour Logan stagger around at 6 am."

"What do you mean?" Willa asked. "He was drunk?"

Alain nodded. A crow screeched overhead. It landed on a gnarled branch in the one-time shelterbelt of lodgepole pines west of the house. "I know times is tough, but he called me a goddamn camel herder. People got no respect for what I do even though I'm the one keeping them alive."

Willa sighed deeply. "How's Adèle?"

"She's okay. Takes care of the grandkids a lot while my son and daughter-in-law look for work."

"Sorry to hear they're still looking." Willa glanced at her watch. "Wanna come in for a minute and brag about the grand-kids? I've got fresh biscuits."

"No. *Merci mille fois.* I'll be lucky to get my run done by supper." He secured the cistern cap with a hard twist, re-attached the nozzle to the back of his truck, and headed for the truck cab. He lingered with a foot on the truck's step box long enough to wave to Calvin coming out of the barn. "You take it easy, Willa. Get some rest. I'll see you next week."

As he settled into his seat and slipped on his dust mask, Willa called up to him. "Hey, Al. Don't let the name-calling get to you."

He gave her a thumbs-up. Willa watched the tanker bump through the U-turn behind the house and back up the road. As she turned toward the milking shed, she almost collided with her husband.

"Hey there, pilgrim."

"Calvin, you scared me," she said. Saskia, their Great Pyre-nees, ran up and pushed her muzzle into Willa's hand.

"Sorry, ma'am," Calvin said. "Just wanted to say hello. You're a jumpy gal, ain'tcha?"

His uncanny impressions usually made her laugh, but she didn't recognize this one and didn't ask.

Absent a reaction, he said, "I guess my John Wayne must be slipping." He planted a kiss on top of her head, a gesture made easy because he towered over Willa. Even then, she was tall herself, a strong Dutchwoman.

The wind swept his hair around his head like a storm cloud. With his square jaw and a slightly crooked nose from breaking it when he fell off a horse once, Calvin looked the nonchalant old cowboy. He habitually imitated the ones in his favourite Westerns from the so-called Golden Age of Hollywood a century ago. Not their scruffy looks, though. He abhorred beards and whiskers and let his thick silver hair fall almost to his shoulders. Willa, with her curls still bright chestnut even now in her fifth decade, didn't believe stress turned hair grey. If it did, Calvin's would still be blond and hers would be silver.

"Wish we had a cavalry to get the provincial and federal governments to cough up bigger water subsidies," Willa said.

Calvin shook his fist and, this time, mimicked the whiny indignation of Alberta's Minister of Water, Ross Cameron: "Inadequate federal transfer payments!"

Willa pulled off her mask. "I asked Alain to come two days early, because we were low. I keep having to flush out all the equipment before I milk. Can't keep the sand out." She crouched down to pet Saskia, who immediately rolled over in the dirt and waited for a tummy rub. "How are we going to pay the bill, Calvin?"

"Love ..."

Willa wanted to laugh. Sure, she thought. They'd pay with love.

"We'll be fine," he continued. "Stop worrying. You and I are strong and healthy, the goats are in good shape, what more do we need?"

Willa jumped up. "Money! We could end up penniless. I'm not stealing away from this farm in the middle of a dark night the way so many others have abandoned theirs." She raised her arms to indicate the surrounding land but quickly lowered them when she realized how preacher-like she looked. "What's not to worry about? This isn't one of your Westerns, Calvin. Where a miracle happens, and everyone rides off into the sunset." She placed her hands on her hips and pawed the dirt with her boot. "I talked to Daniel last night after you went to bed. He's interviewing for a job with Crystel, so he never has to come back to this lousy farm — his words, not mine."

Calvin's blue eyes were placid, imperturbable. "He doesn't mean it, Willa. He's caught up in his own world. Besides, we can manage on our own. We shouldn't worry Daniel with any of this. He needs to live his own life." Urgent bleats floated from the barn. "We're being paged," he said and strode off. He refused to wear a dust mask, saying that if he were susceptible to Valley Fever, it would have struck him down long ago.

Willa followed him as far as the milking shed. "My goat whisperer," she mumbled. Even when Calvin injected animals with hypodermics full of dewormer and supplements, they stood still for him, unruffled. "Everything's gonna be all right," was his refrain. Willa's father had sometimes referred to his son-in-law as Mr. Micawber, Charles Dickens's incurable optimist in *David Copperfield*. But in those days, rain fell at regular intervals, glaciers filled alpine basins, and optimism bloomed like spring flowers.

Turning mid-stride, Calvin walked backwards a few steps. "Forgot to tell you. I spoke to Fred Butterfield yesterday about getting an order of silage for feed this summer. He got an extra water subsidy for his corn last year and said he'd give us a good price." He finished the turn and sauntered toward the main barn, trailing fine powder from slapping his work gloves against his coveralls.

A wave of nausea surged through Willa. Her heart pounded in her ears. As far as she could tell, they'd be flat broke in a couple of months, unable to afford their own food let alone any new feed. She gripped the door of the milking shed to steady herself while she hung up her dust mask. After flushing out the milking equipment, she passed into the main barn to collect the first batch of goats for milking. The entire herd lived in the massive structure, except for the buck, Duke, who had his own quarters in a separate outbuilding. Half the barn had a peaked roof with a hayloft. Below the hayloft, a row of pens housed the weaned kids and yearlings. A storage area held feed and a few tools. In the other half of the barn, where the roof sloped low, a large loafing pen housed the does and kids. Willa and Calvin and Daniel had constructed part of the main barn on stilts over a downslope to give the does and their young a place to shelter under the building when they went outside, which they rarely did now that dust and wind-born fungus threatened the animals' health as much as their keepers'.

Milking does crowded around Willa, and she grinned in spite of herself. Their bleats said, 'Pick me, pick me!' She pulled the door shut after the first dozen had piled through. She dipped the does' teats in an iodine compound, then hooked them to the milking cups. The sound of goats happily munching grain while she drew their rich milk soothed her. She and Calvin split the chores: she milked and kept up the breed and milk records; Calvin did handstands to keep the herd healthy, drawing on his experience as a vet tech. They shared the heavy lifting, especially all the repair work. The relentless drying wind regularly tore shingles off the barn roof and punched gaps in the siding. One news article titled, "They call the wind pariah," reported the number of "severe wind warning" days in the Fort Macleod area had spiked by eighty percent in the last twenty years.

Willa opened the one-way gate behind the milking stalls. The milked does hustled through it back to a holding area adjacent to the main pen. Willa returned to the other door and let the next dozen does tumble into the milking area. If only hard work were enough.

WILLA AND CALVIN'S FARMHOUSE, made of hand-hewn spruce logs, stood stalwart against Alberta's unremitting gales. Her father had hauled the house up the hill when the glaciers began to melt in earnest and overflowed the banks of the Oldman River. He had never bothered with the expense of moving it back when the river receded and eventually dried up. Despite its travels, the house looked exactly as it had when Willa's grandparents built it, right down to the 1970s faded green Formica countertops and four-seater breakfast nook where Willa and Calvin now sat. Only the floor had been replaced, with porcelain tiles that, as her father put it, would easily outlive him.

The aromas of steeped tea and fresh baking hung in the air like false promises. They suggested a normalcy not reflected in the world beyond the walls of the house. The scent of pine wafted up from the lit candle in the centre of the table, nudging distant memories at the corners of Willa's mind. The sappy smell of sun-warmed lodgepoles. Thickly needled branches waving in the breeze. She watched her husband butter his biscuit, a sparing layer right to the outer edges. A smile played at the corners of his mouth. She coveted Calvin's blind optimism. Two nights ago, as they lay side by side in bed staring up at the ceiling, he said, "All we need is each other and this patch of land — our heaven on earth."

Where he saw heaven, she saw Armageddon. While he lived moment to moment, she imagined herself hunkered down by the picture window in the living room with a rifle cocked at an approaching squad car. Refusing to leave the land she and her family had toiled over.

"Calvin, we've got to talk about the loan. We've missed two payments now."

"You worry too much, Willa." He scooped and spread honeyberry jam on a second biscuit, savouring a bite before he added, "We'll get Ian Mason to work something out for us. Extend the loan; reduce the payments. We're having a good breeding season. I've got that lead on selling fifteen kids this month. We'll get back on our feet. Others are worse off than we are. God, these biscuits are good."

"We already renegotiated the loan once. I think we should have a plan for if—"

"Let's see what Ian says on Monday, love." Calvin placed his knife neatly beside his plate. "Now, I've got to get out there and disbud the new kids. Hope the milk truck shows up on time to drain the tank." With biscuit in hand, he kissed the top of her head and went outside. She heard him step into his rubber boots, whistling "Don't Fence Me In." Calvin's steaming cup of tea sat untouched on the table.

Only the tick-tock of the Dutch wall clock in the living room broke the silence in the house. Willa thought about the federal government's upcoming buy-out program. Landowners in Southern Alberta would have from July to December 2058 to cash in their land: twenty-five percent of its current assessed value, itself a fraction of land values a decade ago. She couldn't betray her father by selling his land for a pittance. Still, the word "foreclosure" reared in Willa's mind, bucking all other thoughts away. She tensed her stomach muscles to quell an eruption of sick dread. She anchored her hands on the edge of the table. Fixated on her tea mug, with its picture of a blue bird resting in a twist of jade vines. Her headache, which had subsided, crept back in. As she watched, one of the vines became a snake. It writhed and wound its body around the delicate bird, squeezing. Willa swiped the mug away. Tea sprayed her leg and the floor. The cup smashed on the tiles.

Willa gaped at the dark spatters and ceramic shards. With trembling hands, she retrieved a broom from beside the fridge and swept up the mess. She put the broom away and leaned her back against the fridge, looked at the floor streaked with tea stains where she'd swept.

"It's only an interview," she'd said to Daniel. "If you don't get the job, you should come home for a while. We can build another barn, buy more goats, up our milk output." "Mom," he said. "I gotta go." Willa had stared at the screen until "Call Ended" stopped flashing. She decided to follow up with a text. "Sorry, Daniel. It feels like we're losing you." Then she stopped. Backspaced the message away.

As a toddler, Daniel had run around the barn yelling, "cha-cha," his way of saying 'cat.' Willa sighed at the memory of her boy who grew up and left. Her father had passed away.

Her mother and sister had moved to Calgary. An image flitted through her mind. Her mother fingering the four-way medal on a chain around her neck. She never took it off. Trusted the fervent prayers and devotion it inspired to fix everything. But the cross hadn't fixed anything. This land had once belonged to Willa's industrious paternal grandparents. Determined immigrants from the Netherlands. Her father had persevered to keep the Van Bruggen dream alive. Willa knew what she had to do. Unflinching devotion to the land, and working as hard as her forebears had, that made sense. Drought and strange visions be damned.

2

YOUNG WILLA STRETCHED her arms across the wall of sandbags and peered into the rising Oldman River. She should have been milking the Holstein, Dolly. Instead, she stood glaring at the roiling, muddy waters that had ruined her thirteenth birthday. Papa and Mama and her ten-year-old sister, Sophie, hadn't even sung Happy Birthday to her. Her ears had been filled the whole day with the roar of a backhoe engine and the slap-slap of sandbags being piled one on top of the other.

The river had turned on them again, bursting its banks as it had every spring for the last three years. Still, the stormy heat waves turning glaciers into raging rivers didn't make her insides quiver as much as the battle between her mother and father did. Her father said everything would be okay, but Willa couldn't remember the last time she'd seen her mother smile. The other day, her mother had called the ranch a "godforsaken, waterlogged piece of land." The glares that shot out of her eyes made Willa feel like throwing up. She eyed the willows by the river. Swaying wildly in the wind, they looked like they were trying to lift up their roots and run away as water crept further and further up their trunks. They must be furious at the river, she thought.

Willa leaned forward over the retaining wall to spit into the river. Her life had cracked in two. There was then: horseback rides with Sophie. Ducking under branches in the aspen groves where leaves clicked together in the breeze like tiny castanets. Picnics at the Western Crest, a viewpoint on the Van Bruggen ranch overlooking the Rocky Mountains with their frosting of snow. Her grandparents were buried near the Western Crest; Willa kept their graves free of weeds and debris. Placing fresh daisies and wolf willow sprigs by the headstones. And there was now: endlessly crying skies. Sandbags. The musty smell of damp animal hides and hay. No time for play. Her mother always on edge, fingering her cross and whispering prayers. Her father too preoccupied for jokes or card games.

Sophie ran up and grabbed her arm. "Mama said I could finish my homework later, Willa, so I can help you."

Together, they milked Dolly and mucked out the horse stalls. While they worked, Sophie threw out question after question. "How high will the river get?" "Will the cattle drown?" "What if the house floods?" "Will we have school tomorrow?" Willa reassured her as best she could. Mostly she said, "I don't know, but try not to worry about it." She was old enough now to protect Sophie like a big sister should. They were almost the same ages as Laura and Carrie in the Laura Ingalls Wilder book, *The Long Winter*. Sophie resembled Carrie, thin and delicate. Willa shared Laura's strength and determination, her father said.

By the time they cleaned themselves up, their father had returned with their neighbour Bill Bradford and his son, Logan. Vince Brookes, the veterinarian from Fort Macleod, and his son, Calvin, were there, too. They had left before first light to drive the Bradford and Van Bruggen cattle onto high ground. She'd wanted to go with them, but her father said no — she should care for Dolly and the other animals in the barn. Now he sat down heavily beside her on the sofa in the front room. In the kitchen nook, Sophie snuggled up against their mother, whose paring knife assailed the potatoes. She was trying to study her spelling, but every few seconds her head popped up as if to do a nose count.

"They were up to their bellies in muck when we got to them," their father said. "We hauled most of them out with ropes tied to the horses. We had to leave a few bawling near the water, too stuck to be pulled out."

Willa saw Sophie's lower lip quiver.

Her mother frowned. "Must you share the grim details with the girls, Gerard?"

"They're tough enough to know the truth, Marilyn. Right, girls?"

Sophie stared at him, wide-eyed, but Willa bit her lip and nodded. "Of course, Papa."

After her father and the men had had their breakfast and a few hours' sleep, they reinforced the sandbag wall along the banks of the Oldman River where it had risen another two feet since yesterday. In the afternoon, Bill Bradford set off for home with his son, Logan. Calvin, the vet's son, rode off on one of the Van Bruggen paint horses to check the roads. Willa watched him through the picture window as he galloped across the field. He rode better than anyone she knew. Calm and confident. Every horse seemed eager to obey him. Too bad he couldn't make the river do the same.

Sophie clicked her Legos. The lid on the potato pot clacked softly as the steam escaped. Classical music played on the smart speaker, as it always did when her father was in the house. He and Mr. Brookes scoured their phones for weather reports. No one spoke. The pages of *Little Town on the Prairie* fluttered as Willa turned them, though she could hardly take in what she read as she waited for someone to say something.

After a while, Calvin Brookes stepped quietly back into the house. "Looks like the dam's busted," he said. His voice drawled with calm, but his eyes skittered from one adult face to another. "Just east of the entrance to the Bradford ranch, the Range Road disappears into a lake. The Van Bruggen and Bradford ranches are surrounded by high water."

Calvin towered over the men in the room — a thin lodgepole pine among paper birches. The fact he kept his blond hair long made him stand out, too. Calvin looked at his father with blue eyes that made Willa think of last week's English lesson on clichés. *Like still pools.*

"How are we going to get home, Dad?" he asked.

Calvin's even tone floated over to Willa first so that it took her a moment to process his dire words.

"What in heaven's name are we going to do, Gerard?" her mother said, ignoring Calvin's question and slapping her hand on the kitchen counter. Willa jumped. "Three years we've battled a river that's determined to drown us all." Her mother's face and neck blotched red, as if she'd put rouge in all the wrong places.

Silence again. Finally, Vince Brookes cleared his throat. "Mind if we use your canoe, Gerard?"

Her father nodded, never looking up, just standing there, scrubbing mud and sand off his arms at the kitchen sink. The vet turned to his son. "We'll paddle up the Range Road in Mr. Van Bruggen's canoe and call your mom to pick us up on the other side."

Pulling a kitchen towel off a hook on the wall, Willa's father turned to her mother. He rubbed his arms vigorously, his face expressionless. "Don't worry, Marilyn. The water will recede, and they'll repair the dam in no time. We just need to be patient."

They exchanged silent stares for a moment, then her father said, "Willa, we have something for you."

"Oh yes," her mother said. She disappeared into the office and returned with a parcel wrapped in paper covered in pictures of brightly coloured balloons. Handing it to Willa, she began to sing "Happy Birthday" — the notes thin, shaky — and the others, including Mr. Brookes and his son, joined in. Inside the package was the last book in the Laura Ingalls Wilder series: *These Happy Golden Years.*

LATE THAT EVENING, long after she should have been asleep, Willa tiptoed past her sister's bed to go to the bathroom. On her way back, she heard her parents' voices and pressed her ear to their bedroom door.

"…waiting for better times," her mother said in a fierce whisper. "I love you, Ger, but I'm through fighting nature year after year. How can we make money when our pastures turn into swampland and our cattle keep drowning?"

Willa shifted slightly, causing the floor to creak. For a moment, she heard nothing and wondered if she'd betrayed herself. She held very still.

"See? You don't have any more answers. That's the time to give up. When you've run out of options."

"You're wrong, Marilyn." Her father's voice was soft but deliberate. "This land has been knocking people down and raising them up again for generations. It's no different now than ever."

"This is different. You can't face facts. This isn't a minor economic downturn."

"Boom and bust. That's Alberta. These bad times will pass as the others have. We can choose to bend in the wind or be felled."

"Glaciers melting at record rates. Southern Alberta pounded every year by once-in-a-century storms. Forest destruction from raging late summer fires. Pine beetles devouring what's left."

Willa pictured her mother counting off the disasters on her fingers.

"Fish dying in streams and lakes where the water is hot as the tropics. A *Calgary Herald* columnist said yesterday all we need is a swarm of locusts and Alberta can write its own bible."

Willa thought her father might laugh at that, but he didn't.

"Disrespect aside," her mother continued, "the columnist is right. These are climate catastrophes of biblical proportions." Drawers bumped open and slammed shut. A rapid back-and-forth of footfalls. Willa no longer needed to press her ear to the door to eavesdrop. "We need to sell now while someone's still willing to buy a piece of the famed Palliser's Triangle."

"I think you're being overly dramatic, Marilyn."

Silence again. Had they seen her shadow under the door? She stretched up on tiptoe in a panicked effort to hide her feet.

"You're obsessed, Ger. Mark my words. This place will destroy you sooner or later, but I'm sure not going to let it destroy me — or the girls."

Willa drew a breath at the word "girls."

Her mother's voice rose, the words pinched together to squeeze past her tears. "My sister says I can stay with her as long as I like. When the highway reopens, I'm taking Wilhelmina and Sophie to Calgary."

Willa froze. Her heart, already beating at a canter, sped into a full gallop. Her mother's rant droned on, but she heard nothing after the word "Calgary."

THE NEXT MORNING, Willa attacked the knots in her thick curls with her hairbrush. Her mother stood behind her in the bathroom, her arms crossed, hands in tight fists. "We'll be close to a school and shopping malls. You and Sophie will have a much more stable, predictable life there."

Willa stared at her reflection in the bathroom mirror, silently commanding herself not to cry. "This is our home, Mama. How could you even think about leaving and dragging me with you?"

"Life is about choices, Wilhelmina. One thing or the other. In this case, stay or go. So, do we stay where there's no future or go make one somewhere else? We're slowly drowning here, so the choice seems clear to me."

Willa heard in those words all the stiffness that was her mother. Always certain about everything. When Willa begged to stay home from church one Sunday, her mother said yes, but only if she worked hard at something. "Idle hands are the devil's workshop," she said. "God will be watching." Willa had asked how she knew that. Her response: "That's just a fact, Wilhelmina."

"Conditions are better in the city," her mother continued. "There's a park near Aunt Agatha's place and lots of pathways to ride bikes. I'll buy you a brand-new bike as soon as we have money for it. I may have a chance to work in Aunt Agatha's church, because the secretary there just quit."

"How can you leave Papa?"

"I'm not happy leaving your father." Her mother picked up the towel that Willa had dropped after her shower. She folded it carefully in half lengthwise and hung it over the towel rack. "As I said, life is about choices."

Willa sniffed and tossed her head. "Well, I choose to stay." She waited, expecting her mother to shoot down the idea and march her out of the bathroom and right up to Aunt Agatha's. But she didn't.

"If our family's going to be broken," Willa flailed on, her defiance gaining speed, "I'd rather be broken here than in some stupid place where people are squished together like chickens in a coop." She glared into the mirror and saw relief flash across her mother's face. She had the same look when she dug up a tough weed and discovered she'd gotten the whole root.

"You don't want me to come with you," Willa said.

"Don't be silly. Of course I do. Shall I braid it for you?" her mother said, reaching for her hair.

"No thank you. I can take care of it myself." Willa walked out the door, then paused and looked back, each new word its own sentence. "I'm. Not. Leaving." She turned on her heel. Just before she closed her bedroom door hard, she heard her mother say, "Willa, wait." Willa waited for a knock, but it didn't come.

THREE WEEKS LATER, Willa's father announced that the water had receded enough to uncover the Range Road. He said it the same way he told them a calf died. Willa knew her mother and sister could now leave any time. In the intervening weeks, she and her mother hadn't spoken much, though she'd prepared Willa's favourite dish, nasi goreng, three times. Willa happily devoured the mixture of rice, vegetables and chicken, but the meals hadn't weakened her resolve. Her mother had made only one other attempt to convince her to join them, saying it would be easier for Sophie to settle in if Willa came, too.

One dreary July morning, as drizzle dripped from the eaves, Willa and Sophie stood at the living room window watching their mother and father pile suitcases and boxes into Aunt Agatha's SUV. The girls' hands locked together, fingers interlaced.

"We'll see each other all the time, right, Willa?"

"Of course we will. Nothing will change between us. You'll always be my little sister."

"What if I don't make any friends?"

"You will."

Sophie stamped her foot. "I just want to cut myself in half and give one half to Mama and keep the other half here with you and Papa."

Tears welled in Sophie's eyes.

"You'd bleed all over the place, silly," Willa said.

"Eew," said Sophie.

"You'll have fun living in the city," Willa said, though she couldn't imagine it. "Like Mama said, there'll be shopping malls and bike paths." Even as she uttered the words, she wondered what the big deal was about shopping. And she couldn't imagine a bike ever being as good as a horse.

They watched their mother load the cat carrier into the car. "At least I get to take Madeleine with me." Madeleine, one of the barn cats, had the personality of a lamb. Sophie had gentled her from birth, and the cat often slept with her. Sophie leaned against Willa and sobbed into her shoulder. "Come with us. Please." Sophie drew the 'please' out so long, Willa wondered if she'd ever stop. She stroked Sophie's long blond hair, fine as down, and thought of the countless places she would miss her sister. In the bedroom they had always shared; on the school bus; on the Western Crest; in the barn. She couldn't imagine life without her. She wondered for the hundredth time whether she should move for Sophie's sake. But she didn't want to be locked away in the city. Her mother was right — sometimes you just had to choose.

Part of her wanted to wail, "You should stay with us," but a bigger part of her didn't. If her mother insisted on leaving with Sophie, then go. She'd have her father all to herself. She couldn't help being selfish about it. "I can't come with you, Sophie. You know Papa needs me. I'll look after him and you look after Mama, and then we'll know they're both okay. It's just a different way of being a family."

Sophie nodded slowly. Willa grasped one of the front panels of her long plaid work shirt and wiped dry the dusting of freckles on Sophie's cheeks. She caught Sophie in a hug and held on. None of it seemed real. Any minute, her parents would unload the car and come back inside. They would all giggle at their ridiculous play acting and tuck themselves into the kitchen nook to play that Dutch card game, *Jokeren*, like they used to. Her mother would make vanilla pudding as she often did on Sunday nights. It would all be *gezelig* again. Her father's favourite Dutch word — it had no one-word English translation, but meant cozy, comfortable, pleasant. Willa felt a hand on her shoulder.

"It's not too late, Wilhelmina," her mother said. "You can still come with us."

She noted a tinge of impatience in her mother's flat tone. She clamped her teeth together and shook her head. Sophie pulled away, and her mother stepped forward. Willa glued her arms to her sides, making her body rigid as a barn board to receive her mother's cool embrace.

She stood with her father in front of the ranch house and watched the wheels of the SUV churn up muddy gravel as it pulled away. Sophie had unclipped her seat belt. She leaned over the back seat, staring miserably at them through the rear window, waving limply. Willa and her father both raised their arms high and waved back until the vehicle had crested the hill on its way to the highway and faraway Calgary.

That evening, Willa lay face down on her bed with her arms a double shield around her head when her father knocked softly on the door.

"Come in," she said into the comforter.

"Hey, lieverd," her father said. "I brought you some supper."

"I'm not hungry."

"It's a P, B and J. I'll leave it for you."

She heard him place the plate on her desk. After a while, she knew he hadn't left because she could hear the scrape, scrape of his calloused hands rubbing together. His hands were always busy — roping, hammering, pitching hay, branding calves. In the evening, his fingers whisked cards around the table in games of solitaire. When he read, his fingers tapped the book cover. Even when he took a nap on the couch, his hands twitched as if all his dreams were about work. When she tipped her head up, her father sat down and placed a hand on her long braid.

"You okay, lieverd?"

"Yes. I guess."

"I'm sorry our lives took a turn."

"I know."

"I love you very much. And your mother loves you too.

We'll look after you as best we can. I can't say it's going to be easy, but if we help each other ..."

His voice trailed off, and Willa turned over. She pulled herself up against the head of the bed. She looked at him expectantly.

"Remember Oma's stories about the war in the Netherlands?" her father said.

She nodded.

"How they had to eat tulip bulbs during the *Hongerwinter?* And a Nazi soldier once pointed a gun at her while she scrounged for firewood with her older sister. They went through much harder times than we ever will. Remember how they had to eat sugar-beet pulp, the stuff left over after the syrup was squeezed out?"

She wrinkled her nose in distaste and her father smiled. "That's exactly how Oma's face looked whenever she told that story. You and I are Van Bruggens. We're like her. Tough. You and I can make it here. I know we can. We just have to work together."

She waited, hardly breathing. Water dripped down the drainpipe outside her window. The window and the room belonged to her now, not her and Sophie. She thought that would make her happy, but it didn't. The furnace kicked in, and, after a while, shut off. She lifted the collar of her shirt up to her eyes to wipe away the dampness. "And we'll never, ever give up, right?"

"That's right," he said. He held his hand up and she high-fived him. "Never, ever give up. We'll be fine, the two of us. Life goes on. You have to make the most of the cards you're dealt."

She smiled. Her father rarely won at Solitaire, but he kept playing anyway. When he did happen to win, he cried out, "*hete hond!*" That was Dutch for 'hot dog!'

He lightly patted each of her knees and stood up. "You can see your mom and Sophie a couple times a month on the weekends."

"Sophie can come here. I don't need to see my mother."

Her father shook his head in vigorous contradiction. "No, no. You don't mean that."

She shrugged and he sighed, still shaking his head. "We'll see. We'll see."

He left the room. She burrowed her face into her pillow. Sophie would be at Aunt Agatha's now. Holding fast to Madeleine, no doubt. Willa pictured her aunt's house. One in a row of many. A tiny playground at the end of the street. Poor Sophie, she thought.

THE NEXT MORNING, Willa dressed and went to the kitchen for breakfast, as usual. Her father had already gone out to do the morning chores, but on the table, he'd left her a belated birthday cake, sunken in on one side as if someone had started to sit on it by mistake. Her father had slathered on frosting in gloppy heaps and embedded thirteen Smarties in the vanilla moonscape. She sat down at the table. As she stared through the rainy window, she picked the Smarties off the cake and ate them, one by one.

She'd just finished her last one when her father came inside. She heard him kick off his wooden shoes at the side door. When he came into the kitchen, he beamed at her. "Morning, Willa. I have an idea."

"What kind of idea?"

Her father swiped a finger across the top of the cake and licked off a dollop of frosting. "Mmm," he said, laughing. "Not bad if I do say so myself."

"Thanks for the cake, Papa."

Her father squatted down in front of her, balancing on the balls of his feet. "We need to move the house."

"Move the house?" she said in alarm. "But I thought we were keeping the ranch?"

"Yes, yes," he said. "I'm sorry, lieverd, didn't mean to startle you. Of course we're staying, but we need to move the house further away from the river. Then if the water rises again, we won't need all those sandbags."

She nodded her understanding.

He bobbed back up to his full height and looked out the kitchen window. "I know just where we'll put it. And we'll plant a shelterbelt of lodgepole pines to keep the wind off us, too. And a hedgerow of caraganas behind. Weather's good today. Let's go into Fort Macleod and get the trees."

"Today? Before the house is moved?"

He grinned. "If not now, when?"

At Merry Weather's Greenhouse and Garden Centre in Fort Macleod, they bought thirteen lodgepole pines. Over the next two weeks, her father dug the holes, eight feet apart, and together they planted the perfectly straight row of fledgling pines. They attached three guy wires to each tree to hold them steady in the wind. Behind the trees, they planted a hedge of caraganas as added protection.

"Trees talk to each other," her father said after the work was complete. His voice was hushed, the way her mother talked about Jesus at Christmas time.

"What language do they speak?" she asked, skeptical.

"The language of chemistry. They emit chemical signals that other trees pick up on so they can raise their own defences. Against an invasion of insects, for instance. I read once that trees have been known to keep the stump of a long-felled companion alive by sending a sugar solution through the root system. No one knows why." He pointed at the shelterbelt. "Conifers like these have survived in one form or another for fifty million years. I guess you have to be pretty adaptable to survive that long."

She chuckled at the small, slender trees that showed no hint of their grand history or of one day growing taller than the house. "They look more scared of the wind than anything." She watched the tips bending almost double in the breeze. "Like they'd rather bury their heads in the sand."

Her father smiled and gave her braid a gentle tug. "They'll grow tall and withstand the strongest windstorms. Just like you." He tapped the shovel on each of his wooden shoes and laughed. "And when they're finally done growing, we can turn them into footwear."

She looked up at him. It was hard to imagine any of the coming years being happy or golden for her family, but she loved Papa with all her heart. Maybe that would be enough to make everything right.

3

DANIEL BROOKES GRIPPED the railing as he crossed the Langevin Bridge toward downtown Calgary. A hefty west wind kicked dust around the dry Bow River riverbed. He passed through the castellated wall that encircled Calgary's core. Built to resist flood water from storms and melting glaciers, the wall now imprisoned the city's hollow-eyed skyscrapers. Surging oceans, ruinous storms, and crippling droughts had finally sent developed and developing countries into backflips to curb carbon. Oil barons had been chased out of Calgary's plush offices in the 2040s by the world's intolerance for unconventional oil and its untenable footprint of emissions and tar ponds.

As Dan strode up Macleod Trail toward Stephen Avenue, he skirted an overturned sedan, half-on, half-off the sidewalk near the Municipal Building. A single file of commuters bypassed the derelict car. Most wore dual-cartridge dust masks, as he did, a line of ants weaving around an obstruction. Unfazed, single-minded. He found comfort in the pad and click of their shoes on pavement. The sound of order and determination.

Calgary had become a study in extremes: serene by day and frantically agitated at night. City police couldn't keep up with the chaos caused by rowdy hordes that came out after dark to hurl rocks and insults about uncaring governments. A nine o'clock curfew had done nothing to quell the violence and destruction. Just that morning, Mayor Vaillancourt announced they couldn't afford to hire more police officers. He declared a state of emergency and said he had appealed to the federal government to deploy Canadian Forces personnel to patrol the downtown core. The mayor said City Council would make sure the light-rail transit system kept running. As if the whirr of electric arms stroking overhead wires and the hum of Ctrain wheels on shiny tracks signalled that Calgary was still a civilized place.

Dan pushed his hands further into the pockets of his dress pants. Paper bags, food wrappers, and bits of fluffy pink insulation swirled in windy eddies around his legs as he rounded the corner onto Stephen Avenue. On Olympic Plaza, a wide outdoor court built for the 1988 Winter Olympics, a man half-sang, half-shouted through a bull horn about his saviour, Jesus Christ, who would help them all get back on their feet again. A long queue of ragged men and women snaked through the plaza. They shuffled patiently toward sandwiches and paper cups of water. Bull-horn Man had one hand on a wooden cross with the words "repent" and "believe" painted on the cross-bar. A banner hung on each side of the serving table. One read, "Jesus is coming back." The other listed the Ten Commandments. As someone with no religious affinity, Dan was curious what motivated the proselytizers to help the downtrodden — charity or conversion. He supposed it wasn't either-or, but a complicated marriage of the two.

As Dan strode up the mall, he sidestepped islands of broken window glass and homeless people strewn along the sidewalk like monuments to a failed society. Most of the mendicants had signs propped beside them begging for money and bottled water. He imagined himself in their place. Time was ticking down on the two months' grace Mrs. Winstead had given him on his rent after his grant money ran out. His student loans would be due soon. None of that could be managed on short-order-cook wages at the Breakfast Barn.

Outside the Telesat Convention Centre, a man sat cross-legged on the sidewalk. The mug he held out contained a few coins. His sign, neatly printed and correctly spelled, read: "Help me get back to business." Dan tossed a quarter in the man's cup. "God bless you, son," the man said, grinning, a gap where his front teeth should have been. Dan looked around. Little separated him or his parents or the people scurrying to work from this man's fate. Dan would be thrilled to get the job at Crystel, except for the catch. A surge of nerves kicked him in the belly.

"I'll get you the interview," Percy Dickinson had told him, "but if Landrew hires you, I want you to be my eyes and ears at Crystel. On the sly, of course." Percy's intensity radiated through the phone screen. "The corporation has its own fucking coffers at heart, not the plight of Albertans. They'll fucking divert our pipeline water to the thirsty U.S." About Crystel's CEO, Adam Landrew, his friend said, "A bead of sweat wouldn't dare cross the man's brow. He'd sell his grandmother for a loonie."

Dan made his way up Centre Street to 9th Avenue. A crowd milled about outside the Fairmont Palliser as Dan passed by on the other side of the street. Like most hotels in the downtown core, the Palliser had been recommissioned as a homeless shelter until the city could get back on its feet. People tramped the red-carpeted steps day and night, clamouring for one of the coveted luxurious beds.

When Dan arrived at Crystel Canada Square at 9th Avenue and 4th Street, two burly security guards equipped with handguns and batons stopped him as the revolving door spat him inside. The man's neck formed a thick, sinewy junction between his ears and shoulders; the woman wore a grimace made more ominous by a fat halo of black liner around each eye. Dan pulled off his dust mask and told them he had an interview with the CEO of Crystel. They looked him up and down in scornful disbelief. Each of them held one of his arms as they led him to the reception desk, apparently to disprove his ridiculous story. Assured of his peaceful mission, they showed him to the elevator and stood, arms crossed, until the doors closed.

Dan shook his head as the elevator started up to the 33rd floor. Security had become a growth industry as mountain snowpacks and ancient glaciers evaporated. When thousands of Albertans lost their jobs in the oil sands, civil unrest had crept in the way cold settles in the bones. Alberta, and all of Canada for that matter, had dragged behind the sustainability innovators. Bladeless wind turbines developed in Spain and Germany dotted urban and rural landscapes. American-made rooftop solar panels on homes and many cars kept high capacity Japanese nano-batteries juiced. Cheap natural gas from China heaped efficient fuel on the transportation sector. Alberta needed to rise from the ashes. The water pipeline would be a good first step.

The elevator beeped its arrival. The doors opened onto a bright white reception area, a sharp contrast to the garbage-strewn sidewalk and boarded-up store windows at street level. Dan sniffed the air. Minty fresh with a hint of rosy sweetness.

So unlike the cocktail of stale dust, distant forest fire and chemical Porta-Potty disinfectant that hung like a dirty sheet over the city streets. He cleared his throat and smiled at the receptionist. "Daniel Brookes to see Mr. Landrew."

She smiled back with glossy red lips and snow-white teeth. "I'll let him know you're here. Please have a seat."

Dan's shoes squeaked on the glimmering marble floor as he took a seat on a row of chrome and black leather chairs. He glanced around and thought, minimalist. Not a plant or sculpture in sight. A lone painting hung on the wall behind the reception desk: white canvass with a black squiggle across the middle. A small plaque pronounced the title: Horizon. His mom would have shaken her head at the room. "Hardly what you'd call gezelig," she'd say. But it didn't need to be gezelig, Dan decided. Business is business. Emotion had no place in that. He simply had to find out for Percy if something more nefarious was going on.

Dan felt the receptionist's gaze on him, and he turned to reciprocate her smile. Did she see guilt in his eyes? He looked down, spotted a hangnail on his thumb and picked at it.

How could Dan say no to his friend, a man he'd known for ten years? Percy had risen swiftly through the ranks to become Senior Communications Advisor to Alberta's Water Minister. He had enough clout in water circles to recommend Dan for this interview. Still, Dan considered himself an ordinary guy with good grades, high ideals, and more country hick left in him than he liked to admit. Hardly spy material, and he'd told Percy as much.

"Mr. Brookes, would you like a refreshment?"

He looked up, startled. He hadn't noticed the receptionist walking over. "I'm sorry?"

"Water? Tea?"

"Oh, no. Thanks anyway." He felt himself blush. If he were still alive, Opa wouldn't approve of the spying, but he'd have faith in Dan to carry it off. "You've got your head on straight," he used to say. "Get away from these damn goats and put your brain to good use."

The receptionist still stood in front of him, tapping her toe. "Please follow me," she said, ushering him into an expansive conference room. Her bleached teeth flashed. Was he sure he didn't want coffee or a bottled water? Dan shook his head.

"Mr. Landrew will be with you shortly, Mr. Brookes."

The meeting room rivalled the reception area in sterility. Only the conference table coasters with the Van Gogh Starry Night motif broke the monotony of marble, chrome and fluorescent lights. He licked his dry lips, wished he hadn't refused the bottled water. Five hundred millilitres of Crystel spring water, bottled in Ontario and Quebec, on sale for $8.50 thirty-three floors below.

Dan tapped his fingers on the conference table. He wished he'd gone to the bathroom before he left home. If he got the job, he'd be using Crystel's toilet trailers, the most luxurious facilities in the downtown core, with running water and floral-scented soap for washing instead of the usual hand-sanitizer dispensers. Indoor flush toilets in Calgary had gone the way of the polar bear during Dan's second year at Mount Royal University. Some people carted their waste from small portable enzyme toilets inside their homes to dumping stations around town, but most dug outhouses or purchased Porta-Potties for their back yards. Dan's landlady had installed one of the bright blue stalls behind the house. The 'honey wagons' that sucked up Porta-Potty waste rivalled the number of electric buses on Calgary streets. Everywhere, the pong of glutaraldehyde gusted around with the dust.

Dan was checking his phone when Adam Landrew stepped into the room. Twenty-five minutes he'd kept him waiting. Dan stood up. Landrew towered over him even more than he'd expected. Dan hadn't inherited his parents' height; his head barely reached the man's chin. The whisk of grey hair at Landrew's temples perfectly matched his silver-grey suit, finely tailored with a fine white pinstripe. A cloud of cologne wafted in with him that made Dan stifle a cough as the man gripped his hand.

"Adam Landrew," the tall man said in a melodic tenor. "Good to meet you, son."

"Good to meet you, sir. A pleasure. Really. I ... I was looking forward to it." He was babbling like a fool.

"Sorry for the delay, but the closing of the downtown core again yesterday for high winds got me behind. I wish they wouldn't do that."

Wish they wouldn't do that? Really? Flying building debris had killed five Calgarians in the last year.

"Now," Landrew continued, poking a manicured fingernail on the tabletop. He made no motion to sit. "I've heard good things about you."

"Thank you, sir."

"Thank Percy Dickenson. He said you finished top of your class."

"I was fortunate enough to work three summers with Percy and a few other provincial experts mapping out the confined and unconfined aquifers in the Slave Lake area. The ones with the best chance of rapid recharge when the drought ends."

45

"Yes, yes," Mr. Landrew said, waving his soft, slender hand in mild annoyance. "He said you were quite an asset."

Dan willed himself not to fidget.

"I need employees who know water science, Dan," Mr. Landrew said, staring into Dan's eyes. "We'll get water from the coast and whatever we can from the northern bowels of this province and make sure it gets to the people."

Dan blinked and suppressed the urge to ask, Which people? "I'll do my best, sir."

"Well, a recommendation from Dickenson is good enough for me. I'll get one of the techs to show you around the rest of our offices and the lab. That's where you'll be most of the time — unless we need you in the field, of course." He offered his hand again. "Welcome to Crystel."

"Thank you, sir. I look forward to the opportunity ..." But Landrew had already strode out the door.

Dan took a deep breath. He could learn to be smooth like that, couldn't he? So no one would know why he was really there?

"Oh, god," he said, and crumpled into a chair to await the grand tour.

4

FIVE DAYS HAD PASSED since the tanker turned tank and the snake came to life on Willa's coffee mug. The return to sanity put a spring in her step. That evening, Calvin backed the pick-up with its hay trailer up to the barn door. Willa hoped his beatific smile meant he'd got a good deal on the load of hay that appeared to contain more fodder than straw this time. Maybe it would last them longer than a week.

Calvin stepped out of the truck and bent forward into a deep bow. "Well, good evening, ma'am. You're a sight for the sore eyes of a poor goat farmer. I hope your husband isn't due back soon."

Willa smiled. "You came at the right time," she said. "Do you want to unload, or eat first?"

"Work before pleasure," Calvin replied. "Took a long time today. I had to drive to Red Deer for this load. Paid through the nose for it, but there isn't much good hay around."

Paid through the nose. Willa felt as though the entire load of hay had dropped onto her shoulders. Calvin pushed the button that lowered the hydraulic conveyor and turned on the belt. Alarmed bleats echoed in the barn walls as the groan of the motor sent goats scurrying in their pens. Calvin looked at Willa and raised his eyebrows inquisitively. "You want to work the conveyor and I'll go up top?"

With a vigorous nod, she hauled the dust mask up from around her neck and covered her nose and mouth. "I'm good to go."

Calvin chuckled. "Will-ah, I am your husband," he boomed, breathing stentoriously like Darth Vader in the old Star Wars movies.

"You promised you wouldn't do the Dark Lord anymore. Besides, gunslingers are your specialty."

"Okay, no more," he said. "Scout's honour."

"You were never a scout."

Calvin smiled and shrugged. He loaded a few hay bales onto the belt before climbing the ladder to the loft. For a while they worked in silence, Willa on the trailer dragging bales onto the conveyor and Calvin running feverishly back and forth up above to organize them into neat stacks. "I saw Logan Bradford this morning," he shouted from the mouth of the loft on one of his return trips.

"Where?" Willa called up to him.

"I popped in to the Wholly Grill to see my sister this afternoon." He disappeared for a moment to stack a bale. "Logan staggered in, three sheets to the wind." .

Willa jumped down from the trailer and hit the button to kill the conveyor.

"What's wrong, Willa?"

She looked up at him in the loft. "Was Peter with him?"

"What?"

"Damn this mask." Willa pulled it down. "I said, did you see Peter?"

"No. Logan was upset because Peter had gone to stay at a friend's house to celebrate his birthday instead of staying home with his 'broken-down old dad,' as Logan put it."

"The boy is fourteen now. What does Logan expect? I'm worried about the two of them, Calvin. You're the second person this week to see Logan drinking in the daytime. He never drowned his sorrows in booze when Kelli was alive."

"I'm sure they'll both be fine. Peter's tough. He'll come through okay."

"Oh, Calvin," she said. "The way you make light of the direst events."

Calvin peered down at her. "Direst? The man drinks a bit to ease his sorrows. You're too quick to worry, Willa. C'mon, let's get this done."

"Too quick to care, maybe," she said. She regretted the sanctimonious tone, but Calvin had disappeared into the loft again; perhaps he hadn't heard her. She pulled the mask back on and they didn't exchange another word until they'd finished the job and sat down in the nook, each blowing on their steaming spoons of goat stew.

Willa let the spoon hover in front of her as she weighed her words. "Logan's in bad shape, Calvin. He's not the man he was. Remember what a rock he and his father were for Papa and me? And Logan bought all that land off us when we converted to goats."

Calvin frowned. "He likes to keep to himself now, that's all."

Willa stared into her stew. "I'm not sure who I'd call to help him. Kelli used to drive up to Fort McMurray with Peter to visit her parents, but they're gone now. She had a brother there. And a sister, too. A Lisa? Or Leia? Anyway, I'm not sure what will become of Peter if Logan goes on this way. The boy has a tender heart, like his mother did." Her voice trailed off and she finally put the spoonful of stew into her mouth and chewed thoughtfully.

"I'm sure Logan will be fine," Calvin said. "He's sensible enough."

"Yeah, when he's sober. But Peter's just a boy, Calvin. What kind of example does that set for him? To see his father drowning in booze. We've hardly seen Peter since Kelli died. Daniel was like a brother to him. I don't know how you can be so casual about ..." She stopped, exhausted by her own snappish, dramatic tone.

Calvin set his spoon down beside his bowl. "What?"

"Forget it. I'm just worried about Peter."

Calvin went to the counter and measured water into the kettle. He got out a plate for their after-dinner ritual of tea and cookies. "What do you think of the new hay racks?" he asked at last.

"Great," Willa said, stirring tired circles in her bowl. "The way they hinge out from the wall to dump the old hay. Great." She'd found her way back from the dramatic to the mundane, but it felt fake. Fake it 'til you make it, she thought.

"I noticed you covered each end with chicken wire," Calvin said. "Much safer and the hay stays put. Nice. The yearlings are eating well, and our milk supply is good. Milk prices are up again. Let's trim hooves tomorrow. If we could give them pasture time, I wouldn't have to do it so often, but so be it. The new kids are looking a bit weak, I thought. Got to finish disbudding them, too, before the horns get too big. Catching them is a bugger."

Willa strained the bad news from the pile of innocuous facts. Picking nits from a mink, her father would have said. "What do you mean the kids are weak?"

Calvin spoke to the teapot, his back betraying not a hint of tension. "Nothing serious. The newborns are sinking through their knees a bit is all."

"How did I not notice that? What's the problem?"

"Floppy kid syndrome. A stomach ailment. I saw it a few times as a vet tech. We can buy a couple bottles of Pepto-Bismol when we're in town tomorrow. It sounds crazy, but that always helped."

He turned and ran his tongue over his lips. Willa stared at a tiny hole in the shoulder seam of his shirt. Calvin scratched at his stubbled chin, making a rasping sound. The clock in the living room counted the seconds for them. Tick tock tick tock ...

"Listen, Willa. I can go over and talk to Logan this week. See if he needs any help with the sheep. Other than that, it's best to let people be, and they'll come through all right."

Without another word, they both went to the door to put on coats and boots. Willa headed to the milking shed to collect milk from the pasteurizer. Calvin strode to the toolshed, muttering about hoof clippers. The teapot and cookies sat forgotten on the kitchen counter.

5

WILLA'S LABOUR STARTED at the July 2033 Goat Industry Symposium in Lethbridge, Alberta. She sat with Calvin and her father, Gerard, in the third row of the large meeting room at the Coast Hotel and Conference Centre, listening to the keynote address about the benefits of transitioning from cattle to goats.

"My father always said," the speaker recounted, "never keep goats in anything that doesn't hold water, because Houdini must have learned all his escapist tricks from them."

Calvin and Gerard laughed along with the audience. Willa clutched her abdomen and groaned into a powerful contraction. She grabbed Calvin's hand so hard that he cried out, which turned a few heads.

"Calvin," she whispered fiercely, "I think the baby's coming."

He calmly shook his head at her. "That's impossible, Willa. You're not due for another two weeks."

She widened her eyes at him and stood up, pulling his arm so he had no choice but to follow. Gerard looked up in surprise, hurriedly picked up Willa's handbag and followed them. Willa glanced back and saw him stumble along the chairs, crouching down so as not to disturb the people in the row behind. He needn't bother, she thought. His tall pregnant daughter and towering son-in-law had already walled off everyone's view of the keynote.

That night at 11:54, Daniel Gerard Brookes entered the world at the hospital in Lethbridge. Despite his early arrival, he and his lungs seemed robust enough, but a nurse tucked him into an incubator anyway to give him a "shot in the arm," as she put it.

The next morning, Calvin drove back to the farm to check on the cattle and horses, and to collect the baby accoutrements he and Willa had stockpiled. On his return, he plopped down in the hospital chair next to his father-in-law's as Willa fed Daniel his evening meal. "The Oldman has risen again," he said, "but the house is fine, and the cattle are safe. The Oldman Dam is holding." Calvin smiled at Willa. "I talked to Kelli. She can't wait to see the baby. Says you had a lot of nerve not holding on until you got home and she could put her midwife skills to use."

"She called me about an hour ago," Willa said, laughing. "Said she'd help as long as it didn't involve diapers."

"Right," Calvin said, giving Willa's father a slap on the shoulder. "That's what grandparents are for."

Gerard raised his eyebrows at Calvin. "You're the vet tech with the deft fingers. Must be a natural. How's the trailer?"

Willa and Calvin had moved into an old converted ATCO trailer they installed near the Van Bruggen ranch house when they got married.

"High and dry," Calvin said.

"We need to trade places," Gerard said.

"You want my chair?"

"No, no. You and Willa need to move to the house, and I'll live in the trailer."

"No, Papa," Willa cried out. "The trailer's plenty big for us. The crib is all set up in our bedroom."

Gerard raised his hand, palm-down, in front of him. "The tremors are getting worse by the week. I won't be much good to you soon. You two will be taking over, and you should have the house."

Willa focused on Daniel's suckling, his delicate translucent eyelashes and busy cheeks. She sniffed his sweet baby scent. "That's ridiculous. You're being dramatic. The L-dopa is helping your symptoms; you said so yourself. They're doing trials all the time on new treatments."

Gerard stared at Willa, his hand quaking between them to prove the pointlessness of her optimism.

Calvin gently pressed Gerard's hand back onto the man's knee. "When we switch to goats, the work won't be so heavy. There'll be lots of it, but it won't be so heavy. This operation will be yours longer than you ever dreamed."

"All the same," Gerard said gruffly. "You should have the house." And with that, Calvin and Willa knew the matter was settled.

LATER THAT NIGHT, Calvin and Willa sat in the glow of the streetlight shining through the hospital room window, holding hands. Gerard had returned to his motel room down the street. The feathery snores of Willa's roommate floated through the privacy curtain.

"He's so beautiful, isn't he?" Willa said quietly. The nurse had just picked up Daniel to return him to the incubator.

"And so are you." Calvin leaned forward from his perch on the edge of the bed to kiss her. After a few minutes, he pulled away, but only an inch or two. "I'd like to show you just how beautiful I think you are."

She wrinkled her nose and tilted her head toward the other bed. "Not sure my roomie would approve." She leaned in for another kiss.

She caressed his workworn fingers. "Are we ready for this? Parenthood, I mean."

He laughed softly. "I'm almost thirty and you're not far behind. If not now, when? Besides, it's a bit late in the game to be wondering, isn't it?"

"Just want to do a good job, you know?"

"You will. Are you going to let your mother see the baby?"

Willa let go of his hand. She leaned back against her pillow and closed her eyes. "No. She's not welcome in my life. His life."

Calvin sighed. "Is that fair?"

"That limb may not hold you, Calvin." Willa narrowed her eyes at him. "But you know that. Did Papa talk to you? The cavalry or the U.N. or whatever you two might think you are isn't going to save us. We don't need saving. We both made a choice. Sometimes people are just done with each other. It happens."

"I guess I was just thinking about my own mother and how she can't wait to hold her little grandchild."

"Oh, I forgot to tell you, she called me, too. Said she'll do whatever she can to help. And I video-chatted with Sophie while you were picking up the baby stuff. She said she might be able to take a week's vacation to come visit us."

"Aha, I think we've found a few volunteers for diaper duty."

Willa laughed quietly and laid her hand on his again.

WILLA STARED AT THE RAIN SPITTING onto the windshield. She turned her head every few minutes to look in the back seat. Her father had insisted on riding beside Daniel, saying it would give Willa a well-deserved break. His arm draped across Daniel's car seat. The baby's hand gripped his calloused thumb like a stick shift, and she couldn't help but smile.

"He's got you in high gear, Papa." She turned forward again and looked down the slick highway.

"Will you contact your mother about the baby?" Gerard asked from the back seat of the truck cab.

They'd travelled fifty kilometres from Lethbridge and Willa imagined her father had been chewing on that statement for most of them. "Papa," she said, then shook her head to relax her jaw. She turned to look at him and shook her head again, this time to answer no.

He gave a half-shrug.

"We need to keep the cattle for now," Gerard said after a while. "Alberta's still solid beef country even though prices are down now that everyone else has jumped on the 'certified humane' bandwagon. Business will improve again."

Willa turned to him. "But they say the rivers won't last another ten years. Goats consume much less water ..."

He cut her off. "I know what the experts are saying, Willa, but I don't think we need to panic yet. Costs will go down and prices will rise. As they always have."

Calvin reached his hand across the front seat and covered Willa's. She knew what the gesture meant — he would keep his vet tech job at his dad's practice for now. They would make it work with the cattle as long as that's what Gerard wanted. Calvin knew well enough that what her father wanted, Willa wanted too.

OVER THE NEXT FEW WEEKS, Willa and Calvin made the transition into the house and settled her father into the trailer. Calvin returned to work. They received plenty of help from Logan and Kelli Bradford and Calvin's mother. Willa's sister, Sophie, came to stay at the farm the second week in August, but she had to return to Calgary to prepare for the school year. Daniel's cries, she said, prepared her well for the blare of instruments in her junior high school music classes.

Her father had endless chores to do, so Willa was alone most of the day. But she didn't feel lonely or frightened of being on her own with the new baby. In fact, as she lowered Daniel into the kitchen sink for his bath one early September morning, her heart sang. His pudgy palms slapped the water. Sunshine streamed through the window. She glanced outside, drinking in the unbroken blue sky. The tree-studded foothills gently rose and fell. A mosaic of a million greens lay over the Van Bruggen ranch and beyond. The shelterbelt of lodgepole pines glittered in the sunlight. Their thickly needled branches waved in the breeze. In the field beyond the barn, cattle lumbered through tall timothy grass, attacking their lunch with vigour. Willa grinned down at her beautiful boy. The thick corn-silk hair that had sprouted on his head reminded her of a western pasqueflower gone to seed. After gently patting him dry, she tucked him into a fleece sleeper.

"My beautiful baby," she cooed.

Life bulged with the presence of ample water. Yes, glaciers ebbed away each year in overflowing rivers. And sometimes too much rain fell. But all that could be tolerated, managed, appreciated even, in a fecund world whose ever warming springs and autumns stretched the growing season. Newborn calves had no trouble surviving when the wind blew mild and the ground wore a shroud of morning frost instead of tall snow-drifts. They'd been able to stagger their cattle breeding over a longer period to spread out the calving season. Land that could be seeded grew plentiful crops reaped with ease under a balmy harvest moon in early December. Timothy and alfalfa hay flourished, and, if the fall stayed relatively dry, which it usually did, the hay would be plentiful. The Van Bruggen ranch grew fifteen acres of alfalfa for subsistence feeding. Willa knew they would have plenty of hay to winter their three hundred head of Angus and Belgian Blue this year.

Daniel burbled, his eyes locked on Willa's. A bubble formed on his lips. Willa smiled and began to sing.

Over in the meadow in the stream in the sun
lived an old mother fish and her little fishie one.
"Swim," said the mother, "We swim," said the one,
and they swam all day in the stream in the sun ...

As she sang, she felt as if motherhood were a magic elixir that had lain dormant and could now flow freely through her body.

6

DAN SAT DOWN AT the back-corner table of the nearly deserted
Starbucks at Crowfoot Centre in northwest Calgary, enveloped
in the sultry aroma of roasted Arabica. The coffee franchise
had slowly declined; few could afford a fifteen-dollar macchi-
ato anymore, so only a handful of stores remained. Dan knew
Percy Dickenson liked the finer things — he was no working
stiff. His friend strutted in at 4:30. Prompt as always, Dan
thought, glancing at his phone. Percy gave Dan a wave and
pointed at the counter to indicate he would grab a drink first.

"What do you want?" he called out.

"Tall Zen Garden," Dan replied. He knew his stomach could
use the suggestion of harmony, and Percy could afford to buy.

Percy walked slowly to the table with Dan's mug of tea and
his own cup — double espresso, by the looks of it. Percy called
it his water conservation effort. Despite being marshmallowy
around the middle, he dressed like a cover model for GQ: crisp
white shirt, narrow red tie and black dress pants with a razor-
sharp pleat. His auburn hair, glistening with gel and hairspray,
hung in tiny ringlets to just above his earlobes. Every time Dan
saw him, he sported a new pair of expensive-looking earrings.

As Percy sat down, the ceiling pot lights glinted off his diamond studs. One dark eyebrow, then the other lifted as he looked around, rooting out eavesdroppers.

"Music's fucking loud, but I guess that serves our purpose," Percy said quietly as he leaned forward, pushing Dan's Zen Garden across the table like a chess piece. "Here's your wussy tea. Time you got into more manly drinks, my friend."

"Hello to you, too. Good meeting with Water Services?"

Percy rolled his eyes. "The City of Calgary wants us to lobby Crystel for bargain basement water prices from the new pipeline. While we're at it, we'll tell the National Gallery to buy the Mona Lisa for Calgary City Hall and tell the Royal Canadian Mint to print them some money. People think Crown corps are for the people, but that's bullshit. They're instruments of power. Petro-Canada never gave anyone free gas. Pierre Trudeau set it up to avoid defeat; Brian Mulroney privatized it to get into bed with Albertans and their oil companies."

"Petro-Canada?" Dan asked.

Percy shook his head so hard his ringlets vibrated. "Never mind. Poli-sci crap. So, what did you think of Landrew?"

"Smooth. Terrifyingly smooth."

Percy laughed and sipped tentatively from his steaming cup. "He only seems scary 'cause he's all puffed up with his own self-importance."

"The man golfs with the prime minister," Dan replied. "His self-importance is well founded. And I, a mere mortal, am supposed to keep tabs on him?"

Percy nodded, eyes closed, and brought his hands together below his chin in a prayerful pose.

When Percy opened his eyes, they shone with excitement.

As if he'd actually communed with the Almighty. "Don't worry, man, I've got your back."

"You think I can really help you?"

Percy looked casually around and, clearing his throat, leaned across the table again, a chain of gestures Dan recognized as the start of a verbal blitzkrieg.

"Alberta is flat broke. We're totally dependent on federal fucking transfer payments and Crystel pipeline jobs. Tar sands clean-up in the north is sucking up royalty reserves like a dog gulps his dinner. Our dear Premier Hamady is a pathetic dreamer. She believes the rains will return to save our aquifers, which, at this point, is about as likely as the Second Coming of Jesus Fucking Christ."

Dan felt the urge to say, *we can hope*, but stopped himself.

"Hamady maintains Alberta has a constitutional right to waters within its borders, but that only covers surface and groundwater. Every drop of water in the pipeline belongs to Crystel."

"But the pipeline sits on land annexed by the provincial government," Dan countered. "The province only leases the land to the feds, so Hamady has control over where and how far the pipeline goes."

"Yes, but that's where politics enters the picture, my friend. If the price is right, Ms. Hamady will let the federal government lay pipe wherever it pleases." He swept his hands up to press the point and nearly tossed his espresso off the table. Unfazed, he steadied the rocking cup and continued. "Especially as we get closer to next year's election. The prime minister says he opposes water exports, but his voter base, along with a shitload of tax revenue, died with the oil industry. It's just a matter of time before his fan base in Ontario and on the 'wet' coasts say,

'Let those prairie bastards die of thirst.'" He stopped, not for breath, but to kick back the rest of his espresso.

"So how do we make sure we don't?" Dan asked.

"We need the end of that Crystel pipeline to stay in Alberta. My water supply damn well better not dry up," Percy said, spitting out the words. He wiped a shirt sleeve across his mouth. "That's where you come in. We need you to find out what Crystel's grand plans are."

"And how do you suggest I do that?"

"Keep your ear to the ground. Get close with people you think might have inside info." Percy stopped to speak to the muddy coffee stain on his sleeve. "What the fuck?"

"What if they get the idea I'm snooping? And, by the way, who the hell is 'we'?"

Percy stuck a hand up as if to deflect a punch. "Uh-uh. That's need-to-know. I don't want to compromise you."

Right, thought Dan. *I could tell you, but then I'd have to kill you.* He decided to retreat to moral high ground. "I know this sounds corny, Percy, but I want to do some good here. My parents are having a hell of a time making ends meet. And, of course," he added, "I need the job."

Percy's tone softened. "I know you do. And you will make Alberta better. Quit worrying. Do the job they hired you for, which you're more than qualified to do. I'll be in touch. I know you — you're cool under pressure and I can trust you." He laughed. "Read a spy novel." He clapped Dan hard on the shoulder. "I gotta run. My plane leaves in an hour. Here's a phone for you to reach me. Don't use it for anything else. It's registered to Phil Anthrop. Get it? Phil-anthropy?" He sniggered at his own cleverness, then immediately turned deadpan. "My number's programmed in. Call, don't text." He pointed at Dan with his index finger that bore a nail bitten to the quick. "Don't worry. It's gonna be great. We're going to save the fucking province. Just get me the goods."

After Percy left, Dan took his first sip of tea and bobbed the bag up and down in his cup. A classic Mercer Avenue track — Smoke and Mirrors — came on. He exhaled sharply through his nose. Rubbed a hand through his hair. His days as a short-order cook were over. On Monday, he would start his dream career wearing two faces; he would be the scientist he'd studied to become, and he'd pay for the lucky break with subterfuge. When trouble loomed, Opa had always said, "You can bend in the wind or be felled by it." Time would tell whether Dan's decision to take the Crystel job proved him flexible or stupid. It already felt deeply unethical.

The tea had turned tepid and bitter from ginger. He gulped it down out of a deep-rooted habit of waste not, want not. Outside, daylight tiptoed into the shadows. He cast off the comforting smells of the shop and hurried to the Crowfoot Ctrain station, keen to get home before the city turned manic again.

7

AS WILLA FINISHED the evening milking, the wind suspended its shrieking. She stepped outside and thought wistfully of midnight bareback rides with Calvin before drying winds sucked the life from the land and they had to sell the horses. A walk to the Western Crest would surely clear her head, and walking without a dust mask would be freeing.

She called to Calvin as he pitched hay to Duke in the buck pen. "I'm going to take a run up to the Western Crest. I'll be back soon." She thought he acknowledged her, but she didn't turn back to check.

Saskia panted with delight, trying to incite Willa into a shared state of delirium by zipping back and forth ahead of her, raising a great cloud of grey dust on one abrupt turn. The dog halted and gave Willa her usual isn't-life-splendid Great Pyr smile with her tongue lolling out the side of her mouth.

"You're crazy, girl," Willa said, and it struck her that the evidence was piling up to include herself in that description. She leaned down and stroked Saskia's back to encourage her into a calmer trot, and they walked on together side by side.

Willa headed north up the hill toward Logan Bradford's property. A hundred acres of his land used to belong to Gerard, Calvin, and her. Before they sold the cattle. Before her father passed away. And Kelli Bradford. The land seemed to have died with them, because every last one of those hundred acres now lay fallow and windblown.

She and Saskia veered westward at a grove of aspen trees that reached gothic brittle fingers to the sky. A few minutes later, they reached the Western Crest. A small fence enclosed her father's and grandparents' graves. Her Opa and Oma would be shocked by the view of foothills surrounded by sand dunes. A vast landscape punctured by dead trees. Beyond the foothills, the jagged lead line of the Rocky Mountains no longer shouldered snow. She could see the front ranges tonight, the peaks visible for a change as a rare light breeze from the east thinned out the dust and smoke.

As a teenager, she used to come here when she missed Sophie. Most of the time, she mustered a measure of gratitude for what she had. For her sister, even though she lived far away. For her father. The ranch. She watched minnows flit in silver streaks in the nearby sinkhole during the flood years. Bright sunlight sparkled on the water. Chickadees darted about, crying "oh dear me, oh dear me." The intoxicating spice of pine and fecund grasses saturated the air, then.

Now, the shadowed filigree of leafless bushes draped across the nearby gravestones. The sun hung low and opaque. The air smelled empty. A quotation floated through her mind like a thread of mist from a long-ago morning.

Green Acadian meadows, with sylvan rivers among them
Village, and mountain, and woodlands; and, walking under
their shadow ...

Longfellow. Someone her father used to quote. She turned up the collar of her fleece coat and crossed her arms against an involuntary shiver. More like the valley of the shadow of death, she muttered. Would sylvan rivers ever flow through Alberta again? She had to hope so.

As she turned for home, she spied movement in the dead shrubbery. Cold sweat rose on her skin. She grabbed Saskia's collar. The dog sat still beside her, panting contentedly, her Great Pyr smile intact. Willa peered deeper into the tangle of branches. The flick of a cougar's tail. Two glinting yellow eyes. Glaring, assessing, analyzing. Its shoulders rippled with sinuous muscle. Willa's feet seemed frozen to the ground. Why was the animal unperturbed by the dog? And vice versa? Willa's panic eased. Perhaps the cat was only another nightmarish mirage. But cougar sightings had increased lately as the predators emerged from their traditional mountain habitat in search of food. Even so, they were elusive, unless injured. Or starving. Move, she commanded herself. Mustn't look like prey. Make yourself big. Wave your arms. Make noise.

"Don't you see it, girl?" Willa said loudly. Finally, her feet belonged to her again, and she backed away, dragging Saskia by her collar. The cougar took two skulking steps toward them. Willa yelled, "Leave us alone. Get away."

Saskia barked then. As they retreated, Willa toppled backwards, releasing Saskia's collar. The dog trotted off toward home. Willa scrambled back to her feet. She waved her arms madly over her head. Though she couldn't hear the snarl, she saw the cougar's lips curl back. But it stayed put. Willa half-ran, half-stumbled after Saskia across the potholed fields. The nearly two kilometres felt like twenty. Every few moments, she glanced wildly back over her shoulder to make sure they weren't being pursued. She fell once more, over a survey post installed to demarcate a second barn that should have gone up six years earlier. When she and Saskia burst at last through the screen door into the kitchen, Calvin bolted up from the table, alarmed.

"What's wrong?" he cried.

Willa fell into his arms. "A cat," she gasped. "I think. At the Western Crest." She looked around in jerks. "I thought Saskia would pull free and be killed."

"Sit down. Catch your breath." He stroked her back and picked a twig from the sleeve of her pullover, brushed dirt from her jeans. Then he led her to the nook to sit and he poured her a glass of water.

Willa tipped the glass back and let the coolness flood her throat in one long draught. "I thought ..." she wheezed, "... he'd come ... after us." Her chest barked out a string of coughs. Calvin retrieved her puffer from the medicine cabinet in the bathroom, and she inhaled gratefully. She stared at the puffer in her palm. "I haven't used this in months."

"I'll go out this week and track the cougar," Calvin said. "Right now, I'll pour you a cup of tea." He brought the pot and cups to the table.

"I launched myself across that field," Willa said.

Calvin smiled uncertainly as he sat down and poured the tea.

"I haven't run like that in a decade," she said. *What if it wasn't real? How worried would Calvin be then?* She broke into a fit of convulsive, cackling laughter. Saskia came over to investigate and nosed her leg.

Calvin pushed her cup of tea across the table. "Take it easy," he said. "You've had a bad scare. Have another sip of water while you wait for your tea to cool."

A frown creased Calvin's normally smooth forehead. As she sipped, she drank in his look of concern.

"Can I get you anything else?"

She shook her head and squeezed his hand, holding on.

THE NEXT MORNING, despite the early June heat, Willa breathed warm air onto her chilly fingers as they drove through Fort Macleod toward the bank. The town seemed like a dear old aunt who smiles valiantly through illness, fighting to retain her last vestiges of charm and vibrancy. The streets looked dustier and more deserted than they had even a month ago when she'd come in for groceries. The empty glass eyes of the old library and the Prairie Serenity Day Spa stared each other down across Main Street, as if competing to see who could avoid sagging and fading before their rightful occupants returned. The Drynoch Inn, which used to cash in on the town's status as Alberta's only Designated Historic Area, now struggled to fill its rooms. Fluorescent lights blazed in the windows of the Goodwill store — a reliable old friend to failing farmers and cash-strapped townsfolk. Others catering to the unfortunate included Dr. Hector Clyde, Family Physician, Brian Pinkster, Chartered Accountant, and Jeff Oliver, Q.C., who occupied an office above Dr. Clyde's clinic. Rumour had it only the owner of Keeler's Pub made any real money.

Calvin pulled into a parking spot in front of the sandstone bank building, taking pains to make sure the front of the truck faced west. Insurance companies had sent bulletins to their Southern Alberta customers telling them to park their cars into the wind to avoid damage to car doors and adjacent vehicles from violent gusts.

The bank manager's glassed-in office sat like a giant ice cube behind the tellers and the reception desk. Ian Mason pressed his warm, damp palm against Willa's cold hand. She took a seat beside Calvin in front of Ian's desk and inspected the man's face for hints of potential leniency. She saw only a smooth high forehead, dark staring eyes, a pencil straight mouth. Calvin shook Ian's hand as if they'd popped by for a drink.

"Good to see you two," Ian said with a smile that flashed across his face so fast Willa wondered if she'd imagined it. He raised his eyebrows, scrunching the front of his grey crew cut. "I hated to ask you to come, but we've been friends a long time, and I thought we'd better have a friendly chat."

The piling on of all those polite words made Willa light-headed. She'd known Ian since grade school and had never seen him so formal. She gripped the armrests of her chair.

"Let's take a look at your situation," Ian continued, dragging out the *a* sound in the word "situation."

"Now, Ian, we know we're late," Calvin said, his voice tinged with John Wayne ease. "But we thought we could work it out. Extend the loan, reduce the payments."

Ian looked as though a burr he'd sat on had found its mark. "Gosh, Calvin. Willa. We renegotiated six months ago, and I just can't do any better than the payment plan I set up for you."

Willa leaned in slightly and murmured, "Are you saying there's nothing you can do, Ian? I mean, our water bill alone is nearly $4,000 dollars a month. We've cut back on every-thing else. We're still working hard to grow the business." She glanced at Calvin, who sat still as a rock in high wind. "Milk prices are down again."

All of Ian's finely shored up facial features collapsed in a heap. "I can stretch it out four or five more months because I realize how hard you've worked to make a go of it. But I'm going out on a limb here. They'll foreclose ..." He glanced at the calendar on his laptop. "... end October latest if you can't stick to the payment schedule. What I can do is fold the missed payments into the next four months, but that's the best I can do. I'm sorry. My hands are tied by our head office out east. These are tough times for everyone. Have you thought about selling to the federal government come July?"

Willa concentrated on bringing oxygen into her body. In and out. In and out. "No way, Ian. I can't leave. Besides, we couldn't make a start anywhere with what they're offering." She had grown tired of the phrase 'tough times.' She thought about the utter inadequacies of language in the face of catastrophe. She tightened her grip on the chair and looked to Calvin for a sign that the universe hadn't entered a tailspin. His face burned red — with rage or pent-up frustration, she couldn't tell — but his voice came out like a quiet song.

"Look, Ian," he said. He paused to lick his lips. "Willa's right. We can't leave the land her family has held onto for nearly a hundred years. We've done everything right. We converted to wind power and nano-solar panels. We're giving back more to the grid every month than we use in a year. We installed the composting toilet, the grey-water filtration system. We dug a hole the size of Vancouver Island to put in the cistern. The truck's electric. We got rid of our water-guzzling cattle, and now we raise some of the finest disease-free goats in southern Alberta. Our milk is the best there is. What else are we supposed to do to stay off the street?"

His words bounced around in Willa's head like so many ping-pong balls. Ian's eyes were locked on Calvin's.

Willa looked around in a frenzy, desperate to park her eyes on something solid, immutable. When they lighted on Calvin's face, her insides quivered. His face looked like it had been struck by palsy. His skin slid downward. Bubbling plastic under a blow torch. The puffy mounds under his eye sockets drooped and stretched until she thought they would release the glossy orbs within. And then they did.

Calvin turned sharply in his chair and held her by both shoulders. "Willa. Willa. What's wrong? For Christ's sake." Willa slumped forward against him.

"Get us some water, quick," Ian Mason barked at the assistant outside his office. The young man hurried in and set a bottle of Crystel spring water on the desk in front of Willa.

"Thank you," she breathed. "Just give me a sec. I'll be fine." All three men stared at her as if horns had sprung from her temples. "I'm fine, for heaven's sake. A bit lightheaded is all."

At long last, the young man cleared his throat and returned to his desk. Calvin and Willa got up. She shook Ian's hand, which lay limp in hers. Calvin draped his arm around Willa's shoulder and guided her between the desks of the bank employees toward the front door. Calvin tossed a wave over his shoulder when Ian called after them that he'd draw up the papers. Willa pasted a wan smile on her face and tried to make friendly eye contact with the two tellers. Each of the women smiled weakly, then busied themselves on their computer screens.

8

As they crested the last hill toward home, Calvin finally spoke. "What the hell was that all about, Willa?"

Willa had been sitting with her eyes closed ever since Calvin ran into the store for Pepto-Bismol and a few groceries on the way home from the bank. At first, it felt restful; now she dreaded what she might see if she opened them. Holding still and quiet seemed the wisest course. "What do you mean?" she said, mustering a tone of innocence and surprise. He had enough to do without worrying about a crazy wife. She would go see Dr. Clyde; he would know what to do. "I felt faint is all. The air in the bank was oppressive, wasn't it?"

"And that's why you screamed like a banshee?"

She turned to look at him. "What?"

He looked at her in utter disbelief.

"Watch out, Calvin," Willa cried.

He twisted the steering wheel to pull back from the ditch. "We'll get through this, you know." He repeated the words as if doing so would make them true.

Willa couldn't wait to be freed from the confines of the truck and busy herself with the milking. She hungered for the warmth and soft scratchiness of goat hair under her hands. She had the strength to work but not to deal with the demands of the world beyond their property. A world that punched her in the face for trying to salvage her family's livelihood.

AFTER THE EVENING MILKING, Willa watched Calvin head north from the barn with his Ruger Mini-14 resting on his right shoulder, the stock and barrel gripped firmly in hand. Off to track a cougar for her. A cougar she wasn't sure existed. She marvelled at his unequivocal devotion. He had worked the better part of his life to keep the Van Bruggen dream alive. At first, they had been indomitable — especially while her father lived. Now, the world was closing in on them like a black fog. They groped for a foothold on a piece of property that blew away millimetre by millimetre with each passing day.

She forced her attention back to work, the one sure way to clear her mind. As she entered the barn, Willa took a breath. The pungent smell of soiled straw and the sweet aroma of fresh wafted alternately around her as she shovelled and pitched. Shaky finances didn't seem so insurmountable with a farm tool in her hands. They had won the battle to keep Johne's disease and other goat ailments at bay by keeping the barn meticulously clean. A brigade of barn cats controlled rodents that might be carrying viruses. Diseases like caprine arthritis and encephalitis, that had once been widespread in the industrialized world, had been largely eradicated through better breeding and herd management. Still, Valley Fever and asthma posed new health risks.

Willa pushed fresh hay under the noses bleating expectantly around her. Her father had scoffed at the prospect of goats becoming a staple in Alberta. But a cow drank on average sixty litres of water a day and a goat a mere nine, so he'd finally relented. Now only government ministers and heads of corporations could afford imported beef products and cow's milk. She, for one, loved goat's meat, milk, and yogurt.

She set about chasing down the twenty-five kids in the nursing pen to give them their dose of Pepto-Bismol. Despite their weakened state, they leapt about and squirmed in her arms. When she finally finished giving the last one its pink moustache, she sat down in the straw to catch her breath. As she sat companionably among them, the kids socialized happily. They stumbled around her on their weakened knees, nibbling at her laces and pant legs. "Sure, now you're my best friends." She stroked their velveteen ears. "I hope Calvin is right about the Pepto," she said softly, as if gentle words might help soothe the malady away. "We need you guys to thrive."

Willa stood up at last. She sniffed deeply the musk of animals and straw, and pulled her dust mask over her nose and mouth. The wind whistled shrill threats through the cracks in the barn. As she checked the does' automated water trough, bells rang out over the wind. The tinkling sound filled Willa's ears the way comfort food settles in the belly. She and Calvin had purchased a dozen small cow bells, called *trychlen*, from a Swiss couple they had befriended at the Fort Macleod farmers market. Made of hammered sheet metal light enough for goats to carry around their necks, the *trychlen* purportedly kept predators away. Willa used them to mark the family's special goats. Dolly, the ungainly old dear with a large pendulous udder, yielded record amounts of milk; Sophie, Charlotte, and Anne were the prettiest Saanen sisters among the dames, and produced the prettiest offspring; Becky rivalled Saskia in her friendly, affectionate nature.

Willa barred the barn door against gales and predators. Saskia followed her to the buck pen, where she led Duke by the ear into the outer enclosure so she could clean out old hay and pitch new. She enticed him back into the pen with a small prize of grain. "My dear boy," she chided, "you are the stinkiest thing on four legs." With musky scent glands near their horns and a nasty habit of urinating on their legs and beards, bucks won the prize for foulest smelling creature on a goat farm. She doubted predators ever ventured near old Duke. His previous owner had not disbudded him, so, if Duke did have to face danger, he also had his horns for self-defence.

Night stalked the sky as Willa slid the bar across the buck's barn door and hurried back up toward the house. She wondered again about the phantom cougar. Perhaps Calvin would find paw prints. Or not. She felt as though her rational mind were being hijacked. She needed to regain control of it.

She glanced toward the lodgepole pines she'd planted with her father thirty-seven years ago. They had succumbed a few years back to an airborne infestation of mountain pine beetle and now just waved their bare arms in the wind. She stopped dead. A tall figure stood among the trees, staring at her. The ghostly form gave her a friendly wave. Willa's scalp crawled. "Papa?" she said. He waved again, and her feet took her toward him. She passed the barn. The sensor lights flashed on, blinding her, but she stumbled on. When she reached the shelterbelt, the phantom figure had disappeared. She ran along the length of it, touching branches as she went as if to conjure his form from the rough deadwood. She stopped to catch her breath, holding onto a branch. She leaned slightly down on it and then had to catch herself as the branch snapped off. She pitched the branch as far as she could, swearing. On her walk back to the house, she paused every few moments to look back and scour the treeline for signs of her father in the waning light. Inside the house, she leaned against the door frame with her eyes closed. She should leave the door unlocked for her father, realizing even as she thought it how ridiculous that was. She turned and locked the door. Calvin could use the key under the flowerpot to get in if she happened to fall asleep before he got back, which seemed unlikely given her pounding heart.

In the office, Willa turned on the tablet computer while the wind rattled the window like a brazen prowler. Sophie had left a message. They'd never talked as often as Willa thought siblings should. Growing up apart had created a chasm between them. Lately they'd talked more because of their mother's illness.

Willa sat down at the computer. She said, "Search. Valley Fever." She read through the Health Canada entry and saw no evidence that the disease caused hallucinations. "Search. Dealing with extreme stress." The computer voice droned on with the top result, but Willa's ears perked up at the line, "don't battle stress alone — ask for help from a friend and, if necessary, a professional."

"Stop search." Willa looked up and stared at the picture on the opposite wall: her father with one hand on six-year-old Daniel's shoulder, the other helping him hold up a fish nearly twice his size. Her son's smile revealed a gap where his front baby teeth had been. She read the list of common life stressors on the computer screen: ... financial difficulties, poor mental or physical health, occupational stress such as work overload. She sighed. Check, check and check.

Willa glanced at the time. Nine o'clock in Victoria. Ten in Alberta. Where was Calvin? She considered calling him, but he'd just brand her a worrywart, so she video-called Sophie instead.

"Mom's gone, Willa," Sophie said immediately on answering.

Willa stared at her sister's face on the screen. Nothing moved. She registered the window in her peripheral vision. The dusky trees in the shelterbelt seemed frozen, their stripped tips arched mid-sway by the wind as in a photograph. She hadn't seen or heard from her mother in years, but her shadow had always skulked on Willa's horizon. Out of reach but inescapable.

"Her life hung by a thread these last few days," Sophie continued. "I took her to Victoria General on Tuesday, and her condition plummeted."

The trees began to move again, slowly, as if the wind were grinding back into gear. "Are you okay?" Willa asked.

"Yeah. I'm tired." Sophie looked as though she might elaborate, then added, "Really tired."

"I'm sorry for you, Soph."

"I know you are. Listen, Willa. Mom made a big donation to the Pancreatic Cancer Foundation before she went into the hospital, but she left me a little. I'd like to gift some to you. I know you guys are having a heck of a time out there with the drought."

Willa gave a wry chuckle. "I doubt Mom would want you to help *me* with that money."

Sophie hesitated a mere fraction of a second. Every tiny gesture that accompanied the delay — the nervous shift of her eyes, the movement of muscles around her mouth — registered on Willa's keen radar.

"She told you not to give me any, didn't she?" Willa said.

"No, of course not. I mean, no she didn't."

"You don't need to be the buffer anymore, Soph."

Sophie's face crumpled. "I'm sorry, Willa. But that doesn't mean I have to follow her rules. Whatever went on between you and Mom doesn't affect you and me."

Willa shook her head. "You're good to offer, but I wouldn't feel right about it. You took care of her — that's why she wanted you to have it. She and I were doomed from the start. It's nobody's fault. Shit happens in families. Who's taking care of you?"

"My friend Jennie is here. She's staying with me until after the funeral. I'm going to be fine. Thanks, Willa."

The pitch of the last two words brought an echo to Willa's mind. She noted again the uncanny likeness in looks and voice between Sophie and the Marilyn she remembered. *Thanks, Willa.* The last two words her mother had ever said to her. Marilyn had thanked Willa for allowing ten-year-old Daniel to visit her in Calgary before she moved with Sophie to Victoria. Sophie was still recuperating from Valley Fever then. At its height, the virus had spread to her brain. She'd barely survived, and her mother wanted out of dusty Alberta.

"And don't feel bad about not coming to the funeral. I know there are lots of reasons why that wouldn't work."

Something pinched Willa's gut. Not guilt. Not regret. Just the cold absence of familial duty.

"I love you, sis," Willa said. "Call any time."

Just before she signed off, Sophie planted a kiss on her fingers and turned them to Willa.

Willa looked out at the trees where she had just seen her father. Her mother, dead. If she believed in such things, she might think they had found each other again on the other side — whatever that meant. She was more interested in the living. How often had she looked out this very window to see

Calvin and Daniel returning to the house, smiling broadly? Once, teenaged Daniel reached up and tried to fling his arm companionably around the shoulders of his lanky dad. Calvin laughed heartily and crouched down to accommodate the gesture. Parents always wanted their children to get the best of both of them. Daniel had inherited Calvin's calm, capable demeanour. What had she given him? Loyalty? Apparently not. She was loyal. Her father was loyal. A memorable day came to mind. Was she fourteen? Deep mud puddles had dotted the playground at F.P. Walshe School in Fort Macleod, so it may have been after her fifteenth birthday that wet spring.

Melanie Danforth reigned as queen bee at the school. Willa recalled how Melanie pushed the buttons of her fellow students with military precision. That day, she had Willa in her crosshairs. "Willa, how are you doing?" Melanie asked at lunch recess. Willa spotted the counterfeit concern and braced for impact.

"Fine," she said slowly.

"Oh," Melanie said, "I just feel so bad for you that your mother still hasn't sent for you. I can't imagine being away from *my* mother. She loves me so much, she'd do anything for me. Not to say your mother doesn't love you, of course."

Willa's resulting pique had likely been sharpened by the visit with her mother the previous weekend. They had agreed on a bimonthly visitation schedule. A compromise between her mother's suggestion of monthly and Willa's of never. Sophie and her father usually buffered Willa from her mother's critical eye. But that weekend she had admonished her for looking the feral child with hair flying unbraided, untamed in the wind, and her cheeks deeply tanned. She said it with a smile, the way Willa imagined a hyena looked at a gazelle. Whatever the reason, Willa ended Melanie's attack on the Van Bruggens' broken home that day by giving her a mighty shove. The girl fell to the ground, which turned her impeccable pink frock into a muddy mess. She also smacked her head on a concrete parking stop, resulting in a gash that bled more than Willa thought it should.

Melanie went to the nurse's office, calling back to Willa something about being her sworn enemy for life. Willa went straight to the principal's office, where he scolded her for doing something "unacceptable and obviously contrary to school rules and values." They called Willa's father to come pick her up; she was to serve a two-day suspension. He assured the principal that Willa would be summarily punished for her intolerable transgression. On the way home, he asked her exactly what had happened. When she finished her account, she swore she saw a grin flit across his face. "Drawing blood isn't the kind of thing Van Bruggens want to be known for, Willa. On the other hand, perhaps Miss Danforth will choose her words more carefully in future." He hadn't punished her — just took her side. If Daniel had inherited her father's sense of loyalty, somewhere along the way it had dried up. At least where she was concerned.

The phone beeped. Her sister had sent an e-transfer for five thousand dollars. Willa whispered, "Loyalty."

9

WHEN THE LIVING ROOM CLOCK struck eleven, Calvin still hadn't returned from tracking the cougar. Willa tried to phone him, but he wasn't answering, so she left him a worried message. She considered setting out to search for him, but he could be anywhere, and it would be too dark to see beyond the glow of the quad's headlights. Even in the soft night breeze, the honeyberry shrubs, which bore plentiful fruit despite being subject to drought and high winds, played an impatient staccato rhythm on the kitchen window. She would give Calvin another hour, she decided, then call Logan Bradford and ask him to help find her husband.

She sat down on the sofa in the front room and picked up the novel she'd started months ago. In contrast to her father's lifelong love of reading, books didn't hold her interest the way they had when she was young. She tired of the nuance; real life was black and white. After reading the same paragraph three times, she lay down to wait for the rest of the hour to pass, staring at the picture window as if studying a piece of art, seeking stars in the black canvass. Failing, she closed her eyes and drifted away. She found herself rambling with Saskia through a lush jungle — all oversized leaves and crisscrossing vines. Mossy threads grazed her head. The humid air made breathing difficult. Here and there, blades of sunlight pierced the thick canopy. She expected to hear squealing monkeys and screeching birds, but heard only a tapping sound like the honeyberry twigs against the kitchen window.

All at once the gloom deepened. Sunbeams retracted like dying flashlights. Willa's heart tripped. Desperate for comfort, she glanced toward Saskia, but in the Great Pyrenees's place was a cougar, lunging, claws primed, teeth bared.

Willa opened her eyes with a start, and felt the echo of a scream in her throat. She sat up, her eyes scanning the room, seeking an anchor in the wooden rocker and the painting of the golden aspen forest on the wall beside the window. She reached down to pet Saskia, lying in front of the sofa. Almost eleven thirty. Her ears perked, craving the sound of a jiggling doorknob. Other than the insistent buzz of flies along the window ledges, the house stood silent, as if it, too, were listening anxiously. She made her way unsteadily to the bathroom with Saskia at her heels. Leaning on the counter, Willa came face-to-face with her stricken eyes, her pale skin and lips. Her brown curls lay flat against one side of her head. She dampened the corner of a washcloth and wiped her face. Saskia pressed her nose against Willa's leg, and Willa sat down on the edge of the bathtub, scratching the dog under her chin.

"I'm okay, girl." The dog plunked down, laying her head across Willa's foot.

Willa couldn't remember the last time she'd used this old bathtub. 2040 maybe? They hadn't wasted a drop in a decade and a half. They'd spent their provincial government water conservation grant on a cistern to capture rainfall. They pumped filtered grey water to the barn for washing tools and hosing down the concrete birthing pens. They took five-minute showers once a week with sponge baths in between. Restricting Daniel to short showers had been a battle during his teen years, until they installed a timer. Her father had urged her over and over to "give the boy more time." He and Daniel always formed a united front — they had a seemingly telepathic bond. But she saw no reason for her son to live by different rules than everyone else.

Willa went back to the sofa and picked up her phone from the coffee table. No texts or emails. She'd heard nothing from Daniel since he told her about the job interview. She clicked the text mic and recited:

> Hi son, Thinking about you. I wanted to let you know that my mother passed away today. I know you didn't know her well but I'm sorry for your loss. I've been thinking about Opa Gerard too. Our home meant the world to him. I hope you can understand my disappointment that you're not coming back.

Before hitting send, Willa pulled up the keyboard and tacked "How was your interview?" to the front of her message. A few minutes later, Daniel's reply came through.

> I'm sorry about your mom. I will contact Aunt Sophie with my condolences. As for the other stuff, I need you to accept and support what I'm doing. I got the job. Remember Opa is the one who told me to go get an education.

Willa responded: I don't want to fight. I know he did, but I thought you'd come home after that.

Daniel: I'm trying to make a bigger difference. I'll send money ASAP. Will have to pay back rent first. Mrs. Winstead has been very understanding. Plus, I'll have to start paying my student loans back soon.

Willa: Don't get me wrong, son. We don't want to take your money. We might be able to manage. Love you.

Daniel: Love you too.

Willa sighed deeply. Surely those two words — love you — represented baby steps toward a meeting of the minds. She padded to the kitchen and measured two cups of water into the kettle for tea, hoping the action itself might bring Calvin home. Ten more minutes until her deadline for calling Logan. She pressed the button to start the kettle and thought about the Tent Town slum east of Calgary, where foreclosed farm families squatted in tents and old campers. She shuddered as she pictured herself there, putting a pot of water on an open fire. Outside, the white siding of the milking shed reflected light from a woolly waxing moon.

Willa jumped when her phone announced a video-call. Calvin appeared on the screen. His image bounced around from the judder of his phone.

"Calvin? What's wrong? Where are you?"

"Willa, there's been a terrible accident. I'm bringing Peter home with me. We're on our way."

"Calvin, what's wrong? Calvin?" The screen went black. When she looked up, her heart jolted at the sight of movement outside the window. The windsock danced at the corner of the eaves.

SHE STOOD SENTRY at the front window until the sensor light
on the house lit up the approach of Logan Bradford's truck
with Calvin behind the wheel. Peter in the passenger seat. He
sat immobile as Calvin parked and walked around the truck
to open the door for him. Even then, the fourteen-year-old
scraped his feet along the ground like a prisoner with his ankles
shackled. His hair hung in ropey blond strands around his face;
his eyes never left the ground. She hurried to unlock the side
door for them. *Where was Logan?*

"Peter. Hello, lieverd. Come in." She averted her eyes from
Calvin's stricken face. "Let's put on water for tea."

Peter sat down in the kitchen nook, his face impassive. The
stillness in his wiry teenage body made him seem brittle, as if
he might crumble into a heap of dried bones at the slightest
touch. A contrast to Iron Man on his T-shirt, which she recognized as a faded throwback from the Goodwill store in Fort
Macleod. She added water to the kettle, not bothering with
her usual scrupulous measuring. When the pump stopped its
spitting, a charged silence hung in the air.

"Peter, are you hungry?" Willa asked. "Can I get you a sandwich or a glass of milk?"

"No, thanks," he said in a whisper.

"Why don't we get you settled in front of the TV, and you
can watch a movie or something?"

He didn't speak, just stood up and waited to be prodded in
the right direction, even though he'd been in the house hundreds of times when he was young, before his mother died.
Willa put a tender arm around his shoulders and led him to
the family room at the back of the house.

"Logan's dead, Willa," Calvin said quietly when she re-
entered the kitchen.

She grabbed onto the counter to keep the words from dragging her down.

Calvin paced. "The police say they can't be sure yet how he died. There'll be an investigation. I found him inside the pump house." He stopped and held Willa's gaze. "I couldn't find any trace of a cougar, and I told you I'd go talk to Logan, so I headed up to his place and when I walked past the open door of the pump house, there he was sprawled face down in the dirt and I thought, shit, there's probably gas in there so I called 9-1-1. Then I went to get Peter from his room. The fire department and police came. And paramedics. They pronounced Logan dead right there."

Calvin looked at her with unspeakable anguish. She hurried to him and led him to the bench in the nook. She made a pot of tea and brought it to the table. "It must have been an accident," she said.

"I don't know." He glanced toward the back of the house. The low tones of a sports commentator floated out of the family room. "They'll get the coroner from Lethbridge to do an autopsy, the police said. They called an environmental team to take air samples and examine the well." He frowned. "They found a whiskey bottle near the body."

Calvin crossed his arms on the table and rested his head on them so that his voice came to her as if from far away. "It doesn't really matter. Either way, he's still dead."

Dead. Willa shivered. She would tell Calvin tomorrow about her mother. She went to console Peter.

10

DAN WOKE EASILY to a soft but insistent knock at his door. He hopped out of bed and threw on his robe. He'd never mastered the art of deep sleep the way his father had. His mother used to marvel that Calvin Brookes slept the sleep of the dead until the alarm brought him back to life. "How can anyone's soul be that placid?" she'd asked his dad once. He'd grinned and said, "Clear conscience." Opa Gerard called the way Dan and his mother slept *hazenslaap* — hare's sleep, brief and light.

"Hello, dear," Mrs. Winstead said, smiling as he opened the door. "Do you think you could fetch my water for me today, please?"

Dan had fetched her water every Sunday at one o'clock since he'd moved into her basement suite two years earlier. For the last month, she'd asked him practically every day if he'd be going to get it. He'd given up on reminding her of their arrangement. He hoped she wasn't spending fretful hours on Sunday mornings wondering where her next drop would come from if he happened to be at work instead of within earshot of her anxious knocking.

"Be happy to, ma'am," Dan replied.

Mrs. Winstead tilted her head and curled up the corners of her mouth. "You're a true gentleman, dear."

Dan felt Opa's bone-deep influence on him again. "With your hat in hand, you can get through the whole land," he always said, a phrase directly translated from Dutch, and that meant civility earns you the keys to the kingdom. To Gerard Van Bruggen, nothing beat a good adage.

"Is one o'clock okay?" Dan asked Mrs. Winstead.

"Oh yes, dear," she answered. "That would be fine."

He thought she looked more pasty than usual. He suspected she wasn't eating much fresh food. Of course, the moratorium she'd given him on his rent wasn't helping her. The staple in Calgary grocery stores was bread made from barley grown in irrigated Saskatchewan and Central Alberta fields. Potatoes and other thirsty crops had to be abandoned when Southern Alberta's groundwater supply started running dry. Dan wrote a paper on the topic in his first undergrad year. Some farmers resisted a measure like switching crops, as if their own arteries were spliced with the roots of their favoured plants.

Mrs. Winstead clutched the railing as she hobbled back upstairs. Dan thought her arthritic knees must be bothering her. He closed the door to his basement suite. His mind began to churn as it had the night before, which had made falling asleep in the first place a three-hour, toss-and-turn ordeal. Perhaps he could make a real difference by blowing the whistle on a plot to send water south of the border. But how? Didn't he need gadgets to spy on Crystel? A pen that blew up your enemy after three clicks. A spike umbrella. A trick briefcase with a rifle, twenty rounds of ammo, and a throwing knife hidden inside. Dan's self-image turned on a dime these days from worldly activist to artless hick. The artless hick made himself toast, and, between bites, picked over his meagre wardrobe to tease out another shirt and pair of pants that would suffice for an office job. He washed and rinsed the grey neckline and faded armpits of the green dress shirt he'd worn to Friday's interview in two cups of water — one soapy for washing, one for rinsing — and hung it on a hanger in the bathroom to dry. He decided his rose-coloured short-sleeved shirt would suffice as an alternate. Then he sat down to check his email.

Oblique encouragement from Percy Dickenson, who wrote, "You can do it!" A Greenpeace request for money to save the pronghorn. And an email from Crystel's HR department with a form to fill out and submit online for his security clearance.

At one o'clock, Dan headed to the nearest Crystel water station a kilometre away. He rattled along 1st Avenue NE, pulling the cart he'd picked up for Mrs. Winstead at the hardware store for hauling water. The wagon measured about the size of a coffin and had been designed with a light steel frame, sturdy rubber wheels, and a six-inch metal railing around a thick plastic floor. For the effort of carting Mrs. Winstead's water, he had the use of the conveyance for his own. He strung bungee cords through the handles of the sixty empty four-litre jugs to keep them from scuttling around and leaping off the cart. He squinted into the ubiquitous west wind. The dust mask kept grit out of his nose and mouth, but the wind struck his forehead like repeated slaps from a sheet of high-grit sandpaper.

He met few people as he made his way through the neighbourhood. Bridgeland had once thrived, boasting trendy shops and restaurants. Now, many of the storefronts were boarded up. Only a few other people were out, all heading to the water station with their carts. Dan recalled how, on his visit to Calgary at the age of ten, the pathways along the river had teemed with people pushing strollers, rollerblading, biking. Now there was no river to stroll or ride by. He peered into the shadows between the squat old buildings. Thugs occasionally broke the relative daytime calm, roaming the streets for the chance to steal water from someone. Recently, the police approved pepper spray as a civilian defence. Dan fingered the safety clip on the spray cannister that hung from his belt.

He came upon a man sweeping his driveway. Dan had seen him before and wondered if the man was house-proud or just a Don Quixote, waging a futile war against the wind. "Howdy," the man called out, wiping his sleeve across his forehead.

"Hey," Dan said.

"Another heavy load going home."

"I don't mind."

The man swept his upturned hand over the driveway. "Can't believe my parents used to wash this down with water. Of course, back in 2020 a litre of potable tap water in Calgary cost pennies." He shook his head and resumed conjuring his cloud of dust.

The lineups at the water station snaked back only six-deep at each pump; six months ago, it would have been double that. With the water pipeline drawing ever closer to Calgary, people conserved even more than usual in the hope that the price would drop. For now, it held steady at sixty cents per litre. Every Calgarian had a water allocation permit for 140 litres per week. If you drew your full allotment, monthly water bills totalled 364 dollars per person. Dan wondered how families possibly managed. Of course, you only had to look at the growth of Tent Town east of Calgary to see that many weren't managing at all.

The Crystel attendant stood impassive in his bullet-proof booth in the centre of the island of pumps. Outside the booth, the sign above a display of monochloramine bottles read, "Plan to drink it? Disinfect it!" Crystel only strained the water through a 20-micron sediment prefilter; the end-user had to add disinfectant — at ten times the price of water — to render it potable.

In Dan's line-up, a man had just pulled up to the pump to fill bottles in the trunk of his car. The queues consisted of an odd assortment of conveyances. Behind the car, a woman stood with twenty jugs in a children's wagon. She probably had to fill up every two days, Dan thought. An old man waited with bottles in a shopping cart. Several of its wheels clunked when he moved forward. Behind him, a young man waited in his shiny red vintage 2016 Tesla Model 3. His father's, most likely.

As Dan's queue moved forward, he heard indistinct shouting. One woman seemed to take issue with the amount of water being drawn by another. Of course, you could draw a friend's or family member's allocation. City officials encouraged it — when not kicked over or burned, municipal sandwich signs dotted city streets, imploring residents to "Be a hydrangel ... Deliver water to neighbours in need." Still, spending too much time at a pump irked those waiting behind. When the women started shoving each other, the next man in line jumped between them. A smattering of applause followed.

Twenty minutes later, Dan wheeled up to the pump and tapped Mrs. Winstead's ration card to the reader. He filled her jugs, then tapped his phone on the reader to begin his transaction. He flicked the safety off the pepper spray and dragged his load back up the street. As he passed Langevin School, he spied five young men leaning against a wall. They smirked, exchanged a few words, then jumped away from the wall and started toward him. As Dan instinctively raised the pepper spray, it slipped from his hand and, thinking it might discharge, he leaped sideways. The boys turned back toward the wall, howling at his panic. Dan put the cannister back in its holster and trudged on.

On his return home, Mrs. Winstead smiled gratefully. "Thank you, dear. What would I do without you?"

"I don't know how I'd lug my water without your cart, so we're even." He carried her 112 litres into the house, sixteen litres at a time, up the concrete steps, through the little front hall and into the kitchen, the bathroom, the linen closet, stowing it here and there as Mrs. Winstead directed, a new plan every week.

He accepted with thanks the container of soup she offered him and told her he'd be starting a new job on Monday, so he wouldn't be around in the afternoons as he had been ever since he finished school. She nodded, smiling in a vague way that made him wonder if she understood and, if she did, how long she would remember. Feeling her motherly eyes on him as he left, he wondered what she did all day. Most elderly Calgarians spent their days shut up inside their homes, waiting. Waiting for the Bow and Elbow Rivers to refill. Waiting for the streets to be safe again. Waiting for their taps to run.

He sat down at his computer at the tiny kitchen table and opened the folder of online material he'd compiled to bone up on Crystel. Annual reports, articles, speeches, agreements for water services, including the pipeline that would soon make its grand entrance to Calgary. No one had ever wanted oil pipelines in their backyard, but everyone clamoured to give easement rights to have a water pipeline close at hand.

When Dan was young, Southern Alberta had abounded in water. Rationing was unheard of then. Everyone had more water than they knew what to do with in the 2030s and early 40s, flooding the fields, souring the soil. By the time he finished junior high school, global temperatures had risen by four degrees from the year 2000, and glaciers melted at a rate of eight percent per year. When the Oldman River that flowed through his family's farm began ebbing away, majoring in hydrogeology had felt more like a calling than a post-secondary choice. He drank in his course work at MRU. In his first term, he studied David Schindler, a prescient limnologist and advocate for sound water management and water conservation in Alberta for fifty years. As far back as 2006, Dr. Schindler issued warnings about the cataclysmic turn climate would take. "To a water expert," he said, "looking ahead is like the view from a locomotive, ten seconds before the train wreck." Dan read every word Schindler had ever written. Despite all the dire predictions, Dan never lost hope. The glaciers were no longer the water towers they had been, but if you could irrigate a field, why couldn't you irrigate Southern Alberta?

As Dan flipped through the other files, he noticed something he'd missed on his first time through. "Crystel CEO zips to Bruderheim" said the headline of a small article from a two-week-old edition of the *Calgary Herald*. Landrew had made a quick trip to the desalination plant from which all water flowed to southern Alberta.

Mr. Landrew met with engineers for three hours this morning, then returned to Calgary by private jet. No press release was issued and, when questioned about the short get-together as he headed out to his plane at the nearby airstrip, Mr. Landrew said, "I'm a hands-on guy. I want to make sure my staff are happy."

IT MADE SENSE TO Dan that Landrew would want to personally check in on the Crown corp's plant operations. The squatters in Tent Town and the people lined up at water stations around Calgary knew how important the pipeline from Bruderheim was.

He read until his eyes burned and then collapsed on his bed and promptly fell asleep. He dreamed of walking into Landrew's office, realizing only after he'd shut the door behind him that he wore no pants and his green shirt hung in tattered strips from his torso. Landrew regarded him with a steely gaze. "I wish you wouldn't do that, Dan." When Dan awoke from the dream, he clapped a hand to his forehead. "That's obscure."

11

THE EVENING AFTER LOGAN'S DEATH, Willa sat down in the office just after six to video-call Daniel.

"Hi, son. Looks like you just woke up. Am I disturbing you?"

Dan rubbed his fist across his eyes. "No, not at all. What's up?"

"I'm afraid I've got more bad news. Logan Bradford died yesterday. Your dad found him in his pump house last night."

"What the hell? Is Peter okay?"

"Yes, Peter's here with us. Well, he's not okay, but he's not hurt. They don't know how Logan died. Police suspect gas poisoning from his well. He spent a slew of money on drilling. He had the deepest well around."

"Mom, that's terrible. I'm so sorry to hear it. It's likely the water level dropped. A drawdown will lower the pressure in the well and could allow methane to be released from the water. It's an asphyxiant if the concentration is over fifty percent of the air in a confined space."

"I see," said Willa. "Maybe the autopsy will prove your theory. The funeral will be sometime next week. Will you be able to make it?"

Dan averted his eyes from the screen and took a deep breath. "Sorry, Mom. With the new job … I can't ask for leave. Logan isn't, I mean, wasn't a relative. Even at that, Oma's funeral is out of the question too. I just can't leave right now, even if I was made of money."

She ignored the reference to her mother. "He was one of our closest friends." She paused. "A huge help to us over the years."

"I know, Mom. I'm sorry."

She sucked in a breath. "There's more. Your dad and I are flat broke. The bank will foreclose on us the end of October if we don't make our loan payments by then. But we think we can do it as long as we have your help." Her words came out rapid-fire like rifle shots. She knew Calvin wouldn't approve of her tactics, but she had no internal safety. "Fred Butterfield is giving us a good deal on a load of silage. We'll have to buy that on credit of course. He also said he'd lend us his herd of forty or so does for milking, but we need to rebuild the tarp shed to keep his goats quarantined. We can use the same milking equipment for ours and his if we clean it immaculately between milkings. But of course, we can't do it alone, especially with Logan's affairs to settle. Peter needs us, too. I think Kelli's brother and sister live in Fort McMurray, but I don't know …"

"Mom … Mom, you're going a mile a minute. Let me catch up."

"Of course. Sorry. I'm a bit strung out with all the goings-on."

Dan blew a breath noisily through his lips. "I can't help you right now," he said softly. "Not in the way you want."

"What did you say, *lieverd?*"

Louder now. "I said I can't. I can't. I don't know how to make you understand, but this job is a really big deal. You think this is easy for me? It's a big step. Some days, I feel like a stupid farm kid who doesn't have any business being a scientist. Maybe you and Dad should take the federal government buyout? That program kicks in in July. It came too late for the people in Tent Town, but you can cash in before the December deadline. Foreclosure is a terrible option."

"They're offering a quarter of the assessed value. It wouldn't even begin to cover our debts. We shouldn't give up. If you can't do it for *me*, can't you do it for the sake of your Opa? He's the one who poured his soul into this place. He gave himself to it. And to you and me. He never let go of the dream ..."

"He did let go, Mom. Listen to me. He's the one who told me to leave and make a difference in the world."

"He told you to get an education. Not to leave for good."

"Yes, he did," he shouted, then shook his head and lowered his voice. "And he let go of everything, Mom. He gave up. Gave himself over to a handful of pills." He pressed the heel of his hand against his eye sockets by turn.

Willa stared at the screen. "Pills? Daniel, look at me. What are you talking about?" He put down the phone. She heard him shuffle away, then come back. When he picked up the phone, she watched him drink deeply from a glass of water. When he finally looked at her, she almost turned away. This was not the Daniel she knew. His face contorted. Tormented. She wished she were beside him, not two hundred kilometres away speaking through a tiny, cold screen. She wanted to hold onto him and never let go. "For god's sake, Daniel. What's wrong?"

"I didn't want to tell you this way. I never wanted to tell you. Opa wanted to die, and I helped him."

Willa's senses all shifted into high gear at once. The howling wind filled her ears. The smell of the old wooden desk coated her nostrils and throat like a bitter resin. Her eyes perceived every feature and muscle contraction of Daniel's image as if he were sitting across the desk from her. Her heart pounded in her chest. She braced for the hallucination, betting it would come if she continued the conversation. Yet she couldn't break away, even as she wondered what strange and uncertain turn her mind would take. She took several deep breaths. Her voice assumed a low, flat timbre in a desperate attempt at calm.

"You're wrong, Daniel. Opa Gerard died of Parkinson's disease and an infection from those awful bedsores. He was old and frail, and his body gave out."

"No, it didn't." Dan took a deep, halting breath. "I hoarded his pills for him so he could take them all at once, except he couldn't do it alone, so he asked me to help him."

"How could he do such a thing? How could you …?"

He cut her off. "Because he didn't want to suffer any longer." He was crying now. "You couldn't see what was happening to him. He was always and ever will be a god to you, but he wasn't a god. He was just human and couldn't stand what he'd become after being strong all his life."

Willa looked away from the phone. She recalled that day. She and Calvin had just passed through Medicine Hat, crawling along the highway so as not to stress the new goats. The four-way flashers clicking lethargically. That's when she got the call from Kelli that Gerard had passed away. The sun had half-sunk below the horizon by then. The sky gulped up the dusky light so that the fields around them turned grey. Even the headlights seemed to swoop upward, leaving the highway ahead ominously dark. She had turned to Calvin, her mouth forming incomprehensible words. "Papa is dead." Calvin reached his hand over to squeeze her shoulder. "I'm so sorry,

Willa." Then she asked Kelli, "Is Daniel okay?" "Yes, he is," Kelli said. "He's the strongest fifteen-year-old I've ever met."

A hundred times after hanging up, Willa wanted to leap from the truck; their progress with the goats was so slow it seemed running the rest of the way home would be faster. When they finally arrived, she wrapped her arms around Daniel and wept. For him, for her father, for herself. Dr. Clyde signed the death certificate. Cause of death: "Severe infection as complication from Parkinson's." She had sat with her father before the ambulance took him away. Held and kissed his wrinkled hand, vowing to be as strong as he had always been.

Daniel's voice broke through the memory. On the phone screen, she saw that Daniel had stopped crying. "Mom, what kind of life did he have anymore? No strength to move. To clean himself. He didn't feel he had a choice."

His words computed slowly in her brain. Her father hadn't asked her to help him die. He knew she would have refused. She loved him too much to have lost him that way. "Daniel, why didn't you come to me. Tell me what he was planning?"

"Don't you understand? That would have meant betraying him." He looked miserable again.

The pain of what her father and Daniel had done crushed Willa back into her chair as if they had both run into the room and were holding her down. "You loved him more than you love me, is that it?" she asked, regretting her own words as they came out. Unable to retract them, she flailed on. "Life is about choices, Daniel. It's wrong to take your own life. Or to help someone end theirs. You should have come to me about this."

Just as she said it, tar began dripping down the walls of the office, engulfing the books on the bookshelf, the picture on the opposite wall. First, black goo coated her father's head.

Then six-year-old Daniel and the fish he held proudly on the end of the line. As the tar hit the floor and oozed toward her, she heard Daniel's voice and turned her gaze to the phone.

"Jeez, Mom, of course I love you. It's not that black and white."

Part of her knew she should tell him she was sorry about all of it. As a mother, she should be able to put herself in his shoes, shouldn't she? Tar surrounded her. "I'm not feeling well, Daniel. I have to go." She clicked out of the call and lowered her forehead onto her folded arms on the desk, wondering how long she'd have to stay there before she could be certain the tar was gone.

12

DAN PUT DOWN THE PHONE. His mother didn't understand any of it. The nuances, the complexities. Should he call her back? Try again to explain it so she would understand? But he had no strength for it.

She had changed. Whatever happened to her being his ally? She used to defend him at every turn. When he was in Grade 3 at F.P. Walshe School, his teacher, Miss Hargraves, caught him chewing gum in class. She ordered him to stand in front of the class with the gum on his nose. Instead of complying, he threw a book at her and ran out of the classroom, out of the school. The principal called his mother, and Willa picked Daniel up along the road. On the way home, he explained what had happened. She said, "Wow, what a throwback. The 1900s called — they want their teacher back. I'd like to see Miss Hargraves stand in front of the class with gum on her nose." They laughed about that image all the way home. The next day, she gave Miss Hargraves a piece of her mind.

Now, she couldn't see things his way at all. He sat for a long time listening to the hum of Mrs. Winstead's refrigerator through the ceiling. At last, he climbed the stairs and stood out in the dark yard, wishing the wind could blow the heaviness from his muscles and joints. How long had that heaviness been pulling on him? He did the math: eleven years, one month, and two days.

YOUNG DANIEL WOKE to his parents' phone alarm in the family room, which had been converted to a third bedroom when Opa moved back into the house after he'd fallen twice in his trailer, leading to the diagnosis of stage four Parkinson's. Daniel hoisted himself up on one elbow to check his own phone for the time. 5 am. He collapsed back onto the pillow, slung the crook of his arm across his eyes. He would be in charge of everything today: milking the does, pitching straw to the yearlings, and bottle-feeding the weaned kids. And he would be looking after Opa Gerard. Washing him. Feeding him.

His mother and father would be gone most of the day on a twelve-hour trip to Saskatchewan. A retiring goat farmer near Swift Current had put her certified disease-free herd of sixty-two goats up for sale, and the Van Bruggen farm had put in the winning online bid. The herd of Saanens were proven milkers with solid breeding records.

The Bradfords lent his parents their cattle trailer. It took a whole day to get it ready. They scrubbed it clean, tightened loose metal fittings and flooring so nothing rattled. They strapped foam padding over hinges, latches, and other supports inside the trailer so the goats wouldn't bruise themselves if they accidentally fell against the side. Rubber hosing wrapped around the portable loading chutes would prevent them from banging together. All measures to reduce stress on the goats during the trip. It would take his parents forever to get back. His dad would ease around every curve, braking gradually to keep the animals from losing their footing. They'd be terrified enough as it was. After checking each goat over with a fine-tooth comb, his mother would monitor the trailer cam on her phone to make sure nothing went amiss on the way back.

Daniel sighed. The farm work would be manageable, but the thought of what Opa Gerard would need turned his stomach into a knot of barbed wire. The man's hands shook so much from Parkinson's that he could no longer hold a glass or a spoon. He wasn't the Opa Daniel once knew—skilled and capable. The one who'd held a gun steadier than anyone to shoot a deer. He'd taught Daniel how to handle a rifle like a pro but didn't mind that he refused to shoot anything except bottles and targets. One time, Opa had lain calm on the ground when an angry first-calf heifer knocked him down and straddled him to make a point; she'd taken offence when Daniel hauled away her offspring for castration. Nothing had ever rattled Opa, but now, he spent much of his time in tears. Called himself a "hopeless wreck." Sometimes, hallucinations caused him to speak randomly, as if to ghosts. Only Daniel knew how desperate he was to end it all.

Daniel hurried into his clothes and headed to the kitchen.

"Morning, son," his dad said. "This'll shake the cobwebs out." He handed him a mug of coffee before heading outside.

His mother emerged from the bathroom. "Morning, lieverd. You feeling okay about today? It's a lot for a fifteen-year-old."

"Don't worry, Mom. We'll be fine."

She made a couple of pieces of toast for herself and Daniel. Stood at the counter hurriedly devouring hers in large chunks. Her foot tapped an arrhythmic beat on the floor. "Well, call us any time for anything," she said between bites. "Kelli said she'd be around all day if you need help. You're sure it's not too much for you?"

Daniel nodded. He left his half-eaten toast on the table and walked his mother out to the truck. A pink haze washed the eastern horizon.

"Now, you're sure you and Opa Gerard will be all right?" his mother asked. "I checked on him and he's sleeping easily for now. You know he needs to be fed slowly so he doesn't choke on his food. He needs to sit as upright as possible. I've put extra pillows in the room so you can prop him up in bed. And he needs help drinking now, too, even from a ..."

"Straw. Yes, I know, Mom. I've got this. I'm not a kid anymore. You're forgetting I looked after him when you guys went to Banff for the day. And when you and Dad are busy."

"Yes, I know." His mother tilted her head and looked him up and down. Even stretched up to his full height, she could still kiss the top of his forehead. He'd always jokingly wondered if being short proved he was adopted.

A week ago, she'd winked and told him his strength and smarts and the twinkle in his eye would win a girl over sooner than she'd like. He'd waved off her compliment, saying he was too busy for girls. Even when he went off to university, he said, he didn't plan on making time for a relationship. A shadow had flitted across her face again, as it did every time he said "university." Agricultural college, that's what she wanted for him. Then he could meld the latest research with his grassroots experience to improve their hay harvest and milk production.

"Go, go," Daniel said, closing the truck door after she hopped in beside his father, who waited patiently in the driver's seat. "Go get those goats so we can make a fortune and build your new dream barn."

His mom reached her hand out the window. "Hand-hug," she said. She looked at his dad. "Do you think they'll be okay, Calvin?"

"Nothing will happen that Daniel can't handle. Let's go before they sell those goats to someone else."

She released Daniel's hand. He waved and watched them drive down the gravel lane to the main road. Turning back toward the house, his gaze took in the farm buildings. Cold morning sun shimmered on the rooftops. The Oldman River clutched the gloom in the valley below. Today, the farm was all his. He imagined his mom at his age. Standing in that very spot, she would have been thrilled with the notion that this would all be hers one day.

Staring at the river, he thought about the caverns and tunnels that lay deep below the shadowed surface and the riverbed. He ate up news stories, articles, and documentaries about the world's reservoirs and how water shifted around above and especially below ground. The Marshall Islands had been swallowed by the Pacific Ocean a year ago. Waterfronts in cities like Victoria, New York, and Los Angeles had been swamped by seawater. A seven-metre-high wall kept Lake Ontario from drowning Toronto. In Alberta, the glaciers were mostly gone. Calgary had built a wall, too, to keep the Elbow and Bow Rivers out of downtown. Everyone knew global warming was real, but no one knew what to do about it except to blame everyone else. A news report last week said a group of scientists from the University of Alberta had sent a letter to the prime minister warning that a few years of drought would turn Alberta into a desert. His mother and father didn't believe it. They said precipitation ebbed and flowed. Still, they said switching from beef to goats just made sense in the face of dire predictions. Opa had finally relented too. Daniel was intensely curious what turn the future of water would take.

He redirected his mind to the tasks at hand. His grandfather and his parents had bought a used wheel-line irrigation system to pull water from the river to the barley and timothy grass fields. Later, he'd have to turn the system on and check it every hour to make sure the automated system for rolling it across the field wasn't glitching, as it so often did. They'd planted a new drought-resistant variety of barley to reduce the need for watering. Without Opa Gerard's help, Daniel and his parents had more work than ever, and they did everything they could to make the operation efficient.

After the morning milking, he made more toast and peanut butter for himself and warmed the oatmeal his mother had made for Opa Gerard that morning. He slipped into his grandfather's dark bedroom, stifling a cough from the fusty smell. Classical music played on the smart speaker, as it did twenty-four seven.

"I'm awake, Dan," came Opa's croaking voice.

Morning light seeped wanly through the grey curtains. Daniel opened them, revealing the ghostly forms of furniture and his Opa's frail form under the bedcovers. He pulled Opa into a sitting position, nestled him against four fluffy pillows.

"Is it still warm enough?" Daniel asked after lifting a spoonful of oatmeal from the bowl on the breakfast tray into his grandfather's mouth.

Opa chewed and swallowed with care, then nodded. "Fine, son." He always spoke slowly to be clear and not have to repeat himself.

Daniel alternated taking bites of cold toast with helping Opa eat. He talked almost non-stop about the chores he needed to do after he'd settled Opa in for the morning. Opa smiled. "You're a fine person, Dan."

Daniel eyed the man miserably. He knew why Opa's eyes sparkled. "Don't make me do it, Opa. How can I? I can't."

Opa put a hand on his. "This is the best chance we'll have. I can't do it without you. This is the hardest and kindest thing you'll ever do for me." He broke off to catch his breath. "But not right now. I want you to wash me up first. Then we'll talk about it."

His mother had washed her father's hair the night before, but Opa liked to be bathed every morning to clear what he called his own "sickly smell" from his nostrils. Daniel brought two plastic basins of warm water into the room, one frothy from baby shampoo. He removed Opa's pyjamas. His mother had doubled over a large washcloth and sewn up two of the open sides to make a sort of glove, like the kind that people in the Netherlands used to wash up with. Daniel slipped the washcloth over his hand and dipped it into the soapy basin.

"Now, I'm not made of glass so don't worry you're going to break me," Opa said, as he did every time Daniel washed him.

He smiled. "I'll try not to remove too many layers of skin."

A laugh erupted from deep in Opa's chest, but it deteriorated immediately into a gurgling cough. When he recovered, he said, "My mother took a few layers off me once. Papa bought me a kid's dirt bike. For my eighth birthday. I lost control. Ended up in the mud hole behind the barn. Full of cow piss and shit." He paused to catch his breath. "Mama used the kitchen scrub brush and dish soap to clean me up. Then hosed me down."

Daniel laughed just as he had the other times Opa told that story. He washed Opa with delicate, methodical strokes, keeping him covered as much as possible. He took special care not to jostle the tube that drew urine from his bladder. He worked around the bed sores that the nurse came to dress three times a week. Daniel noticed several new ones low down on his spine, between his shoulder blades and on the back of his leg. Opa instructed him to daub them with a saline-soaked gauze pad and cover them with a gel dressing. Daniel's heart skipped each time Opa winced from the pain. Then Daniel helped his grandfather into fresh pyjamas and changed the sheets. Opa stayed quiet while he worked, patiently allowing Daniel to move his emaciated limbs as need be to get clothing and sheets around his body. Even after Daniel had cleared the room of the soiled linens and emptied the urine reservoir, the room still smelled sour like grain left to rot in a wet field, tinged with the sweetness of fresh linen.

"There's something I want you to read," Opa said, still catching his breath from the bathing efforts. "Longfellow is on the nightstand. Page fifty-two."

Daniel picked up the book, worn and tattered from a lifetime of being handled, read and reread. "This is so old school, Opa," he said, laughing. "Don't you have a million books on your tablet?"

Opa answered, eyes closed, his voice slurring from fatigue. "If the digital age hasn't killed paper books yet, it never will."

"You're not too tired?"

Opa raised and lowered his hand in response.

"The Castle-Builder," Daniel read.

A gentle boy, with soft and silken locks
A dreamy boy, with brown and tender eyes,
A castle-builder, with his wooden blocks,
And towers that touch imaginary skies.

A fearless rider on his father's knee,
An eager listener unto stories told
At the Round Table of the nursery,
Of heroes and adventures manifold.

There will be other towers for thee to build;
There will be other steeds for thee to ride;
There will be other legends, and all filled
With greater marvels and more glorified.

Build on, and make thy castles high and fair,
Rising and reaching upward to the skies;
Listen to voices in the upper air,
Nor lose thy simple faith in mysteries.

"That's you," Opa said. He opened his rheumy eyes, regarded Daniel intently. "You have castles to build beyond this farm. You're always at the top of your class in science. I know you read every article you can on what climate change is doing to Alberta." Opa pointed to the window and then at the floor. "You can make a bigger difference out there than you can here. Our family legacy is important, but if you can contribute to the greater good, you should do it."

Daniel picked up the oatmeal bowl and planted a gentle kiss on Opa's forehead. He eased some of the propping pillows away one by one. "Get some rest," he whispered. "I'll be back at lunch time and we can talk."

Opa's eyelids closed as if all morning they had been holding up great weights.

Daniel found swallowing difficult as he drove the quad out to the field to turn on the irrigation system. Hope filled his mind, but not the uplifting kind. Maybe Opa would die in his sleep. He knew little about prayer, but he heard himself utter, "Please, god."

13

IN BETWEEN CHECKS to make sure the water spurted out as it should, Daniel shoveled soiled hay out of the loafing area and pens, pitched fresh hay, filled the nipple bucket with pasteurized goat's milk for the weaned kids, and cleaned out and refilled the water troughs. All the while, he thought of the small plastic bag in his night table drawer containing twenty orange pills. Could he do it? His mother loved Opa so much she would hang on to him until he wasted painfully away — and his dad wouldn't go against his mom on anything to do with Opa. But was it love when you let someone suffer?

Opa had once shot his favourite horse, a Dutch Warmblood named Brabo, who had shattered his leg stepping into a gopher hole. Opa had called Daniel's mother to bring a rifle out to where he'd fallen off the horse and dislocated his shoulder. He told her to bring six-year-old Daniel, too. Daniel had gone eagerly, not understanding what was happening until Opa aimed the barrel high up on the horse's head beneath the forelock. Opa instructed his mother to help hold the gun steady, which she did. Daniel had been too young and shocked to ask questions. The sight of the animal prone on the ground fought with the familiar image of Brabo happily grazing with the rest of the herd. Daniel covered his ears with his hands but had forgotten to close his eyes. The scene seared into his young brain. The horse's jolt from the fatal shot. The instant ooze of blood from the wound. The spasm of the horse's legs in the moments after. Then utter stillness. His mother climbed back into the quad and held him close. Opa, clutching his arm, put a foot on the running board of the quad and bent forward to Daniel's level. "That's mercy," he said. "A horse's leg doesn't heal right because the bones are thin so they can run fast. And it kills them slowly to make them lie around trying to heal. Do you understand?" Daniel hadn't torn his eyes from the dead horse. Just nodded, tears streaming down his face. When he finally looked at Opa, he saw tears in his eyes, too.

Opa had tried to get him to help him take the pills once before. When his parents took a rare break from farm work to go to Banff and ride the gondola up Sulphur Mountain. But Daniel couldn't go through with it then because it would have felt too much like pulling the trigger on his own grandfather. But now the man who had ignored his own dislocated shoulder to euthanize his horse couldn't even feed himself. And although Opa never complained, the pain from the bedsores had to be unbearable.

It was well past one by the time Daniel returned to the house. He looked in on Opa. Found him snoring softly. The sour-sweet odour, intensified by the closed door, wafted out. The muscles in Daniel's throat convulsed, and tears stung the back of his eyes.

In the kitchen, Daniel pulled out a container of his mother's home-made goat soup from the freezer. He ran water over the bottom to release the frosty lump, then put it in a bowl and zapped it. After mixing up and baking a batch of baking powder biscuits, he sliced several, still piping hot, and spread a generous dollop of butter on each half. The oven warmed the kitchen, filling it with the comforting aroma of fresh baking, but nothing could unwind the wire from Daniel's belly. He heard Opa groan. Daniel placed a bowl of soup, the biscuits and a cup of hot tea with milk and sugar on the meal tray. Then he retrieved the plastic bag from his night table.

Opa smiled when Daniel entered the room and placed the lunch tray on the end of the bed. "My boy, you've brought a meal fit for royals. Mooi in geuren en kleuren."

Daniel narrowed his eyes, trying to place the phrase.

Opa laughed. "Beautiful in smell and colour."

Daniel grinned as he packed the pillows around Opa's back and put the tray in front of him. He heard his phone announce a text message and went to retrieve it from the kitchen counter. "Everything okay?" his mother asked. "All good. Serving lunch," he texted back. She replied: "Love and hugs to both of you." He put the phone in his pocket.

Daniel sat on the chair beside the bed. He tore off a piece of warm biscuit and placed it in Opa's mouth. While Opa chewed, Daniel picked up the bag and fingered the orange pills through the plastic. It had become Daniel's job to help him eat and take his pills — Opa had insisted on that. But instead of Opa taking the morphine, Daniel had hoarded the pills his mother gave him.

"I know we have enough," Opa said. He had searched the Internet for information about that long before he needed it.

The bag slipped from Daniel's fingers, and he leaned forward, pulled Opa's hand to his cheek. He rocked on his chair. With each forward motion, he sobbed, "I can't."

Opa's hand trembled against Daniel's cheek. "Daniel. This is not something for your heart to decide. You've got to listen to reason. I talked to Dr. Clyde about assisted suicide. He wanted me to go to Lethbridge for palliative care." He reached up and touched the side of Daniel's head, resting his quaking fingers in the boy's hair. "But I want to die here. *Oude bomen moet men niet verplanten.* Old trees mustn't be transplanted." He hesitated, whether to catch his breath or collect his thoughts, Daniel couldn't tell. Opa's arm fell onto the bed.

"You can ... you must do this. I can't take the pain anymore. The infections are much worse now. They'll think that's what took me. I don't think the antibiotics are doing anything, and the nurse talked to me last week about moving me to the hospital if things got any worse. I told her not to tell your mother, but the nurse won't stay quiet about that for long."

'Took me.' The words jerked around in Daniel's mind. No one was taking Opa anywhere. He was here. The pills would drain the life from him, but he would still be here, only dead. Daniel recalled the horse's eyes after Opa's mercy killing. The shooting itself hadn't bothered Daniel as much as the animal's empty gaze. Gone but not.

"I can't go on ..." Opa's voice trailed off. A few breaths later, he resumed. "You're tough enough to do this. Remember what to do after. Clean up any traces of the crushed pills. Don't sit with me. Leave the house for a few hours. Then come back in and check on me. I'll be gone by then. Call Mrs. Bradford and she'll come over." He leaned back against the pillows, gasping for breath. His eyes remained closed for some time before he opened them and stared unseeing at the bedroom door. He muttered something, his voice modulating with intensity. Every now and then, a word jumped audibly out of the fray:

"hand" and "field" and "rain." Opa sparring with old ghosts again.

"Opa," Daniel whispered. He cradled the old man's cool, bony hand and studied it. The blue veins between knuckles and wrist looked ropey and gnarled, like the exposed roots of the trees in the shelterbelt.

Opa turned to him, his red, watery eyes suddenly alert. His voice rasped. "Crush the pills with the handle of the butcher knife, and I'll drink them like we planned, with broth from the soup." His hand dropped back onto the bed, but his voice insisted, "Please, Daniel. Now."

THE CUTTING BOARD TURNED white with pale orange flecks as he crushed one pill after another with the butt of the knife. He drove the tears away with his sleeve. He stirred the orange-flecked mound into a cup of lukewarm broth with a straw. He had begged Opa not to make him do it the day his parents went to Banff. *Second time's the charm.* Opa's twist on the old phrase that said it took three times to get something right. He used to say, "If you try something once and fail, a second try is all you need to get it right as long as you're confident enough." He'd been right about that. At least where it concerned things like roping calves, cooking steak, and artificially fertilizing does.

Daniel knew he couldn't refuse again. He wouldn't be able to bear the silent weeping, the betrayal reflected in his Opa's eyes. The timing was right. His parents would be gone the rest of the day. Where were they now? Leaving Swift Current, probably. But maybe he should wait and talk to his mother, make her see the reason in Opa's request. Even as he thought it, he knew she would only be horrified. What a choice: horror or grief. He slapped the counter. A wandering mind accomplishes nothing, Opa would say. He gripped the cup of slurry and carried it to the bedroom.

A month before, Opa had said to Daniel, "You need to be strong for me when the time comes. Parkinson's is the devil at my heels. I don't want to go too soon, and I don't want you blamed. We'll know when the time is right." Daniel had thought it would never come. How could you contemplate the death of a heart still determined to beat?

Daniel sat down on the chair by the bed. Opa smiled at him. A thousand smiles in one. Camping at the Western Crest together. Horseback rides. Calf births. The first kid born on the farm. School exams Daniel had aced. How often had they high-fived each other? Must be a million by now.

"I'm not really leaving you, you know," Opa said. "I'll always be with you — my blood runs through your veins, and I'll always be in your heart. You've got the best of me and your mom and dad in you."

Daniel nodded.

"It's time," Opa rasped. "I want to listen to Swan Lake." Daniel called to the smart speaker to play Opa's favourite music. His hands shook as he placed the straw in Opa's mouth. Opa held up his gnarled right hand and grazed the bottom of the cup. Free will in the faintest touch of skin on ceramic. When the last of the granules had been stirred up and swallowed, Opa's hand sank onto the bed. He let out a sigh. The puff of his putrid breath reached Daniel like a gust of wind across a heap of grass silage. He breathed it in.

Opa opened his eyes. "*Bedankt*, Daniel," he whispered. "I love you. My grandson."

Daniel registered the feeble squeeze of his hand, then Opa's head lolled back on the pillow. Daniel watched the sluggish pulsing of the artery in Opa's thin neck. He eased some of the pillows from behind his back so Opa could lie comfortably. He sat back down, watched his grandfather's chest rise and fall in shallow breaths, held his hand. Two parts of himself began to silently scream in opposition. *Breathe. Stop breathing. Breathe. Stop breathing.* After a while, he knew, as Opa had, that he couldn't bear to watch the battle play out in his opa's body. He picked up the tray and carried it to the kitchen. Dumped it onto the counter. Painstakingly washed Opa's cup and the cutting board, as he had instructed, and set them in the cupboard. "You won't need to say anything to anyone about what we did," he had said. "Call Kelli afterwards. The adults in your life will take care of everything once I'm gone." Daniel ran outside. The exertion invigorated him, like his body had never moved before and now thrilled in the freedom of it. He raced up to the shelterbelt and lay down panting between lodgepole pines. Wild grasses enclosed him. The branches overhead flapped as if the trees were trying to fly away. Opa had told him about the hidden life of trees. How they talked to each other. Kept each other alive.

TWO HOURS PASSED, and still he waited. When the long pine shadows pointed toward the log house, Daniel heeded their urging. Opa lay as Daniel had left him, but the pulsing in his neck had stopped and his mouth had fallen open. Daniel sat down and grasped Opa's cool hand. He called to the smart speaker to stop the music and pulled out his phone. His thumb quavered as he searched for Kelli Bradford in his contact list.

Twenty minutes later, Daniel whirled around when Kelli placed her hand on his shoulder. Behind her stood her four-year-old son, Peter.

"Oh, sorry," Daniel said. "I didn't hear you come in."

"No, no," she said hurriedly, "I'm sorry to startle you. I called out, but I guess you didn't hear me. Are you all right?"

He stared at her.

"Dr. Clyde is on his way, and an ambulance," she said. "Have you called your mom and dad?"

Daniel heard an alarm blare in his head. "No. Can you do that? I don't think I can."

"Of course I can do that, dear. This is a terrible shock for you. I'm here to help. Your grandfather was so frail. It was just a matter of time. I'm so sorry it happened while he and you were alone."

Peter stepped forward and put his small hand in Daniel's. "Is it time for Opa to wake up, Daniel?" he said.

Daniel turned to him. "No, Peter. We need to let him sleep." He clasped Peter's hand, the boy's small fingers warm against one palm, Opa's chilly flesh against the other. Caught between the living and the dead, Daniel cried.

NOW, AS HE STOOD in the yard outside Mrs. Winstead's house, he marvelled at the detailed memories. The sounds, smells, colours, Opa's words. All of it had gotten lost in the mad effort to clean up the remnants of crushed pills. To call Kelli. His parents coming home. The unloading of goats. Finishing high school. Going to university. In the careful, vital preservation of a lie. Through it all, one image had never faded: Opa's lifeless body, mouth slightly agape, jaw askew. *Oude bomen moet men niet verplanten.* "How could you make me do it, Opa?" Dan said to the darkness. "Make me help you die and carry the lie around with me like a dead weight. How can anyone be tough enough for that?" He hardly recognized his own voice. "Dead weight," he repeated. Then he shouted it. The wind snatched his words and swept them up and over the roof of the house. But now the lie was dead, too. He weighed the two aches — the burden of the lie and pain of revealing the truth to his mother. By the time he went back inside and locked the door to his basement apartment, he felt a lightness in his limbs that hadn't been there for a long, long time.

14

NEWS OF LOGAN BRADFORD'S DEATH, and speculation about what would happen to his son, Peter, spread like a Southern Alberta grass fire. Jeff Oliver, the lawyer in Fort Macleod, called the police to declare himself Logan's executor.

Neighbours stepped up to feed and water the Bradford herd of eighty-five Angora sheep until alternate arrangements could be made. Calvin went with a police officer to the Bradford ranch a couple days after Logan's death. While he packed up clothing and other personal belongings for Peter, the officer scanned Logan's computer. She found his will and plenty of evidence of financial difficulties in the form of payment reminders and an email from a collection agency for an unpaid feed-store order.

Logan's mother had moved into a seniors home in Lethbridge years earlier. Jeff Oliver found out she had advanced Alzheimer's and lived in the secure wing. Staff advised him she would be unable to process the news of her son's death. The lawyer contacted family members of Logan's wife, Kelli, in Fort McMurray, where she grew up.

As she waited for Dr. Hector Clyde in one of the examining rooms, Willa's mind churned over the traumatic turns in Peter's life. She knew only too well how the loss of a parent turned the world upside down. He had lost two in short succession. She sniffed the air, finding the smell of antiseptic ointment and disinfectant cleaner reassuring. As if the air itself were a weapon against the dysfunction beyond the walls, in her own life.

She couldn't even begin to sort out her relationship with Daniel. He had helped her father die, for god's sake. She opened her hands and looked at them. They had been so tightly fisted, four deep nail marks bisected each of her palms. For the moment, she needed to stop thinking about Daniel and focus on Peter and financial solvency.

Dr. Clyde entered the room and shook Willa's hand in both of his. He was a tall, broad-shouldered Samson of a man with a shaggy mane of loose, black curls and a round face. The townspeople of Fort Macleod and the surrounding farmers and ranchers had entrusted the general practitioner with their assorted ailments for nearly thirty years.

"Good to see you, Willa," he said. He swung a wheeled chair toward hers, sat and leaned forward, fingers interlaced. His arms formed a solid bridge between his spread knees. "What can I do for you?"

"Feels like I'm reaching the end of my tether."

"Okay, that in itself isn't unusual given the circumstances around here." He stood up and patted the examining table. "Hop up and tell me what kind of symptoms you're having."

"Headaches, trouble sleeping, easily agitated." She paused to temper the pitch of her voice. He moved around her, checking her eyes, ears, throat, lungs, heart, blood pressure. She'd spent the last few days vacillating about whether to tell Dr. Clyde about the hallucinations. If she told him everything, he might insist on a battery of tests she had no time for. She hadn't had a vision for four days. She felt certain they'd go away entirely if she could just calm her nerves. Medication would take care of that, wouldn't it? "Seeing things."

Dr. Clyde stopped, his cool stethoscope resting on Willa's back. "Seeing things? What kind of things?"

Willa kept her eyes on the green speckled linoleum. "They appear suddenly. The image on my coffee mug moved. I thought I saw a cougar—although maybe that was real."

He instructed her to take deep breaths while he moved the stethoscope around her back. "A lot of my patients have been coming in with problems associated with extreme stress. It can cause all kinds of physical and psychological issues. Do you wear your mask all the time?"

Willa nodded and laughed. "You think Valley Fever's making me crazy?"

Dr. Clyde didn't laugh along. "No, no. What about the asthma?"

"I used my puffer the other day after I lost my breath running, but I was good for months before that."

"Good. You don't need those problems on top of everything else. Seeing things is unusual but not unheard of as a symptom of anxiety." Dr. Clyde sat down at his computer and pulled up some forms. "I'm going to requisition a few tests for you. You'll have to go to Lethbridge for the brain MRI. Delores will book that for you. That should take no more than a month. In the meantime, you could go see a counsellor." His turn to inspect the linoleum. "That would cost you here in Fort Macleod, but it's free if I send you to a primary care network in Lethbridge." He looked up and clapped his hands together. "First, let's see what we can work out together. I'll write you a prescription for Ativan." He reached for his prescription pad. With the promise of a quick solution, Willa hopped down from the table and reached for her waist pack, but Dr. Clyde shook his curls vigorously.

"Not so fast, my friend. We need to talk about this. You need a plan."

Willa sighed and eased into a chair while Dr. Clyde rummaged through his desk.

"We'll start with the long term. Making conscious choices is the foundation of stress management."

She snuffed as he rifled through a drawer. "Making choices is easy enough, Doc. I'm pretty good at making up my mind about things, but these visions aren't about choice. I don't know what I'm going to see and when. It's unnerving, I must admit."

He turned and handed her a pamphlet. "Read this. It's an overview of how to develop stress management strategies to get yourself back in control of your thoughts. It will help you recognize the symptoms of anxiety and give you tools to handle it. Come back in any time you have questions. We'll talk again when I get the results of the MRI. Now for the short term. Here's that prescription for Ativan. It's an anxiolytic. When you feel anxious — your heart rate increases, maybe you start to sweat, feel shaky, your imagination ramps up — put one of these under your tongue. The medicine quickly makes it into your bloodstream, and you should begin to feel better in a few minutes." He looked at her hard and handed her the pamphlet. "Watch for drowsiness. Don't operate heavy equipment and all that. Use it in conjunction with the other strategies. And go for the tests."

"Thanks, Doc. I'll take a look at the pamphlet."

"Good." He walked to the door and Willa followed. "There's no quick fix here. You'll have to work at it." Placing a companionable hand on her shoulder, he asked, "Have you told Calvin how you're feeling?" He scanned her face and added, "Do."

WILLA PICKED UP a few groceries before pointing the truck homeward. She turned the radio to classical music, thinking it might inspire calm. She glanced at the clock. Almost noon. Perhaps she had time to make a new batch of honeyberry freezer jam this afternoon. After she drove over the final hill toward the farm, she pulled over to the side of the road and stopped. Despite the lack of green in the farmyard and surrounding fields, the cluster of farm buildings looked picturesque. The bright red roof of the A-frame log house beckoned Willa like a sweet song. Through the haze, she could make out Calvin, striding to the barn with Saskia at his heels. They'd spared no expense in the transition from cattle ranch to goat dairy. 'You have to spend money to make money' had been their motto. She and Calvin had built the barn after they sold the cattle, which had always taken cover in lean-tos on the other side of the shelterbelt. Before buying their first goats in the forties, they'd installed a tarp shed, too, to shelter the newborns, until the wind tore the tarp off, blowing it and several kids halfway to Fort Macleod. Seeing her home this way made her think of carrying a priceless vase.

Moderato from Act II of Swan Lake filled the cab of the truck. She closed her eyes and tipped her head back against the head rest. Her father's favourite piece of music. He said Tchaikovsky's roller-coaster notes conveyed so well the drama and heartbreak of loss. Willa used to tease her father about being a 'Renaissance rancher' because of his passion for poetry and classical music. He was a sight: dumping bales of hay for the cattle out of the truck with his ancient MP3 player securely zipped into the pocket of his coat sleeve and wired to a substantial set of noise-cancelling headphones over his baseball cap. That's the way she would always remember him.

She opened her eyes and gasped. Fire leapt from the windows of the house. Wind kicked flames onto the roof of the barn and toward the row of skeletal lodgepole pines. She covered her face with her hands. When she finally dared to lower them, slowly, tentatively, the flames had disappeared. Her breathing sounded like Saskia panting on a hot summer day. With trembling hands, Willa rummaged in her waist pack for the vial of Ativan she'd picked up from the pharmacy. She placed one of the small, grey pills under her tongue. In short order, her body relaxed. Her heart ceased its crazed thumping and her limbs felt heavy with the need for sleep.

At long last, she pressed the accelerator. It seemed the Ativan would help. But she did feel terribly tired. When she got home, she tumbled into bed and fell deeply asleep.

AN HOUR AND A HALF LATER, daylight shouted through her eyelids. She leapt from the bed, feeling guilty about lying down at all when work called.

She found Calvin and Peter in the barn, giving the kids their twice-daily dose of Pepto. The stomach remedy was working its miracle, as only a few kids remained mildly floppy.

"Hey, you two," Willa said lightly.

"How was your checkup?" Calvin asked. His smile begged for a positive reply.

"Good, all things considered."

Calvin looked quizzical, then pressed his chin to his chest to focus on inserting a plastic syringe filled with Pepto-Bismol into the mouth of a tiny head writhing under his arm.

"Peter's a big help," Calvin said. "He's quick as lightning at grabbing hold of the kids. Doesn't let them escape before the job is done. He caught the rest of the older kids this morning for disbudding. If this keeps up, I should be able to get all the tattooing done next week."

The boy's cheeks reddened in the glow of the compliments. "Nothing to it when you're used to wrestling lambs to the ground for castration." His ears joined in the blushing, then he rushed to corner one of the remaining kids.

When he returned, Willa handed him a syringe. "Wanna have a go?" she asked. "Place the tip at the back of her tongue so the Pepto can slide down her gullet."

Peter nodded.

Willa gripped the kid in her arms. The boy eased a finger inside its mouth and deftly deposited the medicine.

"Well done," Willa said, putting the kid down. She beckoned to Peter. "Follow me."

Motor oil, old wood, and the sharp metallic aroma of well-used tools perfumed the toolshed. From under a low shelf at the back of the cluttered space, Willa hauled out a grey wooden box atop a frame that had long been separated from its wheels. "How would you like to fix this up so Duke can pull you in it? He's surprisingly well tempered for a billy."

Peter's eyes lit up. "Sure. Have you got the wheels?"

"If you can find them, they're all yours. Mind tidying up as you go? There isn't much room, but it could be better organized."

"Okay," he said brightly. "I'll start now."

"First we eat. No use working on an empty stomach." Willa smiled and gave his arm a light punch. "It's my job to keep meat on your bones, remember?"

Willa served up a late hot lunch of stamppot — squash mashed with kale — and sausages, and a smoothie made from goat's milk yogurt and honeyberries. When they'd tidied up the kitchen, Willa walked Peter back out to the toolshed.

"Need help in there?" Willa asked through her dust mask. Peter had no trouble understanding her muffled words. She wondered if he'd grown accustomed to his father's slurred speech, then felt guilty for the uncharitable thought.

"Nah, I'll find my way around." He grabbed the shed door handle. Stared at it as if he weren't sure of its function. "Aunt Willa?"

"Yes, lieverd."

"Do you think I should go back to school?"

Willa pulled off her mask. She put a hand on his shoulder. "I don't know, love. That's your choice to make. There are three weeks of school left. They said they'd base your final marks on the work you've done up until now. It might be good to see your friends, but everyone will understand if you need more time and want to wait and go back in September."

He shot her a grateful smile and went into the shed.

Willa hurried back to the house to retrieve the selenium supplement and de-wormer she'd bought in town. As she stepped back into her rubber boots, her phone rang. She fished it out of her pocket. "Willa here."

"Willa, it's Delores from Dr. Clyde's office. I've booked your MRI appointment for August 5th at Chinook Regional in Lethbridge. Does that work for you?"

"I guess so," Willa said.

"Okay, August 5th it is. I'll send you a calendar event as a reminder. You can book the blood test and cardiogram yourself when it's convenient. I sent you the forms by email."

After Willa ended the call, she clicked into email and deleted Delores's messages. No Van Bruggen had ever had troubles that hard work couldn't set straight. Cal was right. They would figure something out. Sophie's gift was a godsend.

It helped that milk prices were up. And now with Ativan on hand, the hallucinations would fade with the worries.

WILLA SPENT THE AFTERNOON filling syringes with selenium supplement and dewormer that Calvin administered to the does. They worked quietly while the goats bleated plaintively, clearly indignant at being detained and poked with needles, but lulled by their master's gentle, efficient hands. Willa thought about Peter, his eagerness to help, his trust in them.

"It's good to see you smiling, Willa. You feeling okay? What did Hector say?"

"I was just thinking about Peter. He asked me if he should go back to school."

"What did you say?"

"I told him it's up to him."

Calvin nodded. "If he needs time, he can take it. Now, what about Dr. Clyde?"

"He says I'm stressed. Newsflash, huh? Stop the presses: farm life is tough."

Calvin released Dolly, tossed the disposable syringe in the waste bucket and sat up tall on his stool with his hands planted on his spread knees. He looked at her with such hope, her heart ached. "Exactly," he said with a broad smile. "We've been through tough times before. Like that year we were up day and night catching kids to make our herd disease-free. We got through that. I've been thinking, maybe we can sell a few yearlings and Duke to make our payments by the end of October. Duke's pedigree will fetch a good price. Instead of having our own herd sire, we can use a stud service. Oh, and we have to get the tarp shed up for next week when Fred Butterfield delivers his goats. Fred and his son Quentin said they'd help with that."

Willa stood holding the gate of the doe's pen where she'd been about to round up the next quarry. The top plank felt solid in her hands. Its hardness radiated strength and resolve. "What do you think about my asking Sophie for more help?" she asked.

He rubbed his hands across his scalp, which dishevelled his hair. She longed to laugh and to run to him, stroke the hair back in place, but that required an ease she didn't feel. Tension had calcified her limbs. They moved for work, not tenderness.

"She's already given us a lot, Willa. People in Victoria are struggling, too. The rain we need has swamped their shores. Their taxes have skyrocketed."

"I don't think I have a choice. It isn't like the sale of a few goats and milk from forty extra does will save us."

Calvin's gaze wandered to a spot behind her. She turned and saw Peter standing in the half-open barn door. He seemed to be deciding whether to step inside or bolt, all the while struggling to hold the door steady against the oceanic waves of wind that pommelled the barn. The animals skittered about as gusts swirled inside.

"I just wanted to ... I fixed the cart."

15

DAN'S BOSS, LUCAS HOWSE, frowned at him. Did the man doubt the usefulness of his new employee? Dan wondered. His boss's head rose at least six inches above his own. Lucas Howse's thick arms protruded impressively from broad shoulders. He looked more like a bodybuilder than Crystel's senior director for sciences. With his bulk and clenched brow, Howse would send streetwise punks scurrying into the shadows.

"Good to have you on board, Dan," he said, his professorial tone at odds with his appearance.

"Thank you, sir."

"You can dispense with the formalities, Dan. Call me Lucas."

Lucas led Dan to an empty cubicle along the wall in a large open office area. He showed him his station in the adjacent laboratory. The room reminded Dan of his lab at MRU with its long, stool-lined table in the centre and at least a dozen computer workstations along the outside walls. He knew that Crystel's equipment boasted the latest graphics, mapping, and numerical modelling software. The bank of closets and cupboards at the far end of the room no doubt contained shiny, new Solinst water-level meters, dataloggers, and thermistor strings. His hands itched to get busy. Instead of setting him free, however, Lucas led him to the staff room, where he instructed Dan to help himself to coffee and said he'd be back to take him to the conference room for his introduction to the "daily confab."

Dan puzzled for a moment over the upmarket coffee machine. Lots of secrets to unearth, he thought. That morning, he had reported to human resources to scan his electronic fingerprint onto all the forms necessary for employment with Crystel. Identity verification, direct payroll deposit, tax withdrawals, confirmation of fieldwork insurance, and a document swearing him to secrecy.

I, (type name of employee) _____ , solemnly and sincerely affirm that I will faithfully and honestly fulfil the duties that devolve upon me by reason of my employment in Crystel Canada, and that I will not, without due authority, disclose or make known any matter that comes to my knowledge by reason of such employment.

He should have anticipated the formality. The moment he told Percy Dickenson anything, he'd be breaking the confidentiality agreement he was signing. The gum-chewing young clerk who administered the forms looked like he'd rather pound sand in the Bow riverbed than deal with neophyte employees. When the clerk pointed out where he should place the pad of his index finger on the computer screen, Dan responded, "of course," which came out as "of curse." He chuckled nervously, but the young clerk only raised a bored eyebrow.

Now, as he waited for Lucas to return, Dan had the sensation of teetering at the top of a flight of stairs with Percy's hands flat on his back.

"All right, then, let's join the rest of the motley crew," Lucas said. He handed Dan a tablet. "This is loaded with all the latest hydrogeological and security software."

Dan was the newest of thirteen employees in the sciences department of the Calgary office, which had been established six months ago to support the imminent arrival of the pipeline in Calgary. Landrew apparently spent half his time at the head office in Edmonton and half here. Three employees stood at the front of the conference room by the smart board. Lucas introduced the two men as hydro engineers and the young woman as a public relations specialist.

One of the men, named York, differed from Dan in every physical way possible: Dan was stocky and blond as the sun; York was tall, thin, and dark. Everyone Dan knew dressed from the second-hand stores that outnumbered regular retailers now, but York wore tan slacks and a navy dress shirt open at the neck, both of which looked brand new. The other man, Xavier, was also tall, but wore too-short pants and shirt sleeves. Both men looked to be a few years older than Dan — late twenties or early thirties. They apparently knew each other well, because they murmured to each other and locked eyes periodically to smirk at a private joke.

Lucas introduced the young woman standing with them as Ursula Myers, Public Relations Specialist and recent import from Crystel's Edmonton headquarters. She was, Dan guessed, about his own age. Her short auburn hair framed her oval face. Unlike the two men on her left, whose eyes darted from face to face around the conference table, she scanned the room placidly, from Lucas to some point over the heads of the other employees scattered around the conference table, to the floor in front of her and back to Lucas. She had the poise of someone who never questioned whether she was a worldly activist or an artless hick. Dan guessed she went about things purposefully but never frantically. Opa would have said someone like that liked to "see how the hares walk" before deciding how she fit into the warren.

"Here's the latest new kid on the block," Lucas said, pointing at Dan. He gave the group a rundown of Dan's education and work experience documenting aquifer data in the Slave Lake area. "Jot down any questions you have on the tablet I gave you, Dan."

Lucas nodded to the threesome under the smartboard to begin their presentations. Snazzy dresser said, "Operations at the desalination plant in Bruderheim are stellar."

"The new pipeline has progressed as far as Innisfail," Xavier reported. "If all goes well, it should arrive in Calgary, as planned, by the end of October."

"We did have trouble with the water pressure readings in the desalination plant," Ursula added. "That would present problems for our northern clients as well as for people who rely on a good supply into Red Deer. The problem appeared to be a grave anomaly compared to our models, so it was concerning. However, it proved to be a faulty sensor, and it's been resolved. At any rate, York and Xavier are reviewing all the data inputs for the models to make sure there are no screw-ups along the way. Water pressure, obviously, is the key to successful conveyance, and the key to my ability to communicate the success of the pipeline project."

Dan was impressed. Ursula knew a lot about model data.

He'd never met a PR person, but he'd assumed most didn't have much of a grounding in science.

After the presenters sat down, Dan learned what had prompted the sudden parachute landing of Landrew at Bruderheim.

"Crystel has received a third terror threat," Lucas said. "The Northern Water Army says it intends to blow up sections of pipeline south of Red Deer in the next three weeks unless the pipeline is capped where it stands. Needless to say, we're not planning to acquiesce to their demands. There's been no sabotage so far, and we've beefed up security at the pipeline construction site north of Olds, at the Bruderheim plant and at the new Calgary pumping and distribution station, which is still under construction. Plus, we're flying additional armed drones over the entire pipeline extension. With the ribbon cutting for the pipeline and pumping station in Calgary scheduled for late October, Mr. Landrew wants to ensure there's no trouble and that water flows like milk and honey into the Promised Land."

Lucas looked at Dan. "Any questions, newbie?

Dan looked down at the only question he'd scribbled down on the tablet and blurted it out before he lost the nerve. "Who monitors the drones?"

"As you probably know, Crystel reports to the federal environment minister. She arranged for the Canadian Forces to back us up with their drones. They're being monitored from a location in Ottawa. That's all I can tell you with the level of security clearances in the room."

DAN'S CUBICLE ABUTTED those of York, Xavier, and Ursula.

"You three want to join me for lunch at Frank's?" Ursula asked. She looked at Dan. "Coffee shop around the corner."

"Sure," Xavier said, and York nodded.

Dan hesitated. He couldn't afford to eat out, but knowing what made his colleagues tick would help him gather intelligence. The thought felt immediately ominous and foreign, as if he were an actor in a stage play he'd never seen a script for. He topped up his water bottle at the Crystel water cooler on the way to the elevator.

Down on 9th Avenue, Ursula strode alongside Dan with the other two men behind. "This job is a dream come true for me," she said. Rather than pick her way around the swirling garbage, she kicked whatever got in her way.

"No shit," Xavier blurted out. "York and I were laid off from the City's water services department five years ago. We did odd jobs before landing at Crystel."

Dan wondered if perhaps the two were a couple until York said he'd moved back in with his parents in Mount Royal. The upscale neighbourhood explained his stylish garb.

Frank's Café offered booths with faded vinyl benches, reasonable prices, and quick service. All that and a guard at the door to keep undesirables out. Ursula, York, and Xavier ordered coffee and grilled sandwiches; Dan opted for a honey-berry muffin.

"I grew up in Calgary," Ursula said between bites, "but I moved to Edmonton to do a PR degree at the U of A. Did a year there for Alberta Environment, then two with Crystel. I jumped at the transfer to Calgary. Missed my family."

"You live with yours too?" York asked.

Ursula nodded. "Parents, grandparents, brother."

York laughed. "Me too. I didn't think I'd have all the relatives hanging over my shoulder at thirty-one."

"So, you worked in Slave Lake," Ursula said, directing her attention at Dan for the first time since they sat down.

Dan choked on his muffin. He took a sip from his water bottle, but before he could answer Ursula's question, every head in the place turned toward the main door. An old man, staggering drunk, tried to push past the guard.

"Get outta here, old man," the bouncer said. Sharp tongues abounded whether at the water stations or in the downtown core.

"... gotta right to eat here like everyone ..." the old man slurred.

"Not in your condition." The bouncer grabbed the man by the arm and roughly steered him outside. As he staggered away, the man landed on his back in the accessible parking spot. Several passersby stopped to gawk at the him. Inside the café, a few patrons sniggered.

Dan didn't join in the laughter, though he noticed York and Xavier did. He was arguing with himself about going out and helping the guy. He helped Mrs. Winstead, didn't he? He prided himself on his polite upbringing. He gave the occasional coin to the homeless that lined Calgary's streets. But he had a job now. One he wanted to hang on to. His colleagues barely knew him. What would they think if he leapt up? No one else made motions to help the old man. Ursula was frowning. Was that for the old man's state or the heartlessness of the bystanders? Either way, she didn't move. What would he do for the man anyway? Where would he take him? Dan clenched his teeth. He had to stay with his colleagues. Get back to the office.

Eventually, the old man dragged himself to the curb. The lunch crowd turned their attention back to sandwiches and coffee.

Dan took another sip of water and turned his focus back to his colleagues. "Yeah, I worked at Slave," he said at last. "We did assessments for long-term viability of supply at current depletion rates. They won't run dry for a while; by then, the drought might be over."

Ursula's eyebrows went up. "You think there'll be natural water sources in Southern Alberta again?"

Dan shrugged. "I don't know, but I'm hopeful. Unlike the South Saskatchewan basin, the north has gotten at least some rain and snow in the last few years. Of course, right now, the aquifers at Slave can only supplement the seawater flowing into the desalination plant. Crystel has to get that southern extension built. People in Southern Alberta are suffering, and that pipeline will prevent a lot of foreclosures."

Xavier laughed. "You'll be a good company man, all right. You'll be the suck-up employee we'll all have to emulate."

This was the problem with getting to know each other, Dan thought; sometimes you didn't like what you saw. "Just want to help where I can," he said. "And actually, I do believe the drought will end. The glaciers are tapped out, but there's no reason to give up hope." He almost told them that he came from one of those farm families on the brink of bankruptcy. The less said the better, until he knew who these people really were. Maybe they were all spies like him.

Ursula ignored Xavier. "Couldn't agree with you more, Dan. You're from the rural south?"

Dan nodded slowly, wondering what had tipped her off: his clothes, the way he spoke, something in the way he sat, ate, walked. "Between Fort Macleod and Pincher Creek."

"Lucas mentioned that to me. Your connection is a personal one." She didn't wait for a response. "Alberta's aquifers have certainly taken a beating. When I worked for Alberta Environment, I was posted in Fort McMurray, spinning the clean-up of toxic tailings that escaped the Lapstaff end pit lake. What a mess. Don't know how they'll ever clean it all up. Or who'll pay the bill."

"Depressing," said York, who had stayed mostly quiet through lunch.

"Thoroughly," Ursula fired back, although she didn't seem inclined to depression. "With well samples and boreholes, engineers followed a trickling subterranean stream of sludge to gauge its chances of tainting the Mackenzie River and getting into the Beaufort Sea."

When she paused, York asked, "So, will the sludge reach the Beaufort?"

"Don't want to talk about river mortality," Ursula said, wiping her mouth with a paper napkin. "I've got a positive message to spread here, and I'm glad of it. You guys ready to head back?"

Outside, Dan glanced at the old man on the curb. At least no one had called the police. Or maybe that would have been better. Let him sober up and get a decent meal behind bars.

As they neared Crystel Canada Square, Dan said, "Need to make a pit stop." The others headed inside while he made use of the restroom trailer.

As Dan washed his hands, the fragrant soap reminded him just how out of place he felt in corporate Calgary. Opa would have slapped his back and told him to enjoy the creature comforts. Dan's insides tightened reflexively. The conversation with his mother had opened a wound. But she wasn't the main issue. Opa had asked him to do the unthinkable, and Dan was still suffering the consequences. How could he resolve his anger at someone who'd been dead for more than eleven years?

16

ON JUNE 5, Calvin, Willa, and Peter shoehorned themselves into
Jeff Oliver's office, a cluttered room above Dr. Clyde's clinic.
Peter insisted that Willa and Calvin sit on the only two chairs
for clients. Willa hoped the agenda wouldn't prove too emotionally charged for the boy. She could discern little from his
face — a pale mask as smooth and unmoving as plaster — but
his hands were tightly fisted at his sides.

Oliver, a small, grizzled man in a crumpled suit and faded
Bugs Bunny tie, spoke in a languid tone as if he hailed from
Texas, not Fort Macleod. "I'm sorry that there are difficulties
involved in sorting out the legalities. It's unfortunate. I hope
I can help make all this as trouble-free as possible."

To Willa, his words promised to pave the way for a speedy
and sensible outcome to Peter's sad circumstances. She wondered whom Logan and Kelli had named as Peter's guardians.
Perhaps someone in Kelli's family up north.

"Now, I've reviewed Logan Bradford's Last Will and Testament," Jeff Oliver said. "No one other than Peter is named
therein as beneficiary. Still, extended family members may
have an interest in Peter's situation. Not financial, necessarily,

but emotional. Of course, there is always a process for contesting a will in court." He tugged briefly at his right earlobe. "This is not a simple case. There's the question of what the insurance company will do. How they'll ... uh ... work things out."

The delicate language worried Willa. She fervently hoped the autopsy would prove Daniel's theory about methane poisoning, and not drunken negligence.

"There are assets involved in terms of the land, the sheep, and the home," Jeff Oliver continued. "Unfortunately, there is also a substantial amount of debt. I will need to work out with Peter's legal guardians how all that is to be settled." He cleared his throat.

Willa sighed. Perhaps things weren't so clear-cut. "Who are his guardians, Mr. Oliver?" she asked.

Jeff Oliver pulled on his earlobe again. "Well, that's the thing, Ms. Van Bruggen. You and your husband are."

Willa and Calvin stared at him.

"That makes sense," Peter said.

All three adults turned to the boy.

"Mom said if I ever needed anything or anything ever happened to Dad that I should talk to Uncle Calvin and Aunt Willa. She said they would take care of me. I used to talk to her on the phone when she was in the hospital, and that's when she said it. During one of our talks."

"Of course we will, lieverd," said Willa, seeing tears well in his eyes. She wondered why her friend hadn't asked them herself. Perhaps she thought Logan would. Kelli's prescience about her husband ran down Willa's spine like a drop of ice water.

Calvin glanced at Willa and said, "We'll do whatever is in Peter's best interest."

Willa squeezed Calvin's hand.

"Well, then," the lawyer said, "unless you have any further questions, we'll leave it there for now. I'll prepare a detailed portfolio of the Bradford estate, and, as is directed in the will, consult with you on any further decisions in that regard."

AS THEY DROVE out of Fort Macleod, Calvin said, "We can stop by your house any time you want to pick up more of your things, Peter. Just say the word."

"Okay. Now."

"Well, okay, then," Calvin said with a smile. "No time like the present."

As they pulled up to the house, Willa found it hard to fathom that both Kelli and Logan were now gone. She hadn't been to the house since Peter's eleventh birthday party three years ago. As soon as Calvin opened the door, Peter darted in, almost knocking over the large pot containing a dried flower arrangement Kelli had made.

Willa and Calvin waited in the living room near the front hall. The moaning wind sliced between the jambs and the front door. Willa spoke to cover the mournful sound. "He'll miss living here. I hope we can do right by him."

Calvin nodded.

Willa glanced out the French doors to the deck, and froze. Her father was striding across the farmyard toward the Bradford house. He wore jeans and his best shirt that he saved for Christmas and birthdays. Green with creamy stripes. She turned to Calvin to point him out, but stopped herself. She closed her eyes and took three deep breaths. When she opened them, Calvin was staring at her.

"You okay, Willa? You're white as a sheet."

Before answering, she glanced sidelong out the doors again.

The wind whipped wisps of yellow grass in the empty yard. She busied herself zipping up the waist pack where her hand had been madly groping for her vial of Ativan. "I'm fine. Just a headache. Looking for Tylenol, but I'll wait until I'm home."

Peter came down the stairs, bumping a heavy suitcase behind him. Calvin hurried to help. They locked up the house and left, leaving the crying wind to fill the silent void within.

17

THE WIND WHEEZED PAST the window of the laboratory on the thirtieth floor of the Crystel office tower. Dan and another Crystel hydrogeologist, Brad Lyman, had been assigned to study the aquifer records of Southern Alberta and review the proposed pipeline route for potential glitches. Crystel would orient the projected southern extension of the Northern Gateway pipeline across the large aquifers that had depleted last, so that when the groundwater returned, the most accessible underground reservoirs could be tapped to supplement supplies.

Dan kept Percy up to date on his activities. His friend had no interest in the fact that DND deployed and monitored the security drones via an office in Ottawa. And there wasn't much more to tell. Dan had seen emails and reports on the company's intention to support the Alberta Government's plan ultimately to direct the pipeline toward Lethbridge. Not a whiff of anything about a nefarious plan to siphon off Alberta's water supply to the United States.

At noon, Dan stepped out to buy a new shirt. He returned a few minutes late. When the elevator opened onto the thirtieth floor, Lucas fairly leapt at him. The man's voice rang high with urgency. "Emergency meeting. Now." The others had already assembled. Dan slunk into the only empty chair.

"The shit's hit the fan," Lucas said. "A half hour ago, a suicide bomber got control of one of our Crystel vans carrying bottled water to our pipeline work site near Olds. They got close enough to blow up part of the pipeline and kill two employees. Police haven't been able to identify the terrorist in the van. Let's say there wasn't much of him or her left to identify. Police will run the DNA to check for a criminal record."

Lucas sucked on his water bottle.

"That's not all. At the same time as the explosion," he continued, "a group of Northern Water Army militants overran the security hub at the desalination plant in Bruderheim. They killed a security officer." Several people gasped. "We know of twenty employees being held hostage, and there may be more. From what we understand, the NWA is fanning out its rebels through the plant to place the entire operation under its control. Police SWAT teams have the place surrounded. The media have converged on the main gate. We have no proof yet, but it looks like the two acts of terror were coordinated." He scanned the faces in the room, seeming to gather his thoughts.

He went on at full throttle. "Mr. Landrew asked me to assemble a team of scientists to head to Bruderheim after the police regain control." He pointed a finger at the senior scientist, Crake Watkins. "Crake, you'll head up the team."

"Yes, sir."

"We'll need to do a full inspection of all equipment. Make sure nothing's been tampered with. And fix anything they fucked with."

Crake nodded grimly.

"As soon as we get the plant back, you'll take Jim and Adira with you to supplement on-site and Edmonton personnel."

He turned to Xavier and York. "You two stay here and work with Janelle and Callam to make sure the pumping station in Calgary has all its i's dotted and t's crossed."

He turned to Ursula, then immediately directed his eyes at Dan. "Ursula and Dan, you'd best get packed 'cause you're heading south. Mr. Landrew said this is the best time to kick-start the Crystel public hearings on Southern Alberta's water supply. The federal environment minister wants us to take the lead and show those shithead terrorists that we won't be deterred from our mission of mercy in the south. The feds will be offering landowners an out with their buy-out program, but it's our pipeline that might convince people to stay."

Ursula nodded. "So I'll be in charge of communications and media relations?"

"Right. Dan, you're the only one I can spare right now to be their science officer." Dan tried to nod as assuredly as Ursula had, even though he appeared to have been chosen by default.

"This is a collaborative process," Lucas went on. "Besides you, there'll be a chair and a regulatory and pricing expert from the Alberta Government. Security will be handled by the Alberta Provincial Police. Once the other panel appointments are made, there'll be two weeks of research and briefings. The hearings will assess public concerns and take suggestions about water distribution and pricing in the south. The idea is to calm the waters." He frowned. "No pun intended."

"How long will the hearings last?" Ursula asked.

"You'll be gone through the week and home on weekends, although, further south, furloughs will be unlikely. Estimates are the hearings will take four, maybe five weeks. You and I will determine which towns we'll hold hearings in. Any other questions?"

Unspoken queries hung heavy in the room, but everyone seemed too shell-shocked to articulate them. Dan wondered how they could calm the waters when everyone's worst fears had just been realized.

"Okay, ladies and gentlemen, we're off to the races. I'm counting on you to keep Crystel's plans on the rails."

THAT NIGHT, Dan texted his parents. "Hi Mom and Dad, Crazy about the explosion and the plant takeover. Crystel is holding public hearings on the water crisis. I've been assigned as science liaison. We'll be travelling through Southern Alberta for most of July. I'll stop by when the hearings land in Fort Macleod."

His dad answered immediately. "Good for you on getting the position. Things are getting wild up north. Take care of yourself, son. Your Aunt Sophie gave us a shot in the arm in the form of a cash gift. You don't have to worry about us."

Dan replied to his dad and copied his mother. "So glad to hear Aunt Sophie was able to help. I will too as soon as I can spare the cash."

To avoid just sitting and waiting for his mother's reply, he video-called Percy Dickenson on the 'Phil Anthrop' phone. Percy answered immediately. "S'up?" he asked.

"This is insane," Dan said. "I don't think anyone took the NWA's threats seriously, and now people have been murdered."

"Folks feel strongly about this," Percy said. "Environmentalists used to blow up oil pipelines, too, remember?"

"'Folks' isn't exactly the word I'd use for people who blow up other people. The NWA is crazy if they think they're going to block Crystel's plans."

"What's your news?" Percy asked.

"The public hearings on the water crisis are getting underway in a couple weeks. I'm part of it, because there isn't anyone else."

"You like to sell yourself short, don't you?" Percy said. "This is perfect, man. You'll be on the ground for all the pipeline news. I'm sure you'll be able to nose out some facts on the feds' plans to piss away our water."

"Nothing else so far," Dan said. "But I'm still pretty new. I can't see how anyone would let something slip around me. Our PR person, Ursula, is the one who has her finger on what Crystel is doing and what we can say publicly."

"Ursula Myers?"

"Yeah. They moved her from Edmonton to Calgary three weeks ago. You know her?"

"I ran into her about a month ago, when a few of us from the provincial water ministry met with Crystel staff. She's smart and doesn't ruffle easily. One of our communications guys complained about the lack of cooperation in the messaging about the pipeline, and she got all up in his face. Said although there's no requirement for Crystel to coordinate with the provincial government about the Crown Corp's activities, she sent him a copy of her last news release for comments but never heard back. Shut him right up."

"She's unflappable, from what I've seen."

"I shook her hand for that later. Told her anything she needed from the Alberta Water Ministry, she could call me. Stick close to her and see what you can find out. Talk to you soon."

Dan's screen went blank. What the hell had he agreed to?

THREE DAYS LATER, the Alberta Provincial Police, with the help of the Royal Canadian Mounted Police, regained control of the desalination plant in Bruderheim. The APP reported the terrorists weren't well organized. Several had surrendered to the RCMP after two days when vending machine food ran out and no one responded to their pleas to airdrop supplies into the complex. Headlines varied between north and south online news outlets. The *Calgary Herald* proclaimed, "APP and RCMP rout terrorists," but the *Edmonton Journal* said "Bruderheim secure while tensions mount."

Crystel staff breathed a collective sigh of relief. The Crown corporation redoubled its security efforts. The federal government posted army reserves around the pipeline construction site as the clean-up from the explosion got underway. Security procedures for all vehicles, including Crystel's own, were expanded from a mirror check of the undercarriage to a complete inspection of the interior and contents by personnel and bomb-sniffing dogs. Only those people with the highest Canadian site access security clearance drove onto the site after a thorough going-over at the gate. All other employees and contractors proceeded through full-body scanners, then hopped shuttle buses to the worksite. Site staff, supplemented by engineers from Crystel's Edmonton and Calgary offices, set about making repairs and getting the pipeline schedule back on track.

The families of the murdered workers held their funerals. Premier Saffron Hamady, Water Minister Ross Cameron, and Crystel's CEO Adam Landrew made impassioned speeches. They vowed to continue with the project, bring down the NWA, and root out all its hidden collaborators. An editorial cartoon in the *Edmonton Journal* showed the trio as the three wise monkeys sitting on a powder keg, covering their mouth, eyes, or ears with their hands. Nearby stood a masked man holding a match to a fuse connected to the keg. The masked man's shirt read "NWA."

18

THE DAY OF Logan Bradford's funeral smouldered into a full burn by eleven o'clock. Willa, Calvin, and Peter ate a light breakfast after milking the does and locking Saskia and all the livestock up with fresh water and hay for the day. Willa asked Peter how he felt.

After gulping down a spoonful of oatmeal, he shrugged. "It's not like when Mom died. She and I were pretty close. Dad and I never talked much. Lately he drank a lot and fell asleep in his chair most nights."

Willa shook her head sadly and covered his hand with hers.

After breakfast, Calvin fussed with the knot in his tie while Willa patted clean the dusty shoulders of her black dress. She'd last worn the dress at Kelli's funeral. Peter was eleven then. Now he was fourteen and burying his father. The dress pricked Willa's nose, as if she were breathing in brittle fabric fibres cracking apart in the dry air.

"It's too hot for these damn things," Calvin said.

"Shh," Willa whispered. "This is going to be hard enough for him without you complaining about the heat."

Calvin pulled the ends of his tie apart to start again.

"It isn't the heat," Willa added. "You're just not used to wearing a suit."

Peter knocked on the bedroom door, seeking help with his tie, which Calvin provided.

They made their way out to the truck, shielding their eyes from the sun, which hung like a high-watt bulb from a bright blue ceiling. The lightest of breezes trickled through the desiccated branches of the trees in the shelterbelt. The wind had decided to stay quiet and solemn and keep the dust devils still on this day of mourning. Willa happily left her mask at home. The truck's electric motor barely hummed as they drove off, but the crunch of tires on the driveway gravel stirred up a sooty puff of crows from their perch on the pasture fence. Willa thought she counted seven, a lucky number she hoped cancelled out their reputation as harbingers of doom. Peter didn't need any more calamities, and neither did she and Calvin.

The parking lot at New Life Church was already full. Pickups lined Main Street in both directions. Townspeople and farmers alike had come to pay their respects. Calvin parked in a spot near the door reserved for immediate family.

Calvin had made the funeral arrangements with Pastor Mike. Oscar, Calvin's brother-in-law, would perform the eulogy. He and Calvin's sister, Susan, owned the Wholly Grill, a restaurant that served as the hub for the region's information superhighway; the couple knew everyone, and everyone entrusted them with their news and woes. That meant Oscar could be relied upon to be both discreet and diplomatic. Calvin had asked Pastor Mike and Oscar to keep the service short, for Peter's sake.

Willa sat on the front bench between Peter and Calvin and glanced back in each direction. She nodded at familiar faces.

Many congregants fingered dust masks, having brought them out of habit or because they had walked to church.

Willa hadn't been to New Life Church since Kelli's funeral. She couldn't say for sure, but she imagined many of those assembled attended church dutifully every Sunday to ensure their salvation. They believed in a vengeful god who sent trouble for people as punishment.

Before Willa's mother left with Sophie, they attended services at New Life Church every Sunday. Willa mostly went with them. If she was stubborn enough, her mother would let her stay home, but only if she busied herself with some chore. "Idle hands are the devil's workshop," she'd say. Willa's father remarked once that if a vengeful deity existed, he or she had done a fine job transferring that personality trait to humans. Her mother said without a hint of mirth that he would need all his fancy words to talk his way into heaven one day.

The service began only a few minutes late. Pastor Mike was predictably solemn. Oscar, with signature grace, delivered a respectful homage to a hard-working rancher who had fallen on hard times. On behalf of the community, he extended warm condolences to Peter. To lay to rest rumours of drunken recklessness, Oscar expressed his deep regret that Logan had died trying to keep his farm alive with a well drilled deeper than any in the region.

"He had water longer than anyone. When he went to check the water level on the day he died, it had fallen too low, and the pump house filled with toxic gas. He will be remembered as a dedicated husband and father." Willa glanced over her shoulder. Oscar's emphasis of the word 'will' set off a ripple of bowed heads in the pews. She was grateful for Peter that the autopsy had been conclusive on cause of death. She could only hope incidents of Logan's drunkenness would not cloud his legacy.

After the local funeral home removed Logan Bradford's coffin for cremation, many people proceeded to the church hall in the basement for refreshments. There, they socialized and commiserated, all the while fanning themselves with funeral programs.

Willa stood chatting with Calvin's sister, Susan, when she saw Jeff Oliver, the lawyer, speaking with a woman who looked familiar. As the woman approached, Willa remembered her from Kelli's funeral as the sister from Fort McMurray. They looked alike, although the cut of this woman's clothes contrasted sharply with Kelli's down-to-earth style. This woman wore black pumps, which would have gleamed but for a light misting of grit. Her chic long black skirt and jacket suited a cooler climate. Her hair, rinsed blond with auburn highlights, was cut in a stylish bob and tucked behind her ears. She hesitated several times on her way across the room, each time frowning slightly and moving her lips as if she were trying to convince herself of something.

"Aunt Lily," Peter exclaimed from behind Willa and Susan. He stood up from where he'd been sitting with some friends from school.

"Hello, Peter," the woman said with a skittish smile. "It's good to see you, dear." She embraced him awkwardly from the side, squeezing him so hard it launched his opposite shoulder up toward his ear. "I'm so sorry about your father."

She turned her jittery eyes on Willa. "You're Wilhelmina Van Bruggen, aren't you?"

"Yes, I am."

She smelled of flowers and something musky, like the scent of lilacs laced with sweat. She touched her hair and straightened her jacket before she spoke, releasing more of the offending aroma. "Lily Emerson. From Fort McMurray."

Willa held out her hand, which the woman took in a brief, tight shake. "Of course. We met at Kelli's funeral." Lily. Aloof, citified younger sister. Married well. A man with a highly successful reclamation company in Fort Mac. "Good to see you again, Ms. Emerson. This is my sister-in-law, Susan Brookes."

The woman nodded at Susan but said nothing. Susan nodded back.

"I'm glad you could make it for Logan's funeral," Willa continued.

"Such a sad thing. I hadn't seen him for a long time. Listen, Ms. Van Bruggen. I don't want to cause any trouble, but ..."

Willa felt a chill sweep through the sweltering hall; in her experience, anyone who said they didn't want to cause trouble usually did. "Please call me Willa." She turned to Peter. "Can you tell Calvin that the lemonade needs refilling? Thank you, lieverd." Willa turned back to the woman. "The boy's been through so much. Shall we sit?"

"Yes, please."

Willa gave Susan's arm a squeeze and led Lily Emerson to a row of orange plastic chairs along the wall. The woman sat down on the very front edge of one of them. Her hands stayed busy wringing out a pair of black leather gloves, twisting them first one way, then the other.

"We think Peter should consider ... Hmm ... We think we'd like it if, well, he could come and live with us in Fort McMurray. Instead of here." A sweaty sheen on her upper lip reflected fluorescent light from the ceiling.

Willa's head began to pound. As Lily spoke, the hall had filled with chickadees, soundless and flitting above the heads of those assembled. Willa tried to focus on breathing. In and out. In and out. "Will you have lemonade, Ms. Emerson? Can I take your coat for you while we talk?"

"Oh yes," Lily said, futilely fanning herself with her wrinkled gloves. "I mean, I'll leave my coat on, but lemonade would be nice."

Willa walked slowly to the lemonade dispenser. Glancing around to make sure no one was watching her, Willa reached into her waist pack, unscrewed the top of the vial of Ativan and slipped one under her tongue. *Peter's home is in the south. His friends are here. His memories.* Willa took one more deep breath and filled a paper cup with lemonade. As she walked back to the row of chairs, the chickadees vanished.

"Thank you, Ms. Van Bruggen," Lily said when Willa handed her the cup.

While Lily drank deeply, Willa tried to ignore the extreme fatigue overtaking her body. "Don't you think we should discuss this somewhere else? If you tell me where you're staying, I can get in touch with you at your hotel."

"Yes, the Drynoch Inn. I spoke to Mr. Oliver. He pointed you out and said we should meet."

"And so we should, Ms. Emerson," Willa said. "I'm sure Mr. Oliver can arrange something."

The woman shot to her feet. Gave the half-empty cup of lemonade back to Willa. "Thank you, Ms. Van Bruggen. I'll see you in the next day or so." She strangled her gloves one more time and walked away.

Willa closed her eyes and rested her head back against the wall.

THAT NIGHT, while Calvin watched *Forgiven*, one of his favourite old Westerns, with Peter, Willa sat down at the computer and searched, "Lily Emerson Fort McMurray." The website for Lily's freelance editing business rose to the top. She specialized in all genres, spanning fiction and non-fiction. The list of her previous clients included high-profile Canadian authors. Lily had a presence on several social media networks. She clearly saw no need for security settings, because all her information was public access. Her "about" page: Forty-five years old; earned a master's in English literature from the University of Alberta; married to Roy Many Horses. Willa found only a few timeline posts. Links to writing tips from famous authors and publishing professionals. A few notifications for authors' book launches in Edmonton. Willa found it hard to reconcile the image of a serious professional wordsmith with the glove-wringing woman she'd met at the funerals.

When she did a search for Roy Many Horses, his company, Big Plume Environmental Remediation, Inc., topped the list. The "about" page provided a company overview: "Specialists since 2045 in insitu technologies to remove/remediate chemical contaminants present in soil and groundwater. Current projects include active remediation of oil sands tailings." The "contact us" page listed Roy as president and chief executive officer. In the accompanying picture, Willa saw a handsome man with long black hair, serene eyes, and a wide smile. The website also included a before and after picture of a remediation site: the first showed a large pond of black sludge, the second, green grass and trees and a plaque that Willa zoomed in on but couldn't read.

She didn't need to search for pictures of Northern Alberta. News reports in recent years had covered the extent and cost of the oil sands clean-up. But she called them up anyway and found grim displays of boreal forest burnt black. Tar ponds ten times bigger than the one displayed on the Big Plume Environmental website. Willa scowled and thought, *I'd take barren prairies over that mess any day.* She hoped Peter would see it her way.

CALVIN, WILLA, AND PETER waited in a cavernous meeting room at the Drynoch Inn in Fort Macleod the next morning.

Jeff Oliver hustled in a moment later. He jerked his body to right a small file folder sliding off the tablet computer he carried. "Good afternoon, Calvin, Willa, Peter." He glanced around the large room and gave a quick laugh. "Room's big, huh? Lily booked and paid for it without asking about size because time was short, and she considered my cramped office out of the question."

He shook each of their hands and pecked about the table, setting down papers, opening his computer, lifting the papers again and setting them down elsewhere. Given the state of his nerves, Willa assumed he knew Lily Emerson and her husband wanted to become Peter's guardians. Calvin and Willa had forewarned Peter of his aunt's request so he would have time to mull over his reply.

"Thanks for coming on such short notice. I went through Logan's will with Lily yesterday." He seemed intent to say more about that, but looked up instead. "Here she is now."

Lily Emerson crossed the room to the small table with short, determined steps. She reminded Willa of the upland sandpipers that scurried along the shore of the sinkhole she used to visit as a youngster near the Western Crest; the birds would run amok competing for the next buried bug treasure.

Lily shook hands with Willa and Calvin and smiled at Peter, giving his shoulder an affectionate squeeze.

"Good afternoon, everyone," the lawyer said, giving his right ear lobe a few yanks. "Thank you for coming out to accommodate Ms. Emerson's schedule."

Willa wondered if he expected them to acquiesce to all of Lily's demands.

He cleared his throat and continued loudly. "We'll get right to it. We are all familiar with the contents of Logan Bradford's Last Will and Testament."

His words echoed in the enormous space. He paused after each sentence, seeming to wait for his voice to ricochet back to him so he could use it to speak again. His right ear lobe turned a deep shade of pink from being repeatedly pulled, and Willa wondered whether it might come off if the meeting went on for any length of time.

"Peter is sole beneficiary by default," Oliver concluded.

On impulse, Willa grasped Peter's hand where it sat fisted on the armrest of his chair. He gently extracted it, laced the fingers of both hands together and hung them between his knees. The rebuff, though mild, threw her off balance, and she adjusted her position in her chair to re-centre herself.

Oliver reminded everyone that Kelli and Logan designated Calvin and Willa to be Peter's legal guardians. Willa perked up again. Perhaps he would put a quick stop to the notion of Peter moving away after all.

"If no one has questions about the will, Ms. Emerson wishes to speak, as long as everyone is in agreement."

Ms. Emerson stood up and acknowledged the assenting nods with a brief smile. She spoke haltingly, as if she'd had only seconds to rehearse her words. Her eyes darted around like

tiny blue hummingbirds with nowhere to alight. "We were
thinking how nice it would be ... that is, Peter, would you
consider coming and living with your Uncle Roy and me in
Fort McMurray? We have a lovely home. I'm sure you remember it from the last time you visited. We have a hot tub. And
there's a high school nearby and a movie theatre." When she
paused, Willa thought perhaps she had covered the waterfront
of Fort McMurray's virtues. But then she added, "And there's
your Uncle James and Aunt Greta. Their children are a little
younger than you are, and they'd be thrilled to live close to an
older cousin."

Peter directed incredulous eyes at Oliver. "Can I really
decide where I want to live? I only just turned fourteen."

"In consultation with your legal guardians, you are entitled to determine what kind of life you want for yourself and
which responsible parties will be best able to support you in
that course. All the proceeds from the sale of your parents'
assets will be held in trust until you turn eighteen; a monthly
stipend, to be drawn from those funds, will be awarded to your
guardians to cover your living expenses until you reach the
age of majority."

Willa examined Peter's face to see if Oliver's legalese made
sense to him. To her surprise, he wasn't the least bit puzzled.

"In that case, I want to visit my aunt and uncle to see how it
would be to live up there. Aunt Willa, will you come with me?"

Lily Emerson looked as if she'd been punched in the gut,
but she made a swift recovery. "Oh, well, I suppose that would
be — yes, of course — we'd love to have you. Both of you. I'm
sure we'll have a wonderful time together." She leaned over
and hugged Peter before wringing a pair of invisible gloves in
her hands.

Willa's ears rang with the echoes of Lily's words. *Both of you.*
We'll have a wonderful time. She stickered a bright smile on her
face. "Well, Peter, I guess we're going to Fort McMurray." Only
after her impulsive response did Willa wonder how Calvin
would manage the farm and the goats without her. How her
mental health would fare so far away from her normal routine,
far from the stability of home and work.

19

TEN DAYS LATER, it rained. Just enough to quench the thirst of dragonflies and ground squirrels. The dash of rain would also produce more Valley Fever spores to be tossed around by the wind.

Peter returned to school to complete the last two weeks of Grade 9. Before dawn on the Saturday morning after Peter's first week back in school, Willa leaned back in her chair in the study and rubbed her fingers against her eyes and temples. Calvin and Peter were still in bed. The house creaked, seeming to brace its stalwart self against the west wind that had resumed its attack the day after the funeral. The tick, tick of sand particles against the windowpane chafed Willa's eardrums. She'd been going over their finances. Income from milk and goat sales versus the mortgage, water, hay, grain, satellite service, and minimum payment on the twelve-thousand-dollar credit card balance. Willa sighed. The extra milk from Fred Butterfield's forty goats helped. Although she couldn't bring herself to ask Sophie for more money, her sister's injection of funds had covered the mortgage payments for July and August. Maybe they could turn things around yet.

Calvin and Willa had found a buyer for the Bradford sheep. Proceeds from the sale had made a dent in Peter's family debt. Willa and Calvin received a small stipend for Peter's care, drawn from the loan the lawyer, Jeff Oliver, arranged against the eventual sale of the Bradford land and ranch house. If no buyer came forward by the end of November, he would arrange for the sale of the land to the Crown at their cut-rate price. Either way, the proceeds from the land sale, minus guardian's payments and settlement of debts, would form a trust fund for Peter for when he turned eighteen.

Staring now past the figures on the computer screen, Willa imagined Peter fifteen years down the road, doing her work and Calvin's, ready to inherit their farm. He could carry forward her father's legacy as an adopted family member. In her daydream, rain — plentiful and regular — returned. They planted a new shelterbelt, and green branches caressed each other in the light breeze. Birds twittered and nested in the trees. Fish flashed silver in the Oldman River. The fields around the house and the barns and beyond undulated with lush, fragrant grass. She could almost smell it. She saw herself and Calvin leaving the log house to Peter and his young family and moving to the old mobile home down the hill near the river. She savoured the reverie, so unlike her wild hallucinations, as if it were a caramel dissolving slowly on her tongue.

Peter popped his head into the office. "Morning, Aunt Willa."

"Good morning, lieverd," Willa said, her voice warm and rich from pleasant imaginings. "You're up early."

He nodded, rubbing his eyes.

"Wanna help me with the milking this morning?"

"Sure," he said, yawning.

Willa stood up from the desk. "We have time to eat," she said smiling. "I put a barley loaf in the bread machine last night, so we can have warm bread and honeyberry jam this morning."

Together, they went to the kitchen. Willa tipped the fresh loaf out of the baking pan and sliced it. Her feet felt light and antsy, almost itching to dance. She'd slept better in the last week, which seemed to have calmed her enough to diminish the frequency of hallucinations. In fact, four days had passed since her last vision — her rubber boots filled with writhing garter snakes. She'd observed them impassively, almost with fascination, and the image had disappeared almost immediately. She hoped this stable state of mind would last through the trip to Fort McMurray, planned for early July. Peter would visit for two weeks; Willa would travel up with him and stay three days. Lily and her husband, Roy, had already booked their tickets. They'd go by bus to Calgary and then fly north.

Peter took the plate she offered and set about devouring three slices of bread with jam.

She smiled at him as he ate. "We need to clear out the tree today. The one that knocked out part of the fence around Duke's pen. Wanna help me?"

"Sure," he said before taking another big bite of toast.

His appetite had increased exponentially since the funeral. He seemed to stand taller and pitch hay more vigorously. Keeping the outbuildings in good repair was easier with Peter's help. The boy clearly loved farm work. Calvin's demeanor had rubbed off on him so that the goats were calm when Peter trimmed their hooves or gave them needles. In fact, he reminded her of her hard-working son. Her stomach flipped at the thought of Daniel. How could she ever dissociate him from her father's death? She veered away from the thought.

Peter was her focus now. He'd settled in well with them. Had become indispensable, really. Surely, he would choose to stay in the south.

CALVIN CLEANED THE goat pens and attended to barn repairs while Willa and Peter did the morning milking. Afterwards, Willa took the chainsaw from the toolshed, and the two of them headed to Duke's pen. Saskia wanted to join them, but they relegated her to the barn with Calvin so she wouldn't get in the way.

"Duke will be happy to be let out again," Peter said.

"Right," Willa agreed. "Must be getting stir crazy in his shelter. Have you worked a chainsaw before?"

"Nah. Dad said a few years ago I was too young, and we never talked about it again."

"You can give it a try if you follow my instructions and you're careful."

His eyes lit up. "Yeah, I'd like to."

"Calvin filled the bar and chain reservoir with oil last night." She pointed at the fuel reservoir. "He keeps it gassed up so it's always ready to roll. To start it, you turn the ignition switch to 'on,' and open the engine choke. Now, place the chainsaw on the ground like this and put your foot into the handguard." She showed him how to pull the starter handle repeatedly until they heard the engine pop. It took five pulls. "That's pretty quick, actually," she said, smiling. "Then, close the choke halfway and pull on the starter handle until the engine runs." The machine sputtered to life. She demonstrated cutting off a few branches, then turned it off.

After running through a list of precautions, she gave the chainsaw to Peter to try. He followed her instructions and started it on the first try. "Good job," she yelled over the roar. In an hour, the tree had been cut up. After they had cleared away the last piece of wood, Willa and Peter high-fived each other. Willa laughed. "Let's go tell Calvin it's time to put his fence-building skills to the test."

THAT AFTERNOON, Willa and Peter strolled through the does' pen. The tinkling of *trychlen* competed with the whistle of the wind trying to elbow its way into the barn. Willa felt the bellies of several does that she thought might be ready to freshen in the next few days.

"I think Charlotte will kid today," Willa told Peter, as he stroked the doe's back. Charlotte bleated wistfully as if to confirm Willa's prognosis. The goat had positioned herself in the far corner, away from the others. A sign, Willa told Peter, of discomfort and imminent birth. "See if you can feel any tensing in her womb." She showed him where to place his hand on the right side of Charlotte's belly. With her hand beside Peter's, she said, "The tightness in her belly doesn't seem too pronounced, but it's hard to say exactly." Willa walked around the animal. "Ah, look," she said. She pointed to the area around the birth canal below the doe's tail. "The ligaments are softening, so we should move her to the birthing pen."

"You can help with the birth," Willa said, as they led Charlotte to her new temporary home. Peter had helped Willa render the pen as sanitary as possible, and they'd lined it with chopped straw to make a soft birthing surface. "I know you've seen lamb births. Goats do most of the work themselves too, but now and then they need human intervention to help move things along. I figure even a goat needs a midwife sometimes."

Peter nodded gravely. "At least the weather's warm. Some-times my mom and me took lambs into the house in late winter if a difficult birth made it hard for them to stay warm. We'd make a bed for them in the bathtub." He smiled at the memory.

"Your mother was one of the kindest people I've ever met," Willa said. "She always knew just what to do and say to make things right." She reached up and stroked his cheek. "You are your mother's son." He blushed. Willa smiled and said, "I need to go empty the pasteurizer. Wanna stay here for a while and keep Charlotte company?"

Peter nodded again.

An hour later, Willa was filling feeding buckets with pasteurized milk for the weaned kids when Peter rushed into the milking shed, breathless and flushed with excitement.

"She's having her baby," he shouted.

"Okay," Willa said matter-of-factly. "Go wash your hands and arms. I'll join you after I deliver these nipple buckets to the weaned kids."

Her calm melted into him. "Okay," he said, and walked back outside.

When Willa arrived in the birthing pen, Charlotte had already managed to deliver one kid without help. Now, still upright, she licked her newborn with a determined tongue. The earthy, vinegary aroma of birthing fluid filled the air.

Peter gently patted Charlotte's flank and said, without looking up, "So you think there's another one?"

"We can tell for sure by bouncing her." Willa grinned when Peter frowned up at her. "I'll show you."

Willa stood behind her and, bending forward, wrapped her arm around the goat's belly. She gently bounced the belly up and down. "It's an old, reliable trick. If you can feel a hard, lumpy thing shaking around inside, you know there's another baby coming."

The doe slipped from Willa's grasp, bleated loudly, and collapsed in the straw.

"I guess she wants to get this one out lying down," Willa said, laughing. She pulled on an elbow-length glove and reached inside the birth canal. She handed Peter a clean glove. "Put this on and you can feel the baby's hoofs and head. Like lambs, they usually come out in a diving pose with the head between their front legs."

Peter felt around inside, eyes gazing at the corner of the barn as if seeing in his mind's eye what his hand felt. After he pulled his hand out, he declared, "A little smaller than a lamb."

Willa fist bumped him. "The voice of experience."

"Never pulled any out, though."

She reached inside again. "Okay, watch. When Charlotte's belly contracts, I can pull gently on the front hooves to help her push her baby out."

Several contractions later, another kid emerged with Willa firmly holding her front feet. She told Peter to use the clean rag she'd brought to wipe away the mucous from the baby's snout. The baby snorted and gulped air as soon as Peter uncovered her nasal passages.

"Well done," Willa said, laying the squirming kid by her mother's nose. "Now we can let her mama do the rest by licking her off. I always clean the area up so the doe concentrates on her baby and not on the goo, which they always want to clean up themselves."

Peter wrinkled his nose.

"I know. Gross, right?" Willa gathered up the used rag and replaced soiled straw with fresh. "Well, it's milking time, and then I have to make supper. Are you going to hang out here with the ladies for a while? Charlotte will expel the afterbirth in a bit."

He beamed up at her and nodded. "I can handle it."

Willa smiled. "I know you can."

WILLA HERDED THE LAST of the does into their milking stalls and poured a half cup of silage into each feeding container. Peter burst through the milking shed door again.

"She had another one," he said, his eyes full moons in their sockets. "I got him out."

"What?" Willa said, frowning. "Another baby?"

"Yes," Peter said emphatically. "And he's fine. I pulled him out. Charlotte is licking him now."

As Willa hopped down from the milking platform, Peter rushed toward her and flung his arms around her. She hugged him back, feeling his body tremble from shock. Her mind reeled back to the day her father put his horse down after it broke its leg. He had insisted Daniel join her when she delivered the rifle. "He's tough enough to handle it," he said. How old was Daniel then? Six? She had held him tightly after the mercy killing, his body shaking from the hard lesson. When Daniel was old enough, her father had taught him how to handle a gun, though he hadn't taken to shooting. He showed him how to grab and flip a rifle up lightning fast in case he encountered an animal primed to pounce. Death lurked in farm buildings and fields the same way life did, but Daniel had never wanted to be the grim reaper's instrument.

She turned her attention back to Peter. "Okay, *lieverd*, help me finish up this last group here, and then we'll go see Charlotte and you can tell me all about it."

174

They attached the hoses to the udders, and for a while the air resounded with hydraulic suction and flowing milk. After dipping each teat in disinfectant, they released the does back into the barn.

They cleaned the equipment, and then Peter and Willa plopped down in the straw next to Charlotte and the triplets in the birthing pen. The two simultaneously took a deep breath, laughing at the unison of their sighs.

"I knew you wouldn't be able to come," Peter began, "since you can't leave the milking machines once you start them, so I knew I was on my own." His face glowed. "Charlotte started bleating like crazy, and she kept looking back at me as if to say, 'do something.' So, I put on the glove and reached in. I felt hooves, but I couldn't feel the head, so I waited another few minutes, wondering what to do."

Willa shook her head in amazement. "It was breach? Backwards?"

"Yes, but don't rush me."

"Okay, sorry," Willa said, patting his knee.

Peter shifted around in the straw, appearing to be organizing his thoughts. "I had no idea what was happening; I thought I must be feeling wrong, so I reached in again and when I saw Charlotte's belly contract, I gave the hooves a tug. I kept doing that until it was halfway out and then, out it slid. That's when I saw it was backwards. So I tried to wipe off its mouth with my hand, but it still wasn't breathing, and I started to panic, but then I held its nose under Charlotte's mouth. She started licking, and suddenly the baby started breathing and bawling." He finished the story with a triumphant clap of his hands.

Willa turned to face him and took his hands in hers. "Peter, this kid might have died if it weren't for you. He might have suffocated in the birth canal or after he came out. Calvin will be amazed when we tell him what you did."

Peter smiled proudly. They sat quietly watching Charlotte's newborns root for their milk. Outside, the wind howled its discontent, but there in the birthing pen, peace prevailed. Still, Willa's heart ached. She breathed in the sweet smell of fresh straw and new life. How could Daniel have helped her father to his grave?

LATE THAT EVENING, Willa stood at the kitchen window watching the shade of night draw down over the outbuildings. Maybe they could survive after all. Keep providing quality milk to the milk dealer. Do their part to keep the family farm alive in Alberta. The next day, Calvin would deliver fifteen kids to a buyer. Fred Butterfield's forty goats were now housed in the tarp shed heavily anchored to the ground adjacent to the milking shed. Calvin had arranged for Fred's son, Quentin, to deliver the load of Fred's corn sileage on the morning after Willa and Peter left for Fort McMurray. They would transition the goats gradually to the new feed. The young man would stay and help Calvin while Willa was gone.

Lacing her hands behind her head, she smiled at the darkened kitchen window. Fort McMurray wasn't for Peter. It wouldn't take him long to realize how much he missed his old friends. The farm animals. The open expanses of prairie and sky he'd known all his life. She wouldn't press him to stay. That much she'd learned from trying to get Daniel home.

A soft, feathery sensation spread through her body, which made the onset of the headache all the more surprising. Willa steadied herself on the counter as the contents of the kitchen began to turn periwinkle blue. Instead of panicking, she plucked the vial of Ativan out of her pocket and placed one under her tongue, then watched, spellbound, as colour suffused every surface in the room until her own clothes and arms matched floor and ceiling, counter and cupboards. Calvin came into the kitchen a few minutes later. He too was blue.

He stopped and looked at her quizzically. "You look perplexed. Are you okay?"

"Oh," she said, walking quickly past him. "Yeah, I'm fine. Bit of a headache. Time for bed." Willa went straight there, not even stopping in the bathroom to brush her teeth. She drifted off to sleep, soothed by the meds, wondering when they would finally set straight her addled mind.

20

DAN AND URSULA MOVED DOWN to the 29th floor of Crystel Canada Square where the people involved in organizing the Public Hearings on Southern Alberta's Water Supply — Water Talks for short — had set up shop.

The panel comprised three members appointed by Crystel's CEO, Adam Landrew. The chair, Nancy Weston, was short and slight with cropped grey hair. She had a brainy, serious look that turned motherly and playful when she smiled. Her weighty resume included decades-long memberships in the Rotary, Elk, and Rancher's Clubs. She'd served two terms as Member of Parliament for Fort Macleod. Her family had owned a ranch near there almost from the time the town sprouted up in 1874 around the headquarters of the North-West Mounted Police — precursor to the RCMP. She had been minister of agriculture, finance, and the environment in various federal governments formed by the Green Party. After failing to win her third election, she gave up the ranch to head up Olds College. She was on leave from the college to take charge of the hearings.

Albert Travis, the panel's regulatory expert from the Alberta Water Ministry, sported a perpetually untidy combover, a beard gone viral, and haughty dark eyes. Dan rounded out the panel as hydrogeologist and pipeline specialist. Support staff included the communications specialist, Ursula Myers, as well as a sound technician, Tom Sinclair, and bus driver Delores Gray, who would shuttle them from place to place for the duration of the hearings. Nancy brought her administrative assistant with her from Olds College, a young man named Ricky Zhang.

At the panel's first organizational meeting, Albert Travis speculated that hard feelings and suspicion would build as the hearings moved south. "They're all going to think we're trying to screw them over," he said, slouching in his seat.

Nancy listened thoughtfully with narrowed eyes, then turned to Ursula. "Please don't plant any questions, Ursula. These small communities are close knit. I don't want people to think we're trying to rig these hearings by co-opting locals. And I certainly don't want outsiders clumsily pretending to fit in. The people coming to these hearings are facing tough times, and I expect all of us to show the utmost respect for them and their plight. If exchanges get heated — and I want our heads to stay cool at all times — the very capable Alberta Provincial Police will back us up." She flashed a warm smile around the room. "None of you need be a hero. Just do your job and do it well."

"Isn't it all just a PR exercise?" Albert said. "I mean, look at Dan, here. He isn't exactly a Nobel candidate in water science." He glanced at Dan. "No offence."

Dan said nothing. Discretion is the better part of valour, Opa would say. Dan had no illusions about his own experience but didn't appreciate the man's pointing emphatically at him as the panel's Achilles heel. Dan pegged Albert a cynical old bureaucrat at best, a gormless jerk at worst. Why dis the public hearings before they even began? Nancy seemed to ask herself the same question, because her smile vanished. She leaned toward the wild beard with her arms crossed on the table. "We're all in this together, Albert. I trust you value team-work as well?" Before he could answer, she forged ahead. "We will listen carefully to the concerns of the people and present them with serious science." She introduced each new sentence with the gentle poke of her index finger on the table. "We want them to tell us how they want their province to look going forward. Their views will be welcome on all topics – from the routing of the pipeline to the price they feel they should pay for their water. I call that thoughtful consultation."

Nancy instructed Ursula to create a background document so that all the panel members had the same grounding in the issues. Ursula also compiled a detailed list of questions and answers – the panel's Q&A bible, she called it, to help them manage what could be fiery interrogations from farmers and townspeople, something Dan could easily imagine from the way he knew Southern Albertans, especially his own mother. At each hearing stop, the chair would begin with opening remarks and then introduce the other two members of the panel before opening the floor to audience questions.

Ursula spent several mornings interviewing Dan for the science-related answers. The questions ranged from common-place to controversial: How deep will the pipeline be buried? How much water will run through it on any given day? Where will the pipeline be routed? Will the volume of water be enough to satisfy everyone's needs?

On the Friday before the launch of the public hearings, Dan and Ursula sat over the prepared documents that now included speaking points for the panel chair, and media briefing notes.

Ursula wanted every answer to be coherent, complete, and comprehensible to the general public.

"I appreciate your help, Dan," she said after they had finalized the documents. "You've been available and attentive, and that's made my life easier."

"This has been a great way to direct my own orientation in Crystel's projects and plans. I can speak to issues around aquifers and recharge rates until the cows come home, but I needed a brush-up on desalination and pipelines."

Ursula laughed. "You'd be talking about aquifers for a long time then, because there hasn't been a cow in Alberta for years."

"Once a country bumpkin, always a country bumpkin," Dan said, with less humour than he'd intended.

She sat back in her chair and crossed her arms. Her head tilted in her effort to size him up. He noticed her auburn hair was even shorter now — a no-nonsense cut for the road. "You're not proud of your rural roots?" she asked.

Dan stared at her. "Well ... I ... I don't know," he sputtered. "I suppose I'm glad I grew up where I did. As far back as I can remember, though, I vowed to pull up those roots. You know, make a difference in the larger world." He pushed his hand through his hair and let it rest on top of his head. "Before he died, my grandfather as good as pushed me out the door. Sometimes I wonder if I should have ever left."

"I suppose your parents are struggling like so many others are." Her green eyes registered genuine empathy.

He nodded, dropped his hands into his lap, began tearing at a hangnail on his thumb.

"Terrible," she said. "I'm an avowed city girl, so maybe I'm romanticizing, but I always thought farmers were the heart and soul of Alberta. Connection to the land is a beautiful thing."

The hangnail tore away, and a drop of blood bloomed.

Ursula picked up her tablet. As she left the conference room, she glanced back. "Thanks again, Dan."

He nodded again and pressed a finger over his tiny wound. A few farm people had seen the hard times coming long before the glaciers seeped away. Gradually, even his Opa had reined in his optimism. He remembered when he was twelve, he and Opa had gone camping on the Western Crest. They'd loaded the tent, their sleeping gear, and a cooler of food onto the quad, and Opa let him take the wheel. He'd roared to the top of the hill, Opa laughing as they tore through the bumps and ruts. Dan pitched the tent, but in the end, they'd spread the sleeping mats and bags on the grass, burnt yellow by the August sun. That night, as they lay gazing up, Opa pointed out the constellations, his arm slightly bent and shaking.

"You know Boötes," he said. "And there's Cygnus, the flying swan. Polaris marks the north celestial pole, the point in the sky around which all stars seem to circle in the northern hemisphere. Vega, Deneb, and Altair form the "Summer Triangle.""

Dan knew them all, because Opa had repeated their names a hundred times, but he stayed silent. He wasn't even looking at the stars. His throat ached as he watched the tremors in Opa's arm. Opa must have sensed Dan's eyes were no longer on the stars, because he pulled his arm down and anchored his hands across his stomach.

"We're getting rid of the cattle," he said, his voice cracking, "and I know it makes sense with dwindling water, but it breaks my heart to see it happen. My advice to you, Dan, is leave." He jerked his head sideways to look at Dan. "Don't you dare tell your mother I said that. She's attached to this place like a growth ring in a tree. This place is her mission and her passion, and I don't blame her. I'm the one who planted that seed, and she'll stay for better or worse. Your dad, too. He's as loyal to her as the day is long. But you have bigger fish to fry. Your life can be so much more than a few acres of dirt."

Until then, Daniel had been a child living in the moment. Opa's words struck a new chord in him. The unnumbered points of light in the sky signified the limitless possibilities of his life. He knew he needed to get his feet off the ground to reach for them. "Okay," he said, an instant, inexorable promise to Opa and himself.

Dan checked the hangnail; it had stopped bleeding. He picked up his phone and sent a text message to his parents, wondering if his mother would answer: "Hearings start on Monday. Love you." As he gathered his files and tablet, his phone chimed.

"Good luck, son," his father wrote. "We are so proud of you." Dan shook his head. "We," he said to the empty conference room.

THAT AFTERNOON, Dan scrolled through his work emails: an organizational change in the Edmonton office, a progress report on construction of Calgary's water pumping station, an invitation to employees to serve a meal at a homeless shelter. He dove into a thread of fifteen or so forwarded to him by his boss, Lucas Howse, with a note that read, "Could be useful for you ..." The subject line read "Pipeline Water Pricing."

The thread had been initiated by Landrew himself, with a simple email message to executives: he would work closely with the provincial government to establish a pricing regime that balanced the costs of the Crown corporation with the needs of the people. Even as Crystel's profits soared from the sale of bottled water in Canada and abroad, the email said, he would contact the Federal Minister of the Environment for a cash call, if need be. He directed their attention to an attachment for their information — a letter from a man named Balthazar Frost congratulating Crystel for investing in the pipeline to transport water through Alberta. Offering his help if they needed it. Saying how they could benefit from bringing the pipeline into Montana and Wyoming to sell water there. Dan glanced around casually, though he didn't really need to worry about prying eyes. The hearings staff were scattered around the 29th floor and no one had a desk near him. He searched "Frost. American businessman." Made spectacular predictions as a young man, about a meltdown in the U.S. housing market. He'd profited handsomely from that debacle. An archived interview in the *Washington Post* quoted him as having set his sights on investing heavily in water.

Dan stayed late that day. After everyone else had left, he took furtive pictures with his phone of Frost's letter and of Landrew's email on his computer screen. He hoped there were no hidden cameras recording his subterfuge. When he got home, he called Percy and recited what he'd captured.

HIGH RIVER, a town as sand-scoured as any south of the City of Red Deer, hosted the second evening of Water Talks. At the morning meeting, Ursula briefed the panel on media coverage from the first hearing in Okotoks. Nothing earth-shattering, she said. Mostly just stories about the mission, the schedule, and profiles of the panel members. The environmental journalist from the *Calgary Herald* hadn't shown because she'd contracted Valley Fever, but another would join the entourage that evening. The only noteworthy coverage appeared in the

Edmonton Journal. The story acknowledged the angry, anxious faces of the hearing participants. It plugged into worries about the influx of terrorism into Southern Alberta unless someone got the Northern Water Army under control. The NWA, the article said, had renamed the hearings the 'Water Tox,' and promised further havoc.

Crystel's "blue ribbon" panel, as Ursula's news release put it, took to the stage in the Medicine Tree Room of the Highwood Centre, an aging brick structure in downtown High River.

Albert and Dan sat on either side of Nancy behind a long table. Both men wore a collared T-shirt and jeans. Nancy had told the hearings staff their dress code was casual with nothing frayed or too worn. She reminded them to speak in a sensible, measured way. "No use raising hackles with flashy clothes and reactive behaviour," she said. She looked composed, as if she were hosting a backyard barbeque and not a highly charged public consultation.

Dan felt anything but nonchalant. He glanced down at the sweat patches blossoming in the armpits of his new cotton shirt. His next paycheque, he decided, would go to improving his wardrobe with wick-dry T-shirts to counter the effects of stress. His eyes scanned the room while people filed in. He did his best to look calm and cool.

On the walls of the hall, posters of waving wheat fields and enormous cattle herds harkened back to better times. A taxidermied bison head looked down censoriously on the crowd. Dan imagined it saying, "I knew you lot would get your due for killing off my kind." A deer head studded each of the other three walls. They might have replied in unison: "Yeah, what he said." The host of assembled faces – townspeople, farmers and ranchers – eyed the stage like angry Angus bulls. Paper fans flapped. Most people had dual-cartridge dust masks in their laps. Despite the pervasive dry, gritty air outside, the air inside the hall hung humid and malodorous from sweat. Dan smelled something more pungent. His own fear, perhaps. He looked at the four Alberta Provincial Police officers with their sidearm holsters, black pressed slacks, and bullet-proof jackets evident under their short-sleeved uniform dress shirts. They had taken up positions around the room. Their presence seemed like over-kill. He wondered why they didn't topple in the heat.

Nancy Weston beamed at the crowd. "Thank you so much for joining us tonight. I hope the folks in the other towns we visit will turn out as enthusiastically as you have this evening."

Snickers pockmarked the ensuing silence. Nervous or deri-sive, Dan couldn't decide. He glanced sideways for a reaction from Nancy, but she remained composed.

"I'll start with opening remarks, and then we will take questions." She introduced Albert and Dan, providing a brief bio for each, then breezed through Southern Alberta's recent climatic history: how the succession of stormy and unusually hot decades had exhausted the glaciers. No one needed a lesson on the current drought that plagued the Prairie Provinces. She noted that Southern Saskatchewan was struggling as well, a comment that elicited nothing more than slow blinks from the audience. Dan knew their own worries precluded them from registering concern for anyone else. Not unlike his own mother. Her single-mindedness had effectively closed her mind to his ambitions and his pain. He forced his focus back to Nancy's words.

"The north has suffered too," she added, "but now they're benefiting from the desalination plant in Bruderheim. And that's what we're here to talk about. Water from the north will flow south through the new pipeline. We want to make sure your cisterns are filled to capacity with reasonably priced water."

As it had in Okotoks, that line launched a commotion of fierce murmurs among audience members.

A voice rose above the hubbub: "Truck, pipeline, they'll fuckin' rip us off all the same."

"We've set up a mic at the front of the room," Nancy called out. "Any questions or comments should be made there. Please use polite language, as there are children present."

Someone yelled, "Sure thing, Miss Manners." Dan saw the hint of a smile play on Nancy's lips.

Several people rose from their chairs and made their way to the centre aisle to line up at the mic. A thin woman in a plaid sleeveless shirt and baggy jeans cinched tightly at the waist stood up. When those already in line moved to let her pass and take to the mic first, Dan pegged the woman a community leader with far more power than her diminutive build would suggest. Dan guessed her to be about Nancy's age. "Peggy Lampert," she said. The p's shot out of the speakers and ricocheted around the room like spit balls.

"We have plenty of reason not to trust neither our governments nor any federal Crown corporation," the woman said, eyeing each of the panel members by turn. "They subsidized putting in our cisterns during the storm years. Vessels designed for capturing rain don't do one whit of good when there is none. Filling them now is taking every last penny we've saved. Some of the folks in this area have already buckled under their debt load. They're now in Tent Town. We don't trust Minister Cameron. We don't trust Premier Hamady. And we don't trust you three. Unfortunately, at this point, we don't have a whole lot of options."

Nancy nodded thoughtfully. "I feel for all of you in these dire times. A few of my old neighbours near Fort Macleod have come to a similar fate —"

"You got money," another voice shouted from the back corner. "You got nothing to worry about, Miss High and Mighty."

Nancy narrowed her eyes ever so slightly. "I'm here to help you in any way I can, but outbursts will not be tolerated." The air prickled with discontent. She let the unspoken threat dangle. "Please continue, Peggy."

Peggy brought her mouth close to the mic again. "Some of us have first-in-time rights that were allocated to our properties way back in 1894 under the North-West Irrigation Act and upheld by the Water Act of 1999." She stood with legs spread, hands on hips. "We feel we should be given priority access to the new pipeline. By getting a better deal. Or by having a pumping station built on or near our land. Can you guarantee that?"

"That's where the playing field has changed. From necessity," Nancy explained. "Albert Travis, can you please explain the Water Charter passed last year by your government?"

The room settled again. Dan was beginning to see a pattern in Nancy Weston's elegant 'we're all in this together' management style. Deferring to a member of the team had neatly diffused the anger in the room. He dreaded the moment when Nancy would redirect to him, and he would have to speak. This wouldn't be anything like making a presentation to his fourth-year seminar class. She hadn't called on him in Okotoks. All the questions had focused on the panel's mandate, where the hearings would take place, and the NWA threat. Time was ticking. Perhaps when Albert finished, they could wrap it up.

"I'd be happy to," Albert said. "As you know, the government suspended all provincial water licenses between the 49th and 52nd parallel three years ago by a unanimous all-party vote pursuant to the emergency powers provisions of the Water Act of 1999. The Charter was passed by the majority government last year as an addendum to the Water Scarcity Bill, which replaced the 1999 Water Act. It outlines the water rights enjoyed by every Albertan."

"Enjoyed," snorted a stout man at the end of the line. He laughed at his own interruption.

Nancy placed her hand lightly on Albert's arm and stared at the source of the outburst. "Please give Albert a chance to explain." Dan saw Nancy glance casually at the Alberta Provincial Police officers who subtly straightened their posture.

Albert continued. "The system of First In Time First In Right, or FITFIR, was instituted to encourage the development of agriculture in the West. It gave priority access to water in times of shortage to the earliest recorded licenses, held by those who had struggled as the first pioneers and endured incredible hardships."

"You want to hear about hardships?" the stout man said.

In an instant, two APP officers stood on either side of the man. He looked up at each one in surprise, and then at Nancy.

"You going to have your goons throw out an old man like me?"

Nancy shook her head. "Sir, can you please tell us your name?"

The man frowned uncertainly. "Reyes. Leon Reyes."

"Mr. Reyes. We want you to stay and we all want to hear what you have to say, but your behaviour is disrespectful to others. Your turn will come, and if you can be patient, we do want to hear your views."

Dan noted the soporific effect of her polite repetitions. It seemed as though the whole audience released a long-held breath. Leon glanced again at the two officers and nodded at Nancy. "Fine. I'll behave."

On Nancy's nod, Albert continued: "Now that water resources, even in Southern Alberta's deepest aquifers, have dwindled, the FITFIR system is obsolete, outdated, and doesn't reflect current realities."

Dan knew Leon Reyes had no tomatoes in his pocket, or the man would surely have thrown them at Albert. Where Nancy's repetition soothed, Albert's triple redundancy bafflegab rankled. Dan wanted to throw something himself. He began to feel protective; these were his people. Normally easy-going and slow to anger, but irritable, impatient, unpredictable when tested.

"Now," Albert said, "water is a commodity just like seed, fertilizer, and hay, but the government regulates it closely to ensure that market prices don't inflate beyond the consumer capacity of those least able to pay. The government is working closely with Crystel in the area of water pricing, which is set based on the actual cost of desalination and distribution, not what the market might think it's worth."

"Allow me to interject, Albert," Nancy said. "As a federal Crown corporation, Crystel is supported by the federal government. The company provides water at cost to Albertans. It's all part of the Federal Government's National Water Program. People in parts of the country where water is plentiful subsidize water delivery in places where water is scarce. Places where market forces would send the cost of the water skyrocketing out of control." She nodded at Albert to continue.

"Crystel's allocations are based on Alberta's Water Charter," Albert continued. "The Charter establishes priorities for water allocation: human needs come first, then small livestock, then agriculture. Each individual gets a minimum number of litres per day to sustain them. If your business relies on water, then you get more depending on your needs. Allocations are made based on your business tax return from the previous year. When water is plentiful, the allotments increase."

Albert glanced at Nancy, who looked at Dan. "Dan, can you tell the folks about where the water comes from that will fill the new southern extension of the pipeline?"

At the sound of his name, all of Dan's muscles instantly felt like they'd been injected with novocaine. His legs, hands, head, even the muscles in his eyes were unresponsive to the voice screaming in his brain, Speak, *damn it*. He managed to turn his head slowly toward Nancy who eyed him with curiosity, which quickly morphed into a concerned frown.

She waited another moment for him to respond, then she gave his arm a friendly squeeze and said, "Dan, you did such a great job explaining this to me the other day." Her face broke out in the kind of loving smile his mother had so often given him. When she was utterly pleased with something he'd done. The feeling whooshed back into his body as quickly as it had evaporated.

"Yes, Nancy," he heard himself say. "What was the question again?"

"Can you please explain where the water for the pipeline comes from?"

"Of course." This was science turf. His feet knew the way here. "All the water for Southern Alberta comes from the pipeline whose endpoint right now is Red Deer. Crystel Canada sources that water from two places. Most of it comes from the Pacific Ocean with a small supplement from deep confined aquifers in the Slave Lake area." Awed by the stillness in the room and the fact that all eyes were on him, he broke off, but only for a moment. "Right, well, Crystel's reverse osmosis desalination plant in Bruderheim receives saltwater from the Pacific through the Northern Gateway pipeline, which consists of two parallel pipelines. The pipe that used to carry natural gas condensate was cleaned using nanotechnology — nano-bots, if you will. Its current capacity is forty thousand cubic metres, or forty million litres per day. The water comes from a marine terminal in Kitimat, B.C. to the inland terminal in Bruderheim. The plant is currently at half capacity. It will be ready to process eighty thousand cubic metres per day by the end of the year."

Nancy smiled and nodded encouragingly when he finished. His heartbeat resounded in his ears. He'd recovered. In fact, to his own great surprise, he'd aced it.

21

THE FOLLOWING EVENING at the hearing in Gleichen, Dan explained again about the parallel Northern Gateway pipelines and how one used to carry natural gas. The man at the mic asked, "Pray tell, what about the other one?"

Dan looked at him. "The other one?"

"The other parallel pipeline."

"Of course. The larger Northern Gateway pipeline carried crude oil. It's currently unsuitable for conveying water. If all goes well, that clean-up should be complete in three years' time and will nearly triple the amount of saltwater entering Alberta."

The man squeezed his eyes shut. "Forty million litres per day will provide water for two million people. And Alberta has a population of three million. That's where the NWA comes in. They think the south isn't worth saving."

"We're all worth saving," cried the man directly behind him. "But I can barely afford enough water to keep my sheep alive, let alone keep myself clean. Wanna know why it stinks in this room? Me."

The audience burst into laughter — but high-pitched and nervous, not genuine mirth.

The man at the mic smiled. "You don't need to tell us, Ronald." He sat down, and Ronald moved to the front, his face instantly serious. He directed his piercing eyes at Nancy Weston. "Forget our problems with the North. We all know what the real issue is here. If Crystel decides to sell water — now a 'commodity' — to the U.S., we're all screwed. Is that what you're planning, Madam Chair?" The question froze all movement in the room. Even the clock on the wall seemed to stop its march through time. "Well," he said, "how are you going to make sure this pipeline won't pass us by altogether, which would hammer the final nail in our coffin?"

Nancy Weston looked like she was mulling over the possibility of the pipeline leading not to renewal but to death. Dan exchanged a glance with Ursula, leaning against the wall near the stage. Then Nancy said, "I can assure you that Crystel has no intention of selling water to the United States. Crystel is a Canadian Crown corporation, with Canadian interests at heart."

Dan thought about the letter from Balthazar Frost, and hoped she was right to be so unequivocal. Maybe Percy could lead the charge to keep water from flowing to the States. That would justify Dan breaking the confidentiality agreement.

Nancy turned her eyes on Dan again. "Do you have anything to add, Dan?"

This time, he was ready. "We're collaborating with the Alberta Water Ministry on research and development of water resources throughout the province. It's true that our traditional water sources — glaciers — are tapped out. But, if history is any indication, this drought will end, and, when it does, we'll be ready to draw water from the healthiest aquifers to fill the pipeline as needed. As you all know, trucking water is incredibly expensive." Another urgent murmur twisted through the room. "The biggest advantage of the pipeline, whether we fill it with desalinated water or water from our own aquifers, is that water will come from much closer by, and so will cost less."

The man stepped away from the mic but remained at the front, staring Dan down. If he wanted to launch a retort, he couldn't seem to come up with one. After a moment, one of the officers altered his stance, which prompted the man to glance at him and finally return to his seat.

The lineup was long, but they heard and responded to everyone: When will the pipeline arrive in Calgary? Mid-November. How will you be sure no one can sabotage the pipeline? Security including armed drones. How can you ensure water quality? A 20-micron prefilter; the customer adds monochloramine to make it potable. How do I take the federal government's land buyout? The Crown corporation can't speak for the Treasury Board of Canada. Visit their website. Why can't we get free water the way Alberta's First Nations do? The Canadian Government has special constitutional, regulatory, and treaty obligations regarding water supply and quality to First Nations groups.

Finally, a large man in a worn lumberjack shirt bellowed into the mic, "Langdon Doround. Tell me how much I'm going to save."

Nancy nodded at Albert, and he said, "As Dan explained, the pipeline will be a much closer source, so that reduces transportation costs by a significant margin. The price of water delivery for those around Red Deer since the pipeline opened in April has dropped by forty-five percent. The same way the federal government provides have-not provinces like Alberta with equalization payments, Crystel will equalize your costs.

Those who live far from the pipeline won't pay more than those whose land it crosses."

Silence permeated the hall as people calculated the cost savings for their own households.

A latecomer slinked up behind Leon as he left the mic. The young man wore a hoodie pulled far forward over his head, which made him look like he inhaled the microphone when he leaned into it. "What about those crazies up there from the Northern Water Army? What are you doing to keep them in line?"

"This is our last question of the night, and I'll field it," Nancy said. "The government will not negotiate with the NWA. We have tightened our security procedures, and the Canadian Armed Forces are now involved in keeping the pipeline project on track. Anyone with any involvement in terror activities will be prosecuted to the full extent of the law."

Someone shouted from the back of the room. "They'd be happy to let us southerners fry in the desert." A smattering of uncomfortable snickers followed.

Dan saw Nancy's assistant, Ricky Zhang, near the main door, quietly stacking crates of Crystel water bottles onto a table.

"Ladies and gentlemen," Nancy said, "I thank you for your interest and attention. Panel members will be at the back of the hall to answer any further questions you might have before you head home."

The participants tucked away their paper fans and rose heavily. They milled in the aisles until the panel members had squeezed their way through to the water table. Nancy smiled warmly and handed each person a water bottle as they filed by. Dan took up a position as near to her as possible without seeming to be joined to her at the hip. He had achieved a level of comfort with the relatively scripted portion of the evening, but the one-on-one segment made his heart race. He worried that a rogue participant or hard-nosed reporter would lob an unanticipated question at him.

Several people stopped to talk to the panel members. A woman approached Ursula and held both of her hands. Though Dan couldn't hear what the woman said, her face registered deep intensity.

Langdon Dersund took a bottle from Nancy, spit on it and tossed it in a trash can as he left the building. The woman behind him picked the water bottle out of the trashcan. She pulled a handkerchief out of her pocket and wiped the bottle clean. Then she took out a small container of hand sanitizer and rubbed a generous dollop onto the bottle before handing it to a woman with a child.

"My husband's worried is all," she said to Nancy. "But we mustn't waste one precious drop. No matter how discouraged we get."

Nancy smiled and shook the woman's hand. "We'll get through this together."

The woman didn't return the smile but nodded stiffly. "I hope you're right."

Albert was speaking to someone Dan recognized. A tall man about his own age with short brown hair and long bangs swept low across his forehead. Dan read "Liam Parsens — Calgary Herald" on his media lanyard. Liam had dated one of Dan's undergrad classmates. The reporter's radar must have detected the stare because he looked over and lifted his chin at Dan.

A woman with long snow-white hair grasped Dan's hand and looked solemnly into his eyes. "Do you really think there'll be enough water for everyone?" The smell of cinnamon on her breath competed with the miasma of body odour in the room.

"Yes, ma'am," Dan replied. "I've been up north myself. I spent several summers in the vicinity of Slave Lake. I worked for the research division of the Alberta Water Ministry during my undergrad degree and master's. We mapped the aquifers within a two-hundred-kilometre radius of the lakebed to determine the volume and stability of the deepest underground reservoirs. Granted, Slave Lake can't sustain the whole province right now, but it supplements the water from the Pacific. The pipeline is the way to make Southern Alberta thrive again."

The woman smiled and patted his hand. Others had turned toward him. Dan felt his face redden in the glow of their attention. Liam Parsens had also turned to listen, and now walked over to him.

"Dan, how are you?" he said extending his hand. "Remember me?"

"I do. We met through Vince a few years back. Be right with you, Liam." Dan turned back to the woman still holding his left hand. "Don't worry, ma'am. Everything will be okay."

The woman looked at him like he was the drink of water she'd been desperate for.

"Thank you, dear. I believe you." She took the bottle of water he offered and walked away.

"Good to see you, Liam. How is Vince? Or maybe ..." Dan's words trailed off as he realized they might no longer be together.

Liam waved off Dan's hesitation. "Married. Six months now. Didn't make a big deal of it. Popped into the courthouse. Vince isn't working. You're lucky to get this gig, my friend."

Dan nodded his agreement. "Congratulations. Sorry, though, about Vince not finding work."

Liam shrugged. "He's doing a second degree in renewable energy engineering." Then his voice turned all business. "You believe what you said? That there's enough, and everything will be okay? That's not public-hearing bullshit?"

"No," Dan said, shaking his head, "it's not. I've seen the recharge data."

"Recharge data?" Liam raised his phone and stylus. "Sorry. I'm playing catch-up. Just got assigned to you guys. I was covering the Northern Water Army."

Then it clicked in Dan's mind. Liam had been in the journalism program at MRU. While writing for the university's paper, *The Reflector*, he broke a story about an elderly, tenured business school professor known for erratic behaviour. In a lecture, the prof had compared Premier Hamady to Saddam Hussein, an Iraqi dictator responsible for the brutal deaths of as many as half a million people in the late twentieth century. The professor had said if the premier's eight years in office were extended, Albertans might as well shoot themselves en masse. The article led to an investigation, after which the professor was forced to resign. Liam had never shied away from reporting the hard facts.

"Recharge data indicates how fast an aquifer will refill after withdrawals are made," Dan said, scrambling for his bland panel persona.

Liam frowned. "Your parents have a farm in the south, don't they?"

Dan marveled at the man's memory. "Yes, they do. Near Fort Macleod."

"How are they faring?"

"They're struggling, same as these people here."

Dan noticed that those who had turned to listen now clustered around them.

"You're one of them," Liam said thoughtfully, emphasizing the word 'them.' He showed Dan that he was clicking the audio recorder app on his phone.

Dan raised his hands. "No, no, there shouldn't be an 'us' and 'them.' We need to collaborate to get the water to Southern Alberta as quickly as possible." He realized with alarm that Nancy and the other panel members were now listening to him as well. "If everyone here gets behind the project and has confidence in it, that will help fight the forces up north that are working against the pipeline. We need a united front. Albertans for Alberta. The science and the stats on Crystel's pipeline back up the claim that we don't have to fight each other for all of us to get the water we need."

Nancy stepped into the fray. "Mr. Parsens, let me show you the schematic of the pipeline's proposed path."

Dan took a breath as Nancy guided Liam away by the arm. Several meeting participants who had clustered around him shook Dan's hand before leaving the building.

An older man in a rumpled dress shirt and loose tie had been hanging on the periphery. Dan recognized him as one of the reporters Nancy had spoken to after the Okotoks hearing. The man moved forward and extended his hand. "Fred Clayton, *Edmonton Journal*," he said. "Those are brave words, son."

DAN'S BED AT THE Sage Crest Motel sagged miserably, and he slept sporadically. He tried to distract himself by wondering what a 'sage crest' might be. Then he shone his phone torch on the picture of an old grain elevator screwed onto the wall opposite the bed. The frame didn't quite cover the bright rectangle that must have once housed a large TV. He finally fell asleep imagining driving through a prairie landscape replete with waving wheat, and a grain elevator in every town.

When he woke up, he grabbed his tablet and scanned the Alberta news. Liam's headline in the *Calgary Herald* read "Panel scientist vows water for all." He shut the tablet off, too nervous to see his own rash words in black and white, or even to check the *Edmonton Journal* headline.

After breakfast, he slouched in a chair in Nancy's motel room, gulping coffee to bring his bleary eyes and mind to life. Most of the Water Talks staff members were assembled, including the sound technician, Tom Sinclair, and Nancy's assistant, Ricky. Even the bus driver. Only Ursula hadn't shown yet.

"We need to realize," Nancy said, looking at each member in turn, "that we're on a good-will mission as much as we're consulting with the public on how to implement a new water regime. Dan started the ball rolling quite successfully last night. He's found the way out of our defensive position."

Dan sat up at the mention of his name. "I'm sorry?" He'd been so certain he'd said too much. Thought the ball he'd got rolling had a lit fuse. He believed Alberta could prosper again, but worried that Crystel — and the provincial and federal governments — might not be able to stomach his grand promises.

"Relaying your experience up north with such optimism lifted the spirits of everyone who heard you," Nancy continued.

Ursula burst into the room holding up her tablet computer. She tapped the screen a few times and handed the tablet to Nancy. "Still waiting for the *High River Times* and the *Red Deer Advocate* to post online."

Nancy read the *Calgary Herald* headline Dan had seen that morning. Then she said, "*Edmonton Journal*. 'Crystel hearings: no need for water war.'"

"Positive publicity will do us and Crystel a world of good," Ursula said.

"Right," Albert added. "We want to win hearts and minds, not light a fire under the wackos."

Nancy shot the man a stern look. "I will not have the word 'wacko' bandied about by anyone in our group. We're about respectful dialogue. Is that clear?"

Albert opened his mouth to speak, but nodded instead.

"Ursula, please write up new key messages along the lines of what Dan said last night so we can all say the same thing. We can't speak to his personal experience, of course. That's Dan's territory. Dan, please work with Ursula this morning on that."

"Shall I tell the media reps that the bus leaves at one for Strathmore?" Ursula asked.

Nancy nodded. "Yes, that will be fine."

Albert leaned toward Dan's chair. "Plenty of doubters there, too, I bet."

Nancy threw him a hard, unflinching stare. "I'm warning you, Albert. Anyone spouting negativity during these hearings will be dismissed. Please go and prepare for tonight's hearing, everyone."

As they swarmed out of the room, Dan's mind reeled. How had he, an unsophisticated farm boy, become the centre of attention at the Water Talks? Opa's voice came to him like a whisper in his ear: "Caution never fixed anything." His life was now perched on a knife edge — was he a fraud or could he be a force for positive change? He needed to jump in and find out.

22

ON THE MORNING OF JULY 5TH, Willa, Calvin, and Peter drove into Fort Macleod for their second Sunday service at New Life. Logan's will had requested that Peter's guardians take him to church periodically because that's what his mother would have wanted. Willa felt ambivalent about the obligation. She was happy to do it for Logan and Kelli's sake, but whatever religious tendencies she might have had went out the door when her mother left, with one exception. She prayed for her father when he got sick. Pastor Mike had visited him when he became bedridden. Despite Gerard's lack of religious conviction, he appreciated the pastor's interest in thoughtful discussion. The debates fired up his brain and helped him forget his failing body. The pastor was a newly minted man of god then. One morning, when she'd felt particularly desperate about her father's decline, she'd teared up as he left the house.

"I've never been one for prayer, Pastor Mike," she said, clutching his arm. "But I've grown desperate enough to pray for god to spare Papa this horrible disease. But it seems so hopeless."

"God has his reasons for sending people the afflictions he does," Pastor Mike replied stone-faced, patting her hand. "There must be a higher purpose to it. God must know your father is strong enough to endure it. Perhaps he's testing your faith."

She snatched her hand back. "Any god who tests people by making others suffer is sick and sadistic."

Pastor Mike simply shook his head and told her god had a plan.

The salty rage she'd felt that day had resurged when she saw him at Kelli's funeral. And again at Logan's. Willa saw no evidence he remembered their long-ago discussion. At the first service, Pastor Mike had greeted them warmly and told jokes to put Peter at ease. Now, he rushed over when they stepped in the door.

"Hey guys, I have a new one for you. A rabbi, a priest, and a minister walk into a bar. The bartender says, 'Hey, what is this, a joke?" Calvin, Willa, and Peter smiled. "Okay, it's not new, but it's good." He grinned and rushed off to get ready for the service.

Afterwards, he wished Willa and Peter a good trip to Fort McMurray. "Whatever you decide, you know you'll always be welcome here, Peter. Oh, and that reminds me of another one." He glanced around excitedly as he spoke. "After the baptism of his baby brother in church, Johnny sobbed all the way home in the back seat of the car. His father asked him three times what was wrong. Finally, the boy blurted out, 'That priest said he wanted my brother and me to be brought up in a Christian home, but I want to stay with you guys.'"

Calvin and Peter laughed.

WILLA AND PETER'S PLANE rose above the dust and smoke from forest fires in British Columbia to where the sun shone clear and bright. Below, all the muddled hardships of life lay hidden under a duvet of grey haze. As they flew north, the clouds cleared to reveal a grid of brown fields and the curves of dry creek beds and ponds turned dusty craters. Peter's gaze seemed to take in not the drought-drenched land beneath them but the blue heavens above. Sky blue — the crayon young Daniel had always worn down to the size of a thumb tack. Peter's face was placid, but he held his hands in tight fists, as he often did when he wasn't busy at a task.

"What did you think of the take-off?" Willa asked.

"Pretty smooth. You know that most airplane crashes happen just after take-off?"

"So I've heard." Willa shuddered. "Did you enjoy your trips up north with your mom? I know you never flew, but did you have fun with your family up there?"

"Oh, yeah. The car rides were endless, but staying with grandma and grandpa was great. They took us to the pool in their neighbourhood every day."

No mention of Aunt Lily and Uncle Roy. "It's good you remember it so well. You must have been very young then."

"Yup. I always missed home, though. Dad and the animals." He turned his attention back to the inverted sea of blue outside the window. A few minutes later, he crossed his arms on the tray table, lay his head down, and appeared to doze off.

The collage of dull squares now included the occasional bountiful disk. They had crossed over into pipeline land and Willa looked wistfully at the green circles — fields watered by circle irrigation. So different from the south, where plentiful harvests remained a pipedream.

An hour later, Willa gave Peter's arm a gentle shake. "We're landing soon, lieverd. I thought you'd want to be awake for that."

He looked around wildly, his half-open eyes curtained by wispy strands of blond hair. "I had a dream," he said, voice croaking from sleep. Though Willa waited, he didn't elaborate, just pushed his hair back from his eyes and stared outside.

He spoke softly to the window. "Mom always said she would have loved to take me in an airplane."

Willa sat motionless. His revelations were like butterflies she didn't want to disturb.

He went on. "She hated the take-offs and landings, she said, but she loved flying over the clouds because it made her think there was a soft place to land if anything happened."

"Sometimes our imagination can help us when we're scared." Even as she said it, she couldn't help but wonder why hers had turned on her.

"I guess so," he said.

She surveyed the sea of tree remains below. Great swaths of charcoal quills that had once been dense boreal forest before falling victim to fire from dry thunderstorms. Fort McMurray itself was studded with lush green yards and sports fields, all anointed by water flowing from Bruderheim and supplemented by Slave Lake. The town thrived now as it had during the oil sands heyday. Money poured in to facilitate the clean-up of tar ponds. For the federal and provincial governments to restore Canada's reputation as an environmentally responsible nation, they had to demonstrate to the world their commitment to healing the scars of unconventional oil extraction and returning the tumorous earth to Mother Nature. Willa had read that legal battles raged between governments and corporations; projected clean-up costs vastly exceeded available corporate security deposits in the Mine Financial Security Program, which was supposed to protect the taxpayers of Alberta from the liability of industrial development. For now, entrepreneurs such as Peter's uncle, who owned a reclamation firm, lived well off the new boom.

"Fort Mac is even greener than the pictures I looked at online," Willa said.

He nodded.

She imagined pro/con charts forming in Peter's mind. North vs South. The pro-North column getting a check mark for being lush and green. Alive.

Lily Emerson and her husband met them at the airport gate. Lily clasped and unclasped her hands as Willa and Peter approached them. She wore a slim fitting white sundress with green polka dots. Large-rimmed sunglasses perched above her forehead. Her frosted lipstick matched the colour of her shiny pink clutch purse. She reached for Peter and hugged him tightly. "Oh, it's so wonderful to see you, Peter. We're so glad you came."

Lily's husband reached his hand out to Willa. "Roy Many Horses." His hair was even longer than in the company picture, and he smiled just as broadly. His pale jacket of fine linen contrasted with his jeans and beaded belt. She noticed the faint smell of smoke clung to him—but not cigarettes. More earthy, with a light, sweet note.

Willa shook his hand. "Wilhelmina Van Bruggen."

When Lily finally released Peter, Roy shook the boy's hand. The two gazed awkwardly at him, then Lily turned to Willa.

"Good to see you again, Ms. Van Bruggen," she said. "We're glad to have you."

Willa doubted that. "Please, call me Willa."

DURING THE HALF-HOUR DRIVE from the airport to Roy and Lily's house, Peter's eyes were aimed out the window. The unbroken blur of heavily irrigated leafy trees and thick shrubs zipped by outside. To Willa, the startlingly green landscape looked spray-painted and lacquered. Roy rolled down his window. The warm air blowing in smelled so strongly of fragrant flowers and green grass that Willa found it difficult to breathe.

From the front passenger seat, Lily shouted out statistics over the wind. "Summer temperatures average twenty-five degrees Celsius. Only minus-five in winter." She laughed frequently, as if to market her good nature to the back seat. "We have a great minor hockey program up here. Do you still play hockey, Peter?"

"I played Novice and Atom, but it got to be too much travelling. When Mom got sick."

Lily was quiet a moment, then her words scurried on. "I know your mom loved watching you play. We have an arena not too far from us with a league that plays locally." Peter concentrated on opening his window.

Roy said nothing, but silence and subtlety didn't figure into Lily's playbook. Hard sell was more her game. Still, if Peter was adding tick marks to the pro-North column, Willa couldn't tell from his face. She looked out her side of the car. She suspected the beauty before her would need to be curbed once the southern pipeline extended to the Lethbridge area. The desalination plant would have a finite capacity. Alberta could hardly afford to squander productive grain fields in favour of upkeep on Fort McMurray's postcard parks.

Like the other homes in the neighbourhood, Roy and Lily's was stylish, with clean lines and a moat of lush trees and shrubs. A two-storey turret-like structure abutted the rectangular back portion of the building. A wide staircase led to the front door. To the right of the door was a deck with a three-seat swing and terra cotta chiminea. Inside, the turret-like portion of the house contained the front hall and a well-appointed sitting room with a cathedral ceiling above.

"What a beautiful home you have," Willa said.

"Oh, thank you, we couldn't be happier here," Lily replied, her smile bright as a bowl of rosy apples.

Willa couldn't imagine Lily ever having a moment of sadness, not even under torture.

She led Willa and Peter to neighbouring bedrooms on the second floor, overlooking the backyard. Verdant trees encircled the overly large outdoor space. Stranded in the centre: the life-size statue of a lean young man atop a fountain, naked and holding a fish that sprayed water from its mouth. To Willa, it looked like Eden itself, complete with Adam before his and Eve's fall from grace. She assumed the sculptor saw the fish as a fellow creature of god, not as dinner.

After they'd unpacked, Lily took them on a tour. The interior of the house showed evidence of a blending of the two disparate worlds Lily and Roy had come from. Area rugs ranging from modern geometric motifs to a bear skin. An Alex Colville print of a black horse running in front of a church hung next to a painting of an Indigenous man in beaded leather trousers and an impressive headdress sitting on an American Paint Horse. A crystal vase shared a shelf with a ceramic jar, its girth encircled with painted bison. Willa zeroed in on a portrait by Nicholas de Grandmaison, of an Indigenous woman with a sleeping child on her back. Willa stood gazing at the woman's face, which was etched with an equal measure of ferocity and tenderness. The child's arm hung gracefully over the mother's shoulder, a perfect expression of vulnerability and trust. It made her think of Daniel and their terrible conversation. She should call him. But what would she say? Only when Lily called her to come see the library did Willa realize she'd been holding her breath.

Eventually, they spilled out into a large family room in the walk-out basement, complete with a wall-mounted projection TV. Lily directed Peter to the latest virtual reality headset and the smart TV where the games resided. Willa knew he'd never had such luxuries at home, but after brief instructions on how to use the VR headset, he was lost in a world of virtual mayhem. So much better than the real mayhem of becoming an orphan and having to choose his guardians at age fourteen.

Willa glanced at Lily. She pulled her cell phone out of her pocket. "I think I'll go call my husband to let him know we arrived safely."

"Oh, sure. Feel free to roam around at will. Mi casa, su casa." The Spanish words came out high and singsongy.

Willa smiled at Lily, hoping to dissipate the discomfort of two unlike creatures flung together under sad circumstances. "This isn't easy, is it?" Willa said.

"Oh, sure," Lily said, lightning fast. She said it again as if Willa had asked, 'Do you have fresh towels?' Lily spoke to the picture she was straightening. "I put sandwiches in the fridge in case you and Peter get hungry. I'll serve supper at six, but I don't want you to starve before then. Help yourself." She adjusted the perfectly aligned straps of her sundress and turned to leave the room. Willa followed her up to the main floor, where they silently parted ways.

"HOW WAS YOUR TRIP?" Calvin asked by video-call.

"Fine," Willa replied. "We arrived at Roy and Lily's castle an hour or so ago. Oh, it's grand, Calvin. The trees and yard are unnaturally green." She turned in the window seat and aimed her phone camera lens out the bedroom window.

"Oh, my," he said. "Are you settling in okay?"

"The term 'fifth wheel' comes to mind, but I guess it'll be all right. How is everything there?"

"Dolly's developed a mild case of mastitis, but it's subclinical and I'm applying towels soaked in comfrey and milk thistle tea to the affected teat."

Willa smiled at how technical he still sounded after all his years away from veterinary medicine.

"Feeding her kids myself until it clears up," he continued. "Other than that, Quentin and I are doing fine. Nothing seems to faze him. Duke got out tonight, but Quentin slipped a rope around his neck, easy as can be, and led him back inside his pen. Reminded me of Dan. How's Peter?"

"A closed book. Lost in game land. It may be a while before he comes up for air. I should go. I'll talk to you in a couple of days."

"Okay. Don't get used to the green. I want you to come home."

After hanging up, homesickness overtook her. How odd to be so far away from Calvin. Not to have work to do. Not to have her dust mask on hand. She went to the guest bathroom to wash up. Here, water came from a city pipe and not a cistern. She thought the strangeness of the circumstances might trigger a hallucination, but nothing came. She lay down on the bed to rest a while. Perhaps the Ativan was doing its job after all.

23

URSULA AND DAN SAT side by side on the Water Talks bus back to Calgary. The panel members, hearings staff, and media reps had travelled to Okotoks, High River, Gleichen, and Strathmore, all in a five-day period. They now had two days at home to get their lives in order before heading further south for what Nancy promised would be a gruelling schedule of hearings.

"What do you think?" Dan asked Ursula. "Now that we're a few days into this."

"Worrisome," she said, shaking her head. Her voice dropped as she leaned in. "The terrorists up north want to keep all the water; people down here are desperate for it. For now, the terrorists have done some damage, but they aren't particularly organized. The desperate southerners in the city are satisfied with breaking windows and intimidating their own neighbours for a few litres of water. If the mainstream ever decides to join in, there'll be a civil war."

"Don't you think things will settle down when everyone gets what they want? The pipeline will arrive in Calgary, the people up north will see they're getting their fair share. Everyone's happy."

Ursula looked at him in wonder. "You're the genuine article, aren't you, Daniel Brookes? An honest-to-goodness optimist."

Dan shrugged. "I say deal with the bad; hope for the best."

Ursula nodded thoughtfully. "Can't argue with that philosophy. I guess it's how you 'deal with the bad' that counts. Experts predicted long-term droughts forty years ago, but little was done to protect the headwaters of either the North or South Saskatchewan River Basin. The FITFIR system made the environment pay whenever water became scarce. Not to mention how the oil sands used and abused our water resources." She took a breath. "I'm preaching to the choir, aren't I?" She turned away, and Dan followed her gaze out the window.

Dust devils swirled around fallow fields that extended to the horizon. A brown desert broken only by the occasional stranded farmhouse, stand of dead trees, or tumble-down shack.

She spoke again, more quietly this time. "We can't even grow the most drought-resistant crops down here anymore."

"Two hundred years ago," Dan said, "explorer John Palliser said this area was too arid for agriculture or even significant habitation. I think we proved him wrong."

She smiled slightly and shook her head.

Condescension? he wondered. "Of course, then we screwed it up. But what's done is done. We just have to try and do it better from now on. When we get the water back, I mean."

Ursula laughed. "No wonder our audiences love you."

He noticed for the first time that her front teeth overlapped slightly. Also, a softness lurked behind her stern green eyes.

"My grandmother was a political advisor to several Calgary mayors," she said. "Our visits to her house on Sundays came with plenty of serious dinner conversation. Turned me into a cynic, I guess." She directed her gaze out the window again.

He stared, too.

"My grandmother did inspire in me a sincere love for my hometown and for Southern Alberta." She turned and winked at Dan. "You and I are not so different that way."

Dan smiled at her, and they settled back in their seats, quietly watching the dry flatland race by.

DAN AND URSULA called for a rideshare from where the bus let them off at Crystel Canada Square, as they both lived in the northeast quadrant of Calgary. Ursula said she lived in a large two-storey house in Taradale. Dan told the driver his address, which would be the first stop.

Her grandparents had taken them in, she told him, when her father lost his job at TransAlta five years ago. "You can't run dams without water," she said with a sad shrug.

The car crossed the 5th Avenue Flyover and turned up 1st Avenue NE.

"Bridgeland is a great part of town," Ursula said.

"Rougher than it used to be," Dan said as they passed Langevin School.

When the car pulled up in front of Mrs. Winstead's house, Ursula said, "Nice house."

"The house is nice, but I'm below ground," Dan said.

"Basement suite, huh?"

Dan chuckled at her. "Well, 'suite' isn't the word for it, and I'd love not to live like a mole, but I'm barely keeping my head above water financially. And I'm not sure I could leave Mrs. Winstead high and dry." He looked at Ursula sidelong, frowning. "Ever notice how many water-related clichés we have in the English language? Anyway, I haul her water when I get mine. Right now, I've got a friend from university days helping

her out. Not sure if anyone would take over permanently if
I moved."

"That sort of kindness is in short supply these days, Dan.
Good on ya."

"You can credit my parents and my Opa for that." He
climbed out of the cab, then leaned back down to smile at
Ursula. "They taught me to cast my bread upon the waters.
Sorry, couldn't resist."

Ursula smiled and rolled her eyes. As the car pulled away,
Dan knocked on the front door to check in with Mrs. Winstead.
An unfamiliar face peered through the front window.

"Dan Brookes," he called to the woman. "I'm the tenant."
When she continued to look at him uncertainly, he pulled his
driver's licence from his wallet. He held it up to the peephole
and heard the deadbolt click.

The woman opened the door and invited him into the
front room. As she took a seat in one of the large wing chairs,
she introduced herself as Mrs. Winstead's daughter, Madison,
from High River. Dan took a seat on the sofa, patterned with
faded roses.

"She's broken her hip," Madison said. Dark half-moons under-
scored her eyes. "She was on her way to visit a friend down the
street and came upon a group of young men harassing a girl.
She told them to stop and they pushed her down and stole her
purse." She shook her head. "The girl called an ambulance."

"I'm so sorry. Is your mom at the Foothills?"

Madison nodded. "I don't know how we'll find the space,
but I'm going to have to take her home to High River. We've
already got my husband's parents living with us." She busied
her hands stroking her dress across her lap. "I'm sorry, Dan, but
we're going to have to put the house up for sale. We may not be

able to sell it, but I must try. Mother has been quite depressed. Even before the attack, I mean. Quite frankly, my husband and I would worry about her state of mind and her safety if she continued living in the city." Madison studied Dan's face, perhaps wondering if he would take offence at her condemnation of Calgary.

"I understand," Dan said. "I assume I can still direct deposit rent payments to her account until you sell?" When the woman nodded, he asked, "Is there anything I can do to help?"

"I don't think so," Madison said. Her eyes swept around the room. Ancient ornate cabinets and bookcases lined the walls. In the centre of the room, stacks of magazines sat on a coffee table anchored by scuffed claw foot legs. Dan noted several magazines dating from the 2010s. Two *Maclean's* headlines read "The Year That Winter Died" and "'Environmentalism has Failed'." Bold, all-cap typeface on an *Alberta Views* cover blared, "If all humans lived like Albertans, we'd need four planets." He couldn't imagine old dire news helping Mrs. Winstead's state of mind.

"I have to figure out how I'm going to get all her stuff to High River, and where I'm going to put it when it gets there. Anyway, I'll give you as much notice as I can."

"Thanks," he said.

She went from nodding to sadly shaking her head.

DAN STEPPED THROUGH the sliding doors at the Foothills Hospital and took the elevator to the twelfth floor, where Madison had said he would find her mother.

"Dan," Mrs. Winstead said, the brightness of her voice defying her limp grey hair and pasty complexion. "Aren't you a dear to come and see me."

The stale, sickly scent in the room evoked bittersweet memories of Opa during his final agonizing months. But Mrs. Winstead's decline had been sudden. Only a few days before, she'd felt powerful enough to stand up to a gang of hooligans. Now, she lay prostrate and fragile.

"How are you, Mrs. Winstead?" he asked, handing her a get-well card.

"Thank you, dear. I'll be all good soon enough. Be glad to get back home."

He smiled and nodded. Madison hadn't told her yet that she wouldn't be going home.

"I suppose I shouldn't have gone out to see Abigail," she said. "Bridgeland used to be such a nice place to live." Her eyes drifted to the window and gazed at it as if it were a giant screen replaying the history of her community.

"You came to that girl's rescue, Mrs. Winstead," Dan said softly. "You're a hero. Bridgeland will be safe again. When water prices drop, so will crime."

"I don't think so, dear," she said. All evidence of her previously bright voice had faded. She let her head fall back on the pillow and closed her eyes. "I don't think so," she said again. When she opened her eyes, she became more animated. "Did you have a good trip, dear? I saw you on the news. The lady who's running that panel seems quite competent."

"She is," Dan said.

"I'll be glad when that pipeline gets to Calgary." She closed her eyes again. "You're doing good work, Dan. Important ..." Dan stood beside her until her breathing turned to delicate snores. He picked up the envelope from where it lay on her belly, opened it, and sat the card upright on the table beside the bed. As he walked down the corridor toward the elevators, he wondered if Opa would have been better off finishing out his life in a hospital or hospice. How did dying at home measure up against making your fifteen-year-old grandson feel like a murderer? Would he have to get old and sick to figure it out?

WATER TALKS RESUMED the following week. First stop: Vulcan. An hour before the scheduled start of the hearing, the meeting room in the Cultural-Recreational Centre filled to capacity. So many people were still lined up outside that the town clerk opened the County Central High School gym instead. The APP officers took their place at the rear entrance of the gym while the panel members took their places on the stage and Tom Sinclair set up the sound equipment. Even those who had already endured the security check to gain entry to the rec centre were given a pat down and bag search. By the time the last person had been admitted, the meeting had eclipsed its start time by an hour and a half.

The gym had not been used since school ended, but the musty smell of teenage athleticism still clung to the walls. Gradually, the stale, tired body odour of working-class people down on their luck won out. Nancy started the meeting as she had the previous four with a welcome, an introduction to the problem, and the solution of the pipeline. She posed the same questions, and a queue formed at the mic.

A short bald man with a red moustache spoke first. "I have a question for the young man in the blue shirt."

Dan sat staring until he realized the man meant him. Then he leaned forward toward his mic and said, "Yes. Yes, of course. What's your question?"

"Have you done the research on which aquifers in the south depleted last? These would no doubt be the first to fill when the rain returns."

A sonorous groan rippled through the crowd, and the ubiquitous paper fans flapped angrily. The word 'rain' had become taboo. Uttering it, people believed, could only irk whatever gods ruled over such forces of nature.

"That's correct," Dan said. "The proposed pipeline path takes into account those exact parameters. You'll notice on the schematic posters we've hung around the gym that the pipeline does not follow a straight line south, but jogs southeast from High River toward the aquifer under Lethbridge that dried up three years ago. We anticipate that aquifer to replenish first, thereby taking pressure off supplies coming from Bruderheim."

The bald man nodded as another elbowed him aside. Taking his cowboy hat off, the new speaker held the crown and pointed the brim accusingly at Dan. "Ain't gonna be no rain. Aren't you giving people false hope?"

"With respect, sir, I don't think so," Dan said. "The pipeline will bring water regardless of future trends. Favourable weather just means cheaper water."

"How will the pipeline ever get here," the man continued, "when they keep blowing it up?"

Nancy leaned into her mic. "The government is using the latest in drone technology to monitor the existing pipeline. Crystel is on track to bring it into Calgary only two weeks later than planned because of the terrible explosion. In a year and a half, water will flow through High River to Lethbridge. We don't anticipate any possibility of further sabotage, because we're prepared for it."

Dan studied Nancy's profile, utterly inscrutable as usual. If she ever harboured any shadow of a doubt about what she said, her face and gestures didn't betray her. The man had continued to brandish his hat while she spoke, trying to insert his doubts with interruptions of "but" and "yeah, right" without success. He walked away, muttering and shaking his head.

Two dozen more people had asked questions when Dan glanced at his phone to check the time. 11:30 pm. He would recall that moment later when questioned by police, because just then a woman pushed her way to the front, pulled a small pistol from the front of her shirt and aimed it point blank at Nancy. "You're killing the north," she shouted, and pulled the trigger.

An APP officer raced to the front of the room and disarmed the woman just as Nancy tumbled from her chair.

People screamed, and Albert Travis shouted, "Someone call 9-1-1." The scene turned slowmo. Out of the corner of his eye, Dan saw the police lead away the shooter in handcuffs. Ursula hopped up onto the stage and crouched down beside Nancy. She drew her hand back from Nancy's shoulder and gazed at the splash of crimson on her palm. Dan pulled off his T-shirt and squatted down beside her, pressing the shirt over the patch of blood on Nancy's blouse. He placed Ursula's hand onto the shirt so she could wipe off the blood.

"I'll keep the pressure on," she assured Dan.

Nancy's eyes fluttered open. "It's not right," she said. "It's not right."

"You're going to be fine," Ursula said.

"An ambulance is on the way," Dan added. A moment later, a siren sounded outside.

A DOCTOR AT THE Vulcan Community Health Centre dressed the right side of Nancy's clavicle where a small calibre bullet had grazed the bone. The other panel members had gathered in the waiting room. The doctor told them she was extremely lucky.

Dan decided to call his parents' phones despite the late hour. He left a voicemail for his mother. His dad answered groggily, but jolted awake at Dan's news.

"Are you sure it's wise to continue your work with the hearings?" his dad asked.

Dan assured him security would be tighter than ever, then asked quietly, "How's Mom doing up in Fort McMurray? She didn't answer my call."

"She may have turned her phone off since she's staying with Peter's aunt and uncle."

"Or," Dan said, "she doesn't want to speak to me."

"Why would you say that?"

"We had a fight."

His father didn't respond immediately. "I'm sure whatever happened between you will blow over, Dan. Everything will be fine. Just be careful."

THE NEXT MORNING, Nancy agreed with the doctor that she'd been extremely lucky, but insisted on continuing as Water Talks chair. She called a staff meeting in her hospital room.

"Anyone who wants to can bow out," Nancy said. "You won't be judged for it."

She apologized for the deterioration of the situation into violence as if she had shot herself instead of being the victim of the attack. Those who did choose to stay would be safer, she assured them. RCMP officers would be joining the APP security detail. Metal detector wands would be used in addition to patting down hearing participants as they entered a meeting space. No panel or staff member accepted Nancy's offer of an out.

"Shit happens in troubled times," Nancy said. "Now let's get back out there and untrouble them."

That afternoon in his motel room, Dan was scanning the briefing documents again when the echo of an Opa Gerard aphorism came to him. Not Dutch this time but borrowed, he said, from a writer named Anaïs Nin. 'Life shrinks or expands in proportion to one's courage.' His life was expanding. It's what he'd always wanted. Wasn't it?

Just then, his phone buzzed with a message from his mother: "Be safe, Daniel." He vacillated for a few minutes about calling her but didn't have the foggiest notion what he would say. Shouldn't she be calling him? She had abruptly ended their terrible phone call by saying she wasn't well. He texted back, "Hope you're feeling better."

24

ON THE MORNING OF their second day in Fort McMurray, Willa tiptoed down the stairs in the quiet house and punched the numbers into the security panel the way Roy had shown her. She held her breath until a computer voice intoned, "System disarmed." She stepped out the back door onto the patio. Her body swayed, intoxicated by the damp smells of green grass and flowers and the tang of chlorinated water wafting over from the hot tub. She marvelled at how all this natural bounty could be fed by desalinated seawater pumped through a secondary pipeline from a town 385 kilometres away. About the same distance between her farm and Calgary. Was she looking at her future? She could hardly believe it.

The lack of wind unnerved her, and she tucked her curls behind her ears by reflex. She sniffed deeply and recognized the aroma of tree oils. The sharp, musky scent of jack pines and balsam firs. The scents of lilac and Alberta wild rose hovered sweet as syrup. She stepped onto the grass, freshly baptized by the sprinkler system. Her feet became instantly soaked. She crouched down and wet her hands. Took several deep breaths and felt lightheaded again.

LILY SERVED BREAKFAST on the deck.

"Sorry, Roy isn't here," Lily said, as she set plates of bacon, eggs, sweet potato hash browns, and whole grain toast in front of Willa and Peter. "He had to go into work for a few hours this morning. He did take these two weeks off, but something urgent came up. The government wants plans for the reclamation of another tar pond."

"So, tar ponds are his specialty?" Willa asked.

Lily nodded. "Uh-huh. He did his environmental engineering PhD on that at the University of Alberta. That's where we met. He figured the oil industry would be dead by 2045." She shook her head, perhaps pitying his contemporaries who'd been foolish enough to do PhDs in petroleum engineering. She turned to Peter. "Uncle Roy and I are wondering what you want to do while you're here. Fort Mac has an amazing museum on the rise and fall of the oil industry. I can teach you how to play tennis." She jumped up from her chair. "And I have a present for you."

Peter looked up from savouring his meal. His eyes sparked to life. "Really?"

His enthusiasm reflected in Lily's over-wide blue eyes. "I'll get it."

Peter shot Willa an excited grin. Lily returned a few minutes later with a large brightly wrapped box that contained a Hendo 6.0 hoverboard.

"It has a remote control," Lily said, wringing her hands. "Five hours of battery life. Easy to control. There's a great skate park downtown where you can try it out."

Peter's mouth hung open as he fingered the skull motif on the top of the board. "Wow, thanks, Aunt Lily."

They spent the rest of the morning at the skateboard park. Peter fell twice before getting the hang of how to operate a toy he'd never dreamed of owning before. Willa noticed he no longer clamped his hands in tight fists. She presumed the pro-north column now boasted a few additional checkmarks. Lily and Willa strolled around the park across the street. The two women had exchanged scant words since the previous day. Willa had thanked Lily for breakfast and offered to help clean up, but Lily had declined with a declaration that Willa and Peter were guests. Now, Willa tried to engage her with questions. How long had she and Roy had been married? How long had they lived in their home? When would the tar ponds be cleaned up? Lily offered short, polite answers: fifteen years, fourteen years, and even Roy didn't know.

Silence settled on Willa and Lily. After a while, Lily spoke up. "He's such a lovely boy." She twisted a scarf in her hands as she walked. "We would be so happy if he chose to stay. Roy can't, that is, it turned out that we're not able to have children of our own."

"Yes, he is a lovely boy," Willa managed. She thought it bad form for Lily to blurt out Roy's culpability for their lack of children.

Lily seemed to regret her faux pas because she said, "Roy is kind and smart and successful, and he would be a great dad."

PETER'S DEMEANOUR AT dinner matched his unclenched hands. He asked an endless string of questions about the town and its offerings, and listened with rapt attention to his uncle's explanations. Willa didn't think the Oil Sands Museum would hold his interest, but she was wrong.

Roy accompanied them to the museum the next day. There, he became a passionate tour guide at the 'before, during, and after' oil sands landscape display. "Oil was the life-blood of

Alberta for over a hundred years. Pipelines crisscrossed North America from coast to coast. But it all came at a huge cost." Peter drank in the narrative.

"The land bore the brunt of this thirst for oil sands crude," Roy explained. "Ground water contamination. Greenhouse gas emissions. High concentrations of heavy metals and arsenic in traditional First Nations food like muskrat, duck, and moose. One study found high levels of mercury in birds' eggs in the Athabasca River basin."

He pointed to a 3D display showing the migration of contaminants in ground water from Fort McMurray to the Mackenzie River.

"Every last penny of the Mine Financial Security Program has been used to reclaim the land here and downstream on the Athabasca. And more will be needed. Project closure costs far outstrip the security collected over the years to cover the environmental liability. In 2018, the Alberta Energy Regulator estimated clean-up costs for the province's oil industry would total fifty-eight billion dollars. The actual amount to date is two hundred and sixty billion dollars. The government has taken companies to court, but the clean-up is a collaborative process. Instead of the government making all the decisions, Premier Hamady appointed a Joint Action Group eight years ago. It includes environmentalists, health workers, business-people, labour, education and religious reps, Indigenous people, and every level of government. They're monitoring everything from health studies to our contaminant solidification process to defend the public interest."

Whether Peter had the capacity to digest all Roy's words, Willa couldn't tell, but it seemed irrelevant, because he hung on every one of them. Willa thought about her father. He'd been her patient teacher. She felt a hundred feet tall when he confided in her about a ranch business conundrum or concern about an animal, as if she were the only one who could understand. She'd done the same for Daniel, hadn't she? She'd been so busy looking after her father ...

After the museum, they drove to one of the reclamation sites for a helicopter tour of the operations area. They climbed in and donned headsets so they could hear Roy's voice-over that continued through the flight. Roy climbed in the front seat beside the pilot. Willa claimed the middle seat in the back from nervousness. Lily and Peter sat on either side of her. Willa clasped her hands tightly together and stared out the front window toward the solid horizon. Her stomach convulsed as the helicopter lifted off and swung off into the sky. Maybe she should have stayed on the ground. She glanced at Peter, who looked awestruck.

Roy's voice came through the headset. "This is the Milton Lake Settling Basin. We are in the process of reclaiming this site using a process of solidification and stabilization of the tailings. We add a mixture of cement and other compounds. Once it hardens, we'll top it with soil and plant trees. A site in Sydney, Nova Scotia called the Sydney Tar Ponds was cleaned up this way forty-five years ago, and the long-term results are positive. We've already reclaimed other smaller sites around here. The museum we went to sits on an old tailings pond. Milton Lake is the biggest my company has tackled so far."

Willa looked down at the enormous expanse of black sludge. "How much concrete compound will it take to harden this lake?" she asked.

"At least 200,000 cubic metres," Roy answered. "That's roughly five times as much concrete as they used to build the

231

CN Tower in Toronto. We're also doing research into the use of nanotechnology and magnets ..."

Roy's voice faded away. Willa's head ached. She grasped the seat restraint, grateful for its secure hold. She tried to breathe deeply, and thought about the Ativan pills in her waist pack, but was loath to let anyone see her extracting them. She glanced at Peter. Instead of a headset, a giant vice grip now clamped his head. Sunlight glinted off the silver handle that turned of its own accord, squeezing his skull. Willa reached over and hauled the vice grip off the boy's head. She clutched it to her chest. Peter's lips formed words, but the wap-wap of the helicopter blades filled her ears. Lily turned from her window view and frowned at Willa in puzzlement. Willa glanced down and saw Peter's headset in her hands. She gave it back to him and looked straight ahead. She focussed on catching her breath. When she felt more or less composed, she turned to find Lily still staring at her. Willa said into her microphone, "I thought his headset was falling off." After they landed on the helicopter pad, Willa asked to be directed to the nearest washroom. There, she placed a pill under her tongue. She stared at her pale reflection. Moments later, the medicine ironed away the lines of alarm between her eyebrows. "Get a grip, Willa," she said.

ON THE THIRD DAY OF Willa and Peter's stay, Lily's younger brother, James, and his wife, Greta, and their three young children joined them for dinner. They welcomed Willa as warmly as they did Peter. Willa remained on high alert, watching for the knockout blow that would keep Peter in their clutches.

Lily served pork roast, scalloped potatoes, and fresh green beans for dinner. Swiss chocolate cake with vanilla ice cream for dessert. Willa was glad to see Peter eating so well. Still, she worried that the way to the boy's heart was through his stomach. She'd scarcely spoken to him, given his aunt and uncle's preoccupation with fulfilling his every spoken and unspoken wish. She didn't dare speak to him about coming back with her for fear of saying something that would just sour him on doing so. She and Cal could only give him an IOU for a brighter future. Roy and Lily's was ready-made.

Willa excused herself immediately after supper. She sat at the open window of the guest bedroom, rubbing her forehead. Her mind reeled — a tiny net grasping at a million crazed butterflies. It would be so calming if she could give over to some Supreme Being the way others did. God, if you're up there … But if harm was perpetrated by people — sometimes by those you trusted most — you had to count on people for good, too. Her faith lay in Peter to make the right choice.

She counted her Ativan. Six left. She read the label. "As required," it said. She picked one of the tiny pills out of the vial and slipped it under her tongue. Soon, a pleasant drowsiness overtook her, and she lay down on the bed.

She awoke to the buzzing of an incoming video-call. Still groggy from the pill, she picked up her phone.

"Hi, Willa," Calvin said. "Sorry, did I wake you?"

"No, no, it's fine," she assured him.

"How are things?

"Fine, I guess."

"Has Peter decided?"

Willa sat up and rubbed her eyes. The pro-south column had check marks, too, damn it. "No, but I'm sure he wants to go back home as much as I do. You know how much he loves working with animals. There's the memory of his parents. Kelli and Logan chose us as guardians. The prairies are the only home he's ever known. Roy and Lily will be sad about him leaving. They adore him. But he can always come back and visit them."

Calvin frowned but said nothing.

"It's right that Peter should live with us, Calvin," Willa said. "I know what Kelli would say. The will all but confirms it."

"I hate to see you get your hopes up."

She ignored the remark. "I'm certainly not happy here. Everything's been planted and trained and preened and pruned to grow a certain way. The colours are garish, and the leaves on the shrubs rustle in a way that sounds so, I don't know, orchestrated. I miss my spindly, bony lodgepole pines. Does that sound crazy? My hands are so twitchy I can hardly stand it."

"Sounds like you need to get back to work."

She heard a soft knock. "I have to go, Cal. Someone's at my door."

When she opened it, Peter's eyes skittered about, and his face was blotchy.

"Come in, lieverd." She went to the window seat and patted the upholstery beside her.

His face exuded nervousness, misery, and excitement in equal measure. "I've made a decision, Aunt Willa. I'll miss the prairies, but I want to live in Fort Mac. Don't you think it's amazing here?"

Willa swallowed hard several times as he spoke. "Yes, Peter," she said, squeezing the words past the lump in her throat. "It's beautiful."

"That's why I wanted you to come. So you would understand if I decided to stay. I know you wanted me to stay with you. I'll come and visit you and Uncle Cal whenever I can."

"I know you will, lieverd." He hugged her and left the room.

Willa immediately video-called Calvin with the news.

"Are you okay?" he asked.

That made Willa cry. "What are we going to do?" she sniffed.

"Go on as we always have, love."

Willa shook her head. "Maybe we should legally block his decision."

For a moment, Calvin said nothing. "That could cause a lot of damage. I think you love him too much for that."

She nodded and looked around the beautifully appointed guest room. Outside, life pulsed. Lush branches swished in the breeze. A bird chirped, perhaps calling its mate home. Willa thought it might be one of the goldfinches or bluebirds she'd seen in the trees around the deck. She took a heaving breath and smelled smoke. Roy had just sat down on the steps of the deck. Pipe smoke curled upward. She stifled her sniffles and closed the window. "Roy and Lily have this amazing life, Cal. They are so successful. Maybe we could ask them for a loan."

"I don't know, Willa. You mean … as if Peter was our collateral?"

Her head still ached. She moved to the bed and lay down with the phone to her ear. "I don't know." She rubbed her forehead again. "They adore Peter. They might consider it a way to retain a connection for him to the land, to the life he had. The Bradford farm was as important to Logan and Kelli as ours is to us. We should do it for them. And it would only be a loan."

"That might be worth swallowing some pride for," Calvin said.

She remembered something her father had said. "You have to be pretty adaptable to survive that long." She would do it for him, too.

PETER INFORMED HIS aunt and uncle of his decision at breakfast the next morning. Willa braced herself for an emotional display. True to form, Lily unleashed an avalanche of joyful tears. She ran around the table and hugged each of them by turn around the neck from behind. "Oh, it's wonderful," she crooned. "Simply wonderful." Then she sat down and dabbed at her eyes with her serviette, sniffing and beaming.

Willa donned a drama mask of quiet calm. When Lily asked when Willa would be able to send up the rest of Peter's belongings, Willa assured her she would do so as soon as possible.

After breakfast, they included Calvin in a video conference with Jeff Oliver. The lawyer recommended Willa and Calvin retain formal guardianship, in keeping with Logan and Kelli's wishes. They could help Lily and Roy and Peter make decisions about his future, he said. A token formality, Willa thought miserably. Roy and Lily said they had no need for a stipend for Peter so that money could be safeguarded for his trust fund.

After they had dispensed with the legalities, Lily insisted on taking Willa and Peter to mass at St. Agatha's Church in downtown Fort McMurray. Willa wanted to beg off the church service, but they would be taking her directly to the airport after, so she couldn't refuse.

As they drove up to the front entrance of St. Agatha's, Willa assumed the architect had intended the church to upstage all the surrounding mansions. A wide stairway led to two sets of enormous solid wood double doors. High on the wall above sat two round red windows with elaborate steel armature. To Willa, they looked like a pair of bloodshot eyes.

A choir sang them inside, and everywhere people smiled beatific greetings. The interior proved as grand as the exterior. Every magnificent architectural feature and each brilliant rainbow that shot from the stained-glass windows seemed an insult to her own grey world. Were these people oblivious to the suffering of their fellow citizens?

A half hour in, Willa noticed Peter fidgeting in his seat, opening and closing the hymn book and tipping back the kneeler with his feet and letting it fall silently back onto its thick padding against the pew in front of them.

After the fourth hymn, the minister said, "Before I begin the sermon, our devoted sister Margaret Saddler, who has served as head of St. Agatha's Women's Council for the last fifteen years, asked me to update you on her condition. She came through her surgery and radiation well, and has been declared cancer-free."

Willa wondered if the mention of cancer would trigger Peter, but he didn't seem to be listening.

"Clearly," the priest continued, "God has looked favourably on our devout sister and heard the many prayers of the members of this congregation. Mrs. Saddler wanted me to extend her gratitude for your devotion."

Willa bolted to her feet. Prayers as currency. A simple, ridiculous equation. A speech formed in her head: *Your fellow Albertans in the south are worn out. If God has the power to save us, why doesn't he do something? We could use a little rain if he's not too busy.*

The minister looked at this standing, silent stranger and smiled. After a moment, he droned on. Willa scanned the startled faces around her. She sidled awkwardly past the knees in her row. As she stepped into the aisle and looked up, numerous eyes locked onto her. She strode, self-conscious, down the long centre aisle and burst out the main doors.

Her knuckles blanched from gripping the railing at the top of the wide steps. The sky, without its umber mask of wind-blown dust, sparkled like a polished sapphire. She stood eye level with the leafy canopy. Branches waved gracefully up and down the street. These trees were some of Alberta's luckier citizens. They had been saved from the onslaught of fire and insects and desiccation by an armament of piped water.

One of the church doors swung open with a creak. "You all right?" Roy Many Horses said.

Willa nodded. "Sorry," she said lamely. He stood beside her, looking out over the trees.

"I appreciate your hospitality, Roy. I'm sure it wasn't easy for you and Lily to have me tag along, but I can't wait to get home. Does that seem crazy to you? That I can't wait to get back to the dustbowl?"

"Not at all. I come from the Tsuut'ina Reserve near Calgary."

Willa ceased throttling the railing, and turned to rest against it. She looked at him with new eyes. "Oh, I didn't know. I thought you were from around here."

Roy shook his head and smiled. "My people originate from the Dene Tha' First Nation, so you're almost right. They migrated south during the 1800s."

"Do you miss home?"

He nodded. "My dad is the chief of the Tsuut'ina Nation. He wants me to come back. He's ready to retire and wants me to run to replace him. Part of me wants to go. Some people there don't think I'm loyal enough. But I still consider Treaty 7 land home."

"You're doing good work to restore this area."

"I was telling Pete about the water warriors among our people — the ones who worked hard to save it — and he said your son is one, too."

Willa thought about that. "I suppose you could call him that."

Roy tucked his hands in his pockets. "I hope he can make a difference. For my people, that good work paid off, but it took blockades and years of legal action. First Nations on the Athabasca told the world about our polluted traditional lands and rivers. I employ a lot of those people now. They helped put an end to Big Oil. Wasn't enough to stop the effects of climate change, though." He took his hands out of his pockets and took hold of the railing. "My company is my way of honouring my heritage. My life's blood, my breath is to fight for the land. My dad says concrete factories aren't great for the environment either. I don't blame him. It's complicated. And he has his own problems."

"Your people are suffering too."

Roy nodded.

Willa sighed and relished the clean, moist air. "The federal government has its treaty obligations, right? Could they relocate your people?"

"Do you want to move?"

Willa shook her head. She was saying all the wrong things.

"Even if we did want to move," Roy said, "I doubt relocating all First Nations from the Prairies would be very popular in the rest of Canada. We just have to hope the drought ends. And that the climate improves and stabilizes. Isn't that what you're hoping for?"

The breeze pulled at Willa's hair. She tucked her curls behind her ears. "I thought you were going to say 'praying.'"

"Hoping; praying. Maybe they're the same thing."

Willa tilted her head toward the great wooden doors on the church, remembering why she'd stormed out. "I'll bet most of these congregants wouldn't say so. There are a lot of people who believe in god, the cosmic repairman. Pay him enough prayers and he'll fix anything. If that's true, why didn't he save Logan? Or Kelli? She had lots of people praying for her." Willa couldn't seem to stop blurting out her words.

Roy stared up at the sky. "I suppose people want to do something when they feel powerless. I mostly come here for Lily. Some of my people are Catholic or Anglican, but I prefer the traditional ways. Sage and sweet grass smudging. The teachings of our elders. The purification of the sweat lodge. My pipe. When I pray, the smoke carries my prayers to Creator."

Willa looked down at her feet. "I'm sorry, Roy. You must think I'm awful."

He raised a hand in a faintly dismissive wave. "There are lots of ways to look at the world. Honesty is a good thing. I always appreciated that about Peter's mother. You and Kelli were close, weren't you?"

Willa nodded.

"It can't be easy for you to say goodbye to Pete. Lily can't see it. She's been working hard to make him feel at home."

Pete. Willa pursed her lips and nodded.

"You and Calvin have been good to him."

She saw an opportunity blossom. "Roy, I'm not sure how to ask you this." She paused, madly riffling through her mind for the right words. A delicate phrase that would conserve her pride, yet inspire charity. She took a deep breath and gave her tongue full rein. "You and Lily seem to live so comfortably, which is amazing to me because I don't know anyone else like that. Would you consider giving Calvin and me a loan to try and keep our farm going? I realize you hardly know us, but I thought you might do it for Peter. To make sure there's always a connection there. To his other life. I know it's shameless but ..."

She watched him carefully as she spoke, but if he did consider her shameless, he didn't show it. When her words trailed off, Roy pulled out his phone. "We weren't sure if we should offer. How much do you need?"

We. He and Lily had talked about it. "It's just a loan, of course. I don't want it to seem as though you're paying us for Peter. It's just that we're really quite desperate."

"We guessed as much but it's Peter's choice to stay or not. It's not transactional."

"Is six thousand dollars too much?"

"We can do that."

She gave him her email address. As if on cue, the church bells began to chime, and St. Agatha's congregants surged out onto the landing and down the stairs. One of her father's expressions sprang to mind: *Zoals het klokje thuis belt, belt het nergens.* No clock chimes the way it chimes at home.

Lily and Peter emerged.

"Are you all right, Willa?" Lily asked, her face taut with concern. "I knew you looked pale on the helicopter ride. Are you sick?"

Willa shook her head. "Thanks, Lily, I'm fine." She caught Roy's gentle smile. Peter would visit. She and Calvin were emotionally connected to him, and legally too. And with Roy's — and Lily's — loan, they'd have some room to breathe.

25

"MY GRANDMOTHER HAULED my mother to church every Sunday," Ursula said. "Or at least that's the way Mom described the experience."

She and Dan again shared a seat on the Water Talks bus, this time en route to Lomond.

"I hardly knew my grandmother," Dan said thoughtfully. "She left the ranch with my Aunt Sophie when my aunt was young. My Opa Gerard raised my mom. I visited my grandmother once in Calgary when I was ten. Anyway, my Aunt Sophie told me when they still lived on the ranch, she went to church with my grandmother every Sunday. She said my mother was wilful enough that she got to stay home most of the time as long as she worked hard on some ranch chore. 'Idle hands are the devil's workshop,' my grandmother used to say, apparently."

Ursula laughed. "My mother's hands had to be busy holding a missal. What about your granddad – your Opa? Was he religious?"

Dan's turn to laugh. "Not a chance. He found religion in the steamy lowing of his cattle on a cold fall morning. The stars in the firmament. The view of the snow-capped Rockies, when they were still snow-capped." He did a quick search on his phone and read:

Such songs have power to quiet,
The restless pulse of care,
And come like the benediction
That follows after prayer.

Ursula looked at him questioningly.

"Henry Wadsworth Longfellow. His favourite among many."

"Your Opa was a literature buff?"

"Oh yeah. We ... my parents still have some of his old books. He had thousands on his tablet. I don't think he ever had time to read even a quarter of the books he collected. Loved classical music too. Total renaissance man."

"Your eyes light up when you talk about him. You were close, huh?"

"He was my best friend." Dan's throat thickened. "My parents were always so busy, and I understood that, but Opa Gerard was there for me."

"Sounds like he was lucky to have you, too."

Dan shifted in his seat. "I guess so." They fell into silence. Talking about family made his heart ache to resolve the rift with his mother, even though he didn't know how. "Excuse me a sec," he said. He pulled out his phone and texted his parents. "Hi Mom and Dad, Heading into Lomond for our next hearing. Security's tight so don't worry. Love you."

When he entered his motel room a half hour later, he took out Percy's 'Phil Anthrop' phone and sent a message to Percy. "Hey, Perc. In Lomond. Nothing to report. Will keep my ear to the ground." Percy called him immediately. "If you're near anyone, don't speak. No texts, goddammit. Too easy to trace.

Anyway, keep at it. And suck up to Ursula. She may let something slip." Dan clicked out of the call. Subtle as a freight train, he thought.

His parents had responded. "Thanks, keep us posted," his father said.

His mother wrote: "We should talk."

THE HEARING IN LOMOND that night passed without incident. Once again, the reporters tagging along with the Water Talks swamped Dan with questions. He had settled into his spokesperson role, finding his own comfort zone by speaking from the heart.

"Expansion of the desalination plant will guarantee sufficient water for most of the personal, agricultural, and industrial needs of Southern Alberta."

"Crystel wishes it could place a pumping station in every community, but since that's not possible, the corporation will ensure no one is geographically disadvantaged."

"Water is provided at cost as part of the National Water Program."

"The Crown corporation is keen to get input on where to lay pipe, and on what measures will help Southern Albertans thrive."

The lines Ursula wrote for him came naturally now. He simply imagined his parents as the ones needing reassurance and the rest came easily. As he got into bed at the motel in Lomond, he checked his phone and found another message from his mother. She said she was heading back home, and that Peter had decided to stay in Fort McMurray. Was that just information or a passive-aggressive reference to his own decision not to return home? She didn't elaborate, and he didn't even want to ask. He wondered how they'd ever thaw the wall of ice between them.

NANCY BEGAN THE MEETING in Brooks, Alberta with a joke. "At least one of our panel members feels comfortable here." She opened her hand gracefully in Dan's direction. "Dan Brookes, everyone." Scattered laughter filled the room, and someone shouted, "Welcome home, Dan," which drew more laughter. The questions now echoed those in other towns and villages, and all the panel members relaxed into a routine.

Later that evening, Ursula knocked on his motel door. "Want to come for a walk?"

"Sure, let me throw on my runners and jacket." They hadn't gone more than twenty steps beyond the building when an RCMP officer got out of an unmarked car.

"Sorry, but we don't want you leaving motel property. We'd like to keep an eye on you. One shooting is one too many."

They nodded, and the officer settled back into his vehicle.

They circled the small inner courtyard. As often happened in the evening, the wind had died down to a light breeze. They both pulled off their dust masks. After a few rounds of the courtyard, they stopped by a rusty swing set in the centre.

"Think it'll hold us?" Dan asked with a grin.

Ursula folded her arms and looked the old swing structure up and down. "As long as we don't try to swing around the top bar, I think we'll be okay."

They sat down gingerly and laughed when both swings held. Ursula reached over, holding a vending machine bag of peanuts. Dan opened his hand, palm up, and she shook a few peanuts out of the bag. They swung back and forth, pushing off lightly with their toes. The sky glowed raspberry, tapering to cherry red along its western reaches. The air evoked quiet ease, as if the strong smell of smoke came from a nearby backyard fire pit, and not from raging forest fires.

Dan pointed to Ursula's mask. "Have you had Valley Fever?"

"Mild asthma. The mask is preventative, really. You?"

"Preventative. My Aunt Sophie contracted Valley Fever years ago. She lives in Victoria now, far from the dustbowl. In her case, the infection spread to her brain, but antifungals helped her body overcome it. My mom and I both wear one." He thought of her text, ominous in its simplicity: "We should talk." Ominous or not, talking was the only way to resolve anything. He planned to get home the first chance he got, but it wouldn't be soon. The hearings would first take them southeast to Medicine Hat, not west toward home. They wouldn't make it to Fort Macleod for another two weeks.

"I guess no days off for a while," he said.

Ursula looked unperturbed. "I suppose that means we'll be done faster. It'll be good to get home and see my family. Tell me more about your grandfather."

Dan chewed thoughtfully on a couple of peanuts. "Well, he didn't have it easy. As I said, my grandmother left him with my mother around 2020, the start of the 'deluge decade.' My mother refused to leave and still does, even now that there's hardly a drop of water to be had above or below ground, and there's no money to fill the cistern."

"She got her determination from him?"

"In a way. But he was a pragmatist. She won't admit that the farm is finished; she wants to keep it all going for the sake of his memory. She always wanted me to take over. Not surprising, of course, but Opa said I should move on. He still taught me a lot about living off the land, though. Like how to shoot. I never took to it, though. Biggest thing I ever shot was a rabbit, and it broke my heart. He respected that. He stood down a cougar once on one of our campouts. Cocked his rifle, but waited to see if the thing would leave before he had to shoot it. It slinked away."

"Sounds like a good role model."

Dan nodded. "I'm lucky I got to spend so much time with him. After he was diagnosed with Parkinson's, he kept working as long as he could. My mother fretted over him endlessly. She worshipped the ground he walked on. I guess I did, too, to a degree." Dan looked at Ursula. *What would you think of me if I told you I killed my own grandfather?* He rubbed the peanut salt from his hands. "He encouraged me to leave, and I did. Things have worked out pretty well so far."

Ursula smiled at him sidelong. He couldn't interpret her expression in the waning light. Did she think him arrogant?

"Thanks for the walk, short as it was," she said, standing up from her swing and holding out her hand. "Between the bus, motels, and hearings, I'm developing some serious cabin fever."

He let her pull him to his feet, then she let go and tucked her hands behind her back as they walked toward the motel door under a bruised purple sky.

26

PETER PULLED WILLA ASIDE at the airport and whispered earnestly, "I don't want to move here just for the house and the vr headset, you know."

"I know that, *lieverd*."

"I mean, I like Aunt Lily and Uncle Roy. Maybe I can go into business or environmental engineering or something."

Willa saw Roy's fingerprints all over his dreams. What could she and Calvin give him? Scorched earth. Looming bankruptcy. Love subsumed by hardship.

"I'm sure I'll meet some people I like. Edmonton isn't far. It has a great university. I can come and visit you and Uncle Calvin sometimes. Christmas, maybe."

"You won't have any problem making friends. Of course you can visit."

"Maybe I'll start back into hockey. I did miss it for a while. Having the arena and the school nearby is great, too. Aunt Lily said she's going to buy me a bike next week. I'll even be able to bike to class."

What a sales pitch it had been.

"There are lots of advantages to moving here," she said as firmly as she could. "I'm sold. It's beautiful. I can even breathe easier. We will miss you terribly, but we understand why you made the choice you did." She sighed and glanced over at Roy and Lily standing a short distance away. Lily tried to look casual, half-faced away, but Willa saw her take regular glances over her shoulder. "I do miss home, though. Uncle Calvin, of course. I'm looking forward to the sound of all those kids bleating and *trychlen* tinkling."

Peter didn't react. And why would he? He wasn't coming home, and that was that. How could he possibly miss the goats when dust and dead trees and that relentless strafing wind lurked just outside the barn?

On the flight back to Calgary, Willa couldn't stop her hands from fidgeting. Peter's face swam in her mind. He'd looked so sad. And something else. Guilty. As if it were a sin to want a better life for himself. She flipped through the inflight magazine without reading a single word or registering a single picture. Several times she took the vial of Ativan out of her pouch, then put it back without opening it. *How many do I have to take before I get better? Or addicted?*

South of Red Deer, the familiar checkerboard of parched earth crept into view. Willa's heart swelled. How strange, she thought, to feel love and pride for a dying world. But this wasn't its first time on the brink. Perhaps Alberta would rise again as it had done so often before. At the Calgary airport, she climbed onto a southbound bus and leaned her head against the window, enjoying the vibration of wheels on pitted pavement against her temple. The wind had picked up and dust clouds swirled around the bus as it sped down Deerfoot Trail. Roy was right, she thought. It's no Eden, but it's home.

She took out her phone. Roy had e-transferred ten thousand dollars, four thousand more than she'd asked for. Willa smiled as she accepted. His security prompt read, "The boy we love."

WILLA STEPPED OFF THE BUS in Fort Macleod and looked around for Calvin. She circled the building twice, then sat down to wait for him on a bench inside. The wind whistled loudly through the frame around the sliding doors, so she heard only snippets of the music piped in through the speakers. As she tried to discern the song, she realized someone had joined her on the bench. Assuming that Calvin had decided to sneak up on her, she turned to smile and found herself gazing into the eyes of her father. His face lit up in a broad grin.

"Papa?" she said slowly.

His hair hung past his ears, the way it looked when he'd been too busy for the monthly haircut she gave him. He stroked down the front of his shirt—again the one with green and cream stripes.

"Willa, I'm so sorry." Calvin grabbed her hand, and Willa cried out and drew it back as if she'd touched fire.

"Calvin, you scared the life out of me."

He sat down on the bench beside her. "Sorry, love. Are you okay?"

She looked around, blinking rapidly. "Yes, yes. I must have dozed off."

He folded his arms around her and pulled her close.

"You'd think I'd been away a year," Willa spluttered. She should have welcomed the embrace, but it emblemized the chaos of the times they lived in. Calvin hadn't performed a cowboy impression in weeks and had always eschewed public displays of affection.

"Feels like it," he said. He stood and handed Willa her dust mask. He picked up her suitcase. "Ready?"

"How's home?" Willa called out through the mask and over the wind as they walked to the truck.

"Quentin helped a lot. He replaced the dry-rotted boards in the buck barn and built a new hay rack for Duke. He reminds me of Peter and Dan — damn handy and doesn't mind getting his hands dirty. Found a buyer for Duke, by the way."

Willa took a deep breath and held her hands out in front of her, turning them over and back. "Can't wait to get back to work. My hands have softened up a bit over the last few days, but they come bearing cash. Roy loaned us ten thousand dollars."

Calvin held his fist out for a bump, and she obliged him.

"How's Dolly?" Willa asked. "Has her mastitis cleared up?"

"It has. Must feel dry here compared to up there?"

"Peter said compared to here, you can practically drown in Fort McMurray just by breathing." Willa laughed as she wiped the tears that seared her eyes.

THAT NIGHT, as she brushed her hair, Willa considered her reflection in the bathroom mirror. Was it possible to perceive your own madness? Her eyes looked calm, stoic even, above her thin cheeks. Lily was nervous, emotional, a near-manic hand-wringer, but everyone considered her sane.

"Don't kid yourself, Calvin. The north has its own problems," she called to him in the bedroom. "The oil sands sites are still a mess and it'll cost a king's ransom to finish the clean-up." When he didn't answer, she threw the brush in the drawer, flicked off the light and walked across the hall to the bedroom. She leaned her shoulder against the door frame. Calvin sat on the edge of the bed, methodically removing his socks.

"Well," he said, "some people's environmental problems are another's opportunities. It's a boon for Roy Many Horses." He folded one sock on top of the other and carried them to the laundry basket in the corner of the room.

Willa studied him: his relaxed stride, lean legs topped by bright red boxers, his white T-shirt a sharp contrast to his neck and arms. When the sun seeped through the dust, it burnished his skin to nutmeg. She watched him remove his shirt. At fifty-seven, he was still in good shape, his back muscles strong from heaving hay and goats and five-gallon buckets of milk.

Willa slowly walked over to him. He sensed her presence and turned.

"Well, hey there," he said, raising one eyebrow.

She smiled and reached her hands to his chest, feeling small impulses like electricity under her fingers as she touched him. The skin that stayed hidden from sun and wind under his clothes was white as goat's milk.

Willa stroked her hands up until they were clasped around the back of his neck. She brushed her mouth against his. His lips felt rough, and she darted her tongue out to moisten them before kissing him again. When she pulled away, she stroked his freshly shaven cheek. She rested her head on his chest with her eyes closed. Heard him sigh out a deep inhale. A shiver unfurled through the length of his body.

"I really missed you, Calvin. I thought I wouldn't." She opened her eyes and looked up at him. "I'm sorry, but it's true. We're so different. I worry; you don't. I mourn the past; you don't. I feel so off sometimes I can't tell up from down; you make jokes no matter how bad things get."

He eased his arm around her and led her to the bed. She lay down and reached for him to join her. He caressed her for a long time through her faded night shirt. But his touch didn't diminish the heaviness in her limbs, as if her bones were made of stone. After a while they undressed and lay facing each other, fingertips grazing the tiny hollows above collarbones and the soft flesh between hip bones. When their bodies melded, each moved as though the other might break. Each one too fragile to shore up the other.

ONE MORNING, two weeks after her return from Fort McMurray, Willa stood in front of the bathroom mirror, mentally cataloguing her hallucinations as she brushed her teeth. The visions of her father hadn't returned, but several times a day, for a few minutes at least, she saw colours as if she were viewing the world through the various bands of a rainbow. The rattlesnake she'd seen in the barn a few days earlier had thankfully proved an illusion. She reasoned that if she could keep thinking rationally about her visions, they wouldn't feel so frightening. She just had to choose: real or imagined? If the image startled her enough, she could take one of her few remaining Ativan pills. She could always ask Dr. Clyde for more.

She heard Calvin shout her name over the howling wind. She dropped her toothbrush in the sink and ran to the side door in her bathrobe. Her heart jolted when she saw him running through the yard. Calvin didn't run any more than he ever shouted.

He burst through the door and grabbed her shoulders. "Four yearlings are dead."

"Why? What's wrong?" Her heart jackhammered her ribs.

"I don't know." He paced in the small entranceway, frantic. "I'll call the vet. And I'll bring one of the dead goats in for an autopsy. Goddammit, our herd is — was — disease-free. I've put the dead animals in the toolshed for now."

"The milk will have to be tested," Willa said. "We can't put this morning's milk in the tank. Maybe the whole tank is already contaminated. We'll have to test that, too."

She put Saskia in the house. The dog would have to stay inside until they knew what ailed the goats. She got dressed and went out to the toolshed. The rank smell of death whooshed out when she heaved the door open. She crouched beside one of the dead yearlings and stroked its neck. Touched its soft, still nose.

Calvin put a hand on her shoulder, and she looked up at him, his face taut with worry. "We'll find out what's wrong," he said. "We'll fix this. I promise."

OVER THE NEXT TWO DAYS, five more goats died — three does and two yearlings. Dr. Evans, the veterinarian from Fort Macleod, stopped in and took blood samples from the healthy goats. Lab tests deemed the milk safe to drink, but until the vet determined what was killing the goats, it could not be sold. For the time being, Willa pasteurized the does' milk for themselves. She gave as much as she could to Alain Dupre when he came to deliver the water and to Calvin's sister, Susan. They needed no convincing that it was safe to drink. She couldn't bear to waste it. The pasteurizing machine, which normally only processed just enough milk for her and Cal and the unweaned kids, hummed and heated and vibrated nearly twenty-four seven. The freezer was filling fast.

A few days later, Dr. Evans phoned about the autopsy and test results.

"No disease," he said. "No abnormalities in the organs whatsoever. It's a complete mystery."

"So, what do we do now, Zach?" Calvin asked.

"Well, if you have any more dead animals, I want to have a look at those, too. One thing though ..."

He had no answers. Willa toyed with the idea of running away from the conversation so she could take an Ativan.

"The bill so far is four hundred and fifty dollars." Zach cast his eyes down. "I'm in some financial trouble myself, so I'll have to ask you to pay sooner rather than later. Damn. I hate to say that to you, Cal. Your dad's business was thriving when I took it over. I've done my best, but maybe you want to find another vet."

Calvin and Willa had used most of Roy's loan to reduce their credit card debt and had held back eight hundred dollars for emergencies. "No, no," Calvin said. "We can give you the four fifty. Do you want us to pick up the animals we brought over and bury them here?"

"Don't worry about that. I'll cremate them. We'll keep checking into this together. If you do want to stick with me, I wonder if you could give me a few afternoons as a vet tech? It's down to me and Kyle, and I could use the help."

Calvin looked incredulous. "I haven't worked for fifteen years. You think I'd be any use to you?"

"I need a pair of experienced hands; how or when they got to be that way doesn't matter so much. One afternoon a week will help me and take care of your costs."

Calvin nodded. "Okay, it's a deal. I can come over Thursday."

"Good. Keep me posted."

Willa squeezed Calvin's hand. As she walked to the house to make dinner, she wondered how much more bad news she could take before she cracked completely. She wondered what that would feel like. Look like. On her way into the house, she retrieved a pill from the vial in her pouch and slipped it under her tongue.

27

IN MID-JULY, the Northern Water Army issued another threat. They would send secret operatives into the south to scuttle the Water Talks. Landrew countered that Crystel would not be intimidated, and the public hearings would continue. The RCMP confiscated several knives from people attending the hearings in Suffield and Medicine Hat. They found a small pistol on a teenage boy in the town of Bow Island. None were charged as police investigated and concluded they were motivated only by self-defence. As the talks progressed, fatigue and raw nerves plagued panel members and staff like a virus.

At the morning meeting before the trip to Foremost, Nancy told the hearings staff she'd just been informed of another terror attack. "A van driven by a lone radical rammed through a security checkpoint at the no-go zone around the pipeline near Innisfail," she said. "When police fire didn't stop the driver, armed drones blew the vehicle up before it could get close to the construction site. I know these incidents ratchet up the tension around the hearings, but we have to stick to our game plan."

Regulatory envoy Albert Travis said, "These people are nuts. Suicide bombers are the Middle East's stock in trade. Not Alberta's. What happened to being reasonable Canadians? Fuck, we used to be known for apologizing. Now everyone thinks we're a bunch of fucking terrorists."

Nancy didn't correct his language.

"It's water, Albert," Ursula said. "It doesn't take a rocket scientist to figure out how important this is to people."

"Are you calling me stupid," Albert fired back.

"No, of course not. I just think at this point none of us should be surprised about what's at stake."

Albert glared at her.

"That's enough, you two," Nancy said. "We have a few weeks left, and I hope you can all keep it together while we finish what we started."

Dan had noticed the polish and diplomacy fading from Nancy's words. She grew more direct with each passing day.

"Our hearings are a microcosm of a province on edge," she continued. "It's our responsibility to appear calm and orderly." Dan nodded his agreement, feeling self-conscious when no one else moved.

On the drive to Foremost, Ursula picked up a news story about a skirmish outside Crystel's new Calgary water plant. "A group from Tent Town clashed with a busload of supporters of Godwater," she said to Dan sitting across the aisle.

Seated in front of her, Albert swung around. "What the hell is Godwater?"

Ursula scanned her computer screen. "It's a new group from British Columbia that believes pipelines undermine god's will for the climate. They believe Albertans should take his punishment on the chin. All demonstrators have been taken into custody to investigate potential ties to the NWA."

"Religious crackpots," Albert mumbled. "How the hell are a few hearings supposed to turn the tide of extremism anyway? Especially when it's just an empty PR exercise. A bunch of namby-pamby talking points aren't going to save anyone."

Ursula's eyes blazed. "Why are you still here, Albert, if you think we're all so irrelevant? And do you have a problem with my work?"

"No, not at all," he said. "I think you've really blossomed in your job."

"Blossomed?" Ursula spat back at him. "You question my professional integrity and then pull that sexist crap?"

Dan watched their exchange in silence. Albert had chosen the word 'blossomed' to push Ursula's buttons, but Dan had noticed a change in her, too. The same kind of change he perceived in himself. He supposed having to deal with angry citizens and incisive journalists day after day either killed you or made you stronger. When Albert turned and slouched down in his seat, Dan grinned and gave Ursula a thumbs-up.

A few minutes later, they pulled up to their stop in Foremost. Ursula laughed when she spotted the enormous wooden shoe that sat atop a pole outside the motel. "We fit you perfectly" was painted on the side. "This is what I love about rural Alberta," Ursula said. She hopped off the bus and stood admiring the sign. "Character; lots and lots of character."

"Take it from an expert," Dan said. "Dutch people are the biggest characters of all. My grandfather wore wooden shoes in the fields and in the barns all his life. He said he liked to wear them because they kept the woodpeckers off his head."

Ursula grinned at him.

The proprietor of the Wooden Shoe Motor Lodge had bushy white hair and eyebrows and gleaming teeth. He reminded Dan of a *kabouter*, the Dutch version of a gnome. "Aha," the small man said when they entered the office below the shoe, "You're my reservation from Crystel, heh? First reservation I've had in six years. Most people just drop in."

Dan chuckled. The word "drop" sounded more like 'drope' with a heavily rolled *r*. The way Opa Gerard would have said it when he jokingly affected a Dutch accent.

"Right you are," Nancy replied. "We'll be here for two nights."

"Henk Zeldenthuis, proprietor." The man reached out to shake hands with each of the panel members by turn. Henk beamed when Dan shook his hand and said, "*Leuk je te ontmoeten.*" Nice to meet you. Henk turned to his computer screen to assign rooms.

"Love the shoe," Ursula said.

"You can't miss us," the *kabouter* said. "I set aside rooms for the media people in the main lodge, but there are cabins in behind for those who want more space and a microwave. We've got running water from a gravity tank system. Be frugal, because it's metered, and you'll pay for what you use. It's not potable, of course. You can buy drinking water in our dining room."

Nancy, Albert, the support staff, and the bus driver opted for cabins. Ursula said she preferred a room in the lodge to be near the media reps. Dan chose likewise.

"My wife and I will have dinner ready at five if you'd like to join us in our dining room. There's Gordon's on the other side of town, but his greasy spoon can't hold a candle to Rietje's Dutch cooking."

"Sounds good to me," Dan said. "I haven't had an old-fashioned Dutch meal in ages."

"I'm in," Ursula said.

Dan's room was austere except for a large faded photograph of a windmill on the wall above the bed. He pulled a clean T-shirt out of his suitcase and washed up in the tiny bathroom. He used it sparingly, but even so, he relished the rare luxury of tap water, potable or not.

While waiting for dinner, he lay on the bed to catch up on the news. A video clip showed the Godwater clash outside the Crystel pumping station under construction in Calgary. The reporter said twenty-five people were taken into custody after Canadian Army reserve personnel stepped in. The bedlam made him think of Percy and he punched in his number, even though he had nothing to add to their last conversation.

"Sorry, Percy, nothing to report. Just wanted to let you know we've arrived in Foremost."

"How you holding up?" Percy asked.

"Fine."

"How are you and Ursula getting along?"

"We've become good friends, actually." He was surprised how defensive he sounded.

"Maybe there's something more brewing? You two playing hide the salami?"

Dan felt an urge to wash again.

"Real classy, man," Dan said. "We hang out. They don't give us a lot of freedom, though. They keep a tight security perimeter around us all the time. Can't even go for a decent walk."

DAN MET URSULA at the door of the dining room in the lodge just before five pm. They were greeted by Henk Zeldenthuis, and a savoury aroma Dan associated with his mother's favourite dish: nasi goreng.

Delft blue figurines — from tiny thimbles to wine carafes — sat on a high, narrow shelf that circled the walls. An ornate, wooden clock struck the hour. Henk invited them to sit down where they pleased. He bustled about the room flicking switches under the blue caps of small wall sconces, but it remained dusky despite his efforts. A large rectangular tapestry of Rembrandt's dark-hued The Night Watch added to the museum-like atmosphere.

"What lovely porcelain decorations," Ursula said. "Delft, right?"

"Correct," Henk said. "My wife collected them on her trips back to the Netherlands. As you can see, she used to take a lot of trips when we could still afford the airfare." His high-pitched laughter rang out like wind chimes, and Ursula and Dan joined in.

"Dinner smells great," Dan said. "Like home. Can't understand why the reporters went to Gordon's."

"You're a real *kaaskop* then," Henk said, with his unwavering smile.

Dan laughed and turned to Ursula to translate. "Cheese-head," he said. Then, when she still looked puzzled, "He means Dutch. We eat a lot of cheese." To Henk, he said, "On my mother's side. My great-grandparents came to Alberta from the Netherlands in 1968."

"I came over with my wife in 2013 to work for Shell in the Calgary office," Henk said, putting placemats in front of them. "When they shut down, we went through rough times, but family back home lent me money to buy this place. We barely get by, but we get by. We're grateful for the hearings. Brings us some money. Plus, information is power."

"Agreed," Dan replied.

"What would you like to drink? We have beer, water, juice…"

Before he could finish the list, a woman burst into the dining room and pointed an accusing finger at Dan and Ursula. "You'll be the death of us."

"Now, now, Rietje," Henk said, his voice soft and soothing. "Let's not put all that on our guests."

"Why not?" the woman persisted. "Crystel is going to bring the terrorists down on our heads. And they'll siphon all the water off to the Americans and won't leave us a drop." She spoke the last word the same way Henk had said it earlier with a rolling r and a long o, except her tone was livid.

An awkward silence followed, broken finally by Ursula who stood and extended her hand to the woman. "Ursula Myers, ma'am," she said. "Pleased to meet you." The woman looked at Ursula's hand as if it held a switchblade. Without another word, she retreated into the kitchen.

"I'm sorry," Henk said. "My wife is worried about everything that's going on. She's quite straightforward with her feelings."

"It's okay, Henk," Dan said. "We know how strongly people feel. We knew it long before terrorists started blowing things up." He looked toward the main door. "Is it better if we leave? We could call and get the bus to take us over to Gordon's if that's easier."

"No, no, please stay," Henk said, putting a hand on Dan's arm. "The food's all cooked. I've seen the news about the Water Talks. I know you're passionate about getting water here to help us all out. I can understand both sides, you see, so I'm, how do you say it, *tussen twee vuren* — between two fires."

Dan burst out laughing. Henk and Ursula looked at him in surprise.

Dan said, "That's what my grandfather used to say when he talked about my mother and grandmother. They never got along."

Henk's smile reappeared. "I've always considered the Dutch language much more colourful than English. Okay, I'll get you two some supper. No menus. Just good cooking." He walked away, then whirled back around with a look of horror on his face. "You're not vegetarians, are you?"

"Not me," Nancy said from the dining room door. She joined Dan and Ursula at their table. Albert and the panel support staff came, too. They sat at another table. Though Nancy tried to draw them into the lively conversation with Henk, they stayed mostly quiet, and left immediately after dinner. Nancy stayed for coffee but begged off a second cup, saying she needed to return to her cabin for what she termed her "coherent chair" sleep.

Dan and Ursula lingered at the table. When Henk came out to refill their coffee cups again, he invited them to visit with him and his wife in their living quarters. Dan and Ursula looked at each other. Neither one of them wanted to incite Rietje Zeldenthuis to further fits of anger. On the other hand, it was too early for bed, and both were night owls.

More Delftware adorned virtually every surface in the Zeldenthuis sitting room. Two more wooden clocks hung on the wall. One had numbers, hands and a long pendulum all made of brass. The other announced itself as a cuckoo clock when the time rolled over eight o'clock. The aroma of chili peppers, coriander, and cumin hung strong and comforting among scents of wood polish and antique upholstery. Henk invited them to take the brown settee along one wall. Reitje sat in the far corner of the room in a well-worn lounge chair, hemming a pair of pants. Dan sat down uneasily beside Ursula on the settee, wondering if Reitje might fly at them again.

"Your delicious food brought back fond memories, Mrs. Zeldenthuis," Dan said. "Thank you for the meal."

"Call me Rietje," she said, without looking up. "Goat meat isn't quite the same as pork, but it isn't bad." She continued to stare at the needle she deftly poked through the fabric and plucked out the other side. "I get a bit overexcited sometimes," she said, her voice gruff.

"These are seriously difficult times," Ursula said.

Henk told Rietje about Dan's Dutch lineage, and she finally looked up from her work.

Dan thought hard. "*Bedankt voor het diner*," he said. "*Heerlijk*."

"Your pronunciation is good," she said to Dan. "We come from Amsterdam." He smiled. *Umsterdum*. "Henk worked in a farm equipment factory back home."

"I worked long hours and commuted an hour and a half to my job each way," Henk explained. "What a life! I used to live up to my name back then." He looked to Dan expectantly, but Dan shook his head and frowned. "*Zeldenthuis* means 'seldom home.'" His charming laugh filled the sitting room. "I've gone from never home to always home. I need to change my name, don't you think?"

"Oh, Henk," Rietje said, with the hint of a smile. "Your silly old joke."

They talked of their family in the Netherlands. Henk's brother was an engineer who had worked on a series of new dikes to counter rising sea levels. The sun, visible through the west-facing picture window, sank into its sea of pink haze. After a while, Rietje brought in Dutch vanilla custard — *fla* — and a plate of goat Gouda cheese slices. As everyone's spoons tinkled along the bottom of their bowls, Rietje's face turned grave again. "You two had best be careful. The radicals up north would rather that plant in Bruderheim didn't send another drop of water south of Red Deer. They start off sounding reasonable. The next thing you know, they're blowing something up."

"The NWA is still an inept, radical fringe," Ursula said matter-of-factly. "I don't think they've won over the moderates up there yet."

The conversation turned back to family, with Henk asking about Dan's. At ten that night, Dan and Ursula made their way upstairs to their lodge rooms. She had stayed unusually quiet through the rest of the visit.

"You okay?" Dan asked.

"When I lived in Edmonton, I dated one of those northern radicals Rietje was talking about," Ursula said. "He wasn't an extremist when we started seeing each other. He began to hang around with people from the Water Conservancy Alliance at the U of A. Talked about the importance of restoring balance to Alberta. Making sure the south had enough water without jeopardizing overall supply and all that. They seemed pretty reasonable, like Rietje said, but then a couple people joined who spread paranoia about the pipeline and rallied the moderates to their position. That's when the tide turned, and they became the NWA. We broke up then. I heard their meetings got more raucous and inflammatory. They began to talk about 'our' water and how irresponsible the south had been to squander their resources."

"Glaciers up and down the eastern flanks disappeared in equal measure," Dan said. "The north didn't protect its headwaters any better than the south did."

"Try telling them that. They launched a 'Welcome to the Province of Northern Alberta' campaign, and talked about splitting from the south to protect northern interests. Once, they created a giant fabric cut-out in the shape of Alberta hung in a metal frame. They lit the southern part on fire, and it burned up slowly to the point marking Red Deer, above which the rest of it had been made fire retardant. Creepy, huh?"

"Do you know what the guy's doing now?" Dan asked.

"No idea. I haven't seen him on the news or anything, so he may not be ultra-extremist now, but he was pretty into it." They stopped outside her door.

Dan said, "People forget — and our friend Albert is a case in point — that we're all in this together."

She punched Dan playfully. "Whether we're city dwellers or a country bumpkin like you with the manners and the sayings and the old-fashioned values, we all have to get along, right?"

Dan grimaced, then he grinned, tipped an imaginary hat and feigned a Texan accent as thick as baked beans, the way his dad always did. "Ma'am, this ain't my first rodeo. I do admit to always keepin' my saddle oiled and my gun greased."

Ursula laughed.

Dan faced her and grasped her hand. "As I said, everything will settle down when the pipeline reaches Calgary and no one's the worse for wear."

Ursula smiled at him. "Ever the utopian, Mr. Brookes. Still, even people who seem perfectly reasonable can turn ferocious." She squeezed his hand. "Goodnight, my friend."

MORNING DAWNED DEEP PINK in the east, as if a cosmic force had simply swung the evening sky around, using the wooden shoe over the motor lodge as the fulcrum. Dan spent the morning answering emails from reporters, and checked in with his Crystel colleague Brad Lyman about his latest aquifer analysis. In the afternoon, the panel members met to discuss their response to the latest reports of unrest. Nancy said they would stay the course on their messaging. Albert Travis thought they should talk a hard line against people who would stop the pipeline. "Let Crystel and the Department of National Defence deal with the radicals," Nancy said. "We need to keep it positive for the folks down here. Whoever's eking out a meagre living is spooked enough without us ramping up the rhetoric."

Her approach worked well at the Foremost meeting that night. The positive response allowed the assembly to break up by 8:30 pm, instead of the usual ten. By 9:30, the panel staff had all said good night to each other.

At ten, Dan sent a text to his mother. "We'll be in Lethbridge for two days. After that we finally get to Fort Macleod. Can you meet me in town or come pick me up?" Texting seemed a calm prelude to a bitter war. He had been formulating a speech he would recite to her about why Opa had done what he had, knowing all the while she wasn't easily convinced of anything once she'd made a choice about it. Would she play the 'you don't love me like you loved him' card again? Maybe that's the question he should be asking her. Who did *she* love more? He was just reading her response — "Yes, I'll pick you up. Just say the word." — when he heard the swoosh of a piece of paper being slipped under his door.

He walked over and picked it up, frowning. Handwritten on a sheet from a Wooden Shoe Motor Lodge pad, the note read: "Can't sleep. Wanna go for a walk? We can breach the perimeter by sneaking out behind Henk's shed. Leave by the dining room door. U." Dan pulled on his runners and light jacket. With the wind down again, he decided to leave his dust mask behind. He stepped out of his room, chuckling to himself as he looked furtively left and right. More spy stuff. That made him go back inside and grab both his phones. Better safe than sorry, he thought.

No light shone under Ursula's door. He tiptoed past the Zeldenthuis's private quarters and left by the back door in the dining room as the note had instructed. He had just snuck past the shed when someone seized him and covered his mouth with a sweet-smelling cloth that, an instant later, turned foul enough to make him gag. He struggled to get free. Then his legs gave out.

28

DAN WOKE IN PITCH BLACK. His head ached. His nose was pressed to a surface that smelled metallic, tinged with natural gas and dust. The surface jostled him, inflicting further insult on his pounding head. When he first came to, he thought he might be in the trunk of a moving car, but then realized his legs lay fully extended. He touched his jeans pockets, but both his phones were gone. Struggling up onto all fours, he fumbled his way around the space. He toppled several times as the vehicle swerved or hit a rut in the road. He found a wall and leaned back against it, clutching his head in his hands. After a while, he heard a moan.

"Who's there?" he called out, alarmed at the echo of his own voice in the hollow space.

"Oh god," a voice said.

"Ursula? Where are you?" He scrabbled around the floor until his hand brushed her shoe.

"Dan?"

"Yeah, it's me." He crawled up to her head and stroked her hair. "You okay? Are you hurt?"

"If you can lift the anvil off my forehead, I'd appreciate it." She groaned.

"Give me your hand." She did and they held on in the darkness. Every now and then, the shadowy outlines of their barren prison became visible in blade-thin flashes of light coming through a horizontal crack at one end of the floor. They both examined the space on hands and knees. Nothing. No latches or door handles. Dan braced himself against the walls with his knees bent so Ursula could perch on them and feel high up on the walls. She found hinges for a door, but no clue as to how it might open.

"I guess it opens from the outside."

"I think so. And we're driving down a highway. The flashes must be junction lights."

"I take it the note I found wasn't from you?" Dan asked.

"I should have known you'd send me a text," Ursula replied. "Just thought you were joking around old school after your cowboy impression."

They leaned themselves against one of the walls. Sick dread hung between them. Several bone-jarring hours later, the bumping and tossing intensified. They grounded themselves, crablike, on the floor. Light no longer flitted in through the crack. The dust thickened. Their throats grew raspy from thirst. After a while, they lay down, exhausted, with no choice but to succumb to the juddering bumps and ruts.

Finally, the bumping stopped. Dan heard footsteps, a click and slide of metal latches and rods, a door rolling open. Two men appeared, then disappeared in a blinding wash of flashlight beams. Dan flinched from the sudden onslaught and shielded his eyes with his forearm.

"Get out," one of the men growled. "And be quick about it."

Ursula clambered to the edge and jumped down from the truck bed. Dan caught his toe on the tailgate and fell hard to the ground. Ursula helped him to his feet. The men grabbed them and pushed them ahead. In the bobbing flashlight beam, Dan made out a decrepit wooden building. In the field nearby, a wind turbine hummed in the steady breeze. The dusty air smelled less of wood smoke than it had in Foremost. They must have driven east. He looked in that direction and saw the first tinges of dawn. They'd been travelling all night. Maybe six hours. What was six hours east of Foremost?

One of the men pushed Dan and Ursula through the door. He made his way across the room and turned on a generator. It hummed loudly. Dan figured they must have wired it to the wind turbine outside. The strongman flicked on two utility cage lights hooked over beams in the ceiling. Dan squinted at the kidnappers. The man who had turned on the generator was burly with a beefy face and long stringy brown hair. Six two or three. Wearing an old Budweiser cap. He pointed a rifle at them. Ruger Mini-14. The same kind of gun Opa and his dad used for hunting. The other man was bald and hatless. Short. No more than five nine. Skin tanned the colour of coffee. He stood with his legs spread and arms crossed. A boss's posture, although they were dressed the same: black t-shirts and pants. Streaks of black and green showed here and there on their faces and necks, where they'd failed at wiping off camouflage paint.

Dan surveyed the room. The low ceiling required the two men to duck under the cross beams. Faded newspaper covered the walls. Where the strips had tattered, rough boards showed through. In the centre of the room stood a wooden table and rickety looking chairs. In the far corner, a porcelain tub sink with a rusty base plate where a tap had been. A hotplate stood on the counter beside the sink. There were two small windows covered with black paper and one other door. Dan doubted it led to a bathroom with floral-scented soap.

"Facilities are out back," Budweiser man said, as if reading Dan's thoughts. "Hope you can piss and shit with a rifle aimed at the outhouse door." He laughed. "Or maybe that will make it easier."

"Who are you, and why the fuck did you bring us here?" Dan said. He rarely dropped the F-bomb but, under the circumstances, it rolled easily off his tongue and helped him muster his bravado. He glanced at Ursula. Her face wore the same inscrutable mask he'd first seen in the Crystel boardroom.

"Pretty boy here swore at us, boss. Should I teach him some manners?"

The bald boss man said calmly, "Not now, Rambo."

Rambo circled one palm over the knuckles of his other hand. "Just say the word, Rigel."

Their tone and manner reminded Dan of the old movies his dad liked to watch, but the fact they came across as caricatures only made his and Ursula's reality more chilling. Dan guessed inexperienced criminals had neither honour nor discipline. He focused on channelling his fear into outrage. "You with the NWA, Rigel?" he asked.

"Shut the fuck up," the bald man shouted.

"Fuck you," Dan snapped. "You'll have the RCMP and the army on your ass if you don't let us go."

"I can assure you it won't be that easy to find you," Rigel barked. "They didn't do a great job of keeping you two out of trouble in the first place, did they? Those guys do security like a broken picket fence."

"So," Dan tried again. "Who the hell are you?"

Rigel made the slightest of motions with his head and Rambo opened the mystery door and shoved Dan and Ursula into the adjacent room. As the strongman slammed the door shut, Ursula lunged for the cage light and flicked it on. She and Dan stood in the centre of the room, surveying their prison cell, hemmed in by the sound of the wind hurling against the outside wall and the loud hum of the generator in the main room. On the floor, two camping mats, each with a pillow and a comforter printed with an Iron Man motif. The child's blankets contrasted ominously with the circumstances. The room had one window, blacked out with paper like the ones in the other room.

An hour later, they heard another vehicle drive up. Two new voices and excited barking. The bedroom door flew open and a woman in army fatigues kicked a crate of water bottles inside. Early twenties, maybe younger. Blond. Untidy wisps escaped from a severe bun at her neck. Bright fuchsia lipstick. She carried a Ruger, too — evidently their weapon of choice.

"For your new home sweet home," she said, her high-pitched voice sounding almost pleasant. "Not much of a view, but you might find a way to keep yourselves occupied in here." She smiled lasciviously.

"Wait, I have to use the bathroom," Ursula said.

"Rigel, what do I do if one of 'em has to piss?" Blondie hollered.

"Take them out, Justina," Rigel said. "That rifle isn't a parasol."

"Out," Justina said. "Both of you."

As they left the bedroom, Dan's heart leapt at the sight of the spitting image of Saskia. He reached for her as if his Great Pyrenees from the farm had been teleported to the old farmhouse. The animal growled low in its throat at his approach. Dan saw gleaming teeth and the intense stare of an animal bred for something quite different than protecting goats. A point reinforced by the Doberman that stood drooling behind Saskia's double.

Justina escorted Dan and Ursula at rifle point to a ram-shackle outhouse. Someone had repaired its walls and roof by nailing on two-by-fours of different lengths so that it looked like a child's first attempt at construction. Ursula took her turn, and scowled as she came out. Dan decided he'd best relieve himself while they were inclined to let him.

"Oh, great," he muttered as he stepped inside. Drifting sand had all but filled the pit. A bench spanned the full width of the space, with a rough hole, sordidly discoloured, cut out of the centre. A roll of toilet paper sat on one side of the bench beside the four-pack it had come out of. A high window allowed in just enough light to be able to see but not enough air to dilute the foul fumes that would soon accumulate from the excretions of six people.

Dan heard Ursula say, "What do you want with us? Maybe we can make a deal."

Silence.

"Hand sani?" Dan said when he came out.

The young woman cackled.

"Charming," Ursula said.

"Move," Justina snarled, keeping her rifle trained on them.

When they re-entered the house, Dan took note of the other new face. A man with a bulbous nose, scraggly grey hair, and beady eyes like a rabid animal sat next to Rigel at the table.

Ursula slowed her steps. "Rigel," she said, "I have a connection with the NWA who might not be very happy you're holding me."

Rigel raised his hand to stop the procession. He looked at Ursula with interest. "Really? And who might that be?"

"His name is Martin Christoph. We dated a while back."

Rigel sat up at the name. "Martin Christoph is a hero to us, Ms. Myers. A legend even."

Ursula said quickly, her voice tight with boldness, "Well, I'm sure he wouldn't approve of my being held here at gunpoint. I assume you'll call him?"

"I'm afraid I must extend my condolences, Ms. Myers," Rigel said, his eyes cold as glacial ice. "Mr. Christoph was good enough to scatter himself around the pipeline construction site for our cause. He planned to escape the van before it detonated, but, sadly, his timing was off."

Ursula's face paled but remained expressionless.

"You know how to pick 'em, girlie," said Rigel's new sidekick with a guttural laugh.

"Shut up, Hick," Rigel said, keeping his eyes on Ursula. "I think Martin would wholeheartedly approve of your being here." At the slight tilt of his head, Justina dug the butt of her rifle into Ursula's back and pushed her into the bedroom.

Like Rigel, Justina slammed the door. Dan held Ursula's shoulders and peered into her face. "You okay? Here, sit down."

Ursula nodded slowly and lowered herself onto a mat. "He blew himself up," she breathed.

Dan marshalled his thoughts. Opa Gerard would say, "Van niets komt niets. Do nothing and you get nothing." Dan grabbed two water bottles from the crate and offered one to Ursula. "We need to hydrate to keep our heads clear," he said. The words sounded strange. Like playacting.

Ursula nodded and took the bottle. "What the hell do they want with us, Dan?"

He paused, listening for movement outside the door. "I think we're the next step," he said, his voice low and solemn. "They want to stop the water flowing south, so they start with inflammatory PR. Website and billboards. Then they stage a short-lived takeover of the desalination plant. They set off a few explosions. Still construction continues. So they ramp it up. Give Crystel and everyone else a very public reason to shut down its north-to-south operations."

Ursula pulled her legs up and hugged them. "Innocent people died in those explosions. There's a good chance they killed the officers who were guarding the motel. The question is, how much are we worth?"

29

BY THE THIRD SUNDAY IN JULY, Willa and Calvin had lost thirteen more goats — six yearlings and seven does, including five from Fred Butterfield's herd of forty. Willa felt ragged from the strain of milking so many does, pasteurizing milk, and worrying about which animal would die next. She had one Ativan left. Her hallucinations hadn't stopped. She endured them as best she could to save the remaining pill for a truly desperate moment. With the farm plagued by deadly disease, she had no time to go to town for a new prescription.

Willa dragged herself out of the milking shed that morning, but hurried into the main barn when she heard Calvin on a video-call with Zach. The vet's face on the small screen burned red with excitement.

"It's the silage," Zach shouted. "It's the goddamn silage. It's contaminated. I'm coming over right now with a load of probiotics. The goats' intestines are overrun with bacteria."

Willa looked at Calvin and felt herself blanch. The freshened does had just feasted on a handful of toxic silage as she drew their milk. Still, she was heartened by the news. "No antibiotics then. Thank god."

"Right," Zach said. "They wouldn't recover any faster and it'd be weeks before you'd be able to sell your milk again."

Willa raced to pull the silage from the feeding troughs.

Zach came by an hour later with the probiotic feed granules and several sacks of starter feed ration with high-quality proteins, vitamins, and trace minerals to mix with it. They spent the afternoon ensuring that each goat ingested a dose of the probiotic/starter mixture. Zach told them, "Three days and they'll be hale and hearty." They called Fred Butterfield with the news. Devastated and apologetic, he said he'd have the pit bunker where he'd fermented the corn inspected and decommissioned if necessary. He refunded half their credit card payment with a promise of a full refund when he could afford it. With the credit headroom, Willa and Calvin bought a small load of clover and alfalfa legume hay, high in protein, vitamins, and minerals, to get the goats back on their feet. Calvin would pick it up from the feed store in Fort Macleod in the morning.

After supper, Willa and Calvin sat side by side on the sofa in the front room to speak to an elated Peter by video-call. "Will we be able to build the herd up again right away?" he asked.

Willa and Calvin glanced at each other. They had no money to replenish the herd, but neither said so. Willa couldn't get past Peter's choice of the word 'we,' and savoured it the way Saskia enjoyed a bone.

"Have you met some young people in your neighbourhood?" she asked.

"Couple. We go to the skateboard park. I'm getting pretty good on the hoverboard."

He didn't look as happy as Willa had expected.

"How are the Bradford trio doing?" Peter said, changing the subject back to the three kids he'd helped Charlotte birth.

"Couldn't be healthier," Calvin replied.

"Sure glad about that. It's strange getting goat's milk from a grocery store and not from the milking shed. Doesn't taste the same, either. And the smell reminds me of Duke. Not much, but I notice it."

"I guess we spoiled you," Calvin said with a laugh.

"How's that new bike Aunt Lily got you?" Willa asked.

"It's good. Nothing like getting pulled by a Duke in the cart though. Is Dolly over her mastitis?"

"Oh, she's fine," Calvin assured him.

Willa could hardly restrain herself from shouting at him, "Come home, lieverd. You don't belong in a town." She imagined him unpacking his suitcase when he got back to his room. He would head to the barn to pitch hay to the yearlings. She focussed her eyes on Peter's face on the phone screen, then something caught her eye. She looked down at her arm and saw her flesh decomposing before her eyes, black and purple and putrid. As soon as she sidled away from Calvin to pull her face from Peter's view, her hands flew to the vial of Ativan in her pocket. They shook as she opened it and slipped the last pill under her tongue. She sat with her eyes closed until her heart slowed to a canter. She sighed deeply, rubbing her hand over the smooth skin on her arm.

Willa heard Peter's voice call out. "Where did Aunt Willa go?"

She slid back beside Calvin. "I'm right here, lieverd." She was shaking. Calvin stared at her and grabbed Willa's hand with his free one. She shook her head slightly and they both turned their attention back to the phone.

Peter looked down. "It's great here, but I miss you guys."

"We miss you too, Pete," Calvin said. "It's been a tough few weeks for us, buddy. We need some rest. We'll talk soon. We love you." He clicked off the phone and set it on the coffee table, then twisted himself sideways to look at Willa head-on. "You okay?"

"I'm good now."

"Willa," he said, his eyes uncharacteristically hard. "I'm really worried about you. What kind of pill did you take just now?" He paused, searching her face.

"Just something Dr. Clyde prescribed for stress."

"We could leave, you know," Calvin said, still studying her face. "Just get what we can for the land and start fresh somewhere else."

"No, Calvin," Willa said, shaking her head. "I can't. Legacies are worth fighting for."

He reached his arm around her shoulder to draw her to him. "My dear Willa," he sighed. She rested her head on his shoulder. A shadow of their embrace loomed on the opposite wall, as a pair of headlights pierced the front window of the farmhouse.

"Who the hell is that?" Calvin asked, turning to look outside. He frowned at Willa. "Alberta Provincial Police."

Willa's heart leapt into a gallop again. She followed Calvin to the side door. A uniformed APP officer stepped onto the side porch.

"Good evening, sir," the officer said when Calvin opened the door. "Can I come in?"

He tipped his police cap at Willa as he stepped inside. "Ma'am." He extended his hand, shaking each of theirs by turn. "Officer Liam Frazier. I'm afraid I've got bad news."

Willa thought her head would explode from the pounding in her ears. "It's Daniel," she said before he could elaborate. "What happened to him? Was there an accident?"

The officer shook his head gravely.

"Thank god. What's wrong, then?"

"I think we should sit down," Calvin said. He led Willa and Officer Frazier into the living room.

"Your son's been kidnapped along with one of his colleagues from Crystel. A young woman by the name of Ursula Myers."

"What? Why?" Willa stuttered.

"The Northern Water Army has claimed responsibility. They're demanding the pipeline construction be shut down."

"Do you have any idea where they might have taken them?" Willa asked. She gripped Calvin's hand to keep hers from shaking. "They're alive, aren't they?"

The officer skirted her second question. "They were taken in the night from a motor lodge in Foremost. Whoever kidnapped them strangled one of the officers controlling the motel perimeter. Apparently, your son and his colleague were lured away by bogus notes we found in their rooms addressed to each other. There was no sign of violence. The kidnappers may have used chloroform or something similar to subdue them."

Calvin and Willa spent the next hour telling Officer Frazier everything they could about their son. They confirmed his address, other vital stats, and the names of friends he'd made mention of. Willa said Daniel had talked about a fellow by the name of Percy Dickenson in the Water Minister's office. That he'd gotten him the job at Crystel. Calvin found Percy's cell number on the contact page for the Water Ministry and gave it to the officer.

"Okay, we'll track him down," Officer Frazier said. "I promise to keep you posted on the investigation."

As soon as the officer left, Calvin called Percy Dickenson's number while Willa put on water for tea. Percy answered on the first ring.

"You don't know us," Calvin said. "Our son is Daniel Brookes. My name is Calvin and my wife's name is …"

"Willa," Percy finished for him. "Yes, yes. Dan and I have been working on and off together for a number of years, and of course he's mentioned you. The CEO of Crystel just called me with the news about Dan. What a fu … terrible turn of events. How are you both holding up?"

Willa found the brusque, no-nonsense tone of his voice calming. "We're so worried," she said, stifling her tears with a quick intake of breath.

"I'll do whatever I can to help the police," Percy promised. "If I hear anything, I'll let you know. I work for the Minister of Water, so I'll be dealing with the Crystel folks on this, too. We'll work as a team to bring them home. Believe me, we'll be calling out the big dogs. We'll find them."

Calvin ended the call and reached his arm around Willa.

"Dan told me you two had a fight," Calvin said, kissing the top of her head. "He didn't tell me what about."

Her ears rang with a sound like rushing water. Calvin's words hung in the air, calm and inviting. But the dam inside her had knit itself tightly together. A barrage of deadfall and boulders holding back a raging torrent. "I'm sorry, Cal. I just can't. Not right now."

They video-called Peter to inform him before he or his family members saw reports of the kidnapping on television or online.

Peter stared at them, utterly stunned. Lily put her arm around him.

"Where?" he asked at last.

"We don't know," Calvin said calmly. "The police are doing all they can to find him. I'm sure he's going to be just fine. We called a good friend of his, too. He's with the provincial government. He said he'd help in whatever way he could."

Peter seemed satisfied by that. "Let me know when you find out anything," he said.

Willa nodded, wishing she could be so easily convinced by Calvin's words.

That night, unable to sleep, Willa snugged her back against Calvin and pulled his arm around her. Despite the warm late July air, her body was beset by a bone-deep chill.

"Wouldn't you feel better if you told me what happened between you and Daniel?" Calvin whispered into her hair.

"I don't want to burden you more than you already are."

"Spill," Calvin said. "You know that's what I'm here for, right?"

Willa took a deep breath but couldn't stop her tears. "It's Papa. He didn't die of Parkinson's. He killed himself with pills, and he got Daniel to help him."

Calvin lay motionless. After a moment, he said, "We were away that day getting the goats."

"Yes," Willa said, wadding up a bit of the duvet cover to wipe her eyes.

"Poor Daniel," Calvin breathed. "I'm so sorry, Willa."

Willa turned over and cried into Calvin's chest. He wrapped his arms tightly around her and held on.

30

THE BLACKED-OUT WINDOW robbed them of a sense of time. They didn't dare disturb the paper cover, and estimated noon by the intense hunger in their bellies. Dan opened the bedroom door. Immediately, Justina jumped up out of a chair just outside and cocked her rifle at his heart.

He raised his hands in surrender. "Hey, take it easy. We just want something to eat."

"You'll get fed when we're damn well ready to feed you," she said, and shut the door. Despite her menacing tone, the door opened again almost immediately, and she handed in several nylon bags filled with bread, peanut butter, power bars, and apples. "This should keep you from starving," she said before shutting the door.

They found a bar of soap in one of the bags. No one offered them water to wash with, so it appeared the precious bottled water was for drinking and cleaning. They washed their hands and made sandwiches — a messy affair without cutlery — then hung the food bags on a protruding nail they found in the wall. With nothing more to do, they sat against opposite walls, quietly contemplating their predicament. After a while, Ursula lay down on her mat. The wind howled through cracks in the eaves but did nothing to dislodge the stifling July air that swamped the room. Every now and then, she swiped at her face.

"Shit," she said. "I think the food's set off the radar of the local ant population."

They moved the mats to the opposite end of the room from the food and tightly sealed all the packaging in the bags.

They both lay down with their backs to each other.

Dan heard a slapping sound.

"Damn bugs," Ursula said. "I guess we should be glad they're not fire ants."

"That's looking at the bright side," Dan said, humourlessly.

She shifted on her mat. When he turned to look at her, she was sitting up.

"Mind holding me for a while?" she asked. She said it the way she had asked him earlier if he wanted a peanut butter sandwich.

"Sure."

She slid onto his mat and lay down with her back to him. When he turned to curl toward her, she drew his arm across her waist and patted it rhythmically. "They don't seem too interested in hurting us," she whispered.

Her tone, half-speculative, half-hopeful, or perhaps the soft tap of her fingers on his, calmed the nerves in Dan's belly.

"No point in harming your collateral."

They passed the afternoon and evening in silent dread. After they were allowed out one more time to visit the outhouse, Dan fell into an uneasy sleep.

THE NEXT MORNING, he woke exhausted. Fear had calcified in his joints so that his body ached with every move. He winced at the sharp pain in his neck when he turned his head to look at Ursula on the other mat. She had moved back to it sometime during the night. She hadn't turned off the light, perhaps to reduce the risk of nightmares. Her brows were pulled together. No doubt she fretted about their captivity in her dreams. He wondered what had woken him, then heard the shuffling of feet and the murmur of voices outside the clapboard door. He tried to set in motion a mental clock to track the passage of hours. Must be around eight in the morning, he thought.

How strange to wake up in terror. He realized how peril-free his life had been up to now. Even when Nancy was shot, the presence of police officers had eased his shock. What had scared him most in his life was helping Opa die. But that held no mortal danger for him. He sighed. Just long-term residual trauma. Stop, he said to himself. Old agonies would only muddle his thinking.

Ursula moaned. A moment later, she sat up and looked around, eyes wide, as if she'd been stung and was looking for the culprit. "What time is it?"

He crawled over to sit on the end of her mat and placed a hand on her shin. "Around eight, I'm guessing. You okay?"

"I dreamed I was at home."

She didn't elaborate, and he didn't ask.

They had only occasional contact with the kidnappers that day. During trips to the outhouse, their captors said nothing. Now and then, they muttered to each other outside the captives' bedroom door, their words inaudible over the hum of the generator. For their part, Dan and Ursula exchanged few words as well. They sat like prey, listening for the sound of an approaching predator. Dan took note of the kidnappers' routine. The smell of cooked food signalled the evening meal. Six o'clock, give or take. He tore a strip of newspaper from the wall and scratched two stripes onto the aged wood beneath. Two days and counting. He turned his attention to the strip of front-page newsprint in his hand. Though yellowed and faded, the type was legible. *Regina Leader-Post.* January 6, 1945. "Enemy resists fiercely," one of the headlines read.

ON THE THIRD EVENING of their captivity, Dan sat down beside Ursula on her mat. He put a finger to his lips, although they were unlikely to be heard over the clatter of pots and now louder voices that filled the main room. One of the captors cooked dinners on the hot plate for the others while Dan and Ursula continued to eat cold food. Of course, the two captives were grateful to be eating at all.

"I was thinking about your question to Rigel," Dan whispered, speaking around a bite of sandwich. He swallowed. "Do you remember Percy Dickenson? Edmonton. Provincial Water Ministry. He said he knew you."

"Percy Dickenson," she whispered back, frowning. "Oh yeah. He came onto me after a pipeline meeting Crystel had with ministry people. Said if I had dinner with him, I could have all the departmental access I wanted."

"Wow." Dan hesitated, knowing he was setting himself up for a fall. "He's an old friend of mind. He got me the job at Crystel. Wanted me to spy on the Crown corp., to get dirt on how they were going to sell water to the States at the expense of Albertans." He cringed at the guarded, suspicious look in her eyes.

"Spy? You agreed to that?"

Dan leaned back against the wall and closed his eyes.

He rubbed his face with both hands. "I'm sorry to say I did. I was desperate for the work. I only ever passed on one email."

When he looked at her again, she had stopped chewing. She balanced her half-eaten sandwich on her knee. "What email was that?"

"I received a long thread that began with a note of congratulations from U.S. businessman Balthazar Frost. He's been investing in water for a long time. Said he admired Crystel's efforts to bring water to Alberta from the coast. Technology winning out over the vagaries of nature, and all that. He said he would be interested in supporting their efforts if it meant bringing water to Montana and beyond." His hands fell to his lap; he shook his head with guilty regret. "Anyway, Percy might be able to help us. After all, he's the right-hand man to the Minister of Water."

Ursula grabbed her sandwich and shifted onto her knees to look at him straight on. All judgement had vanished from her face. "You think they'll let you talk to him?"

He shrugged and stood up, handing her the rest of his sandwich. "Here, hold this. It's worth a try." He knocked on the bedroom door.

"What do you want?" Justina said, as she opened the door and raised her rifle.

"I assume Adam Landrew is making the case for our release. Crystel has a lot at stake here. But I have a friend — Percy Dickenson — who might be able to do more. I don't know what exactly you guys want but he may be able to help you get it. He's high up in the Alberta Ministry of Water."

A few moments later, the boss, Rigel, appeared in the doorway. He handed Dan a phone. "Secure line," he said with a smirk.

Dan took the phone, but as he made to dial, he noticed a call had already been placed.

"Hello?" Dan said.

"Sorry, my friend," came the voice through the speaker. "Change of plan."

Dan almost dropped the phone. "Percy?"

"You proved useless as an insider, so I decided to give you an easier job. Sit tight. I've told them not to hurt you, but this should keep our water north of Red Deer where it belongs."

Dan's heart pounded. He felt lightheaded. Percy's words rang in his head: *My water supply better not dry up.* "Why you fucking two-faced double-crosser ..." But Percy had already ended the call.

The bald man laughed, grabbed the phone back, and shut the door.

"Some friend," Ursula said heavily. She sat cross-legged on her mat with her elbows on her knees. She handed him back his sandwich and hung her head forward.

"How naïve could I get," Dan said. "I wanted to stop Crystel from syphoning off water to the States; Percy wants a civil war."

Ursula looked up at him. For a while, she said nothing. He saw shadows cross her face. Puzzlement. Annoyance. Then scorn. "You call yourself a scientist."

Dan bristled at the insult. "Well, I don't know if I ..."

She cut him off. "How long have forests been a commodity? Resources need to be regulated to make them sustainable and protect the people who need them or make their living from them. If we ever have enough water to sustain all our needs, and we can pad our coffers by selling to the States, then why not do that?" Her tone, a fierce whisper convinced of its own logic, seemed to be drawn from some new well of strength.

He watched her with fascination, forgetting his hurt. Still, he pushed back. "What was I supposed to do? I needed the job."

"Doesn't sound like the Daniel Brookes I know."

"Okay, well, how can you be so sure Albertans' interests will be served before they redirect water to the States?"

She dropped down onto her mat again. "Politics. Any government that tries that will be out on their ass."

"Who's the optimist now? You're sure there won't be any cross-border political maneuvering or court challenges when they want more and we say no?"

She looked at him in surprise. "I thought I was the political junkie." She resumed eating her sandwich. When she had finished, she brushed the crumbs off her jeans. "Okay, maybe that's a bit naïve. I suppose you thought you were serving the greater good."

Where Dan's hurt had been, guilt rushed in. "Well, my own good first, but yes, the greater good did figure into it."

Ursula knelt in front of him and leaned close. "Bottom line, I have no interest in being a pawn in someone's goddamn water war. We have to figure out how to get out of here." She tilted her head in the direction of the window. "It's time we found out how secure this prison really is."

Ursula peeled the paper back from a bottom corner, being careful to keep the sticky tape around the outside edge intact so it could be refastened around the frame. Blurred light glowed on the pencil-straight western horizon. A substantial grove of trees stood to the south. They had noticed it on their trips to the outhouse. The branches were leafless, but the trunks appeared thick enough to hide them while they worked their way through the grove and out the other side. They thought it might buy them some time if the captors thought they were hiding there.

Ursula examined the window itself. Rust encased the latch. There would be no opening it. She scraped at the mortar around the window frame with her fingernail. "It's pretty crumbly," Ursula whispered. "I think we can scour it out with the nail we hang our food on. We can hide the scrapings under our mats."

"Okay," Dan said. "We'll do that while they're eating supper."

THE NEXT EVENING, they waited until knives and forks clicked on plates. Voices rose and fell. Rigel and Hick bantered easily; both spoke in low, booming tones. Justina and Rambo stayed mostly quiet, laughing on cue.

Ursula wriggled the nail until it came free from the wall and got to work. Despite the mortar's crumbly consistency, the layer around the window frame ran deep.

They took to sleeping side by side, having pushed their mats together to better hide the mortar crumbs. With the opportunity to wash so limited, the musky smell that wafted from her skin as she moved in the night grounded him. Sharp and earthy like the wolf willows on the Western Crest. His gut twisted at every recollection of home.

Work on the window progressed slowly. They tore strips of fabric from the undersides of the Iron Man comforters to cover their mouths against the mortar dust. And they could only work it loose when the dinner noise outside the door rose sufficiently to conceal the sound of scraping.

IT TOOK TWO MORE NIGHTS of frantic scraping to remove all the mortar. By the next dinner hour, they were ready to ease the window out of its casing. The wind had calmed, but the waning half-moon burned brightly through a smoke and dust-free sky.

"Not tonight," Ursula said. "We'd be perfect targets."

She pressed the paper back into place.

That night, in the darkness, Ursula shook Dan awake.

He'd been dreaming. About his mother, slashing awkwardly at gigantic leafy wolf willows on the Western Crest with an unwieldy scythe. He had been trying to stop her but was terrified of her hacking blade.

"Try and rest," Ursula said. "When the time is right, we'll need every bit of energy we can muster." She turned onto her side with her back to him, all the while keeping a firm grip on his arm, clasped around her waist.

"RISE AND SHINE," Justina said as she burst into the room. "We need you for your close-up. Getting' cozy again, huh?"

"I think you're jealous," Ursula said, with a small jut of her chin.

Justina glared at her as she and Rambo hauled them out of the bedroom and sat each of them down by turn on a rickety chair against one of the newspapered walls in the main room. They each held a different sign with scrawled writing. Dan's read: "If Crystal builds the pipline, I die." The spelling errors would have been laughable if the message hadn't been utterly chilling. Ursula's read: "Save me!!!! Stop the pipline from killing the north!!!!" Rigel snapped pictures with his phone. As Dan and Ursula were led back into their makeshift prison cell, Rigel hunched over his phone, presumably disseminating the images far and wide. Dan thought about how the pictures would alarm his parents, but at least they'd know he was alive.

EACH NIGHT Dan and Ursula waited for an opportunity to slide the window out and make a run for it, but one of the captors always seemed to be shuffling around near the door.

There were eleven marks now on the bedroom wall. The outhouse reeked. The air in the farmhouse was stifling. The bedroom felt more cramped with each passing day. Dan and Ursula had nothing to eat but peanut butter, stale bread, and bruised apples. The smell of hot food from the other side of the door sent their taste buds into spasms of longing.

Their captors grew surly. Dan and Ursula frequently heard them hurl accusations at each other.

"Why aren't you roughing them up?" That was Justina.

"How long are we going to be stuck in the fucking boonies? And why the hell do we need four people to guard a scrawny scientist and his bitch?"

"Rambo," Ursula whispered.

"The rabid-eyed guy named Hick," Dan said, after a low voice said, "We need more decent grub. Rambo feeds us rations out of a box like we're the prisoners."

"Fuck you." Rambo. "I just cook what I have, asshole. Fuck. This is so not worth it."

Dan and Ursula played games to pass the time. Word games and guessing games. At one point, he grinned and suggested I Spy, which earned him a punch on the arm. They shared stories about growing up, their worst dating disasters, their favourite books and movies and food. They spent hours deciphering the ancient news stories plastered on the walls.

In a rare moment of generosity, the captors allowed Ursula and Dan an hour of outdoor activity. They spent that hour walking circles around the house, always in someone's rifle scope. They estimated the distance between the house and the grove of trees. They listened for high flying drones that might be spotting tire treads on the road leading up to the old farmhouse but heard only the incessant huffing wind.

ONE NIGHT, Dan caught Ursula several times watching him closely as he studied the newsprint on the wall.

"Care to share?" he asked.

"Sorry I was hard on you. Percy the dick is obviously the real villain here."

He smiled. "Nice nickname. Apology accepted. I was stupid to think I could be a player in such a high stakes game."

"We probably shouldn't talk about it," she said.

"What? The high stakes game?"

She shook her head slowly.

He crawled over on his knees and took her hand. "Hey, we're in this together. You can tell me anything."

She concentrated on tracing his knuckles with her fingers. "Are you scared?"

"Hell, yeah."

"Me too. It's like there's an electrical current running through me all the time." He sat down beside her and covered her hand with his.

"People can be scared and courageous at the same time."

She nodded, then frowned. "I've been wondering — why aren't we driving each other crazy, like the crew out there? If we can get through this, we'll probably be friends for life."

"We'll get through this," Dan said in earnest, then he laughed softly. "I come from a long line of determined Dutch people. And you're not exactly a shrinking violet. Opa always said, *Het geluk helpt de dapperen.* Fortune favours the bold."

ON DAY THIRTEEN, tempers flared into a firestorm outside their bedroom. "Where the hell's our relief," Justina said, her voice icy.

"Shut the fuck up," Rigel said. He ordered them outside, presumably to take them out of earshot of the prisoners.

Snippets of their conversation floated over to the prison window, but not through it until finally Justina's high-pitched words penetrated like a bullet.

"I'd be happy to shoot those two cocksuckers so we can all get the hell out of here."

Ursula's fingers clamped around Dan's forearm. Two car doors slammed. Tires spat gravel as a car spun away from the farmhouse. "Justina's gone," she whispered. "Hick, too, I guess."

That night, long after the kidnappers' usual dinner hour, Dan eased open the door a crack. Rigel and Rambo were asleep and snoring on two of the cots in the main living area. A rifle leaned against the head of each cot. Dan thought about tiptoeing out and seizing one of the guns. He would have to make it across the creaky floor without disturbing the dogs, cock the rifle, and shoot before the second man had either overpowered him or put a bullet through his head. Impossible.

"Where are the dogs?" Ursula whispered after he'd eased the door shut.

"Dunno," Dan muttered. "But I don't think we'll get another chance after Rigel finds out Rambo slept through his watch." He looked at her intently. "We can do this."

"Yes, we can," Ursula said, taking a deep breath and letting it out in a slow sigh. "We stay low and slow until we've almost reached the trees."

Dan nodded. He peeled back the paper and eased the window out of its frame. Wind lashed in, and he froze, waiting to see if the men in the other room heard it. Nothing. He lowered the window to the ground outside. Then the two of them climbed out. The crescent moon was too hazy a spotlight to be a threat. The wheezing wind would obscure their footfalls.

They pushed the window back in place to keep the wind from rattling the bedroom door.

Crouching, they headed west, crawling when they got to the corner of the farmhouse. Ursula was ahead of Dan, and moving quickly. Sharp tufts of grass needled Dan's arms and poked through his jeans as he slid forward on elbows and splayed knees. When the farmhouse and wind turbine were dwarfed behind them, he stood up slowly. He called softly to Ursula: "Now."

He'd barely hauled himself to his feet when the beam of a flashlight jerked into view and a set of canine incisors clamped his arm. The Doberman. A few moments later, a fist collided with his diaphragm. When the dog let go, Dan collapsed in a heap, fighting to breathe. As he flattened out to protect the front of his body and covered his head with his free arm, a boot stomped repeatedly on his ribcage and lower back.

Rigel hauled him to his feet and pushed him toward the farmhouse. Rambo shoved Ursula, then they were sprawled again in the bedroom and Rigel tore the door off its hinges as if it were cardboard.

Ursula held Dan's shoulders until his gasping eased and he lay quiet on his mat. She tucked the comforter around his curled body and gently stroked his back. His arm, his gut and his left side throbbed. She washed the bite on his arm with bottled water and tied a nylon shopping bag tightly around it to stem the bleeding. As he drifted at last into a fitful sleep, Dan thought, *What the hell do we do now, Opa?*

31

A WEEK AFTER Willa and Calvin learned of Daniel's kidnapping, a car drove up the gravel lane just as she returned to the house to clean up after the morning milking. She didn't know the vehicle, but when it pulled up in front of the deck, she saw Pastor Mike from New Life Church behind the wheel. Her whole body stiffened.

"Good morning, Willa," he said, stepping out of the car. "I know you weren't expecting me." He held his hands up as if she might draw a pistol from under her long work shirt. "I felt compelled to come."

An old movie line came to Willa's mind: "The power of Christ compels you." She recalled hearing it used in a mocking way by a formerly Christian comedian.

Willa imagined Pastor Mike was on some run-of-the-mill mission to minister to a local. He would tell her to have faith in god to save Dan. "I'm sorry. This isn't a good time. Calvin and I are very busy ..."

"I heard the news about Dan. I wanted to see if you needed anything." His hands retained their defensive pose. "Anything at all."

She looked at the ground. "I appreciate the sentiment, but I can't think what you could do that the police aren't already doing."

Pastor Mike looked back at his car, then at Willa. "Can I come in? For just a minute?"

Willa didn't answer. She started walking toward the house, and the pastor followed. While she didn't want to talk to him, she didn't think Calvin would approve if she ordered him off the property.

Inside, Willa put water in the electric kettle, but Pastor Mike shook his head. "I don't need tea. I won't stay."

She motioned for him to sit down in the kitchen nook and put water on to boil anyway. She remained at the counter while the kettle behind her hissed.

"I'm so sorry about Dan, Willa," the pastor said. "I'm praying he'll be found safe and sound."

Willa nodded and cleared her throat. "The pictures the kidnappers released at least show he and Ursula are alive. Or were ..." She wondered how constricted her throat had to feel before she stopped breathing entirely. Swallowing did nothing to appease the lump that had lodged itself there since Dan disappeared.

Pastor Mike looked out the window. A crease formed between his brows. "So much strife and uncertainty ..."

Annoyance eased a bit of the thickness in Willa's throat. "Strife, yes, but I thought certainty was your stock in trade, Pastor Mike. Don't men of the cloth have all the answers?"

His eyes jerked back to her face, but the hard look she expected to see there didn't materialize. Instead, she saw something akin to affection. "It's been a long time since I was that certain about anything, Willa."

His humility took her by surprise, but his long-ago theory about god testing *her* faith with her father's illness blazed in her mind. "I thought everything happened for a reason?"

Instead of responding, he picked up the pillar candle Willa kept in the centre of the table. He brought it to his nose and sniffed. "Mm, pine." He put the candle down. "Many things do seem to happen for good reason, but that doesn't mean it's preordained. And it doesn't mean we can't change the outcome."

Willa frowned. "That sounds suspiciously like self-determination. Not exactly good fodder for a sermon about the power of god." She turned to drop a teabag into a travel mug and pour boiling water over it. "Here's a question for you, Pastor Mike," she said, her back still turned. "What about changing the outcome by taking your own life or helping someone take theirs? Isn't that a sin?" Only the click of the lid on the mug broke the leaden silence that followed.

Willa turned and leaned on the counter but said nothing. The bewildered look on Pastor Mike's face was oddly satisfying.

"Those are not easy questions to answer, Willa," he said at last. "Issues around life and death rarely lend themselves to a simple choice of right or wrong. Assisted suicide is legal in Canada, but there are clear protocols around the person's condition and who can approve such things. Of course, I'm not an expert on the law. My faith dictates that life is usually worth preserving, but there are exceptions."

Willa's turn to be dumbfounded.

"I don't want to keep you from your work, Willa," Pastor Mike continued, "but ever since you came back to church with Peter, you've been on my mind."

"I think 'back to church' is a misnomer, Pastor Mike. You have to have been somewhere in the first place to go back to it."

"You've always been part of this community, just as the church is. We've been connected by default ever since I came to Good Life."

"I suppose there's logic in that."

"You and I have been at odds. You may be surprised to learn I remember exactly when that started. I loved your father. He was a great man. Intelligent. Had a gentle way and a good heart."

Willa's throat seized up again. She took a sip of tea, knowing full well it would burn her tongue. It did.

"Pastors can be young and stupid like laypeople, you know. I used to spew a lot of foolishness."

She stared at him, feeling her shoulders loosen.

"Getting by as best we can day by day, that's all god wants us to do. To be there for each other." He reached his hand out, palm up, fingers slightly curled. His skin looked soft and pink. She stared at it as if he might perform some sleight of hand. Produce a coin or a dove from thin air. When she reached out, he squeezed her hand between both of his and stood up. "I'll keep Dan — and Ursula — in my prayers, Willa. Just know that I'm here if you need me."

He let himself out. She went to the picture window and watched until his car crested the hill and disappeared.

THAT NIGHT, Willa dreamed about running through a forest of aspen trees, leaves bright as gold bullion. Trying to catch a little girl with hair the colour of the leaves. Always ahead of her. Every few seconds, the girl stopped and looked back. Her eyes crinkled as she shook with soundless laughter. On the next turn, a bitter scowl replaced her smile. The girl pointed a pistol at her. She watched her pull the trigger. Willa jerked awake with the echo of the pistol shot in her ears. Her alarm clock read 3:12 am.

She stared up at the darkness, her mind skittering back to the jumble of horrors in the conscious world. Where was her son tonight? Was he sleeping fitfully too? Would she ever see him again?

When restlessness found its way to her legs, she got up and shrugged into her robe. Made herself a cup of tea and sat down in a chair in the front room with Saskia at her feet. Stared at the blackness of the sky out the picture window. The wind clawed across the house — it hadn't died down as it often did at night. Officer Frazier had called after Pastor Mike left. He said the police had questioned the panel and staff involved in the pipeline hearings as well as the owners of the motel. The sound technician for the Water Talks confessed to sliding the bogus notes under Dan's and Ursula's motel room doors. He said someone named Pamela D'Angelo had PM'd him, dictated the wording for the notes. She had claimed to be a friend of Ursula's and e-transferred him one hundred dollars to execute what she termed a birthday prank to spur on the romance everyone saw budding between the two Water Talks employees. The man was devastated that he had inadvertently helped the kidnappers. The police did not charge him with any crime. He donated the hundred dollars plus an additional hundred to the Alberta Ecotrust Foundation. It struck Willa as strange that he had shared that additional piece of information. Did Officer Frazier want her to know the man had atoned for his part in the kidnapping? If so, her son's life amounted to a two-hundred-dollar charitable donation. Perhaps when Daniel was found, she could forgive the man. But how culpable was she? Had Daniel retreated from her to end up in mortal danger, or had she pushed him away? Regardless, the connection between them had ebbed away, just like the precious glaciers had.

Life had been simple once upon a time. Not easy, but simple. Like painting with primary colours, clear and bold. The year they switched to goats, she and Daniel and Calvin had worked tirelessly side by side, day after day catching new-born kids and separating them from the rest of the herd. Those months were marked by exhaustion from the hardest work they'd ever done on the farm. She would hug Daniel after a long day of exertion and ask him if he was okay — really okay — but he never failed to answer her with a grin and one of her father's sayings: "What doesn't kill you ... will try again tomorrow."

Her empty vial of Ativan sat on the coffee table in front of her. She needed to go see Dr. Clyde. The hallucinations dogged her two, three times a day. The memories of Daniel were real, though. They swept through her mind all day every day like a gulp of swallows.

At the age of twelve, Daniel had built, with the help of his dad, the cart that Peter fixed. They used it to gentle a new buck, a six-month-old, wild-eyed beast. Willa marvelled at Daniel's patience. First, he led the animal around by a halter and then by the ear. Finally, it pulled him in the cart.

His voice came back to her in snippets. *I'm not a kid anymore. Go get those goats so we can make a fortune. I'm too busy to mess with girls.*

They would have made it if he'd stayed. He wouldn't have been kidnapped if he'd stayed. She leaned forward, pressed the nail of her index finger to the pad of her thumb and flicked the Ativan vial. It skittered off the coffee table.

Desperate to calm her mind and her nerves, she got up to find her long-neglected novel. She'd left it in the office. She walked down the hall, Saskia in tow. When she reached the office and flipped the light switch, she stopped cold. Her father sat in the desk chair. He looked as he had at the bus station. This time he spoke.

"Hello, Willa."

"Papa?"

He smiled. His thumbs twiddled, spinning in perfect, waltzing circles without touching. He motioned with his chin for her to sit in the extra chair. She dropped onto it. Her eyes fought with her mind. Real? Not real? But then the need to believe won out.

"Daniel's in danger," she said.

"I know, lieverd, but I think the police will find him."

She narrowed her eyes at him. "Daniel told me what happened. How could you leave me like that? Not even include me in the conversation."

"Where there's life, there's hope? Is that what you mean? Stay alive for the people who need you?"

She nodded.

"I don't blame you for not understanding my suffering."

"How can you say I didn't understand? I took care of you. Wept for you. Prayed for you day and night."

"There are many ways to care, Willa. Did I want to leave you? Of course not. But I had no choice."

"Of course you had a choice. And so did Daniel."

He reached his hands out. "Willa, please don't blame Daniel. It was my decision. You didn't blame me when your mother left."

"Maybe she made a wrong choice," she said, her voice icy, "and maybe you chased her away. I wasn't exactly old enough to know the difference. But how could Daniel help you die when he loved you? When he knew how much I loved you."

"Your mother left because this place made her crazy. She was drowning in her own life. I couldn't blame her for wanting to go someplace where she could breathe. She hated herself here. She certainly couldn't be the mother you needed."

Willa pounded her fists on the desk. "I deserved better."

"Of course you did, Wilhelmina." She recognized the tone — her name a lark's song, the gentle way he had of sorting out her confusion. "I'm saying we all have reasons for the things we do. And they don't always make sense to those around us — especially those who love us the most." He turned in the chair and aimed his gaze out the window. Willa knew what his ghost eyes were searching for in the darkness: the line of scraggly trees. "You did become strong," he said. "But you must also bend in the wind."

"Damn those trees," Willa said, her voice low and fierce. "This isn't about bending. We're talking about what's right and wrong. It's wrong to take someone else's life, and it's wrong to take your own. It's wrong to give up. I learned that from you. Goddammit, Papa. If I can't bend, it's your fault." She jumped to her feet, her body shaking. The realization came to her the way her hallucinations did — suddenly and in vivid detail. She said slowly, "You're the one who told him to go. You sent him away. It's your fault Daniel's in trouble."

Before he could answer, she careened down the hall, stepped into her rubber boots, and out the side door. Too fast for Saskia to follow her. The wind snapped at the hem of her robe as she looked past the barn at the lodgepole pines. Even in death, they were solid, stalwart. The wind pushed its powerful palms against her, trying to hold her back, but she fought it. She followed her shadow away from the shaft of light spilling from the side door of the house. The moment she grabbed the door of the toolshed, it ripped from her fingers, swinging open. She groped for the light switch. Tools hung from hooks or were neatly arranged on shelves. Boxes of screws and nails sat in small tidy stacks. Neatness wrought by Peter's hand. She'd lost him, too. She zeroed in on her quarry — the chainsaw — and carried it outside.

The barn was quiet as she marched past. The sensor light on the north wall flicked on. She followed her own shadow up the hill to the shelterbelt. Then the sensor light flicked off, leaving only the faint glow from the house.

She pulled the choke out and placed the chainsaw on the ground. With her foot on the handguard, she grunted as she pulled the starter handle. Three yanks on the starter rope and the machine roared to life. She stared up at the first tree. Its bare branches swayed stiffly in the wind. She took a deep breath of dusty air and sliced off a low branch. Then another and another to expose the bottom of the trunk. Faster and faster she cut, slicing and hacking from one tree to the next. A baker's dozen, her father said when they planted them. Twelve and one for luck. When she had delimbed the bottom of the thirteenth tree, she turned back to survey her handiwork. Each tree rested on a single bony leg. Branches littered the ground like rats' nests. Toeing a foothold among the shorn limbs, she cut a notch in the trunk of the thirteenth tree. Then she back-cut the trunk just above the notch. She set the chainsaw down and laid both hands on the tree they planted for luck and leaned all her weight against it. The tree toppled. Desiccated upper limbs snapped off as they smashed to earth. The twelfth and eleventh trees fell with equal precision. As she back-cut the tenth trunk, the wind screamed in her ears and she heard a great crack as the tree side-stepped its notch and tore in its own direction. She stumbled out of the way, falling over a branch, twisting her knee, lurching, almost righting herself, then toppling into the maze of branches, banging her head hard against a fallen trunk.

WILLA OPENED HER EYES. Calvin was kneeling over her, his rough fingers moving along her neck, his eyes closed in concentration as he tried to find her pulse. She struggled to sit up, but fallen branches caged her in.

Calvin's eyes snapped open. "Take it easy, Willa. Lie still until I know if you're okay to move."

She did as he said.

"Do you feel any pain or numbness?"

"Bit of a headache."

Saskia lurched over fallen branches and launched herself at Willa's face, trying to lick her back to health.

"Yes, girl, I'm fine," Willa said, reaching an arm around the big dog's neck. "Calvin," she said. "I need to get up." Something was different. A dam inside her had broken open. She pushed Saskia's head away.

"Wait," Calvin said. "Can you move your legs?"

When she did so, a piercing pain surged up from her left knee. "My knee's a bit sore," she said. "I need to go to the doctor. But not for my knee. Well, I guess that, too."

Calvin looked away from her down the pile of gnarled and twisted branches and felled trees. But he said nothing, just put a tender arm around her shoulders and helped her up. She leaned on him, hobbling back to the house in the ashen dawn. He sat her down in the kitchen nook and set about making tea.

"Do you want to tell me what's going on?" he said with his back to her. His tone was deep, and for the first time in all their years together, he sounded artificially calm.

Her first instinct was to lie, but she shook it off. "I do. I'm just not sure how." She exhaled the words, drawing them out. "I think I'm going mad," she said quietly. "I've been having crazy visions. Things that seem so real, and even though I know they're not real, I still react to them as if they are." The truth tasted foreign on her tongue, like unusual food she had to roll around her mouth to decide on its palatability. "I didn't want to tell you. You had enough to worry about."

"So you thought you'd show me?" he said to the kettle. His voice came out in a sighing tone as if his patience were almost spent. He turned and leaned heavily on the counter.

"I thought the drugs would help," she said. "They didn't."

"You hacked the shelterbelt to bits in the middle of the night because of those pills?"

She shook her head as if to dislodge coherent words. "No. No. I don't know. Maybe." She took a deep breath. "Cal, I spoke to Papa last night."

"What?" He looked genuinely alarmed. "Did you talk to Dr. Clyde about these visions?"

"Not exactly. Enough that he scheduled me for a brain scan, but that's not until next week. August 5th. I wasn't going to go, because I thought the pills would fix things."

Calvin looked out the window.

She stood up, wincing at the pain in her knee. She hobbled over to him. Followed his gaze to the wreckage of the shelterbelt. "But they didn't fix anything."

He shook his head and frowned. He was receding from her as surely as if he were floating away. She threw her arms around him to hold him there.

"You shouldn't worry Calvin, I told myself. I thought I was strong enough to handle it all. The financial trouble, the hallucinations, the truth about Papa's death, Daniel's kidnapping. At every turn, I thought there was a simple solution: Peter would live with us; Sophie's then Roy and Lily's money would save us; drugs would fix my mind; Daniel would apologize." She stopped to fight back her tears. "But Daniel is missing. Sometimes – most of the time – life is too complicated for simple answers."

He rested his chin on the top of her head and stroked her hair. "Watershed."

She pulled back to look up at him. "What?"

"People call that kind of revelation a watershed."

She took his hand and led him to the living room sofa. First, she told him about the water tanker turned army tank and the vision of his palsied face in the bank. From there, the rest of the story spilled out, ending with the vision of her father in the office and the anger that had triggered her rampage through the shelterbelt. "I've never felt such rage before, Cal. When it dawned on me that Papa had told Daniel – practically ordered him – to leave the farm, it felt like I had no choice but to cut down those trees of his." She turned to the picture window, as if it were a treasure map with a clue to her son's whereabouts. "I thought what Daniel did was too terrible to bear. Right now, I would bear any kind of pain if it meant Daniel could be found safe and sound."

Calvin kissed Willa's hand. "Me too, love."

32

DAN AWOKE TO Ursula stroking his hand. He narrowed his eyes against the glare of the cage light. "You okay?"

She nodded. "Shaken up, bruised arm from Rambo's vice grip. More importantly, how are you?"

"You don't have to look so worried," he said. "I'm not dead yet, although my ribs and lower back beg to differ."

The corners of her mouth hinted at a smile. "Wanna eat something?"

He closed his eyes. "Two eggs over easy, bacon, and whole grain toast. A pancake would be nice." When he opened his eyes again, she was wiping hers.

"We're in deep shit here, Dan," she whispered. They couldn't see the men in the other room through the door frame, but they could hear them murmuring urgently to each other. "What are we going to do?"

His back and arm throbbed as he turned awkwardly on the mat. "Mind re-inflating this sorry excuse for a bed if I shift onto the floor?"

"Sure."

He eased off the mat and she blew a few puffs into the valve.

Once he was settled again, he smiled at her. "Okay, that helps. We can't get discouraged, Ursula. I haven't told you much about my mom, but I know exactly what she'd say right now."

Ursula looked spent. "What?"

"Life is about choices. When my mom was young and they still had seven hundred and fifty acres and two hundred and forty head, Opa struck off one day to move some of the cattle to new grazing land. The weather turned unexpectedly, and his horse got spooked by a lightning bolt that struck a tree not a hundred metres from where they stood. The horse threw him off. Every few seconds, another lightning flash burnished the sky. 'I thought I'd traded in my Angus for a herd of charred steaks,' he said. He lay there under the black roiling sky and figured, correctly as it turned out, that he'd broken his leg. His horse had run into the herd, scattering the cattle. He lay under the wide-open sky. No one would come looking for him for a long time because my mom wouldn't be back from school for hours."

Ursula's eyes remained glassy from her tears, but she seemed intent on listening, so he continued his story.

"Opa tried to get up but couldn't. Rain started falling, and soon he was, as he put it, the soggiest speck of humanity the universe had ever produced. But my Mom wasn't feeling well that day, and the secretary at her school in Fort Macleod drove her home. Soon after the secretary drove away, Mom realized Opa wasn't anywhere in or near the house, which concerned her because the weather was bad, and he wouldn't be out in it if he could help it. So, she had to choose: call someone and wait, or go look for him herself. She headed out into the storm, and for reasons she can't explain to this day, she rode her horse right to him."

Ursula shook her head with tears in her eyes. "That's a nice story, Dan, but no one's going to ride up to this godforsaken farmhouse and save us."

"It ain't over 'til it's over," he said, setting his jaw and reaching his good arm up to run his fingers through his hair. "I'd kill for that pancake, though."

She started laughing then, snickering at first and then convulsing with loud guffaws. She clutched her sides with crossed arms and buried her head in his chest.

"Shut the fuck up in there," Rigel shouted.

That made her sit up and laugh harder, and she was well on her way to hysteria when Dan reached up and stroked her cheek. Her laugh subsided. Then she lowered her head and touched her lips to his. When he smiled at her, she leaned down again and kissed him.

"Okay then," she whispered, shoving her hair behind her ears. "We can't wait for someone else, so we have no choice but to try again."

"What do you have in mind?"

"If we separate them, we've got a better chance. Do you think you're strong enough to take on Rambo the lunkhead?"

"Who do you think I am? The superhero from the comforters? At the moment, I'm the furthest thing from Iron Man."

She ignored the sarcasm. "Maybe there's a chance you could surprise him. He thinks you're the feeble captive now. I can try and distract Rigel."

"Distract?" Dan asked. "Oh, no. That sounds like a very bad idea."

"I'll be fine. Just play lame."

He groaned. "No problem there." He shifted to raise himself up on an elbow. She reached out to help, but he put up a dissuasive hand. "Listen," he said, peering at her, "if we try again and it fails, they might kill us."

"If we don't try, they'll kill us anyway. I doubt they'll drive us back to Foremost, pat us on the head, and send us on our way."

"Second time's the charm," Dan said. He lay still for a while, then called out, "Rigel. Thanks to you, I have to piss and shit some blood."

Rigel told his cohort to take Dan out. Rambo cocked his shotgun and aimed it at Dan, who limped, hunched over, out the back door. He staggered across the dusty ground, raising clouds as he went, clutching at his lower back. He hoisted himself into the outhouse and closed the door. The sulphuric smell enveloped him like a rank shroud. After a moment's pondering, he pulled down his jeans to just above his knees and sat down over the hole. The advantages of this position were twofold: he couldn't see whether the burning stream leaving his body was bloody, and he was prone, which would help convince Rambo he needed help. "Opa," he murmured, "If you're up there, I could use your help right now."

Five minutes passed, then a few more. Finally, Rambo shouted. "What the fuck you up to in there. Did you fuckin' fall in?"

Dan let out a loud groan. "Try getting the crap kicked out of your kidney and see if you can piss and shit right."

Rambo snarled a laugh. "Hustle it up," he said.

"I'm not in here for the ambiance," Dan called out. For added effect, he jammed two fingers into his throat and spewed the meagre contents of his stomach beside his runners on the floor.

"You retching in there?"

"What do you think, moron? Look, I can't seem to get up. I'm gonna need your help if you want me back in the house."

"Bullshit," Rambo shouted.

Dan imagined him glancing back at the house, wondering if he should call his boss for help. He had already slept through a watch, so Dan doubted that would be an option. And Rambo knew Rigel was busy with Ursula. *Shit,* Dan thought, *he better not be hurting her.* "Well, we can stay here as long as you like," he said, keeping his voice even, "but I'm not going anywhere on my own."

He heard Rambo's heavy scuffling feet on the dusty ground. "Open the fucking door," the man said.

Dan kicked open the door and found himself staring into the barrel of Rambo's rifle. "You gonna shoot me or help me?" Dan asked calmly.

Rambo lowered the gun stock to the ground and grimaced at the stench. "Jesus fucking Christ," he muttered. When he reluctantly reached out his hand, Dan's foot kicked up hard, squarely catching the underside of Rambo's nose. He staggered back, clutching at his face. As the gun fell, Dan lunged for it. He flipped the gun up and around the way Opa Gerard had taught him. *You won't always have your gun at the ready, and sometimes you'll only have an instant to aim and cock it.* The instant passed, and Dan was ready, gun gripped tightly with both hands to minimize recoil. With his head lowered and body leaning slightly forward, he felt fierce. Rambo lunged, and Dan pulled the trigger. Rambo fell onto his back. A blood stain bloomed in the centre of his shirt. Dan had no time to contemplate what he'd done; the two guard dogs burst through the door of the tumbledown farmhouse. Dan shot the Doberman and hesitated only a split second before shooting the dog that looked so much like his own. Then Rigel rushed out, gun cocked.

"Better put it down, Dan," Rigel said, his voice soothing.

"You put it down," Dan screamed, pointing the rifle at Rigel. "Put the fucking gun down. Right fucking now."

Rigel smirked slyly at him. "You won't get very far with your pants around your ankles."

Though he kept his eyes on Rigel, Dan caught sight of Ursula in his peripheral vision. She walked up behind and to the right of the kidnapper. "And you won't get very far with a bullet in your back," she said. "Set the gun down."

Rigel hesitated for just a moment, then slowly put his gun on the ground. Ursula reached for it and backed away with the gun aimed at him.

Dan saw it dawn on Rigel that Ursula had been bluffing about the gun at his back.

"Shit," Rigel said, scowling.

"You okay, Dan?" Ursula said, keeping her eyes and the gun on Rigel.

Dan laughed, high-pitched and wobbly. "Long as I can get my pants up, I'm good to go." He hauled up his jeans, buckled his belt and took up the gun again. "Keys, Rigel. Where are the keys to the cube van?"

They made Rigel drag Rambo's body inside the farmhouse, then they marched him into the back of the van and barred the door.

Ursula helped Dan into the passenger seat, then she hopped in behind the wheel and the truck bumped away across the field on the faint ruts of an old road. Dan said, "Where did you learn to handle a gun?"

"I didn't. I'm a communications specialist. I know what to say and when to say it. If he turned around, I knew you'd shoot him. Once I had his gun, I figured I only had to pull the trigger."

Dan turned toward her, grinning, and noticed several buttons undone on her shirt. He reached over and covered her hand with his.

"He didn't hurt you, did he?"

Ursula looked toward the hazy prairie horizon and said breezily, "No, he didn't." Then she added, "It's 2058. You guys have got to get over your breast obsession."

THE GPS IN THE cube van directed them two hours north of the old farmhouse to Mankota, Saskatchewan, a town with an RCMP detachment. There, they dropped off the van and its human cargo. They sat on the sofa in the staff lounge and waited for the local doctor to arrive. An RCMP constable named Pritchard took notes on their story. She assured them a helicopter had been dispatched to take them to the hospital in Lethbridge. After Dan and Ursula had described the events of their capture and eventual escape, Dan asked if they could make some phone calls.

"Yes, of course," Constable Pritchard said. She gave them each a phone, and Ursula moved away to make her call so Dan could stay on the sofa.

His mother answered almost immediately. She began to cry as soon as he said, "Hi, Mom."

"Oh Daniel, are you okay?"

"Yes, Mom. We're safe."

"Oh, thank heavens. I'm so sorry. So sorry."

"I'll come and visit you and Dad as soon as I can." Dan's hands began to shake, making it nearly impossible to hold the phone steady. Cold sweat erupted on every inch of his skin. "Okay, Mom, I think I better go. I'll talk to you soon. Give my love to Dad."

Even before he could click out of the call, the phone fell from his hand and he collapsed sideways onto the sofa, conscious but worn-out. Constable Pritchard ran over and helped him lay down on the sofa. "Easy, now," she said, just as the doctor stepped into the lounge.

Ursula picked up the phone Dan had been using. His mother was still there. "Ms. Van Bruggen, this is Dan's colleague, Ursula. Your son's going to be fine, but he's hurt and exhausted. He's in good hands now." After ending the call, she hurried over to Dan. The last thing he heard before he passed out was Ursula's voice. "It's all over now, my love."

SOON AFTER, the RCMP helicopter flew the two to the hospital in Lethbridge for a full evaluation. Dan heard the doctors say there were media vans in the hospital parking lot. Crystel's CEO Adam Landrew and Dan and Ursula's boss, Lucas Howse, flew from Calgary to Lethbridge as soon as they heard the news the two were free. Dan and Ursula joined them at an evening news conference on the hospital steps to formally announce Dan and Ursula's freedom. They all stood next to an RCMP sergeant named Thomas Haines, who led the news conference. Dan sat in a wheelchair beside Ursula. A nurse had cleaned and bandaged his arm where the Doberman bit him during their escape attempt. He also had three cracked ribs and a bruised kidney.

"Thank you for coming," Sergeant Haines said to those assembled. He gestured toward Dan and Ursula. "I am happy to report that the two kidnapped Crystel employees, Dan Brookes and Ursula Myers, are recovering well from their ordeal. One arrest has been made so far in this case: Rigel Croft, a terrorist with the Northern Water Army. One of his cohorts was found dead where the captives were held. Our intelligence tells us that Croft may have also spearheaded the explosion at the pipeline construction site. Our investigation is ongoing. Drawings of other suspects have been posted to the APP and RCMP websites and social media networks to enlist the public's help in capturing them." He turned to Adam Landrew. "Mr. Landrew?"

The tall man stepped up to the microphone. "Adam Landrew, CEO of Crystel. Also here with me is Lucas Howse, director for sciences at Crystel. The Crown corporation will support the RCMP and the Alberta Provincial Police in whatever way we can. This terrifying incident does not deter us. We will continue building the new water pipeline and open the Calgary water plant by mid-November. Water will flow to the south, parched now for nearly a decade. As we heard again and again during the Water Talks that these two brave employees were part of, Albertans are united in our fight to keep this province viable in the face of crippling drought. We won't let a handful of radicals keep us from our mission. Together, we will prevail and thrive." He swept a hand toward Dan and Ursula. "I want to publicly commend Crystel employees Dan Brookes and Ursula Myers for their bravery. They endured nearly two weeks of captivity at the hands of these monsters and then overpowered them. They gained their freedom and delivered the key criminal to the RCMP. We'll see to it that these two heroes get a bit of time off to deal with their scars. Thank you, ladies and gentlemen, that's all for now. Thank you again for coming."

Reporters called out questions, but Lucas raised his hand to indicate none would be taken. Inside the hospital, he turned to face Dan and Ursula and put a hand on their shoulders. "Rest up, you guys. You deserve it."

That night, Dan and Ursula were taken under tight security to the Lethbridge Holiday Inn. They headed to their rooms, but Ursula grabbed Dan's hand outside her door. She smiled at the two RCMP officers who would be posted outside their adjacent doors and pulled Dan inside. After she shut the door, she threw her arms around his neck and kissed him deeply.

When she finally pulled away, she sighed. "Hard to believe that nightmare actually happened. I'm proud of us. I know your mother is proud of you, and your Opa would be, too."

He pulled her close. "We couldn't have done it without your extraordinary communications skills."

She laughed. "I've been asking myself," she said, her head nestled against his neck. "Do I find you attractive and want to sleep with you because of the emotionally trying circumstances we've just shared, or because we have some actual chemistry?"

"Excellent question," Dan replied, rubbing a hand over his bruised kidney. "I'm inclined to want to test that theory under strict laboratory conditions, but I think we should put off the investigation until we've had some rest."

"Agreed," Ursula said. She placed her hands gently on his cheeks and kissed him again. When she finally pulled away, she smiled and said, "Preliminary research."

Back in his own room, Dan took out the new Crystel phone Lucas had given him. After entering Percy Dickenson's number, he typed a text message.

"It'll go better for you if you turn yourself in, Percy. Or should I call you Pamela D'Angelo? You sent that message to the sound technician, didn't you?"

A moment later, his phone buzzed: "I'm fucking brilliant, right? What a stooge — did everything I asked for 100 measly bucks. Who knew you weren't a complete candy-ass, though? Why didn't you rat me out right off?"

"You don't deserve the break, you bastard, but we've been friends for a long time. I think you're more misguided than evil."

"I'd make a run for it, but you'd make sure I didn't make it across the border. You're wrong, you know. It'll all go to shit, and then I'll say I told you so."

Dan ignored the prediction. "I'll give you half an hour. When you get to the nearest Edmonton Police Station, tell the officer to call me to confirm your arrest. If I don't hear anything, I'm calling my new best friend, RCMP Sergeant Thomas Haines." Dan hung up. A half hour later, the phone buzzed again. No text this time, but a selfie of Percy in a crisp white shirt and tie, an Edmonton Police crest visible on the building behind him. Percy had raised the middle finger of his free hand to the camera.

Dan stifled the laugh that would have left him clutching his side in agony. A few minutes later, his phone rang from an Edmonton number.

THE NEXT DAY, news outlets reported three more arrests in the kidnapping case. Dan showed Ursula the pictures. She gasped as she recognized Percy's face as well as those of the gun-wielding young blond, Justina, and the rabid-eyed man, Hick, from the farmhouse.

"Percy turned himself in?"

"With a little encouragement. Apparently, he wasn't going down alone. If they don't plead guilty, we'll have to testify."

"I look forward to it," Ursula said.

33

THREE DAYS AFTER Ursula and Dan escaped their prairie prison, the RCMP escorted Ursula back to her family's home in Calgary. They delivered Dan to his parents' farm. Two RCMP officers were assigned to each of the freed captives to provide round-the-clock police protection.

Dan's mother ran to him as he heaved himself out of the police car, leaning heavily on a cane. She held him, sobbing, until he gently extracted himself from her arms in order to clasp his father in a warm embrace. His parents' eyes brimmed so intensely with love that he had to look away. Saskia ran up, and Dan couldn't help flinching from the memory of her doppelgänger at the old farmhouse. She licked his hand, and he patted her head fondly. "Wow," he sighed, looking around at the house and farm buildings. "I can't believe I'm really here." He swallowed hard, as his voice cracked with emotion. "Wasn't sure I'd ever see this again."

His mother and father each hooked an arm through his and helped him climb the wide deck stairs. Over a lunch of nasi goreng with goat's meat, and honeyberry muffins for dessert, Dan sketched out his ordeal, avoiding the grim details, veering quickly to questions about the goats and Peter.

"Peter pumped his fist when he heard you were safe," Willa said.

Dan laughed. "He's a good kid. I'll video-call him myself tonight."

"He'll appreciate the face-to-face," Willa said, her eyes shining. "You're even more of a hero to him now."

Dan smiled. His mother had been effusive with her love since his arrival, but the old tensions lingered. The kidnapping seemed to have blown holes in the wall between them, but the barrier hadn't crumbled.

"The wind is gusty this afternoon," Willa said, looking at Dan, "but do you think you're up for a visit to the Western Crest?"

He nodded slowly. He was happy to visit his old haunt, but what would she say when they were alone?

"We can take the quad," she said.

"Okay. But you'll have to take it easy."

"Promise," she said. "Now before we go, I'm going to take some lunch to the security detail in the squad car. I'll ask if they can guard the fort while we're up there. Is that okay with you?"

"Sure. If anyone suspicious shows up, they'll see them coming."

With lunch delivered and an agreement from the officers that they could watch the approach roads from where they sat, Calvin headed off to feed the weaned kids while Willa and Dan put on their dust masks and set off on the quad. The masks and the wind made conversation difficult, so they kept their own counsel as they made their way west across the fields. His mother glanced at him repeatedly. As they rode up the final stretch to the crest of the hill overlooking the Rockies, she shifted in her seat, seeming uncertain, jittery —

not the stern, unflinching figure she'd become to him in recent years.

When they reached the Western Crest, his mother helped him out of the quad, and they studied the horizon through the haze of ubiquitous dust and smoke. The jagged line of the Rocky Mountains cracked the horizon as if the universe were an egg, breaking open at the middle. "I'm wondering," she said at last after taking off her mask, "if a heart actually swells from love, or if it just feels that way."

Dan removed his mask, too, and smiled, not knowing what to say. More water would have to flow under that bridge before the mother-son bond could fully heal. Her anger had cut him deeply; the wound was still raw and bloody.

The wind erupted again, blowing stiffly across the crest. It whipped dust devils off the distant sand dune foothills. Arm in arm, Willa and Dan walked to the graves of Willa's grandparents. She squatted to tuck honeyberry sprigs against the gravestones, using rocks to weigh them down against the wind.

When they moved to Opa Gerard's grave, his mother took his hand. Her skin chafed his. His hands had once been rough like that, first from farm work, then hydrogeological field work and cooking at the Breakfast Barn. Crystel had smoothed them over.

He looked around, feeling a deep attachment to this place, yet knowing he would never find his bliss here. He wondered if that's how travellers felt when they thrilled in an exotic place of great beauty, all the while knowing they didn't want to live there.

His mother drove the quad back to the leeward side of the hill, out of the worst of the wind, and stopped.

"Thank you for coming up here with me. I haven't visited his grave in a while."

"I don't think I could have overpowered the kidnapper without him," he said.

His mother said nothing.

He spoke again into the welcoming silence. "I never realized it before, but Opa taught me how to be patient and ferocious. How to make sure one doesn't interfere with the strength of the other."

"I used to think I'd never lose you," she said, grasping his hand again, "and then I lost you twice: once to the city and once to those horrible kidnappers." His jaw tightened, but he held her gaze. She scrutinized his face. "Your eyes. I don't know. They're shining, but there's a hardness there I probably deserve."

He noted her humility, but could hardly disagree with what she saw.

"You can't imagine how happy I am to have you home."

He shrugged, waiting for the bullying to begin.

She studied her hands resting calmly in her lap. "I wanted to be the perfect mother. The one I never had." She looked up at him intently. "I wanted to be everything to you that she wasn't to me."

He shot her a rueful grin. "Well, at least you set a reasonable goal for yourself."

She smiled back. "Yeah, didn't work out as well as I'd hoped. I'm sorry, Daniel." She paused. He assumed she was resisting the urge to tack on the word 'but.' "More than that, I wanted to be everything to you that my father was to me."

A cloud had swept in, darkening the sky. He picked up a honeyberry twig from between the seats and began snapping it, in half and then in half again, and again, until only a fraction remained.

"You're wondering," she said. "Can I leave it all behind? The assisted suicide. Getting you to come home. Is that right?"

He nodded.

"I don't think I'll ever understand it," she said. "Part of me will never accept that he chose to end his life, and how he did it. But I love him; I don't worship him. What he asked you to do was an unconscionable burden. You have every right to be angry at me, but also at him."

He looked up at her in surprise. *Unconscionable burden.*

"You not taking over the farm — that hurts too," she went on. "But I know the hurt will fade. I'm just glad you're safe. Nothing matters more than that. Nothing ever will."

"You think I've left you, but I haven't," he said. "I will always be a part of this place." He squeezed her hand. "And Opa wasn't the only one who inspired our escape. Apparently, you've had some influence over me too."

She laughed, a new lightness in her demeanour. No, he decided, it was an old lightness. Like the time she laughed about him throwing the book at his teacher. He smiled at the memory. His mother held his hand, grasped the steering wheel of the quad with the other and drove slowly back down the hill and across the field toward home.

Just before they arrived at the hacked-up shelterbelt, he said, "Stop for a sec, Mom."

She stopped and put the quad in park, then pulled off her dust mask when he removed his.

"I want to tell you about Opa's death," he said.

She sat still and looked at him expectantly.

"He was truly desperate. I saw it in his eyes. He begged me to help him. I didn't want to, but I couldn't stand the idea of letting him down that way. Seeing the lingering disappointment in his eyes." He looked away, unable to absorb any of the pain in hers. "We listened to Swan Lake. He said I should go build castles. 'Make thy castles high and fair.'"

She stroked his cheek then and he turned to her again. She smiled, her face radiant. "You will. Longfellow, right?"

"Opa's favourite," he said.

She looked away, seeming to study the fallen trees. "I did an essay on Longfellow in high school. Some say he was a genius; others say he was just a derivative sentimentalist. I argued he was a genius, but I guess none of us are just one thing or another."

With that, she winked at him, put the quad in gear, and headed for home.

34

DR. CLYDE LOOKED FROM Willa to Calvin with a mixture of warmth and professional concern. "The brain scan is conclusive, Willa. Even without it, your symptoms line up with a diagnosis of Lewy Body Dementia. One of the first signs of the disease is hallucinations. Patients report seeing colours, whole scenes that are startlingly real. As in your case, these visions can progress to actual conversations with phantom figures, the way you spoke to your father. Unfortunately, Ativan can aggravate the condition more often than it helps it. I'm so sorry."

"Not your fault, Doc," she said, shaking her head emphatically. "I held back important information." She looked at Calvin. "From everyone."

"It's not just that," Dr. Clyde continued. "It takes a brain scan to see what's really going on. Extreme stress seemed a reasonable preliminary diagnosis."

"So, what is it, and what can be done?" She placed both hands squarely on her knees.

"That's the thing, Willa." Dr. Clyde's face turned bland. A stony professional mask. He had done that before. The night her father died, after Dr. Clyde had examined his body. His expressionless face had irritated her then, as if he weren't one of them. As if he could slip behind an impermeable barrier and not feel the pain of these people whom he'd known, cared for, for two decades.

She recalled how, on that terrible day, everyone had been spread around the living room, all of them still as death. Kelli in an easy chair with Peter enfolded in her arms. Dr. Clyde in another. She and Calvin on the sofa. Daniel lay on the floor staring at the ceiling, sobbing softly, the tears running down into his ears. "The bed sore infections," Dr. Clyde explained quietly, his mouth a straight line, barely opening to let the words escape. "They progressed ..." He looked down at his loosely clasped hands. "I'm certain he died from septicemia."

Willa said loudly, "I told him he needed those dressings changed more often." Everyone started at her outburst.

Dr. Clyde said, "I think things had progressed too far already, Willa."

Her frustration reared into anger at the repetition of the word 'progressed.' She spat out her words. "Progress means you're getting better, Hector, not dying." She had thought at the time, maybe he wasn't such a good doctor after all. Maybe he could have done more to keep her father alive.

Dr. Clyde uttering the word 'Parkinson's' jarred her from the memory. "Did you say Parkinson's?" she said with alarm.

"Lewy Body is related to Parkinson's. There are new treatments. Medication delivered across the blood-brain barrier to clear out the plaques. It's not a perfect cure. And it's not a simple procedure. In fact, the treatment is delivered in stages. But it's covered under health care."

Dr. Clyde continued in a monotone, as if Calvin didn't

look mystified and her own face didn't reflect terror, which she knew it must. "I will speak to my colleagues at the Neurology Department at the South Health Campus in Calgary and see how quickly I can arrange for treatment. The hallucinations will continue, but now that I know what we're dealing with, I can give you a different medication that might help. There are a couple of options we can ..."

"Why did you bypass the normal requirement for an autopsy on my father?" The words came out of her mouth the instant they came into her head.

"Willa?" Calvin said, seizing her hand. She shook loose from his grasp.

Dr. Clyde's eyebrows drew together in a thick, questioning dip.

Her eyes locked on his. "You said an autopsy wasn't necessary because you knew how my father died, and that would create unnecessary paperwork that would prolong the agony of his passing. Remember?"

Dr. Clyde nodded.

"You knew he committed suicide."

Dr. Clyde nodded again. The motion seemed to judder his unflinching jawline. "I saw no point in making everyone's pain worse than it was."

"And you knew Daniel helped."

"I suspected as much," Dr. Clyde continued, "because I doubted your father would have been capable of taking multiple pills on his own."

The old anger flashed across her mind. But, almost immediately, a surge of compassion chased away the rage. "You did the right thing," she said softly. "I wouldn't have said it then, or even a month ago, but I'm saying it now."

Dr. Clyde leaned forward in his chair. "He had asked me to help him die two weeks before he took his own life. I gave him alternatives. I told him Lethbridge has several excellent palliative care facilities." He shook his head. "Those are the rules — I had to offer alternatives and give him time to consider them. I said we'd talk about it again in about a month." He hesitated but didn't take his eyes off her. "I also upped his acute-pain morphine dose the day he asked for my help. I'm sorry, Willa."

She listened to the wind sandpapering the window. "I don't blame you. Any of you." She slumped, the fight gone out of her. "It isn't easy to say goodbye to someone who's always been in your life. Not a day goes by ..."

When her words trailed off, Calvin filled the emptiness, almost under his breath. "Let's work on getting you well."

At home, Daniel's face blanched when she told him the diagnosis.

"I'm so sorry," he said, putting his arms around her.

"Thanks, lieverd," she said, hugging him back. "It's treatable, and I'm going to be the most cooperative patient you've ever seen."

"Cooperative, huh?" he said, screwing up one side of his mouth. "I'm going to hold you to that."

AUGUST 15TH DAWNED still and overcast, although the clouds weren't heavy enough to release their precious moisture. After milking the does and pitching hay to the yearlings, Willa donned work gloves and joined Calvin, Daniel, and the water tanker driver, Alain Dupre, in the laborious task of taking down the last of the lodgepole pines in the shelterbelt. Alain had brought over his woodchipper to shred the trees to make bedding for the goat pens. She was helping him load branches and stump pieces into the chipper.

After a while, she paused to watch her husband and son. Dan's injuries prevented him from doing much physical labour, but he helped by calculating the trajectory of the falling trees and calling out instructions on where to place the cuts. He'd always enjoyed the process of tree cutting for firewood and was skilled at it. After felling the trees, Calvin was parsing them into manageable chunks with the chainsaw. The sight of the two of them working together warmed her heart. Suddenly, Daniel stopped calling out directions and looked down at his arm. A dragonfly had lighted there. One of the biggest desert whitetails she'd ever seen, its body the colour of alabaster. Her son stood still until the insect flew away. Willa leaned down to gather up a bundle of twigs and smiled, remembering what her father had said so long ago about turning the trees into wooden shoes when they were finished growing. She stood up and paused again, hugging the bundle in her arms. Life was always in flux on a farm.

She tossed the bundle into the chipper, waited for the machine to devour the sticks, then reached for the switch and flicked it off. The men looked at her in surprise. Calvin shut off the chainsaw and silence exploded around them.

"You okay, Willa?" Calvin asked.

He'd been monitoring her closely since the doctor's appointment, hardly letting her go to the bathroom by herself.

"We need to leave," she said.

"Do you have an appointment?"

"No," she said, waving his words away from her face as if they were flies. "*Leave* leave."

"You mean … leave the farm? Move?"

She nodded. The knowledge blossomed in her chest, like a heart attack, like love.

"Câlice," Alain said. "I can't believe it. You of all people."

"Yes, Al. Me of all people."

The men waited patiently, or perhaps they were dumbstruck. She took a moment to compose herself before she went on. She was making it up as she went, gingerly testing the uncertain shifting foundation beneath her words. "We're in freefall, Cal. We're living on borrowed time. And too much borrowed money. We need to get our feet back on solid ground. We shouldn't wait to be forced off while we chase a pipedream."

Calvin looked down the hill at each of the farm buildings by turn, as if he were gauging the difficulty of carrying them off in his arms. Finally, his eyes lighted on Daniel, who looked back at him with a shrug and his eyebrows raised high.

"We can try and sell the goats," Willa continued. "Take the offer from the federal government to buy the land. We can't wait for the pipeline. We'll scarcely last until it gets to Calgary, let alone down here." She looked at Daniel for confirmation. He gave a barely perceptible nod but said nothing. She imagined he didn't want to do anything to dam the flow of her rational words.

Calvin crouched down and patted one of the trunks, snapped off a small branch and stared at it. "But we won't get a quarter of what the land is worth," he said. "Or the goats for that matter."

"Met apemund betalen," she said.

"Say what?" Calvin asked, but he must have recognized the cadence of the words because he added, "Something Opa said?"

Dan's eyes lit up. "Paying yourself with monkey coins."

She gestured at the few remaining skeletal trees. "I've been hanging onto a dead dream. It's time to admit it and move on as best we can. You said it yourself, Cal. Just before the officer showed up to tell us about the kidnapping." She shivered involuntarily.

"Yeah, but you said no," he reminded her. She saw an unsavoury stew of astonishment and doubt in Calvin's eyes. "Where would we go?"

"Maybe Fort McMurray. I'm sure Roy and Lily could help us get settled. You could get a job as a vet tech. I could retrain. Become a vet tech too. Why not? I've spent my whole life around animals. Then I could still get my fix. We'd be close to Peter. And we could visit Dan and Ursula in Calgary." She smiled at her son. The ease in her limbs felt real. Like a small green shoot that, under the right conditions, could flourish.

"I'll get the word out," Alain said. "For sale: best damn goats in Alberta."

Calvin and Dan laughed, and Willa half-laughed, half-cried along.

THEY VIDEO-CALLED Peter that night to let him in on their plans. "I hoped I could always visit whenever I wanted," he said, "Even when I'm older."

"We wanted that too, lieverd," Willa said, "but we can't make it work anymore. Small comfort now, maybe, but I'm looking forward to living in the same city as you. We can spend lots of time together when we get up there. And you can come and visit us here before we leave."

"I really thought I could move back some day. You know.

After I got a career and worked for a while like Dan is doing. I figured once I made money, I could buy a piece of land or maybe move back in with you guys."

A few weeks ago, she would have been elated to hear him articulate his dream of returning to the south.

"That's what I would have wanted, too, Peter," she said. "More than anything. But you have to know when you're licked. And we're licked but good."

She phoned Sophie next. Her sister was as surprised as anyone.

"Oh, sis, what a hard decision that must be. I always imagined your heart buried somewhere in the ground there, beating like crazy to keep you and the land alive."

"Are you upset?" Willa asked. "This is the Van Bruggen legacy we're talking about."

Sophie shook her head slowly. "I was never a farm girl." She laughed. "You got a hundred percent of those Dutch genes. I don't know how Mama ever thought she could live out there. She may have grown up in the sleepy hollow of Fort Macleod, but she had the big city in her soul. And I'm just like her. But I don't need to tell you that."

Willa felt an evolution of sorts in being able to listen calmly to Sophie talk about their mother as if she were reading her grocery list.

"The only regret I will ever have ..." Sophie faltered. "I don't know, should we even talk about regrets?"

"Spill," Willa said.

Sophie shook her head. "You and I were dealt a rift as deep and wide as Horseshoe Canyon."

Willa thought about that and nodded. "Good thing we installed a tightrope."

Sophie laughed. "Good thing indeed." She raised a thumbs-up sign to the phone screen. "I'm glad Mama could help. She owed you."

After her call to Sophie, Calvin placed three cups of steaming tea on the table. He, Willa, and Daniel spent the next few hours making lists of what to do, what to sell, and who they needed to say goodbye to. Willa knew the transition, this new way of looking at and planning for the future, was easier with Daniel there. She had missed him all these years while he was in school, not just because she had always looked at him as the boy who would carry the Van Bruggen torch, but because she loved him, plain and simple.

35

DAN HELD URSULA'S HAND as they entered the bedroom where the mats and Iron Man comforters lay askew, as if still waiting for them to crawl on top for another unsettled sleep in the heat. Even as the whirr of the helicopter told him they were safe, the sight of the marks on the wall threatened to resurrect the trauma of captivity. They returned to the main room. The police had collected Rambo's body just after Dan and Ursula showed up in Mankota. A rusty stain by the door evidenced the spot Rigel had dragged the dead man to after the shooting.

"Hell of a thing," RCMP Sergeant Thomas Haines said. "They had enough fire power here to run a small army. You two should consider yourselves mighty important."

"No, just lucky," Ursula said quietly.

They walked the officers through the events of the nearly two weeks they were there, including the route of their escape attempt. The officers then raked through the kidnappers' stores and set about packing everything in boxes to load onto the helicopter. Dan and Ursula walked around outside while they waited for the officers to finish up.

"I'm really sorry about Percy," Ursula said. "Betrayal by someone you thought you could trust is a terrible thing."

"I thought we were friends. The spy stuff was a terrible mistake on my part."

She shook her head. "You had good intentions. You wanted north and south to survive. His intentions – well, that's another story. I wonder when we'll have to testify."

"Could be a year, the Crystel lawyer said."

"Do you think we'll be able to get back to normal?"

Dan looked at Ursula for a long time. A grin burrowed its way into his cheeks and pushed at his eyes until his whole face felt warm from it. Folding Ursula into his arms, he said, "Chaos is the new normal, my fellow former captive, and you and I are better equipped than most to handle whatever comes our way. What doesn't kill you makes you stronger."

She pulled back and smiled uncertainly. "I hope you're right."

IN THE ENSUING WEEKS, more NWA informants came forward and further arrests were made. Police deemed the NWA's back sufficiently broken for Dan and Ursula to resume their lives without police protection. The panel, with replacements for the two of them, held its final hearings in Milk River, Lethbridge, Fort Macleod, and Claresholm. Crystel judged the exercise a success. Not surprisingly, the kidnapping had raised public sympathies, bolstering Crystel's standing in southern communities.

In Claresholm, the Crown corporation announced the final route and water pricing regime for the Southern Alberta extension of the Northern Gateway water pipeline. Crystel's CEO Adam Landrew held a joint news conference with Premier

Saffron Hamady. They assured the province that Crystel would respect Alberta's Water Charter.

One late August evening, Dan and Ursula made love and lay languid in each other's arms in Dan's basement apartment. Mrs. Winstead's house had not sold yet. She now lived in High River with her daughter, who was slowly sorting through her mother's effects. For Ursula, life would pick up again the following week when she would begin planning the ribbon-cutting ceremony for the arrival in mid-November of the pipeline and the opening of Calgary's new water pumping station. Dan, meanwhile, had resumed work at Crystel Canada Square.

Ursula was reviewing the news. "The quote picked up most by the news stations is: 'The pipeline extension is a watershed in water management. Albertans will have the water they need.'"

"Yours?" Dan asked.

"No. That one's a Landrew original. I hate repetition but you can't argue with sincerity — it eclipses weak writing every time."

"Remember our conversation back at the farmhouse?"

She grinned. "You'll need to narrow that down, love."

"What do you think would happen if Crystel ever decided — or was forced — to sell water to the United States by depriving Albertans of their share?"

Ursula groaned. "More shop talk, huh? Fine, I'll bite. Between you and me, if that happens, we'll see the rise of a sophisticated terrorist cell that will make the NWA look like a kindergarten picnic."

"You think they'll tread carefully."

"We can only hope. I'm more curious what you plan to do with the settlement money Crystel gave you for the kidnapping ordeal."

Dan stroked Ursula's bicep thoughtfully and traced the edges of the ceiling tiles with his eyes. "I offered some of it to my parents to help with their move, but they refused. Said they could hardly take money paid out for extreme hardship and distress." He kissed her forehead and waved his hand in the air. "I guess I'll have to use it to move out of my subterranean Banff Springs Hotel."

"Exactly." Ursula sat up excitedly on her bent knees. He reached to pull her to him, but she stopped him by taking his hands. "Would you consider buying this place and moving upstairs?"

He frowned, about to protest about not having enough money. She put a finger to his lips.

"I know you don't have enough alone, but what if we pooled our resources for the down payment?"

He smiled. "I do believe you're propositioning me, Ms. Myers."

"Someone told me that life is about choices." She placed a hand on his chest and stroked the fingers of her other hand along the side of his head and let them rest there in his hair. "I think you should listen to your heart and succumb to reason."

Without warning, a knot in his belly tightened as if she had reached inside him and pulled both ends of a looped wire. She noticed his discomfort immediately and pulled her hands back into her lap.

"What's wrong, Dan?"

He resumed scanning the ceiling tiles. The corner of one had broken off and he concentrated on its jagged edge. He thought he'd purged the guilt, but there it bloomed, black and billowy on the horizon. Confessing to his mother had been painful but freeing. He had to tell Ursula too. "I've told you a lot about my Opa Gerard."

"Yes. I almost feel like I know him. A good man with a flair for proverbs."

"There's something I haven't told you."

Ursula gathered the sheet around her naked body and sat up tall beside him, waiting. Dan pushed himself up to rest his back against the headboard.

"He had Parkinson's. Advanced Parkinson's."

"Yes, I know. You told me that."

He didn't want the tears to well up, but that didn't stop them. "I helped him kill himself." He couldn't stop his voice from rising either. "When I was just a kid. Fifteen."

She stared at him, then she took his hand and held it still in hers. "Tell me what happened."

And he did. When he finished, she sat exactly as she had when he began, except that she reached up and ever so delicately touched one of the tears on his cheeks. Then she said softly, "Daniel Brookes, you are the bravest, kindest person I know."

He pulled her to him, and, after a while, they fell asleep in each other's arms.

36

WITH THE HELP OF Alain Dupré's networking, it had taken only six weeks to get all the goats sold at a good price. Fred Butterfield took back only half of his herd to compensate for the toxic silage. His twenty and Willa and Calvin's own herd were not all going to one farm, though. They had found several experienced goat keepers in British Columbia who they knew would make good homes for their prized herd. They found buyers for much of their equipment, too, although they took a hit on the milking machines.

They funnelled the proceeds from the sale of the goats and equipment into paying off the rest of the credit card debt and some of the outstanding mortgage debt. Once the administration and legalities involved in selling off their land to the federal government were complete, they would be able to clear away even more of the mortgage. Still, there would be a sizeable shortfall. One of their neighbours advised them to declare bankruptcy, but Calvin and Willa abhorred the notion of having to ask permission to spend their own money for five years. They sat down with Ian Mason at the British-Canadian Bank to establish a new loan for the mortgage shortfall. It would kick in at the close of the land sale to the feds.

With Lily's help, they had secured an apartment in Fort Mac. Once they got there, Willa would work part-time in Roy's accounting department. Calvin would take a few veterinary courses at Fort Mac's Keyano College to upgrade his skills and restore his license to practise as a vet tech.

Roy and Lily told them by video-call to take all the time they needed to repay the interest-free loan. "I know where to find you," Roy said with a laugh.

Willa underwent six treatments in Calgary for Lewy Body Dementia, effectively removing eighty-five percent of the plaque that interfered with normal brain function. Her neurologist said removing every vestige of the disease was impossible, but almost immediately after the treatments began, the hallucinations stopped, and her energy rebounded to levels she hadn't felt in years. Good health buoyed her spirits. The thought of moving had evolved slowly from an unbearable nightmare into a sufferable sorrow.

To allow Peter to say a final goodbye to his two beloved homes, Lily flew with him to Calgary, and they took the bus from there to the Van Bruggen farm. Lily would take the bus back to Calgary and fly home alone. She had arranged for Peter to miss a week of school while he and Willa and Calvin packed the last of their belongings and drove north together.

One evening after milking, Willa flicked on the light in the newborn pens to bottle-feed the last of the new kids that would be picked up along with the remaining does in a few days' time. She was seated in the straw, cuddling a feisty black Saanen male, when Lily walked in.

"I can see why Peter loved it here," she said. "The goats are adorable, and the smell of fresh hay is intoxicating."

Willa smiled. "I'll adjust to a new life, but I'll miss the old one terribly. All the same, we're grateful to you and Roy for helping us."

"We're happy to help." She glanced up toward the cross-beams in the barn roof. "I think Kelli and Logan are looking down approvingly." She stood with her arms resting on the fence around the enclosure, and nodded at the hairy bundle in Willa's arms. "He's got energy to spare."

Willa laughed. "That he does. He's a special one. Good body structure, smart as can be. He's got several generations of good milk producers in his pedigree. The new owners will raise him for breeding."

Saskia nuzzled Lily's leg, and she patted the dog's head.

Willa said, "I'm not sure who will have the hardest time adjusting to living in an apartment in the city — me or Saskia. I guess we'll get through it together."

Lily scuffed at hay tufts with the toe of her bright white sneaker. "Peter wants to live with you in Fort McMurray, Willa."

Willa looked up at Lily. "What?"

"You have a long history with the Bradfords; you and Calvin are more like parents to Peter than Roy and I could ever be. He really misses you."

"But," Willa sputtered, "he hasn't asked us."

"He's not sure you want him back after he ... well, he feels he abandoned you."

Willa released the kid and jumped up. "Of course we want him back," she cried.

"In the end, that's what Kelli and Logan wanted anyway," Lily said. She laughed as the black Saanen pulled ferociously at one of Willa's pant legs. "I'm glad I had a chance to see you and Calvin here in your element and ..." She waved her hand around the barn. "... among these lovely animals."

Lily's voice possessed an ease Willa hadn't heard there before. What a difference it made not to be on opposite sides of a custody battle.

"Those bells have a charming ring to them," Lily said.

"*Trychlen*," Willa said. They're Swiss." As Willa backed out the gate of the newborn pen, the black Saanen did a spinning jump.

Lily giggled. "My, he's delighted with his full belly."

Willa strode into the does' pen and waded through the remaining dozen bleating milkers that would be picked up by their new owner in a few days. When she reached Charlotte, she said to Lily, "This is our favourite. She's an excellent mama — gentle and generous." Willa removed the *trychlen* from around Charlotte's neck. She used the handkerchief hanging out of her jeans pocket to polish the dust and oil off its hammered metal surface. Joining Lily at the gate of the pen, she handed her the bell. "I want you to have this."

Lily smiled. She reached over the barrier and hugged Willa tightly. She held on much longer than Willa thought she would.

As they walked back to the house a few minutes later, Peter ran up behind them. To his obvious surprise, Willa slung an arm over his shoulder and said, "Silly boy. Of course we want you to live with us."

37

DAN BORROWED Ursula's parents' car to drive down to the farm for the final send-off. Ursula's work on the grand opening of the pumping station prevented her from joining him. He insisted he had sufficiently recovered from his injuries to help board up the farmhouse windows and batten down the barn and other outbuildings. He and Peter installed the final plywood panels on the house the day before the final departure for Fort McMurray.

"Do you miss this place?" Peter asked Dan as he handed up a couple more nails.

Dan took the nails and stood still at the top of the ladder to look around the Van Bruggen farm. "I couldn't be happier that I grew up here. Sometimes I wonder how I ever left. Sounds silly, maybe, but I come here in my dreams." He laughed. "It's my happy place, I guess. Still, I don't regret leaving." He hammered a couple of nails in, then looked down at Peter, who peered up at him, shielding his eyes against the brightness of the sky. "What about you, Pete? How do you feel about leaving for good?"

"I used to wonder how anyone could live anywhere else. But that's kid stuff. When Mom and Dad were still alive."

He handed Dan a plank and more nails. "I miss them more than I'll ever miss the place."

"Then I think you have your priorities straight." For a few minutes, the air resounded with Dan's hammering. Then he came down off the ladder, grinning. "You remember that time I babysat you and we took sleeping bags and blankets out to the aspen grove near your house?"

Peter squinted his eyes in an effort to remember. "Yeah," he said slowly.

"By the old pond. You were pretty young."

Peter nodded. "Right. Mom and Dad were frantic when they got home because they couldn't find us."

Dan nodded thoughtfully. "Place makes for great memories."

"But people live in your heart forever," Peter added.

Dan laughed. "A couple months living in the city and the young man becomes a poet."

"No way. I'm going to be an engineer like you."

Dan clapped Peter on the shoulder. "A noble profession, my young friend."

38

OCTOBER 31 DAWNED clear and crisp. A severe dip in the jet stream had conjured cool weather. Skiffs of clouds tossed scant raindrops onto Southern Alberta. "Mother Nature likes to tease," Calvin lamented as he piled the suitcases into the truck bed. They had managed to pack the entirety of their lives — or at least the essential parts of it — into one large rented trailer. The exchange of hugs and best wishes with neighbours had drained Willa. Everyone remarked on the enormous life change she and Calvin were undertaking. It felt like she'd left a hundred times already.

She and Daniel took time after breakfast to say their final goodbyes to Opa Gerard and Willa's grandparents, who would rest forever on the Western Crest.

"Can't wait to meet Ursula," Willa said. "She sounds like a firecracker."

Daniel's eyes softened above his mask.

"You really love her, don't you?"

He nodded.

Willa remarked on the stillness of the barn as they passed it on their way back to the house. "Kinda ghostly when it's empty," she said, twisting her face into a frightened grimace.

Daniel laughed. "Nah, even if there were a dozen bulls in there, you still wouldn't hear them for the thirteen trees worth of wood chips they'd be dancing on." He cried out in mock pain when she punched his shoulder.

"I think Opa Gerard would be happy I cut down all that deadwood."

"*Oude bomen moet men niet verplanten*," Daniel said.

She stopped and stared at her son. She waited for a gust of wind to subside. "I don't know that one."

"Old trees shouldn't be transplanted."

His eyes teared up. She took his hand and led him toward the house for one last wander through the rooms. "Sometimes an old tree has no choice," she said.

CALVIN GLANCED OVER at her as he pulled on the webbing that would secure the luggage during the long drive to Fort McMurray. "No mask?"

She shook her head. "If I'm going to leave my old life, I want an unobstructed goodbye." She looked around at the outbuildings, then returned to the side door of the house to lock up. She hesitated with her hand on the key in the deadbolt. Surveying the boarded-up windows, she had the feeling she was locking her father inside, incapacitated, as he was at the end of his life. She recognized the thought immediately as one based in reasonable emotion rather than irrational thought. She heaved a great sigh.

Daniel walked into her open arms and held on for a long time. "Don't forget to stop in when you get to Calgary," he said.

After Daniel drove off, Willa stepped into the truck cab where Calvin and Peter were waiting. "We're actually doing this."

A frown flitted across Calvin's brow. "Question or statement?"
"You tell me," she said.

He reached his arm toward her but left it resting on the back of the seat. "We are, and it's the right thing to do. Everything's going to be okay."

Everything *would* be okay. She turned to look at Peter in the back seat. Saskia had slung her head across his lap. "Ready?" she asked. He nodded solemnly. Leafy tentacles crept along the ceiling of the truck and over all their heads. Unwilling to leave the dogged honeyberry bushes behind, Willa had uprooted two of them, placed each in a pot and set them on the floor in front of Saskia. Willa would plant them in Roy and Lily's yard. As she turned to look out the windshield, one of the branches caught in her curls and she extracted it carefully and pushed it away.

The truck and rented trailer bumped along the gravel laneway that connected the farm to the rest of the world. They turned onto the main road and headed west up the hill toward the highway. She looked straight ahead until they reached the top of the hill. There, she touched Calvin's leg and he stopped. She hopped out and walked past the trailer for one more unhindered look back. She imagined her father. Hale and hearty. Waving to her from the deck of the old log house. Her hand flew up too. She smiled at the involuntary reflex, then walked back to the open passenger door and hopped in. The truck crawled over the crest, as if Calvin were easing apart the tether between Willa's heart and the land, strand by strand, so it wouldn't sever with a snap.

ACKNOWLEDGEMENTS

I mostly want to thank my husband, Mike Walsh, who tolerated endless discussions about plot and character on the hiking trails, when all he really wanted to do was relax and enjoy some peace and quiet. I'm grateful to my two sons, Connor and Greg, for all those times they patiently waited for supper while I — just one more minute — finished up a chapter. Heartfelt thanks to Kelsey Attard, Anna Boyar and everyone at Freehand Books for taking an interest in this story and for the incredible support they provided throughout the publishing process. The amazing editorial prowess of Barb Howard helped it cross the finish line. Copy editor Naomi K. Lewis aimed eagle eyes at the final text. Legendary writer and editor Merilyn Simonds worked her magic to get this story ready for submission. She and the 2015 Emerging Writers gang at Sage Hill Writing Experience kept listening long after I'd reached my allotted word count. Plus, a pinky-swear with memoir writers Dauna Ditson and Cathy Cooper proved a powerful motivator. Wayne Grady, thanks for that super depressing discussion about Earthly destruction from climate change. Scott King, hydrogeologist extraordinaire, talked to me about recharge rates, dataloggers and thermistor strings. If I got any of it wrong, don't blame him — he did his best with my non-scientific brain. I'm grateful to pharmacist Gisele Scott-Woo for being my tour guide in the world of drugs and disease. No writer can do without her generous early readers! Mine were Lori Hahnel, Rona Altrows, Susan Carpenter, Michelle Phaneuf, John Blair, and Josepha Vanderstoop. Thanks, you guys! Gotta mention the good people at Alexandra Writers Centre Society, who continue to help me, and so many others, hone our craft through workshops and retreats. I must confess that I fell hopelessly in love with goats. Goat breeders Felix and Andrea Mueller, Leila Cranswick and Carolyn Van Driesten, and their families opened their hearths and hearts to me and even let me get my hands dirty so I wouldn't harbour any romantic illusions about the hard life on a goat farm. Even then, my eyes were sufficiently dreamy when I returned home after delivering a goat kid on my own, for my wise husband to firmly and repeatedly close the door on the prospect of being goat breeders ourselves. I am eternally grateful to Cheryle Chagnon-Greyeyes from Muskeg Lake Cree Nation in Saskatchewan, now living in Calgary, and Cynthia Pipestem from the Tsuut'ina First Nation for their patient teachings about Indigenous culture and ceremony. If I am off the mark in any way, it's on me. It takes a village to write a novel, and I'm grateful to all the generous people who contributed to mine.

NOTES

The poem fragment that Willa recalls on page 68 is an excerpt from "Evangeline: A Tale of Acadie" by Henry Wadsworth Longfellow. Daniel reads Longfellow's "The Castle-Builder" to Opa on page 112. On page 244, Daniel quotes Longfellow's "The Day is Done" to Ursula. All poems were sourced online from the Maine Historical Society at http://www.hwlongfellow.org.

Daniel refers to the work of David Schindler, who is a real limnologist. Professor Schindler's 2006 article "The Myth of Abundant Canadian Water" can be accessed online at Canada Foundation for Innovation at http://www.innovation.ca/story/myth-abundant-canadian-water.

DOREEN VANDERSTOOP is a Calgary-based writer, storyteller
and musician. Her short fiction has been published by *Loft on
Eighth* and *Prairie Fire* and has appeared online at *Montreal Serai,
Prairie Journal, Epiphany Magazine* and others. As a storyteller/
musician, she intersperses songs among tales of all genres,
including her own original stories. Doreen performs for audiences of all ages at schools, libraries, festivals, conferences and
more. She leads workshops to ignite in others a passion for
the power of story — oral and written. *Watershed* is Doreen's
debut novel.